The literature on child abuse is extensive, but in *The Blackberry Web* the plot exposes this "crime" not only in our own country, but internationally. The author's literary skill shines through as well as her concern for the exploitation of our young people.

Sister Mary Clare, P.B.V.M. ACSW

This is a powerful, compelling, well-written book about pedophilia and the sexual abuse of children. Christenson has braved the subject at a pertinent time in our history. The research is extensive, and the author has woven a story full of suspense and fact. A must read for teens and parents.

Leah Hoffman, Co-Media Specialist

Ms. Christenson's engaging fictional account of innocence destroyed by the devastating consequences of childhood sexual abuse is based upon an all too real world-wide problem. It is an important wake up call regarding a subject too little addressed by our society in America and by others around the world. Pedophilia robs children of their God given freedom and has dire consequences socially, psychologically, and spiritually for society as a whole. This book deserves to be read by a wide audience.

Donald W. Ogard, MSW, Marriage and Family Therapist, Retired; Kathleen Ogard, MS, Special Education Teacher, Retired

# THE BLACKBERRY WEB

## TANGLED IN THE VINES OF CHILD ABUSE

KELLY CHRISTENSON

*To Ida, my friend & wonderful "roof mate"*

*Kelly C.*

TATE PUBLISHING & *Enterprises*

Published by Tate Publishing & Enterprises, LLC
127 E. Trade Center Terrace | Mustang, Oklahoma 73064 USA
1.888.361.9473 | www.tatepublishing.com

Tate Publishing is committed to excellence in the publishing industry. The company reflects the philosophy established by the founders, based on Psalm 68:11,
*"The Lord gave the word and great was the company of those who published it."*

Book design copyright © 2007 by Tate Publishing, LLC. All rights reserved.
*Cover and Interior design by Steven Jeffrey*
*Edited by Amanda Webb*

Published in the United States of America

ISBN: 978-1-60462-248-5
1. Fiction: Psychological
2. Family & Relationships: Abuse
07.12.05

*Dedicated in loving memory to*
*May Louise Nock*
*Friend and Mentor*
*Who prodded me to write this story*

## Acknowledgments

Because "no man is an island," I could not have written this story without the assistance of the following:

Michael T. Propst, M.D., Pathologist, Anchorage, Alaska, who graciously gave counsel on the autopsy report;

Ellie Sbragia, Director, Arizona Center for Law Related Education, Phoenix, Arizona, who submitted papers on child abuse;

Rudy Kohnle, who introduced me to the computer and never gave up on me;

Iola Larson, my sister and constructive critic;

My niece, Dr. Wendy Larson, who helped with the final submission;

My cousin, Peggy Adams, who gave valuable insights on the content;

My niece, Krista Larson, who helped with computer problems;

Friends, who read the first prototype and gave invaluable suggestions—Anita Coppock, Kathleen Olsen, Leah Hoffman, Sister Mary Clare, Lois Corl, Viola Svart, Marjorie Bielke, Carol Johnson—and just when I was ready to give up, Sue McCorkle, whose encouragement and perseverance made it happen;

To the judges and in-court clerks under whom I worked in the Alaska State Court System in Anchorage, Alaska;

A big thank you to my editor, Amanda Webb, for her guidance, enthusiasm, trust, suggestions, insight, and encouragement; and to the wonderful, professional staff at Tate Publishing.

*Preface*

This short novel is a work of fiction, a story of mystery and suspense involving subjects of which little has been written, other than factually—pedophilia, pederasty, and children exploited in pornographic videos. The names, characters, and incidents are either the product of the author's imagination or are used fictitiously. Any resemblance to actual persons, living or dead, is entirely coincidental.

Though the story is fictitious, the research is extensive, and the facts are real.

- "Kelly" Christenson

Oh, what a tangled web we weave,
When first we practice to deceive!
Scott. *Marmion*
Canto vi.st. 17

*Prologue*

The slick Piper Cub swooped to around 2500 feet as it turned west toward what had formerly been the quiet, peaceful, diminutive town of Stanwood in northern Snohomish County on Puget Sound. A short distance from the languid community, the creamy-colored sands of the once choice, popular Juniper Beach were all but obliterated.

Clutching the binoculars, Rafe leaned forward, scanning the horizon as far as he could see in all directions. Shaking his head in disbelief, he turned to Ken and shouted above the drone of the engine, "Ken, look! Look over there! Can you believe this?"

"No, I can't! It's absolutely crazy!" his friend shouted as he leaned over to stare at the scene.

"This is absolutely unbelievable!" As Rafe pointed, he shouted, "Look over to the west, Ken! Almost every narrow asphalt road in the country for miles has been taken over by the blackberries! It's incredible! They've climbed the sides of practically every building in town!"

Rafe muttered to himself, "What a disaster—abandoned cars, empty buildings—Stanwood dead, absolutely wiped out after the silent, unobtrusive intrusion of an enemy bent on total destruction. Those blasted pervasive, thorny vines! It's as if some evil force caused them to grow completely out of control." In every direction, the scene was one of impenetrable green, like an invading army clothed in camouflage, marching to overtake the enemy. "Wonder how it all happened. Why? Why?" he mumbled.

There was only a faint semblance of the bridge connecting the mainland to Camano Island. The vines had crept up the piling, over the railing, and across the asphalt. The country road heading west out of town to the island looked like a gray-colored thread stretched across a rough carpet of dark green burlap.

"Ken, do you think you could set her down in that field over there so we could get out and look around the town?" he shouted.

Ken nodded in the affirmative. "We'll give it a try! May be rough landing, so hang on!" He banked the small plane and headed for a small clearing in a pasture.

Rafe thrashed around in bed, slashing the green brambles with a machete, as if he were in combat with an aggressive, invading force, a coercive operation utterly out of control and with no objective order of command.

Rafe awoke with a start, disturbed and confused. He sat upright in bed. He shook his head, and a clump of unruly salt and pepper-colored hair fell over his brow. He blinked, rubbed his eyes, and tried to recall every facet of the extraordinary, ominous dream. A wide yawn deepened the lines of his rugged face, a face that other men trusted and women liked.

Hugging his bent knees, he sat, deep in thought, reasoning, contemplating the dream, trying to impose some aspect of organization to his thoughts. His hands slipped over the blond stubble of hair on his legs. The window had been open all night and the bedroom was cold. Shivering, he slid back down into the warmth of the bed again. Hugging the covering beneath his chin, he stretched his legs, reaching outside the circle of warmth his body heat engendered to the cool side. Subconsciously, he was reaching out for someone, for her. Withdrawing, he cuddled like a child in a fetal position, rationalizing, thinking, thinking.

Glancing at his watch, he noted the time—6:00 a.m. He hated to get up, leave the warmth of the bed, and go over to close the window. Under his breath, he whispered, "Well, it has to be done, and there's no better time than the present to drive out to the house." Slipping out from under the warmth of the blue down comforter, and standing erect and tall, he genuflected, stretched, flexed the upper muscles of his arms, and headed for the shower.

Rafe parked his best friend's station wagon about twenty-five feet onto the private driveway leading up to the old-fashioned stone house, opened the car door, swung his long legs out onto the fine gravel, and began to walk slowly, surreptitiously, down the narrow tracks through the dense growth of trees and plants. The early morning sun was rising in the eastern sky, playing hide-and-go-seek in the trees. Shards of light filtered through the branches. Dark, ominous clouds gathered overhead, and Rafe knew that it would soon be pouring. He buttoned his light-weight jacket and, looking up, marveled at the busy sky, which would soon become a battlefield, a battlefield of the elements.

Rafe walked unerringly. Every rotten stick and leaf seemed to shout his passing, and every living twig and branch seemed to be in a contest to restrain him. A blunt blackberry vine barb grabbed the trouser leg of his blue denims; when he reached down to disengage its grasp, a thorn pricked his index finger, drawing blood. Unconsciously, he sucked the petty wound and spat upon the ground.

Tufts of tall grass, weeds, and dandelions forced him to stay on the concealed lane. Rafe paused to pull on a blade of grass, biting off the tender end. As far as he could see there was thick undergrowth—Oregon grapes with their shiny green leaves and dusty blue-colored berries, fronds of dark green sword fern, bell-shaped mushrooms, ivy, rhododendron bushes—all overshadowed, it would seem, by the statuesque Douglas fir and the western hemlock. It was fragrantly moist. He inhaled the aromatic pungent air, exhaling slowly. Mosses blanketed the rocks under a lacy-branched western red cedar, and in and out and through it all, the vines of the prolific blackberry were a maze of tangled green.

At forty-two, Rafe was as erect as the evergreens on each side of the lane. His straight carriage accentuated his six foot-two inch height, and his broad shoulders tapered down to a still narrow waist. His hair, threaded with silver and prematurely gray around the temples, framed a strong-featured face, a striking contrast to his unlined, tan complexion. His blue eyes were disarming, friendly, keen.

Rafe recalled, as he continued down the path, that a wit had commented that if everyone abandoned the western sections of the states of Washington and Oregon, the blackberries would take over within five years. His mom had told him many years before about an article she had read in the *Everett Daily Herald*—something about the blackberries being a thorn in Stanwood's side. The city fathers stated that if the blackberries were not controlled, within ten years the cursed things would invade the town and destroy all other life. It could be the greatest threat Stanwood had ever known. The story was imbedded deep in his subconscious, and had become a reality in his wild dream.

Rafe grinned as he recalled a conversation with Ken several years before. It was shortly after they both married. A pie social was the big occasion at church, and Ann and Kim decided to make blackberry pies. The fellows agreed that the least they could do for their new brides was to pick the blasted things. Rafe was complaining. "Why can't the girls just make lemon pies instead, Ken?"

Ken popped a large berry in his mouth. "I don't know. I think they simply want us to suffer." Laughing, he joked, "Don't forget, Rafe, this is the place to live if we ever get poor. After all, we can always eat these pesky things!" He opened his mouth like a fledgling and stuffed in more of the succulent, delicious berries. "Sure luscious, aren't they?"

"Yeah, by the looks of your mouth, I'd say they're pretty good all right. Come on, Ken, if you keep eating all you pick, it will take us forever to get enough for two pies." A small thorn lodged in his index finger and he tried to get it out with his teeth. "Blasted thorns!" he exclaimed.

"But they are so good!" Ken mockingly grinned, smacking his purple lips.

"Say, my friend, remember what else that guy told us?" Rafe asked.

"What? Can't remember."

"He said that the leaves could be used for medicinal purposes. The Indians had known that for years. I'll just bet the Pilchuck Tribe used them for a lot of ailments. That's probably why Pilchuck Julia lived to be such a ripe old age."

"You really think so? Well, if that were true, think of all the money we'd save if we didn't have to go to the doctor." Ken laughed.

As he reflected, Rafe grinned. It was conceivable all right. Some blackberry vines had crept across the road, and in one place had grown into a natural canopy overhead. Passing under the formidable arch and rounding the curve, Rafe paused, shielding his eyes from the glaring sun that had just peeked out from behind a dark cloud. "Dear God, it looks so—so deserted, so desolate," he whispered. He stared at the two-story old stone residence, which had been his home for so many years.

The early morning sun cast long, eerie shadows on the house as he paused at the cracked cement entrance leading up five, then three more steps to the front verandah. Could it have been only two years since this old home—with the stained glass windows, the large natural stone fireplace, the winding stairway—had rung with laughter?

An oppressive gloom, like a shroud of dark colored gauze, seemed to envelop the house, disguising its facade. Rafe felt the darkness, and at that moment a morass of loneliness began pulling him down, down into an indescribable abyss. It was as though he gazed upon a home that had never been an integral part of his life. Could he ever feel peace and tranquility there again? Without Ann? It seemed so cold, so completely foreign.

Blackberry vines literally encompassed the stately structure, sheltering, protecting the front entrance, the large plate glass windows, and the smaller evenly-spaced windows around the sides of the house. The vines were thickly twined and intertwined around the porch's post supports. They had grown up the sides of the building, and had traversed the gutters onto the roof. The brambles continued over and across the carved double doors, which led into the front entrance hall, defying the intruder.

Rafe stood there as if in a trance, and his innermost thoughts drifted slowly through a kaleidoscope, revealing fleeting glimpses of his life. Then the image froze into a giant panorama—a happy childhood, his father sitting at the head of the table, his mother at the kitchen sink, a group of youngsters playing baseball, classes in high school and college. The end of the picture was indistinct. Captivated, he was transported back in time to a particular evening approximately two years before. It was as clear in his consciousness as though it were yesterday. The house was ablaze with lights, and he could hear the talking, the laughter of closely-knit friends, the voices of the children playing upstairs.

His select group of friends were cast from the same mold, at times a bit boring, but always there for you in time of trouble, sharing sorrows and joys. A special chemistry cemented them together just as the mortar held the bricks together on the old school house. Their parents had been friends, then there was grade school, followed by high school, graduation, colleges in Washington state, engagement parties, wedding plans, bridal showers, marriage ceremonies, baby christenings, PTA meetings, funerals—all an integral part of their mundane lives. Their children were close, scrapping, chasing each other, shouting, trudging to Little League baseball games, pulling the usual childhood pranks in Sunday School class and Vacation Bible School. Though they worked hard, they found the time to hike, ski, fish, dig clams, camp, and swim in Blackman's Lake, Silver Lake, Lake Stevens, and Puget Sound, and now they had come together to wish Ann success and best wishes in her new enterprise which was to open soon—Ann's Jam Jar. It had been a wonderful party, and Ann was exuberant, delighted that her friends were so encouraging and eager to share in her happiness.

Rafe visualized her face—her radiant smile, the way one dark eyebrow always arched when he teased her. To him she was the most beautiful woman in the world. Ann was oblivious to any attention paid to her by men—her dark, long hair cascading over her narrow shoulders, her profile, her figure; heedless of what women admired—her exquisite beauty, the way her clothes fit. How he had loved to hold her, lift her hair, kiss her neck, fill his nostrils with her fragrance, play with her lustrous hair, and mess the wispy bangs. Her skin, a milky white with a pink sheen, was flawless, except for the small mole above her right brow. He knew other women might have envied her, that men admired her, and this pleased him. She was strong, self-reliant, creative, fun to be with, the kind of friend that anyone would covet. And she had always been his best friend.

Rafe closed his eyes and stood quietly, listening, reminiscing. In the recesses of his mind, from a far distance, he heard her voice, *"Ken, how about another piece of blackberry pie? Harry, some cream for your coffee? Kim, bring some more coffee, will you?"* Adult voices, small boy-girl chatter, laughter—how clearly he heard each voice.

Why Ann? Why Julie? His precious little Julie had been a miniature of his wife, an exquisite child. He scanned the blackberry vines again, recalling, with a faint smile, the delicious pies for which Ann had gained such a reputation. No one could prepare as delicate a crust—the pie, not too sweet, just the appropriate amount of tartness. His taste buds began to flow. She was so thoughtful, always taking a jar of blackberry jam whenever they were invited out for dinner or for a social evening.

Rafe paused and leaned against the cold concrete wall, his heart pounding. Head cradled on his arms, he gave way to long pent-up emotions. His body convulsed with sobs as he relived the events of that summer. It seemed, as he leaned on that cold mortar, that his pain and suffering elevated him to a higher plane of existence. He became unaware of time, and in his stupor, the nightmare that had haunted him for almost two years drifted in and out of his semi-conscious state of mind. Would he ever be completely free from this haunting scene, this grotesque play? Must he continually be obsessed by the panic and terror of their cries?

*Ann, Julie, Neil, and some of his closest friends were caught in a patch of the largest blackberry vines he had ever seen. The vines were like a gigantic spider web, spreading, catching, entombing them. They were frantically fighting to free themselves, only to be caught more securely with each move. The unmerciful brambles twined and intertwined around their bodies. Their eyes begged for mercy, but the barbs tightened, crushed, and held them securely in their grasp. The briars were enormous, the barbs like sharply pointed knives—cutting, gashing. The juice from the large berries matted their hair and ran down their faces. Their mouths were open, and the gory fluid that gushed forth was a thick dark magenta color, a mixture of blackberry juice and blood. The wounds from their cuts oozed blood and ran down their frightened faces, making them appear grotesque and unreal. There was no way to escape, no way to extricate their tortured bodies. Their faint cries reverberated incessantly in his ears, "Rafe! Rafe! Help us! Daddy! Help me! The berries are choking me, Daddy! They hurt, they hurt! Please help me, Daddy! Help!"*

"Julie! Ann! Wait—I will help you! I will help you. . ."

Rafe was oblivious of the time. Not realizing how long he had been standing in this position, he became conscious of a muscle spasm in his neck. The muscle tightened like a tight rope stretched from pole to pole in a circus. He raised his head slowly and began to rotate it deliberately, eyes tightly closed. He massaged the back of his neck, forcing the knotted muscle to loosen. He shook his head to erase the dizziness, clear his mind. "God, please help me, please help me," he whispered.

Rafe pushed himself back from the wall and stood with face uplifted, eyes closed. The silence was deafening. He soon sensed an inexplicable peace and calm, and the tension in his body gave way as every muscle relaxed. Then the answer dawned like a bright light illuminating a darkened space. "I know what I must do," he whispered. "I know what I must do. He must pay. He can't get away with it." His fist hit the open palm of his left hand repeatedly and, with a hurried glance at the house, he turned away from the wall. With determined steps he strode back to the wagon, jumped in the car, placed the keys into the ignition, started the engine, reversed the shift, and with deliberation backed out onto the narrow country road. In his mind's eye he saw again the blank stare of his little girl in the video. Oh, the shame of what these innocent children endured.

Rafe drove the car slowly, but his mind was racing—Julie in that pornographic video, the blank look in the eyes of each of the children—the degradation—the sadness—Amanda. It was a race of thoughts in a challenging competition on a speedway with no finish line. Large raindrops hammered and beat the windshield. He thought of the early morning dream. *Hmm, I must tell Ken about that ridiculous dream—his plane, our flying above Stanwood together—Stanwood wiped out by blackberries! Sure crazy—he'll never believe that one.*

It was registration day at George College. Neil Manning, scrubbed, fresh-looking, blond hair neatly combed, immaculately clad in blue jeans and white sport shirt, walked into the cafeteria and glanced nervously around the large, noisy room. Prospective students mulled around. Nervous freshman appeared confused and lost. Sophomores, juniors, and seniors compared schedules and chatted about their summer vacations. There were hugs, shouts, boys punching each other in friendly gestures, and girls talking in loud voices to friends.

Neil glanced at Ginny, a nice looking, red-haired, brown-eyed girl. Yeah, she did look nice, very nice. Then turning, he fumbled through the cards in his hand, proceeded to one of the marked tables, waited his turn patiently, and remarked, "I guess this is where I begin."

Harry Lochrie looked up at him with raised eyebrows. "Freshman?" Neil nodded in the affirmative. "Okay, let's see what you have there. Perhaps I can help you." Hesitating briefly, Neil handed him the cards and hooked his thumbs on his two front pockets.

"Thanks, Mr.—Mr.—er." He quickly glanced at the nameplate on the table. "Mr. Lochrie."

Harry's index finger slid down the list to the M's where he soon discovered Neil's name. "Okay, here it is—Neil Manning." He put a check mark in front of the name. Smiling, he continued, "You're in my class three days a week, Neil. I'll see you next Monday." Glancing across the room to an attractive dark-haired woman in horn-rimmed glasses, he nodded and said, "From here you go on over there to Mrs. Sturtz's table. She will be your English teacher." Harry motioned with his pencil to a table on the other side of the room and handed him the cards.

"Thanks—thanks again, Mr. Lochrie," Neil grinned.

Rafe, who had been standing in the background observing, walked over to Harry's table. "How's it going, Harry? That young man looked pretty promising. Clean cut. Courteous, wasn't he?"

"Yes—yes, he was. Didn't seem to fit the norm," Harry agreed. He took the stack of registration cards and shook and tapped them on the table, as he would a deck of cards. "Registration is looking pretty good this semester, Rafe, and do we ever need the numbers." Glancing at Neil, he continued, "Say, that young man is the recipient of a four-year science scholarship. Why don't you say hello to him? Might make him feel a bit more at ease." Without waiting for a reply from Rafe, he called, "Manning! Neil Manning!" Neil turned around with a surprised look, thinking perhaps he had made some kind of mistake. Harry continued, "Come back a moment—there's someone here I want you to meet."

Neil walked back to Harry's table. "I'd like to introduce you to the head of the science department, Neil. This is Mr. Langley. You'll be seeing a lot of him later in your advance science classes. He won't bite," he added with a grin.

Rafe extended his hand, and Neil took it hesitantly, "Glad to know you, Mr. Langley."

"Nice having you on board, Neil. I hope you'll like it here at George. If you have any problems, don't hesitate to come by my office. I'll be happy to help you any time."

"Thanks, Mr. Langley." Neil fidgeted. "I'm really happy to be here. I—I could hardly wait to come. Well—well, guess I have to sign up for the rest of my classes. Be seeing you." Neil raised a hand in a farewell gesture. "Thanks—thanks a lot."

"Nice looking kid," Rafe remarked. "Did you notice his eyes, Harry? Most unusual—so deeply set, and such a pale blue color, almost gray. Seemed a bit nervous, wouldn't you say? Where's he from anyway?"

"Somewhere over in eastern Washington. Audrey gave me the low-down on him. He lives on a farm—wheat farm I think, over near Spokane. He's a bit shy, but he'll be okay after he makes a few friends and becomes involved. Must have been a good high school student seeing as how he received a scholarship to our prestigious, albeit small, modest college. I hope he can keep it up." As an after-thought, he mumbled, "So many of these kids who come from small schools can't, you know."

Rafe, running his hand through his hair, remarked, "I wonder about his background—small high school I suppose, with not much competition. Well, I hope he can cut the mustard." His glance followed Neil to the next table. Turning, he placed his hand on Harry's shoulder, bent over, and whispered, "You know, friend, I'll just wager we're the only college Profs in this entire country who work registration. Do you think it's because we're the best, or do you think it may be because the school can't afford to pay someone else to do this?"

"We are the best, pal," Harry grinned. "Without a doubt, without a doubt. Sure we're small, but we're good, Rafe. You know that! Besides, I kind of enjoy doing this—seeing the students I've had—meeting the freshman. Remember, we're not the University of Washington. You remember how large those classes were?"

"Yeah, I remember," Rafe grinned. "Of course, if we were at the U of W, we'd probably never get to know any of these kids personally—we'd have such large classes. On the other hand, our salaries might be a bit higher, too."

"Yeah, but how many of those profs at the U took a special interest in you, Rafe? Not very many. I was just a number. So were you."

"Perhaps—perhaps," Rafe agreed. "At least, as an undergraduate student. It was a little better when we worked on our Master's."

"Yeah, I suppose so—you're right." Harry turned back to gaze into the questioning eyes of the next student in line, an overweight nondescript girl with long, lifeless blond hair. She handed him her registration card. He looked at it, and checked her name in the D's. Dana Danworth. "There you are, Miss Danworth." Pointing again to Mrs. Sturtz, he continued, "Go to that table right over there next." With a warm smile, he added, "You're going to like George College. Good luck." Turning his head toward Rafe, he said, "Hey, Langley, coffee at three?"

"Meet you in the faculty room at three, Harry."

"Next?"


It wasn't until the beginning of Neil's third year in an advanced science class that Rafe became acquainted with, and especially interested in, Neil Manning. Rafe soon learned to appreciate his analytical inquiring mind, his eagerness to work, and his positive attitude toward learning. He was confident that Neil had remarkable potential, and would make an excellent teacher.

"Well, Neil, how do you like George College by now? This is your third year, right?"

"That's right. Even though it's not very large, it's a great school, Mr. Langley. I appreciate the fact that the teachers take a sincere interest in you. I like it a lot. Hey, got any suggestions as to where I should take my fifth year—begin work on my master's? I thought about Bellingham, but maybe the U. of W. would be a better choice. What do you think?"

"Well, that would depend on what you get your degree in, Neil. You know, Harry Lochrie and I both attended the University of Washington, and it was great. When that time comes, I'll be happy to work with you—help you make the right decision."

Rafe observed his painful shyness and reticence, and thought he was making progress. Noting that he had filled out considerably since his freshman year and admiring his athletic build, he asked, "Are you into any sports, Neil?"

"Not competitively, Mr. Langley. I like track and field events the best, and I love to run. I won first place in my district for the mile when I was a senior in high school."

"Do you run every day?" Rafe asked, genuinely interested.

"Well, not every day, but I try to run five to ten miles every other day or so."

"Perhaps we can run together some day. Though you might leave me in the dust," Rafe grinned.

"That would be nice, Mr. Langley. I'm sure you wouldn't have a problem keeping up with me." Neil wondered why he was taking this special interest in him, and doubted that the day would ever come when they would actually be running together.

Rafe acknowledged Neil's embarrassment when he talked about his accomplishments. As the year progressed, a well-founded rapport began to develop between Rafe and Neil.

One day, in the faculty lounge, Rafe was chatting with Harry Lochrie, and the subject of Neil came up. "Say, Rafe, you have Manning in a couple of your classes now. What do you think of him?"

"He's a bright kid, painfully modest, reserved, but his grades are up there with the best of them. He's a real loner, Harry. It's too bad we can't channel some of Dave Castle's idiosyncrasies in his direction. That's one kid who is too aggressive. I'm afraid that at times Dave just rubs me the wrong way."

"Yes, I know what you mean, but he'll probably change when he gets a little older. Don't give up on our problem boy yet, Rafe. He's capable, and under that facade he has a great deal of potential."

"Well, I just hope we can bring Neil out of his reserve some way," Rafe said with concern.

"Yes, well maybe we can. I know what you mean. He doesn't seem to have any close relationships, and it beats me why he doesn't have a girlfriend—someone special, I mean. He surely is a good-looking kid, and I'll just bet a lot of the gals would like to go with him. I don't think he ever goes to any of the school functions. At least, I've never seen him there with anyone."

"I think I'll try to draw him out of his shell," Rafe mused, cupping his chin in one hand.

One day after class, Neil was cleaning up in the lab. Rafe glanced up from the papers on his desk. "Neil, do you enjoy swimming?"

"Yeah, I do. I'm a pretty good swimmer I guess you'd say—have known how since I was about six years old. I used to go to the lake with my uncle, when I was just a little kid. He taught me to swim, and I was a pretty good diver, too. Everyone thought my jack-knife was about perfect. Yeah, I like all water sports—fishing, water skiing, swimming. That's the one big reason I accepted the scholarship out here instead of the one back east, and I really wanted to attend a small college, you know. I want be out on the bay and on the beach as much as possible, Mr. Langley. That is, when I'm not hitting the books!" Neil laughed nervously.

"Glad to hear that," Rafe said.

Neil continued the chatter, "I have a nice little boat, you know—fixed it up really neat. Yes, I love the water. Puget Sound is really great!" He shifted from one foot to the other, and walked over to the sink to begin rinsing out some stainless trays.

"Say, Neil, we're going to have one last outing next Saturday at our cabin on Whidbey. How would you like to join us?"

"Gee, you mean it? I'd love that. Could I bring something along? I could buy some chips or something."

"No, you don't have to bring anything—just yourself. And say, if you want to bring a girlfriend along that would be fine with us. My wife, Ann, will have plenty to eat for everyone. And, two other couples will be joining us with their kids. You already know Harry Lochrie, and I'm sure that his wife, Jane, and Kim Ripley will also be bringing food. We—we have a little girl, you know. Her name is Julie. You'll like her—a little princess—course, her parents would think that. Do you have a friend you'd like to bring along?"

With eyes cast downward, he replied, "No, I'll just come by myself I think." Looking up, he asked, "Do you think that I'd have any trouble finding your cabin if I came across on my boat? I have a friend on Camano Island who lets me park my truck there and use his ramp."

"Well, the cabin is pretty well secluded, Neil, but you could probably find it if I draw a map for you. Come here and let me show you." Rafe took a sheet of paper and sketching, remarked, "Okay, here's Camano City. You're at about this point I think. Come across the bay, then south until you…" Neil scrutinized the drawing over Rafe's shoulder. "I'm sure you won't have any trouble. If you get to a small island with a high cliff and one large tree on it, you know you've gone about a quarter of a mile too far."

"Gee, thanks, Mr. Langley. Thanks a lot. I'm sure I can find it. I'll be there."

"We'll be looking for you a little before noon, Neil," Rafe smiled. "The cabin is an A-frame, and there are white shutters on the windows—a large deck in the front, and a dock. I don't think you'll have any trouble finding it." Then, as he walked toward the door, he added, "And, don't forget your swimsuit!"

Neil had little difficulty finding the Langley cabin, though he realized when he saw the small island with the steep cliff and the one lone tree that he had gone about a quarter mile too far south. He turned the craft around and headed back north, chagrined that he had missed it the first time.

Rafe's map was excellent and as he slowed the craft down a short distance from the shore, he spotted the A-frame. Everyone on the beach gave him a waving reception as he pulled up to the dock. After all the introductions were made, he felt quite comfortable, and entered in with the other guests gathering driftwood for the bonfire, helping Ann with the food preparation, and cleaning up after the wiener roast. He made a game of everything with the kids—chasing them in a game of tag— swimming with them—helping them roast their hot dogs, but introducing them to smores was the highlight of the day as far as they were concerned.

The Ripleys, the Lochries, and Rafe and Ann were sitting around the red cedar picnic table on the deck. Ken spoke, "Your new friend seems to be enjoying himself with the kids, Rafe. Is he in one of your classes at the college?"

"Yes, yes he is. He comes from eastern Washington—somewhere near Spokane. His folks have a wheat farm. He's a terrific student, but painfully shy."

Harry interrupted, "He received a four year scholarship to George, Ken. I've had him in several of my classes, a fine student, but he's different. I can't believe he doesn't have a girlfriend. Look at him. He's nice looking, but so bashful and withdrawn."

"He doesn't seem bashful to me," Kim said. "He seems to be right at home with the kids."

"Maybe he's more comfortable with kids than with adults," Ann reasoned.

"Maybe. I don't know." Rafe glanced over at Harry. "You and I have talked about it, Harry. I'm trying to bring him out of his shell. I hope he enjoys himself. He's been such a loner."

"That's just what I like about you, my friend—always taking a particular interest in the kid that needs something special. No wonder you're the favorite Prof at George!"

"Ah, come on, Harry. What do you mean—the favorite Prof at George? You're just as guilty as I am. What about that young man— what was his name—Adam—Adam Weiland? If you recall, the faculty was about ready to give up on him in his freshman year, voted to expel him for drug use, but you fought all of them, went out of your way, lent Adam an ear, and gave him some excellent guidance. Look at him today, a doctorate from Harvard, an outstanding astronomer, an author. It wasn't long ago that I read an article in the Smithsonian that he had co-written. Brilliant! Don't give me that hogwash!"

Harry made no comment, but with a pleased expression on his face, shook his head slightly in agreement.

"Anyone for a piece of blackberry pie? It's fresh—well, just baked yesterday," Ann said.

"You know, none of us can turn your pie down, Ann!" Ken exclaimed. "Make my piece big, will you?" Turning to Rafe, he continued with a big grin, the kind of grin adults reserve for a child's tall tale, "Say, not to change the subject, Rafe, but have you been picking any berries lately? Perhaps from a plank?"

"You'll never forget that one, will you?" Rafe laughed. "That was a pretty frightening experience, funny or not. You might try it some time, Ken. Get a long plank, crawl out, and fall in. Boy, those barbs can hold like a fox trap."

"No thanks," Ken retorted. "I'll let you pick, and I'll just enjoy Ann's delectable pies."

"Kim, come help me, will you? You can pour some more coffee." Ann walked into the cabin.

"Right-o!" Kim replied, as she jumped up out of her chair to follow Ann.

"You don't need my help?" Jane asked.

"I think we can handle it, Jane. Thanks. Your big job is to keep these guys happy, and that's no easy matter!"

"After pie, what say we have a game of hearts?" Harry asked.

"Okay with me," Ken replied. "You won't get away with anything this time, Harry."

"Here come the girls. That really looks delicious, honey," Rafe said with an approving glance at the pieces of pie. "Nothing like this in any restaurant!"

"How true! How true!" Harry agreed, as he picked up his fork.

Rafe was drawn to Neil as a big brother and in the ensuing months, Neil became a regular at the Langley home. Julie was always excited and happy when he came to visit her parents, or sit with her, because he gave her all of his attention. Neil enjoyed reading to Julie as much as she liked hearing the stories, and Rafe and Ann were both amazed at his knowledge of children's literature. He introduced her to the ducklings in the Boston Square, exclaiming, "See, Julie! Look at this picture. All of the traffic stops just so the ducklings can waddle across the street in safety!" *Make Way for Ducklings* was one of her favorites. Funny looking creatures in a book about wild things frightened her, and she squealed when she looked at the strange pictures.

"Those wild things are awful looking, Neil!"

"Yes, yes, they are, but remember, Julie, they're just make-believe," Neil assured her.

After a trip back to the farm, Neil came back to the coast laden with an armload of children's books. Ann questioned him, "Neil, where on earth did you get all of these wonderful books? Some of them are Caldecott Awards."

"Yes, I know. My sister and I received most of them for Christmas and birthdays. I've heard some of these stories so many times I almost know them by heart. Mom thought it would be nice to lend them to you for Julie to enjoy."

"How nice. Be sure to tell your mother how much we appreciate this. We'll take good care of them, and make sure they don't get all mixed up in our collection. I'll write your name in pencil on the inside cover just in case."

Neil always wanted Julie to sit on his lap when he read to her so he could explain the pictures. He liked the smell of her hair. Funny, children seemed to have a unique odor. Their heads had a distinctive essence, not at all offensive—a child smell. Julie was enthralled with the stories about a little island, the snowy day, the biggest bear, and the frog who went-a-courtin'. When Neil read the book about the little girl who picked blueberries, Julie asked, "Neil, are blueberries like blackberries? Did Sal pick blackberries, too?"

Neil smiled, "Not really, Punkin'—they're a lot easier to pick than blackberries, and I doubt that Sal picked them. She had too many blueberries to pick." Ann just shook her head, smiling at the conversation as she walked away.

Julie loved Neil, and took him to her favorite place, a shaded, grassy glen by a narrow creek in the woods behind their home. It was always cool there, serene and peaceful, even on the hottest day of summer. Occasionally, they would simply sit and talk, Neil answering the myriad of questions. When Neil pulled a blade of grass and bit the end off, Julie did the same. When he held a piece of grass taut between his thumbs, blew on it, and made a whistle, Julie tried that, too. She loved the whistles he whittled from the slender birch branches.

One day in early April, during spring break and before Easter, Julie looked up at him excitedly, "Neil, do you want to play 'I Spy?'"

"What kind of game is that?" Neil asked in genuine interest.

"Well, we have to go into the woods to play. We hunt all over for Easter lilies, and the first one that finds one, yells, 'I spy!'"

Ann interjected an explanation. "The kids call trilliums Easter lilies, Neil."

"I see! Well, that sounds like a lot of fun to me. Yes, I'd love to play. Do you want to go now?"

"Okay, let's go!" Julie cried, as she jumped up and down. "We'll bring a big bunch home to you, Mom."

"That will be so nice, honey. I'll put them on the kitchen table. Try to find a pink one—just for me, will you?"

"Okay, Mom—we will." She reached up for his hand, "C'mon, Neil."

Julie had been enthralled the day that Erin Ripley took her to the large hazelnut tree behind the grade school, and she wanted to show Neil the place where she and Erin had gathered nuts. They found a few nuts and then began to play tag on the smooth, worn path around the tree. When Neil caught her, he grabbed her around the middle, lifted her off her feet, and swung her 'round and 'round. Julie screamed with delight.

Neil was working diligently in the lab after the last class of the day. Rafe was at his desk, grading papers. He glanced over at Neil, got up, walked over to him, and sat on one of the high metal stools at the black table. "Neil, you don't goof off much, do you? Come over here and sit down a minute. Let's talk." Neil turned from his experiment, and looking up at Rafe, followed him over to another table.

"Sure, Mr. Langley. Do you need help with something?"

"No, I just want to talk to you for a few minutes." Rafe pulled out a stool for Neil, and sat down across from him. Rafe leaned over and looked directly at his student, "Neil, you're one of the best students I've ever taught. You're conscientious, you're dedicated, you're ambitious, but…" he hesitated. "You—you don't seem to have any close friends, any girlfriends. Don't you ever take time to have any fun with the fellows? Have a date?"

"Sure I do, Mr. Langley. It's fun for me to come out to your place, and sometimes I go with the guys to a movie, or out for pizza. It's just that I have so much studying all the time, I don't have time to fool around very much. Because of the scholarship, I have to keep my grades up, you know. And, taking girls out can be pretty expensive. I don't have any money to throw around." For the first time, Rafe noticed a little brown fleck in Neil's right blue-gray eye.

Slapping his knees, then standing up, Rafe exclaimed, "Well, okay! You know, Ann and I both think a lot of you, but you're so serious all the time. We want you to have some fun, too."

Neil grinned, "Don't worry, Mr. Langley. I'm fine, just fine. It won't be long now until vacation, and then I'll be working on the farm, and when I get back, I'll be out on the bay in my boat again. I love that."

"Okay, Neil—just don't forget, we're your friends, and are here to help you in any way we can. Well, I have to get home. Don't stay too late, will you?"

"No, no, I'll be leaving in a few more minutes. Thanks, Mr. Langley. Thanks a lot." Neil returned to his work.

At the door, Rafe paused and looked back at Neil. "Oh, I almost forgot! Ann and I are planning to drive down to Portland for a conference next weekend. Would it be an imposition to ask if you could stay over with Julie?"

"An imposition? Not at all! You can count on me."

"We'd really appreciate it, Neil. It would be for just one night. Julie loves it when you come. She likes being with you, and we trust you with her care. We'll have a good book ready for you to read to her."

"No problem, Mr. Langley. I'd be glad to stay with Julie. Suppose Ann—I mean Mrs. Langley—could leave us a blackberry pie?" he grinned.

"I'm sure that could be arranged," Rafe laughed. "Well, we'll confirm later, then. Now don't stay too late. That experiment you're working on can keep. Good night, Neil." Rafe walked out the door. Neil began cleaning up the trays, a big grin on his face.

As Rafe and Ann drove south on I-5, Ann looked over at her handsome husband, "I just hope we're not taking advantage of a good thing, darling. Neil has been so generous and willing to stay with Julie whenever we ask him, but you know, I just can't help wondering—wondering why he doesn't have more friends his own age. He doesn't have a girlfriend, does he?"

"No, I don't think so—not yet, but don't worry about him, honey. He's doing okay, and he has lots of time. He's just reserved, modest, frugal, perhaps a bit of an introvert. You know, I think we mean more to him than the students do. He's comfortable around us, Ann. I don't think I've ever seen a young person his age who has so much patience with a child. He taught Julie how to swim, and has taken her fishing, and look at all the books he reads to her. Good books, too."

"Yes, I know, I know. Oh, you're probably right," she admitted rather reluctantly.

"Julie's having the time of her life since Neil came into our lives, Ann. And, remember how he helped pick berries late last summer? Boy, he can take my place there any time. The blasted things!" Rafe reached over and patted Ann's knee. "I sure do love that jam and those pies though, sweetheart."

"Well, you'd just better like my pies," she teased. "Rafe, speaking of blackberries, I want to share some of my ideas with you in regard to the Jam Jar. By the way, do you remember what Shakespeare said in one of his plays—think it was Henry IV—'If reasons were as plentiful as blackberries, I would give no man a reason upon compulsion.'"

"How in the world could you ever remember that? And, could you please explain what it means?"

"I didn't remember—until I came across it in the library one day. Guess it's because I'm a blackberry nut!" she laughed. "Well, that's better than being a seed, isn't it?" Hesitating for the remark to sink in, she added, "That was a puny pun, wasn't it?"

"I'd say it was a pretty good one," Rafe replied with a grin.

"I'm probably a nut and a bit seedy, but, seriously, Rafe, back to the shop. I would like to have cards made up with facts and quotes about blackberries, and perhaps some attractive wall hangings with different quotations done in calligraphy, bordered in blackberry vines—like Shakespeare's quote. You know, it's really amazing—all the information available about blackberries. I've been doing some research and reading in the library, and honestly, Rafe, it's interesting. Did you know that the blackberry is a member of the rose family? I just know that people would be curious and find the factual information fascinating."

"Yes, I did know that the blackberry was a member of the rose family, but I think you'd better forget about that Shakespeare quote. C'mon, Ann, do you really think your customers would find this information fascinating?"

"Yes, I really do—you just wait and see what I've found. It's all in a folder on my desk. I'll share when we get back home. These little extras will bring in added revenue, too. You'll see."

"Could be, could be, my dear! Say, have you given any thought to mugs? You know—like the one you gave me—and perhaps some other pieces of pottery with a blackberry motif painted on them? That might be a possibility, too."

"Yes, I thought of the mugs, and small plates. Who knows? Perhaps we could find all kinds of special dishes with berries on them. That's a terrific idea. Oh, Rafe, the possibilities are endless. Isn't it exciting? Wonder where I could get the pottery."

"It shouldn't be too difficult to find a source. Maybe in Everett or Seattle. Yes, it could be exciting I guess—could be, could be, my enterprising little wife. You know, I do think you're going to be a great success at this, really I do."

"I hope so," she said thoughtfully. "I can hardly wait to get started."

Rafe's thoughts reverted to the college, and to Neil. "Ann, did I tell you that I think Neil may be one of my assistants next semester?"

"Yes, you told me." Ann smiled sweetly at her husband, put her hand on his knee, then looked straight ahead, lost in her own thoughts.

Rafe began to whistle "On the Road Again", and Ann began to hum the tune. "I just love this drive in the spring, Rafe. Did you ever see so many shades of green in your life? So often I think of all those people who live in the center of a large city, like New York, or in the middle of the country, who couldn't imagine such a thick growth of trees, and it goes on and on for miles. It's a gorgeous corridor. I guess they aren't allowed to cut any of the trees unless they are within so many feet of the highway."

"No, they can't. It's the law, and yes, it is very beautiful. They are so thick in some places, though, I wonder how they make it."

"That Scotch Broom is everywhere, and it really is pretty, don't you think? When you look at one of those little blossoms closely it's simply exquisite. You know, I don't think there's another place in the world that I'd rather live than right here in the Pacific Northwest." She took a deep breath and sighed wistfully.

"You really mean that, don't you?" Rafe responded with a contented grin. "Well, I guess I'll have to agree. It's beautiful all right—such a brilliant yellow, but I'll just bet some of these cattle farmers would like to get rid of the Scotch Broom. It's a pest—takes over. What do you think the cows do when the pasture is covered with it?"

"I don't know, Rafe. I don't see any right now, but I just can't get over how colorful it is."

"Ann, glance back over there at Rainier. The mountains are perfect for skiing now—new snow cover, not a cloud in the sky. Be nice if we could go skiing again, wouldn't it? What say we take Julie up some day and give her some lessons?"

"A great idea. She'd love it I'm sure."

"Yes, my darling, this is one great place to live, a great place—except—except for the blackberries."

"Rafe! You big tease. You'll be sorry you said that!" Ann slapped his thigh.

"And, sometimes I think a little less rain would be nice, though it hasn't been too bad lately, has it?"

Ann sighed deeply, and replied, "Well I for one don't mind the rain. That's what makes this part of the country so lush and beautiful." After a few moments of complete silence between them, she said, "Honey, let's stop at the next good restaurant and have a cup of coffee, shall we? I could use the little girl's room, too."

"Sure, I know a nice cozy little place a few more miles down the highway where we can look out the window at Mount Saint Helens.

Too bad she had to lose her top. She was such a perfect mountain before she erupted. We'll be driving over the Toutle River, honey, and you'll be able to get a pretty good idea just how much ash came down from the mountain when you see the area around the highway. Ann, ever hear the story the Indians tell about Saint Helen's affair with Mount Hood and Mount Adams?"

"Hmm—an affair. Yes, seems that I did when I was a little girl, but I would enjoy hearing it again, Rafe, especially if you're telling it. I think she got disgusted with Hood and Adams sparring for her affection so she moved away from them—something like that—right?"

"Right—the story goes something like this…"

Ann was sitting at the kitchen table deep in thought, tapping a teaspoon on the edge of a mug, her mind full of all the business she had to complete in regard to the Jam Jar. Just as she raised the cup to take a sip of coffee, the telephone rang. It was 7:30 a.m., July 17, 1983. She walked over to the desk in the corner of the kitchen and picked up the phone after the third ring. "Langley residence—may I help you?"

"Mrs. Langley? Hi, this is Neil!"

"Oh, hi, Neil! Nice to hear from you again! When did you get back?"

"Just yesterday. Is Mr. Langley home yet?"

"No, Rafe isn't home yet. He'll be back the morning of the twenty-first."

"Well, are you and Julie doing anything special today?"

"No, nothing really special. Why?"

"Well, it's such a great day—I thought you might like to go over to the cabin and go out in the boat for awhile. Maybe we could do a little waterskiing."

"Well," Ann replied reluctantly, "I do have a lot of things I should take care of, but it does look like a wonderful day. It sounds like fun, Neil, and we don't have that many perfect days, do we?"

"No, we don't. I think you should consider my offer."

"I suppose so. Well, okay, Neil, we'll go. I'll make some lunch—sandwiches and cold drinks."

"That would be super. I should be there around ten o'clock or so. Would that be okay with you?"

"Yes. We'll try to leave a little after nine—maybe we can catch the ten o'clock ferry so we should be there no later than ten-thirty or so."

"Is Julie up yet?"

"No, not yet, but I know she will want to go, and I'll get her up right away. We'll see you at the cabin then."

"Great! Bye for now!"

"Goodbye, Neil. See you in a couple of hours."

Ann placed the phone in its cradle and walked to the hall, pausing at the bottom of the stairs. "Julie! Julie!" she shouted. "Get up, honey! We're going over to the island and out with Neil in the boat! Hurry up! Now don't go back to sleep!"

A faint reply sounded from an upstairs bedroom. "Okay, Mom." A couple of minutes later Julie appeared at the kitchen door, still in her Strawberry Girl pajamas, yawning and rubbing her eyes.

"Good morning, Julie. You've really had a good long night's sleep, haven't you?" Ann bent over and gave her a loving hug. Crouching, so she could look straight into Julie's eyes, and placing both hands on her slim shoulders, she continued speaking in a soft, resonant tone, "Julie, Neil just called and we're going to meet him at the cabin. I want you to run right back upstairs, wash, and get dressed. Put on your blue knit pants and that new T-shirt with the blue stripes. Grab your windbreaker and wrap your swimsuit in one of those old beach towels in the bottom drawer of the dresser out in the hall. Can you remember all that? Hurry now! I'll fix some hot chocolate and cereal for you."

Ann planted a little swat on her bottom. Julie hesitated momentarily and, without comment, turned and ran into the hall and up the stairs. *That was funny*, Ann thought. *She didn't seem to be very excited or overly anxious to go.* For the moment, she dismissed the concept and began to prepare the hot chocolate. But, she couldn't erase the contemplative mood, and in her mind's eye she saw Neil and Julie playing in the water. He threw her up in the air and caught her. Then, they would duck underneath the surface together and she would come up giggling and squealing. When he taught her to swim, his hands were around her tiny waist, and at times one hand was spread across her tummy, holding her up. They would dash out of the water, splashing each other. Then they would run and play tag on the beach, or fly the two colorful kites he brought. While out on the deck of their cabin one day, she watched as they romped in the sand. Julie playfully pounded on Neil's chest and shouted, "You take that back! You take that back!" Ann wondered at the time what that was all about, but said nothing. They were always going up and down the beach hunting for unusual shells or agates. She recalled the day they were rolling the ball back and forth on the planks of their pier, and the rubber ball hit Julie between her legs, and she giggled and tried to roll the ball hard so that it would hit Neil, too. He always wanted her to sit on his lap when he read to her. Was she resenting their closeness? Was it absurd to feel a bit annoyed and disturbed over their relationship? She dismissed the distressing thoughts. It was probably just her imagination.

Five minutes later, hair brushed smooth, dressed in her blue pants and striped t-shirt, Julie appeared at the kitchen door. Her windbreaker was over her arm, her swimsuit rolled neatly in her very special old beach towel.

"Oh, that's my girl! You look so pretty, honey! Here, come and eat your breakfast." Ann poured a cup of piping hot chocolate into her Pooh mug and placed a bowl of her favorite cereal in front of her. She poured the milk on the cereal, but allowing Julie to put on the sugar, cautioned, "Not too much now."

"I know, Mom—too much sugar will rot my teeth."

"That's right, Julie. Do you want a piece of toast, too?"

"Yes, please. Could I have some blackberry jam on it?"

"Of course." Ann reached for the ever-present jar of blackberry jam, spreading the jam to the very edge of the toast, just like Julie wanted.

Julie was thinking about the beach and the water, racing in Neil's boat across the bay from Whidbey to Camano Island. He'd built a small box-like cabin on the craft in the event that it might rain, and when she felt a little cold, she loved to go into the big box and curl up in a blanket, just like a bird in a cozy nest. Most of the time, however, she wanted to be right out in the front of the boat, with the wind whipping through her hair, stinging her face. Sometimes Neil would go around in a big circle and then they'd cross over it, bouncing on the swells and waves, just like a roller-coaster ride. She was really glad her mom decided that they should go. If only her dad were going, too, but he was giving a paper at a big conference back east somewhere.

"Julie, will you please clear the table, and put the dirty dishes in the dishwasher while I go upstairs, make the beds, and get dressed?"

"Sure, Mom—just as soon as I finish my cocoa. It's too hot."

"I won't be long, and then we'll be on our way. Thanks, honey. You're a good girl, and I love you so much."

"I love you, too, Mom. You're really neat."

Ann smiled at the remark—and at her daughter's purple teeth and smeared lips. Turning to go, she added, "Don't forget to brush your teeth and wash your face again!"

"Okay, Mom, I will," Julie replied, as she took a big bite of the jam-covered toast.

It was about ten minutes after nine when Ann backed the green Volkswagen Bug out of the garage and turned down their driveway toward the highway. As she pulled out onto the main road heading west, Mr. Ray drove by, honking and waving at them.

"There goes Mr. Ray, Mom. He's a real nice man, isn't he?"

"Yes, he surely is, Julie. It's too bad that Mrs. Ray is so ill. I must remember to take her some blackberry jam tomorrow. Will you remind me?"

"Sure, Mom. Will you let me go along with you?"

"Well, of course you will go with me. Do you think that I would leave you home by yourself?"

"No, just kidding." Julie looked soberly at her mother, "Mom, is Mrs. Ray going to die?"

"I don't know, honey. I suppose she will—some day. We'll all die some day."

"Well, then," Julie continued, "Will Mrs. Ray be ruptured?"

"*Ruptured*? Julie, where did you get that idea?"

"Mrs. Wills told us all about it in Sunday School class. She said that people who died and were buried would be ruptured when Jesus came back," Julie proclaimed.

"Honey, honey, you misunderstood Mrs. Wills. She said raptured, not ruptured."

"Oh—well, will Mrs. Ray be raptured if she dies?"

"Yes—yes, I am sure she will go up in the rapture. I am sure she will. She's been a wonderful Christian all of her life."

Julie said thoughtfully, "That is really going to be something, isn't it, Mom? All the graves will open up—Grandma and Grandpa Sommerfield, Grandma and Grandpa Langley—and all those other people—they'll all go up in the rupture—I mean rapture."

"Yes, Julie, it is going to be something, all right." Ann was amazed at her child's comprehension, and couldn't believe what she was learning in Sunday School. She would have to tell Mrs. Wills how impressed Julie was with the lesson on the *rupture*.

Julie was deep in thought and Ann broke the silence when she asked, "Honey, do you think we'll make the ferry?"

"You'll make it, Mom," Julie assured her. It was as if the subject they had been discussing was too difficult to comprehend. Julie sighed, looked up at her mother, and said, "Mom, could you tell me about the owl and the pussycat again?"

"The owl and the pussycat? Sure. Hmm, let's see now. Do you remember how it begins?"

"They went out to sea," Julie replied.

Ann began to recite the poem that Julie loved so much.

> *The owl and the pussycat went to sea*
> *In a beautiful pea-green boat,*
> *They took some honey, and plenty of money*
> *Wrapped up in a five-pound note.*
> *The owl looked up at the stars above,*
> *And sang to a small guitar,*
> *"Oh lovely pussy, oh, pussy, my love,*
> *What a beautiful pussy you are,*
> *You are, you are,*
> *What a beautiful pussy you are."*

"Whoops, we're almost there. I'll finish on the way across. Okay?"

"Okay, Mom."

The *Cathlamet* was just pulling into the dock as they drove down the hill and into the waiting line of cars at the Mukilteo dock. They stayed in the car on the short ferry ride over to Whidbey Island. It was a gorgeous day—blue sky, fluffy, cumulus clouds playing hide-and-go-seek with the sun, a veil of cirrus clouds just above the horizon. Temperatures were predicted to be in the mid 80s, and the bay was smooth. "Oh, it is so lovely. What a day!" Ann exclaimed.

Julie looked up at her mother, smiled, and sighed, "It's really nice, Mom. Can you finish the poem now?"

"Sure! Let's see now, where did I leave off?"

"You said, 'what a beautiful pussy you are, you are, what a beautiful pussy you are'."

"That's right. Okay…"

> *The pussy said to the owl,*
> *"You elegant fowl,*
> *How charmingly sweet you sing,*
> *Oh, let us be married,*
> *Too long we have tarried,*
> *But, what shall we do for a ring?"*
> *They sailed away for a year and a day*
> *To the land where the balm tree grows,*
> *And there in a wood, a piggy-wig stood,*
> *With a ring at the end of his nose.*
> *His nose, his nose,*
> *With a ring at the end of his nose.*
> *"Dear Pig, are you willing*
> *To sell for one shilling, your ring?"*
> *Said the piggy, "I will!"*
> *So, they took it away,*
> *And were married next day*
> *By the turkey who lived on the hill,*
> *They dined on mince and slices of quince,*
> *Which they ate with a runcible spoon,*
> *And hand in hand, on the edge of the sand,*
> *They danced by the light of the moon.*
> *The moon, the moon,*
> *They danced by the light of the moon.*

"That's all, Julie. 'They danced by the light of the moon'."

"I know. 'They danced by the light of the moon'," she repeated wistfully.

After the ferry anchored, the Volkswagen Bug bounced up the gangplank and sped up the hill out of Clinton, northwest on Highway 525. Julie spoke, deep in thought, "Mom, what's a runcible spoon?"

Ann smiled and hesitated before replying, "I'm not quite sure, Julie, but I think it's just like a big meat fork, only the prongs are curved like a table spoon. Maybe it's a spoon like that one with the holes in it that I use for vegetables. You know the one I mean, don't you?"

"Yes, I think so. The juice runs down through it."

"That's right. When its runcible, it doesn't hold liquid," Ann said. She hoped.

It took them about twenty-five minutes to reach their secluded cabin, up Honeymoon Bay Road and then down tree-lined Fisherman's Alibi Road. Julie always enjoyed this drive. Ann remarked, "If we didn't know just where our cabin was located, we would never find it, would we, honey?"

Julie, one eyebrow raised, looked at her mother, "Mom, you're so funny sometimes. You know we never have any trouble finding it."

Ann had been checking out the oak cupboards in the cabin when Julie, looking out the big bay window, shouted, "I think that's Neil coming now, Mom!"

Ann hurried to the window and put her arm around Julie's waist. "You're right, that's Neil. C'mon, let's go down to the dock and meet him. Here, you carry these towels, and I'll get the lunch."

Neil's Bellboy fiberglass eighteen foot runabout made a swoosh as it came in toward the Langley dock. Though an introvert, he was a bit of a show-off when it came to his boat, and he took great pride in keeping the small craft spotlessly clean and freshly painted. He had lucked out when he found the boat and the tandem axle, galvanized self-loading trailer. Later, through a college friend, he bought the Evinrude outboard motor for a reasonable price. He usually launched at a friend's ramp south of Camano City Beach. It was a secluded place to park the truck safely. Earlier in the summer, he completed the small box-like cabin, which was about four-by-five feet, and which left about two feet of crawl space on the starboard side of the boat. He had christened the small craft the *Webfoot*.

Ann and Julie both stood on the dock as Neil pulled up. "Hi, you two!" he shouted. "Terrific day, isn't it? Here, Julie, put on your life jacket—that's the rule, you know!" Neil helped each of them into the boat, and made certain that Julie's life jacket was securely fastened. Julie crawled to the small seat in the bow, and Ann sat on the bench in front of Neil.

"Neil," Ann asked, "Why did you come back to the coast in July? Isn't this a really busy time on the farm?"

"The real work, the harvesting, begins in two or three weeks, so my dad said it would be okay to come back here and play a little before then. I'll have to go back in August," Neil explained.

"Oh, I see," Ann said. "Well, it's really nice that you thought of us today."

After skimming over the water at full speed for several minutes, Neil cut the motor and yelled, "Ann, do you mind taking over for awhile? I'd like to ski!" They were about ten miles north of the cabin.

"Sure! Shall we go in so you can get your skis on?"

"No, that won't be necessary! I can manage out here! Man, what a day!" Neil stopped the engine and took his shirt and pants off, revealing his swim trunks underneath. He gracefully slipped over the side into the water with his rope and skis. Ann admired his lean, muscular physique. They were drifting. "Okay, Ann!" Neil shouted. "Give her the gun!" She started the motor and they were off with Neil coming up on his skis in inimitable form. Ann determined right then and there to learn to water-ski herself. She had procrastinated much too long.

They paralleled the shoreline of Camano, carved a wide bracelet through the water toward Whidbey, and headed south. Then, they cut a straight course east, after which they turned again and zigzagged across the bay between the two islands. Surprisingly, there were few out skiing, but there were several lazy sailboats skimming the blue waters of Puget Sound. Ann thought, *What a thrill it must be to carve that path through the water—like skiing up at Steven's Pass after a big snowfall.* She was sure she could learn to waterski—couldn't be too much different.

Eventually, Neil motioned that he had had enough, so he dropped the rope. Ann made a big circle and guided the craft back to Neil, idling the engine as they approached him. He swam to the side of the boat, put his skis in, then hoisted himself over the side. Bending over and shaking the water from his head, he exclaimed, "Wow, that was just fantastic! You'll have to try later this afternoon, Ann." He dried himself with his beach towel and sat down to pilot the boat again.

"I think it's a little early yet to have our sandwiches!" Ann shouted. "Do you mind if I slip into your little cabin and take a few winks, Neil? I've been up since six, and the boat's motion is making me so sleepy!"

"Fine! It may be a little cramped, but help yourself. Go ahead! Get a good rest!" Neil yelled.

When Rafe was gone, Ann invariably had difficulty sleeping. She missed their early morning conversation, the cuddling, the loving. Well, he'd be home again in a few more days and their lives could get back to normal. The thought made her smile. She fantasized his return. She was so drowsy.

Neil cut the engine a few knots, and the *Webfoot* gradually slowed. Julie, eyes squinting, was looking out straight ahead, her slick black hair whipping in the wind. She was wearing her swimsuit and the small yellow life jacket Neil had given her the first month they met.

After a few minutes, Neil left the engine and crept up to Julie in the bow of the boat. Gently touching her arm, he whispered, "C'mon, Punkin', come back here and sit with me for awhile. You can help steer the boat." Punkin' was his favorite name for Julie, though he also called her Sweetie Peetie and Julianna.

Julie hesitated momentarily, then crawled back, and sat on the floorboards in front of him. "Here, you sit right down close to Neil." He gave her a hug.

About thirty minutes later Ann awakened, feeling refreshed, and peered out of the makeshift cabin. Inhaling the fresh salt air deeply, and facing the bow of the boat, she realized that Julie wasn't in her usual spot. She crawled out and turned her head in the opposite direction, back to Neil. Her mouth flew open in a startled cry, her beautiful eyes widened in a look of total panic and horror. "Oh, my God!" she screamed. "Neil! What are you doing? Are you crazy? What are you doing to my little girl? Neil! Julie!"

She lunged at them and tore the child away. Julie fell forward, striking her head on the sharp corner of the box-like cabin. The blow knocked her out. Ann did not notice the blood that oozed down the side of her face. She went into a rage, hitting, clawing, pounding Neil's chest. The boat rocked. "You filthy—you filthy, deceitful pervert! How could you make her do that?" She was crazed, possessed by an inner rage she had never before experienced.

Neil, turning the engine off, tried to explain. "Ann, Ann, don't! I wasn't hurting her! Really, I wasn't hurting her!"

"You weren't *hurting* her? Neil, this—this is outrageous! How could you?" she cried, as she continued to pound his chest with both fists.

His hands were on her shoulders, and he began to shake her violently. "Stop it, Ann! Stop it! Julie is hurt! Don't you see! She's bleeding! Quit that! Look at Julie!" he shouted.

The boat, unattended, began to go around in circles. In the scuffle, Ann lost her balance and fell headlong overboard. Neil stopped the motor and looked back to see Ann swimming. In a strong stroke, she reached the craft again and tried to lift herself out of the water and back into the boat. Neil, deranged at that moment, grabbed a stick that was lying on the floor of the boat and struck her, first on her forehead, then on the left side of her neck. She began to lose consciousness. She clung to the side of the boat, but felt her mind drifting, aimlessly wandering. "Neil, what are you doing?" she gasped. Then, she felt his strong grip on her shoulder. She grabbed his arm and tried desperately to loosen his grasp.

"I wasn't hurting her, Ann! Please!" he cried. "Can't you see—I—I—wasn't hurting her!" He bent over and grabbed both of her shoulders. The boat rocked. He tried to push her under, but she clung desperately to the side of the boat until her hands were white and her knuckles bulged.

"Julie! Julie!" Her cry became weaker. "Oh, Neil, don't! Don't do this! Please, Neil—please!"

Arms aching, muscles stretched like a tight rope, she was forced to relinquish her hold, and Neil jumped out of the boat, almost on top of her. They slashed around in the water. He grasped her by the shoulders again, forcing her under. She couldn't breathe, and frantically gulped in air as she surfaced momentarily. She swallowed the salty water. Her mind was racing. *Oh, my God, he's trying to drown me! Please, dear God, help me—help me!*

With all the strength she could muster, she pushed him away. Gasping for breath, her aching head emerged, and she thrashed around in the water, beating him with clenched fists. They continued to struggle, but he was the stronger of the two. In one final attempt, he grabbed her head in both his hands and pushed her under, holding her steadfast, as though his very life depended upon this one act. His eyes were wild.

Kicking with all her might, she surfaced again and gasped, "Neil, don't—please don't! Oh, Julie, my baby!" His grip was like a steel vise, holding her under the surface of the water, a clamp that held her fast. She strained with all the strength she possessed to free herself—to no avail. It was at least five minutes before the fight left her body, until he could feel her go flaccid and limp, until the struggling ceased.

The events of her life flashed before her like a kaleidoscope—*her*

*childhood—her mother and father—their funeral—the young man respon-*
*sible for their tragic deaths—her visits to the jail to talk to him—grade school*
*and high school—Rafe—their first kiss at Ferguson Park—college—her*
*engagement—the pastor's counseling—her wedding day—Julie's birth—the*
*tiny bundle in her arms—the rosebud mouth opening to suck the milk from*
*her swollen breasts—Julie's first step—her first word—the Jam Jar.* "Rafe, oh
Rafe, I love you." Her brain cried out, *Juuuulllliiieee...* She felt her mind
slipping. She was falling, falling, falling down, down—into a chasm, into
the depths of a black abyss. She lost consciousness as she sank into mer-
ciful darkness.

Neil sustained his hold on her long after her body went limp, long
after the fighting ceased, until he felt a pull from beneath. He gave her
a big push. His hands were free, his fingers white, bent, and as stiff as a
board. He flexed them until he felt the blood pulsing to the tips of each
finger. He swam and, grabbing the side of the boat, hoisted himself in
over the side. Ann was gone. He wondered how long it would be until
her body surfaced, until it would drift in with the current.

Sitting, holding his head in both hands, he cried, "Oh, God, I'm
sorry! I'm so sorry! Why did this have to happen? What am I going to
do?" His thoughts were racing, and he began to rub his temples. A shiver
ran up his spine. Goose bumps caused the blond hairs on his arm to
stand erect. He had to think fast. Julie—Julie—what would he do with
his precious Julie?

Earlier that summer Neil had injured his shoulder while helping his
father on the farm. The pain had been intolerable, and the doctor had
given him a prescription to help alleviate the throbbing pain, to help
him sleep. The vial was still in the pocket of his pants. He fumbled for
the container—codeine—took four of the white pills, unscrewed the cup
from the thermos, broke the pills in small pieces, and dropped them into
the plastic cup.

"Mommy? Where's Mommy. Neil?" Julie whispered in a weak little
whisper. He filled the cup half full of water. After the pills dissolved, he
carefully raised Julie's head.

"There, there, Punkin'—got a bad bump, didn't you?" he whispered
sympathetically. "Here, take a drink of this good cold water. Let Neil
wipe the blood off your face. Poor baby..." He gently dabbed at the
blood stains on her face.

"She's okay, Punkin'," he lied. "Here, drink some more." She drained the cup. He cuddled her and stroked her head, playing with her beautiful, dark hair, admiring her long black eye lashes. "Just close your eyes now and rest. You'll feel better in a little while." In a very short time the drug began to take effect and Julie was sound asleep. He kissed her tenderly on the forehead.

Neil thought how lucky for him that he still had some of the drug. Now what? He had to make it look like an accident. The dinghy—he'd go back to the cabin and make it appear as if Ann had been out in the dinghy. Julie would sleep for hours. He would think about what to do with her later. He didn't want to hurt her. How he loved her—his very own little Punkin'. He started the engine and they sped south toward the cabin. Thank God the cabin was so privately located in that cove. No one would see him.

As the boat cut a clean path across the bay, Julie slept soundly, and Neil's thoughts were racing, his mind a clutter of fragmented debris. *Ann, Ann, why couldn't you understand? Why did you have to fight me? I wasn't hurting her. Julie—what will I do with Julie? What will I do with her? I didn't want to harm her in any way. I love her, oh, how I love her. I've never loved anyone in the world as much as I love my sweet little princess. If only we could steal away somewhere together where no one else could find us. She belongs to me. She loved me, too. I know she loved me. But, no, I can't keep her. I can't run away with her. I'd be suspect.* Like a bolt of flash lightning in a darkened troubled sky, he thought of Mr. Jenson. *Jenson, that strange man from Sweden with the patch over his eye!*

*During a dark rainy March night, spring term, Neil had accompanied some of his friends from the college to a party in Seattle in the Ballard District. "C'mon, Neil, you need to get away from the grind for awhile. We won't be out late. We're just going to take a run down to Ballard to see some relative of Bill's. His aunt is throwing a party in this guy's honor. Guess he's some kind of an important person from Sweden or Denmark. What say?"*

*"Naw. I don't think so."*

*"Oh, come on, Neil. Go with us."*

*"Well, I suppose I could go. This studying will keep 'til tomorrow. Okay, okay, I'll go."*

*While at the party, the boys had seen a video, a porno film, a film that shocked and offended him. He was embarrassed and self-conscious, yet he stood there, not commenting, his left hand in his back pocket, his right hand holding* a can of coke, wondering about his own stupidity. Why had he ever allowed himself to become involved? He was mortified and embarrassed; he felt sheepish. Did his friends actually enjoy this type of thing? If only he hadn't come. He couldn't wait to get away, away from this disgusting show. It was gross.

Thankfully, the woman of the house, Bill's aunt, finally came and turned the blasted video off. "Come in the library, fellows, I want you to meet my brother."

"Okay, Aunt Elaine. I've been waiting to see Cameron. How long will he be here?"

"I'll let him answer that, Bill."

Neil had noticed that there were quite a few Scandinavians mulling around the house. He was grateful for the interruption—anything to get away from that stupid video.

Cameron Jenson, a tall, handsome, engaging man, put on a charming facade for those who gathered around him. There was a certain mystique about him, a fascination, a charismatic appeal that attracted others to him. When he talked about the Louvre in Paris, mentioning some of the famous pieces of art on display there, his audience was captivated by his knowledge. Neil wasn't at all interested in the arts, but he was fascinated by the black patch over the man's left eye, and wondered if the eye was gone, or just injured. He had never seen anyone who wore a patch over an eye.

Neil would never know just why this Jenson guy singled him out for a private conversation. When speaking to the group, the talking was intense and exacting, almost like a lecture. He was discussing art museums on the continent, answering questions about famous paintings, talking about distinguished artists. Neil was mesmerized by this man who emanated some kind of royal character, this man who demanded attention by his very presence, this man with the rigid jaw, tight lips, and thin smile. Drawing Neil to a corner of the room, Jenson's personality changed, as a chameleon changes its color. He became more relaxed, more friendly, warm, and amicable.

Jenson questioned Neil skillfully, and drew answers from him that he would have thought incapable of answering. What kind of man was this? One thing was certain. He was confident and knowledgeable about many things. They talked about college, politics, wheat farming, and the beauty of the Pacific Northwest. For some unknown reason Jenson showed an unusual interest in Neil. He told him about his own college days in Denmark, and his interest in photography. "You must try to come to Europe some time, young man. Possibly after you graduate. You could do graduate work in Denmark."

*"That sounds pretty exciting, Mr. Jenson, but for now all I want to do is get my degree and teach science courses in high school." Neil grinned, "Maybe I could get to Europe later—after I've saved some money."*

*"Well, I'm sure you have a lot of good friends and other interests to keep you out of mischief, young man. Say, as I told you, I am very interested in photography, and am presently involved in film production in Europe. Concurrently, we are setting up a new studio in Denmark. I'm always looking for the right girls and boys for my films. Our creations have a great appeal here in the United States, Neil. Right now I'm searching for a pretty little girl about five or six years old for a particular picture, a girl whose parents would agree to sign a contract for a promising film career. By the way, if you know of anyone like that, be sure to get in touch with me. Here, let me give you my card." Jenson reached into his inside jacket pocket and pulled out a snakeskin cardholder. "Perhaps I could borrow your pen?" Neil handed him a cheap ballpoint. "I'll just write Elaine's phone number on the back of it." Handing Neil the card, he added with a half smile, "I may even be able to find a spot in a film for you some time. One never knows. You're a fine looking young man, my friend."*

*Jenson placed his hand on Neil's arm, and gave him a peculiar wink with his right eye. Neil felt a bit unsettled, and thought, Yeah, me in films? That's a joke. Is this guy serious?*

*What had Jenson really meant? The video he had seen at the party flashed before him, and he recalled having had a strange feeling about the guy. Well, maybe he'd find out just what Jenson was all about.*

They pulled up to the dock. Neil killed the engine and bounded out to secure the boat. Julie would still be out for hours. He quickly untied the rope that was attached to the dinghy, jumped in, and rowed out about one-hundred yards. Neil plunged into the cool clear water, grabbed one side of the small boat, and tipped her until she began to take on water. He turned the dinghy bottom-side-up, and swam back to the dock.

When he jumped back into the *Webfoot*, he noticed some of Ann's belongings—one sandal, her shoulder bag, and her blue Cashmere sweater. He hurriedly revved the engine, went out approximately five hundred feet, and threw the items into the water. As he glanced down at Julie, he noticed her beach towel. He'd throw that in, too. They'd find them on the beach later. It would look like an accident. They would obviously assume Julie had drowned, too. He headed east for Camano Island and the boat landing.

Neil plotted and schemed as he sped the short distance from Whidbey to Camano Island. He'd cover Julie so that no one could possibly guess what was under the covering, and put her in the truck. He'd get the boat back on the trailer, park it near the ramp, and they'd head for Seattle. Later, he'd return for the boat and thoroughly scrub it down. He would remember to put the thermos, sandwiches, and soft drinks into the truck. Just then he felt a hunger pang.

The events of the day were racing through his mind as they drove south on I-5. He hadn't meant to kill Ann, but she was acting insane, absolutely insane, and completely out of her mind. If only she could have been reasonable. If only he could have reasoned with her. She should have known that he would never really hurt Julie. What they did was not all that bad. If only she would have listened to him. No one ever really listened to him. No one listened when he was a little kid—no one would listen now. What a wild cat! Strong, too! But, why did he have to drown her? He hadn't wanted to drown her. No, he hadn't wanted to fight with her. He had really liked Ann, but why had she been so irrational? Thank God for the drug. Had Jenson meant what he said back there in Ballard last March? And, what would he do with Julie? He had written Jenson's sister's telephone number on the back of his card. Maybe he wouldn't even be in Seattle. Maybe he would be in Europe filming, but his sister would know how to get in touch with him.

Would Jenson put Julie in a video—in one similar to the one he had seen in Seattle at that party? Well, he would have to leave that all up to him. Julie could become famous if she got the right part in a movie, and some day she would come to him and thank him. She was beautiful enough to be in pictures. He fantasized as he drove along—Julie, a grown woman, a gorgeous, dazzling creature, now an important popular movie star. She had been his female lead in an Academy Award winning film. He held her close. She lifted her face to his own. Her eyes brimmed over with tears, tears that flowed freely down her cheeks. She looked up into his eyes and whispered, "Thank you, my darling—thank you for everything you have done for me. I am yours, yours alone, Neil. There will never be anyone else." He kissed her passionately. He stroked her long black hair. Would Jenson want her? Would he make her a star? Poor little Julie—poor Punkin'—how he loved her.

In the hour it took to drive to Seattle, Neil relived the past fifteen years of his life.

*The Manning farm was picturesque, like a scene from the National Geographic Magazine. All the buildings were painted white, trimmed in red, a striking contrast to the fields of wavy, golden ripe wheat. The combine, tractor, and other farm equipment were never left haphazardly out in a field, but were lined up like tenpins, or stored away in the machine shed like pawns in a game of chess, waiting for the next move. Neil grinned and rubbed his chin as he recalled the confrontation he had one spring day with his father over where his bike should stand when it was not being used. What difference did it make anyway? His parents were perfectionists. The weeds didn't have a chance in his mother's flower garden, and the many planters were always overflowing with flowers. What a great sense of color! He could still hear his mother's voice, "Neil, will you please go out and pick a bouquet for the table? Be sure to pick yellow and blue flowers. I want them to go with that pretty cloth—you know the one I mean."*

*"Yes, Mom, I know—I'll do my best." His mother took pride in her table, and many evenings they ate by candlelight. One evening his friend, Mike, had come over after school to study and Neil's mother had invited him to stay for dinner.*

*Later, Mike said, "Wow, that was really a great meal, but your mom didn't have to put candles on the table just because I stayed for dinner."*

*"She didn't, Mike. We eat by candlelight all the time," Neil responded with pride.*

*"Really?"*

*"Yup."*

*Neil thought of his sister, Laurie, and his curiosity about girls. Now she was sixteen, a beautiful girl, a junior at Luther High, and a cheerleader— popular, too. But, it was Julie who let him know about little girls. At first, she didn't seem to mind at all, but lately she was acting reticent about some of the things they did together. He told her it was their secret and that he would never hurt her. He loved her too much to hurt her.*

*He pictured his home, the wavy golden fields of ripe wheat waiting to be harvested, kitchen smells—home-baked bread, sweet cinnamon apple pie, chocolate chip cookies, the cold, rich milk, and the homemade butter. Family meals at the large round oak table off the kitchen were pleasant, a time for conversation centering around the business of the farm, school, and church. His father reprimanded him if he took even a carrot stick before the blessing had been offered. He could hear his father's voice, "Let us bow our heads and give thanks."*

*The large coffee pot was always on the stove, coffee as clear and sparkling as a morning dew drop. He knew his mom's secret—an egg in the coffee grounds. At ten o'clock in the morning, his father would always come in for a break, and in the summer months when Neil was not attending school, he noticed that his father always gave his mother a hug and a kiss after washing his hands, and before pouring the aromatic coffee into his special mug.*

*"Dad, are you and mom going to Spokane in the morning?"*

*"Yes, why?"*

*"Well, I'd really like to go, too. I want to go to the bookstore and get some more paperbacks."*

*"Not this time, Neil. Your mother wants to take Laurie. We have to send her off to kindergarten looking good—new shoes, dresses, school supplies— whatever little girls need for kindergarten. She's so excited about it." Reaching out to touch Neil on the shoulder, he added, "You know how these women are, Neil. It takes them forever to make up their minds about anything, and I need you to stay here on the farm and watch over everything. Here, have another glass of milk and a cookie."*

*How clearly he could see his dad sitting there in his denim overalls, both hands around the large mug of coffee. His father didn't smoke, but he loved his morning coffee. Neil had begged to go along, but his father shook his head and said he should stay home with the dog. "Your Uncle Ernie offered to come and stay with you, Neil, but I told him I thought you'd be okay alone for those few hours." Neil recalled his relief to learn that his uncle would not be coming. He could read his beloved science fiction books by Robert Heinlein, and cook a hot dog for himself.*

*"Sure, Dad—I'll be okay." He really didn't mind staying alone, but he couldn't help feeling just a bit dejected and perhaps a little jealous of his younger sister. It seemed like his mother and father were always doing things for Laurie and leaving him either with Uncle Ernie or alone.*

*He recalled the conversation after Laurie's first day in kindergarten. "Well, Laurie, how did you like going to school today?" her father asked.*

*"I don't think I want to go back tomorrow, Daddy. I was there all day,*

*and I still don't know how to read."* Everyone laughed. *"Could I please have another piece of chicken?"*

*Uncle Ernie. In front of his parents, Uncle Ernie was always going on and on about what a terrific kid Neil was—smart in his studies, handy with his hands and all that stuff—just like a son to him. He and his Aunt Ellen had never had children of their own. Ellen was his mom's youngest sister, and he really liked her, but ever since he was about six years old, Uncle Ernie fooled around with him, and did some things to him that he didn't appreciate. He never told anyone because his dad seemed to think the world of Ernie, and anyway, he was married to his favorite aunt. Uncle Ernie was a large strong man, always willing to help his father with some of the more difficult tasks on the farm.*

*Why didn't they pay more attention to him? It was always "Laurie this, and Laurie that." She was a pretty little thing, but sometimes he felt like choking her. When she was a baby, his mother would allow him to watch her change her diaper and give her a bath, and he remembered thinking how different girls were. The year Laurie entered kindergarten he would be in sixth grade, his last year in elementary school. He couldn't wait to get to middle school because of the great library they had. He could have lived in the library all day—and all night.*

*Yeah, ever since Laurie had come into the picture, they kind of forgot that he was a part of the family, too—that is, everyone except his Uncle Ernie. Course, his parents were always kind to him, but he surely would have liked having his dad spend more time with him, and if only he could have hugged him once in awhile it would have been nice. Did men ever kiss their sons? He wondered. Would it have hurt anything if his dad would have kissed him? His mom did—once in awhile. They surely kissed and hugged his little sister all the time.*

*Uncle Ernie was good to him—took him fishing, played ball with him and taught him how to bat. He even took the time to put up a basketball hoop behind the shed, and brought him a really good basketball one time for his birthday. He acted like his father. Ernie took him to the lake often, taught him how to fish and row his small boat. One time when he was five, he told him he was going to teach him how to swim. He did, too. That was the first time it happened—when he threw him up out of the water, then caught and held him in that private place. He did this often, but he never harmed him, nothing like that, just laughed, joked around, and played with him.*

*Neil felt funny about some of the things he and Ernie did together; but his uncle was good to him, and he never hurt him, not much, anyway. He'd tell him that it was their secret, just between them. But, things began to get worse and worse, and it bothered him. He didn't like it all, not one bit.*

*Neil recalled his embarrassment the time his sixth grade teacher quietly came to his desk and whispered, "Take your thumb out of your mouth and quit daydreaming, Neil." He knew his face was red as a beet.*

*From his upstairs bedroom window, around ten in the morning, he saw Ernie driving his yellow Chevy truck onto the driveway leading into the Manning farm. He pulled up to the tractor his father was working on, and jumped out of the truck. Neil could hear the conversation. "Good to see you again, Art! Working on this old tractor again, I see. Well, even though it isn't the latest model it still looks just like new. Never knew a man in this world who took such good care of his machinery." Before giving Art an opportunity to respond, he continued, "Say, I have to drive into Spokane later this afternoon and take care of a little business. I'd like to take Neil along for some company, that is, if it's okay with you and Marilyn."*

*"Sure, Ernie. It's okay with me, and I'm sure Marilyn won't mind. Neil can sleep in tomorrow if he wants to—it's Sunday. Go ahead and ask him if he wants to go."*

*"Fine, I'll just do that. Now, don't work too hard, Art."*

*Ernie walked over to the house, up the steps to the kitchen door, knocked, and opened the screen door. "Marilyn! Hi! Is Neil here?"*

*Marilyn recognized her brother-in-law's voice, and yelled from the bedroom, "Ernie? Come in! I think Neil's upstairs studying. He has tests next week, and he's really been hitting the books! How about a cup of coffee?"*

*"Love one, if it's no trouble for you and if you have it made. I'll run upstairs and see Neil first, though—I'd like to have him go into Spokane with me this afternoon. Talked to Art about it, and he said it would be okay with him, if it's all right with you."*

*"I think that would be nice—a good break for Neil. He's been studying so hard—wants to take all top grades into junior high school next fall. You know him and grades!" The voice coming out of the bedroom revealed a particular pride it its inflection. "When do you think you would be back home?"*

*Ernie began running up the stairs as he replied, "Probably late tonight! Just a minute, Marilyn—I'll be right back down for coffee!" Ernie knocked on Neil's door, "Neil, may I come in, son?"*

*Son? Neil thought, shaking his head. "Oh, brother," he whispered under his breath. Then he shouted, "Sure! Come in, Ernie."*

"Hi, Neil. Really hitting the books these days, huh?"

"Yeah, we have our final tests next week, you know. I do want to make good grades. Gee, Uncle Ernie, just think, I'll be in the seventh grade next fall."

"Yeah, you're really growing up, getting tall, and downright handsome I might add. You're going to be twelve next month, aren't you?"

"That's right—twelve years old," Neil replied, with a pleased look.

"Say, buddy, I have to drive into Spokane and take care of a little business this afternoon. I thought maybe you'd like to come along and keep me company. Maybe, after I get through, we could grab a pizza and take in a movie. Would you like that?"

"Gee, yes, I'd like that. But, Uncle Ernie, I really shouldn't go. I think I'd better stay home and study."

"Come on, Neil, you'll get good grades anyway. I'll just bet you'll be right at the top of your class again. You still have tomorrow afternoon and evening to catch up. What do you say? Maybe we could go and see Star Wars. You haven't seen it yet, have you?"

"Star Wars? Gee! No, I haven't seen it yet, and I would love that! Is it okay with my mom and dad?" Neil's eyes sparkled with excitement.

"Yes, they think you need a break from studying. You know, it's been a long time since we did anything together—think it was during your spring vacation, wasn't it?"

"I know, Ernie, but I've been awfully busy with school work." He had purposely stayed clear of his uncle because he knew he would be expected to do things with him that repulsed him. He was getting too old for that stuff. He didn't like being with him anymore. Yet, that movie—he really wanted to see it, and he knew that his parents would never bother to take him. Well, he'd go with him this one time, and then he would tell him—tell him all the things he had thought about in the past year, his last year in elementary school. This would be the last time, absolutely the very last time. He wondered how his uncle would accept what he had to say. Maybe he'd get mad, really mad at him. He'd probably bring up all the nice things he had done for him—make him feel ungrateful, like a fool. Neil didn't think his uncle would ever hurt him, but he might tell him off. Well, one more time, one more time. He simply could not continue doing all those things with him anymore. Someone might find out. He wondered what his parents would say or do if they knew what went on between them. What about his Aunt Ellen? He really felt sorry for her. He *didn't know exactly why, but he felt sorry for her. She surely didn't know Uncle Ernie very well.*

*"Is Aunt Ellen going with us?"*

*"No, she can't go this time. It will be just you and me, son. We'll have a good time—the movie—pizza. You get ready right away, and I'll go down and have a cup of coffee with your mom. Hurry. We have to get on our way because I should be in Spokane no later than three." Ernie slapped him on the shoulder and left the room.*

*Sitting across the table from Marilyn in her sparkling blue and white kitchen, sipping coffee, and munching a chocolate chip cookie, Ernie spoke first. "That boy is something else, Marilyn. I've never known a kid who liked to study as much as he does."*

*"I know," Marilyn said thoughtfully. "We're really proud of him. I only hope that Laurie will do as well."*

*"You and Art have two wonderful kids, Marilyn. I wish we could have had the same luck, but guess it just wasn't in the cards."*

*Marilyn looked at Ernie, smiled, and patted his arm as she rose to get the coffee pot. "Have another cookie, Ernie."*

*"Thanks, I will. They're just delicious. No one can make bread and cookies like you, Marilyn."*

*Neil came bounding down the steps two at a time. Grabbing a cookie, he said, "I'm ready, Ernie. Bye, Mom! See you in the morning, I guess. It'll be late when we get home 'cause we're going to see* Star Wars. *Isn't that neat, Mom?"*

*"Yes, that's wonderful. I know how much you have wanted to see it. I'm glad you can have such good times together." She smiled, as she glanced from one to the other. "Here, take a cookie or two with you, and be good now. Drive carefully, Ernie!"*

*"We will, Mom." As the truck sped down the highway, her words kept reverberating in his ears. Over each black, tarred section of the old highway, he could still hear her voice, "Be good now—be good now—be good now."*

*Neil was fascinated with* Star Wars. *He lived the film. Protocol—protocol—what did that word mean anyway? He would ask Ernie after the show. No, he probably wouldn't know what it meant. He'd look it up in the dictionary tomorrow. He imagined that he was Luke. Luke was blond, too. Eccentric. What did eccentric mean? He'd look that up, too. Luke's aunt reminded him of his own Aunt Ellen—plain, pale blue eyes, straight, light brown hair, kind. Entranced, he sat there as though in another world, on another planet, in another time. He fantasized about being a Star pilot, whizzing from planet to planet. His mind raced as Luke raced out there in the galaxies. The energy field—was there really an energy field surrounding each of us? The Empire was evil. Was The Empire the devil? He loved robots. Would robots ever really be important in the world? Of course they would be—very important. The Force controlled everything in the universe. Was God The Force?*

*Those awful sand creatures—he hoped he wouldn't have a nightmare over them. Wow! He wondered if there really could be life on other planets. Seemed logical. His mind continued to race—just like the space ship,* Falcon. *He wondered if he would ever find his princess. The magnetic field—he hoped he could learn more about it in junior high school. Neil loved the droids. How could anyone love a droid anyway? He did! They were good. They were polite. A droid would make a terrific friend. Boy, even the bad guys realized that they should never underestimate The Force.*

*The theater was almost as dark as a night in December, a night when heavy, low hanging clouds shut out the light of the moon and stars. Ernie and Neil sat about halfway back on the right side, in the last two seats of the tenth row. Ernie's thoughts were not of Luke and his space ship. They were of Neil. The latter sat back in his seat, alert, just as straight as a stick, chewing his fingernail. Ernie cautiously reached over and took Neil's hand out of his mouth. Neil hardly noticed. He was Luke! He was flying through space on a space fighter!*

*Ernie stole another glance at Neil, who sat, resting his right elbow on the seat's armrest. He became increasingly aware of the boy's presence. He leaned toward him, his hand holding his chin, gently rubbing the short stubble of his black beard, his arm brushing Neil's narrow shoulder. He had never seen Neil so engrossed. How he loved that boy, the blond hair, the deeply set blue-gray eyes, the thick, long lashes, the heavy brows, the small, straight nose, the full lips. He had been more than a son to him—much more than a son.*

*Ernie studied the profile. His desire mounted. He slowly, gently laid his hand on Neil's thigh. Neil seemed oblivious to the move, oblivious to Ernie's mood. Ernie found Neil's hand, and slowly began to place it on his own thigh. Neil's hand jerked like a frog's leg in a hot skillet. He pulled it away, and turned his face toward Ernie's. "No, Ernie! No! Not now! Not ever! No! No more!" Ernie had never heard such an exclamation of exasperation, such determination in his voice.*

*"Okay, Neil—shhh—not so loud! Okay, kid!" He stared at the screen, not seeing. He knew his face was red—he could feel the blood pulsating in his*

*temples. He sensed that Neil was staring at him. Ernie whispered, "Shh, shh, okay, Neil! Look at the picture! It's okay, kid! It's okay!" Ernie's thoughts were racing. Neil was growing up. Would he keep their secret? Yeah, he'd be too embarrassed to tell anyone. He was a very private kid. He wouldn't tell. No, he wouldn't say anything. Well, it could be over between them—that special relationship could be over, it could be over.*

*A feeling of complete exhaustion and weakness swept over Ernie's body, and he felt the blood drain from his face. It was the same feeling he had when he experienced that bout with the flu. In his subconscious he could hear Ellen say, "Come on, Ernie, I'll help you get to bed. You poor dear—when you get sick, you really get sick. You really get sick." Yes, it was the same feeling.*

*The movie ended, and the lights came on. Neil turned to his uncle and whispered excitedly, "Luke used The Force, Uncle Ernie! He used The Force! The good guys won! Wasn't it just terrific?" He had seemingly forgotten the incident.*

*"Yeah, it was great, Neil," Ernie grinned. "Well, let's get going. We still have to grab that pizza."*

*Neil was silent, pensive, deep in thought, as they made their way to the truck. He hopped in, fastened the seat belt, and looked over at Ernie. "Do you think the good guys always win in the end, Uncle Ernie?"*

*"Yeah, I guess so, kid," Ernie replied as he slapped him on the knee. He started the engine, and they pulled out of the parking lot and headed for the pizza parlor.*

Neil glanced over at Julie, sleeping peacefully, her long, black lashes like sable brushes on her delicate skin. The minute hand on his wristwatch moved slowly, giving him more time to plan, to think about what he must do, to think about the past. His truck stayed in the right lane. He relived his high school days as though they were yesterday.

*"Neil! Hey, man, who you taking to the senior ball? You are going, aren't you?" Bob inquired.*

*"Naw—I can't make it, Bob. You know me and dancing! Anyway, that night my folks are celebrating their twentieth wedding anniversary, and the church is going to give them a big bash. They've asked me to say a few words—make a little speech—command performance, you know. Can you believe that? Me making a speech? I just couldn't go to the senior ball on account of that. My*

folks would be hurt, ya know. I have to be there." In his heart he was grateful for a legitimate excuse.

Bob raised his brows in question. "That's too bad, man! We're going to have a great time after the dance at John's place—going to stay up all night, Neil, and then go over to Jenna's for breakfast. Her mom is going to make fries, eggs, hot cakes, and ham. I wish you could change your plans and come, Neil. You'd have a great time. Wouldn't your parents understand? Man, who wants to go to an anniversary at church anyway?"

"I know—sounds dumb, but I just can't get out of it."

"Well, I guess I can understand how you feel, Neil, but with your good looks you wouldn't have a problem getting a date. I know a certain someone who would just love to go with you."

"Really? You're kidding!"

"No, I'm not kidding! Too bad. As I said, you wouldn't have any trouble getting a super date. I mean it!" Bob slapped his friend on the shoulder, turned, and ran down the hall.

Neil grinned as he watched his friend running down the hall. He thought, what a joke—having a date—funny, really funny—a date—with a girl? He slammed his gray locker closed, gave it a kick for good measure, and walked toward the science department of Luther High School. He wished he could be carefree and cool, like Bob and his friend John. They always seemed to have so much fun, and they were never ill at ease around girls. Why was he so different? Why couldn't he feel comfortable around girls? In his heart he always knew that he was some kind of misfit—extremely reticent and embarrassed around the fellows in the shower room. At times he hated himself.

"Hey, Manning, are you going to run after school today?" Dale stood by his locker, waiting for a reply.

"Oh, hi, Dale. Yeah, I think I'll run. Are you?"

"Yes, I'll meet you after the bell. Okay?"

"Just give me a chance to change my clothes first. Yeah, I'll be there." That was the one activity Neil loved—running—and he excelled at it.

"Great! I'll see you a little after three. If you're not in the locker room, I'll meet you out on the track." Dale turned, and yelled, "See you!" He hurried down the hall. Half way down the corridor, he stopped and shouted back, "Hey, Manning, congratulations on that science scholarship! George College isn't very large, but I hear it's a terrific school!"

"Thanks, Dale." Neil grinned.

*College—psychology class—it was there that he realized that he, Neil Manning, had what the professor termed a poor self-image. Yes, he figured that much out for himself—no one had to tell him. Why was he such a misfit anyway? Why? Why? No one knew any better than he, how he always managed some way to talk his way out of social relationships which made him uncomfortable. He wondered if he would ever find a girl who could really be interested in him—enough to marry him. He knew he would be a teacher someday, teach for a few years, and get on his feet before he thought of marriage. Maybe he'd meet another teacher. One thing was sure—he didn't want to farm. Laurie could have the farm some day. She was so perfect—just like the farm.*

And, then his thoughts went back to Ernie—Ernest. He was Ernest all right! The jerk. Screwloose. He was the only one who really knew what he was like. He would never, never tell anyone what he had done with his dear Uncle Ernie—never, as long as he lived. He couldn't even cry at his funeral. Afterward, his mom made some comment about his apparent lack of emotion.

*"Awe, Mom, it isn't that I don't care. You know, some people just react differently. I guess I kind of keep things inside. I don't show my emotions outwardly. You know what I mean, don't you?"*

*"Yes, I suppose so, Neil. I suppose so."*

*"I'm really sorry that Uncle Ernie got killed in that automobile accident, really I am, but my sympathy goes out to Aunt Ellen. She's so alone. She's the one I feel sorry for."*

*"I know, Neil. I know," his mother replied.*

*It was too bad that Ernie was killed, but that was life—or death, as the case may be. In his heart he was glad he was dead. He hated him. Yet, he loved him, too. Funny. Could one hate and love at the same time? He supposed so. But his Aunt Ellen was something else—such a nice person—always so kind and thoughtful and good to everyone.*

*"Neil," his mother said a few months later, "you know, Ellen has found a wonderful new friend. She started going with this man a couple of months after Ernie was killed. He happened to be a friend of the fellow in the other car."*

*"Really? Well, isn't he married?" Neil asked.*

*"No, not now. His wife passed away a couple of years ago. He is such a fine, considerate man. He has a small spread about twenty miles from here, and he*

*has a daughter. Her name is Angela Scott. She would be much younger than you, but perhaps you remember her from school."*

*"No, Mom, I don't remember her. Maybe Laurie knows her. Does Angela like Ellen?"*

*"Yes, I think so. Ellen loves her as much as if she were her own child. I just think it's wonderful, don't you? At last she has a daughter."*

*"Yeah, Mom, that's great, just great. It was too bad that Ernie and Ellen never had any kids of their own."*

*He wanted his Aunt Ellen to be happy. He supposed that she never really knew the true Ernie. She would never have believed the facts. Neil's folks wouldn't have believed it either. Neil thought he knew why his aunt and uncle had never had children.*

At about three in the afternoon, as Neil neared Seattle, he pulled off the freeway by a telephone booth to make the call. Fumbling through his wallet he finally found the right card. "Yeah, this is it," he assured himself. He dropped the quarter in the slot and dialed the number written on the back. The phone rang four times before he heard a woman's melodious voice. "Anderson residence. May I help you?"

Neil stuttered, "Hello, hello, is this Mrs. Anderson, Mr. Jenson's sister?"

"Yes, who is calling, please?"

"This is a—Neil—Neil Manning. I came to your home last March with your nephew, Bill, and some other college friends. I met your brother, Mr. Jenson, then. Do you remember?"

"Yes, I surely do remember that evening, Neil. It was just wonderful having you boys come for a visit. How are you? Is Bill okay?"

"Yes, I think so. I haven't seen him for a while, though. Say, Mrs. Anderson, is Mr. Jenson there by any chance?"

"Yes, would you believe, he is, Neil! Would you like to speak to him?"

"Yes—yes, I would. Thank you."

"Neil, I think he's out back on the deck. Can you hold on for a few minutes?"

"Yes, Mrs. Anderson, I can wait." He stood on one foot, then the other, and ran his left hand through his unkempt blond hair. Biting a fingernail, he tasted salt.

The voice was curt, "Hello! Jenson here."

"Hello—hello, Mr. Jenson. Nice to talk to you again. This is Neil—Neil Manning. I met you about four months ago at a party at the Anderson home. I was one of the students from George College up north who came down with Bill. I was the blond guy. Do you remember me?"

"Yes, I surely do, young man. How are you? Are you ready to come to Europe to complete your studies?"

"Well, I'm fine, just fine, thank you, but no, no, I'm not ready for Europe yet. Still have another year at George. Perhaps later."

"So you'll be a senior next term?"

"That's right."

"Well, what can I do for you?"

"Well, uh, Mr. Jenson, the reason I'm calling—well, uh, I remember your telling me that you were making films in Europe—in Denmark. Remember?"

The calm reply was, "Yes, I remember."

Neil continued, "Well, you told me that you were always looking for good-looking boys and girls for your films, and if I knew of a pretty girl whose parents—ah—whose parents—would like to put her in films, that—that perhaps you would be interested. Uh, would you be—interested, that is?"

"Perhaps. Yes, that is correct, Neil. I said that. Do you have someone in mind?"

Flushed, Neil answered breathlessly, "Yes, yes, Mr. Jenson—I—I do know a very beautiful little girl who will be six on her next birthday. She's right here with me."

In a reserved voice, Jenson interrupted, "She's right there with you now? Well, Neil, tell me more about her."

"Well, first of all her parents are all for it," he lied.

"Excellent. Tell me more."

"Yes, sir. Well, as I said, she's almost six—I think. She's really a pretty little thing."

"What is the color of her hair, Neil?"

Neil wondered what difference that would make, but quickly replied, "Did you ask what color her hair was?"

"Yes, what color is her hair?"

"She's a—a brunette, long dark hair and light blue eyes."

"Sounds perfect to me. When and where can I see her?"

"Well—a—perhaps you could meet us in a motel. Are you familiar with any up on Aurora, say around eighty-fifth or ninety-fifth? We're not very far from there."

"Yes, I just happen to know of one right on the corner of ninety-fifth and Aurora. I could meet you there in approximately half an hour. It's a small motel, and at this time of day I doubt they would have much business. I'll be in room seven. Would this be favorable with you?"

"Yes, that would be fine, that would be fine. I'm sure that I—I won't have any trouble finding it."

"Excellent. Anything else, Neil?"

"Well, yes—yes, sir. Didn't you tell me that you would pay?"

"I don't recall saying anything about that."

"Well—a—you will pay, won't you?"

"We'll talk about that when I meet you, Neil. Half an hour." Jenson cut the conversation short. "One more thing, Neil. Are you alone?"

"Yes, we are alone. We'll see you in about a half hour then. Goodbye, sir."

Neil shook his head, breathed a sigh of relief, hung up the phone, and ran his fingers through his hair. "Hmm, I think the guy did mean it," he whispered. He jumped back in the pick-up and looked over at Julie, who was sleeping peacefully. Such a pretty little thing, he thought. He'd just sit there and wait. He wanted to play it cool; he didn't want to be early.

Thirty-five minutes later he pulled slowly into the parking lot of a seedy looking motel, and parked in front of Number seven. He killed the engine, jumped out, went up to the door, paused for a moment, knocked, and a young woman of medium height opened the door. She was quite attractive, blond, blue-eyed, a full figure. Neil inquired, "Uh, is Mr. Jenson here?"

"Ja—you are Neil? Neil Manning?"

"Yes. I called. He told me to meet him here. It's about a girl. Shall I get her and bring her in?"

"By all means, Mr. Manning." Neil observed her decided Scandinavian accent. Her lips were full, perfect for pouting, her complexion extremely fair, her skin flawless over high cheekbones full of natural color.

Neil tried to awaken Julie, but fortunately she was still sound asleep. It was probably for the best. He carried her into the shabby motel room and placed her gently on the washed out, pale, rose-colored chenille spread covering the sagging double bed. The brass posts of the bed were discolored by age and long use. He glanced down at the worn, spotted brown rug. The air was musty and reeked of stale cigarette smoke. The cream-colored paint on the dilapidated radiator was peeling, and the maid had not bothered to pick up any of the flakes, which were now imbedded in the rug. He wondered why Jenson had asked him to come to such a disreputable place. He had appeared to be a gentleman of exquisite tastes.

Mr. Jenson came out of the bathroom, and walked over to the bed. His hand cupped his chin as he gazed down upon one of the prettiest little girls he had ever seen, so different than most of the girls, who had either blond or light brown hair. Her hair was raven black and heavy. Her eyebrows were dark and naturally arched, with lashes long, thick, and curved slightly upward. Jenson nodded his approval, and thought perfect, just perfect. He turned to Neil and spoke in a laconic manner, "You were quite right, Neil Manning. She is surely a beautiful child, and you say her parents are in joint agreement that she be in films?"

"Yes, yes, sir. That is correct." They each knew they were acting—acting in a scenario that was a complete farce, an absurd, exaggerated comedy, a comedy of errors. Each was giving an unsurpassed performance in a melodrama about unrealistic life.

"Yes, well, Neil, you were so right about the child. She will be perfect for the film I have in mind. Now may I say something to you that I insist you never forget?"

"Sure, Mr. Jenson. What is it?"

"After this meeting today, you are not to make further inquiry about the girl, or her whereabouts. You are to erase this rendezvous completely from your mind, forget that you ever met with me. Do you understand what I am saying?"

Boy, this was one different guy. He had been transformed. All business. He was definitely not the same man he had met in Ballard. "Yes, I understand." He really didn't. He wondered what they would do with Julie. He thought, *What am I doing? What am I doing to my sweet little Punkin'?* He said nothing. Everything was happening so fast. Neil fidgeted, "I'm really thirsty. Do you suppose I could get a coke or something cold to drink?"

Jenson nodded to the blond, and she stepped out. In a short time she was back in the room with two cokes. She handed one to Neil, who snapped it open immediately and took a long drink. The young woman walked slowly to the window, opened the other can for herself and took a sip. The sunlight filtering through the venetian blinds accentuated her high cheekbones, and her blond hair caught the lights of the neon sign across the street. Neil admired her lovely profile, the lights playing on her hair, and pondered her background. Why would this nice looking young woman be involved with a character like Jenson, a man who bought children? She couldn't be very old. What was in it for her?

Jenson picked up the phone, dialed, and said, "Jenson here. May I speak to Andrew? Yes, yes, but make it fast. Andrew, bring the cash. You know the place. Yes, immediately." Placing the phone deliberately on the side table, he smiled faintly as he glanced at Julie, then turning to Neil, said, "Andrew will be here in about five minutes. He will have the money for you."

Neil breathed a sigh of relief.

After a short and uncomfortably strained period of time, a 1982 white Buick pulled up in front of the door. Jenson drew the musty, stained, faded, green-colored drapery back, and peered out the window. "Andrew is here," he exclaimed. "Astrid, will you please get the envelope?"

The young woman opened the motel door and stepped outside. She accepted a large manila envelope from the man in the car. The girl came back into the room, and handed the envelope to Jenson. He turned his back, opened the envelope, checked the banded one hundred dollar bills, turned, and handed the money to Neil. "There you are, young man— three thousand dollars. I trust this will meet with your approval. You may leave now, Neil," he said with a crooked smile. "I've really enjoyed seeing you again. Thank you very much. We'll take good care of—you said her name was Julie?"

"Yes, Mr. Jenson, her name is Julie."

Neil accepted the envelope, which was bulging with banded one hundred dollar bills. His hand was shaking. Not knowing what else to say, he simply nodded in agreement. He stole one last, quick glimpse of Julie. Jenson guided him to the motel door, opened it for him, and Neil, coke in one hand, the money in the other, stepped out and got into the 1980 Ford Courier pick-up. He threw the money on the seat, rolled the window half way down, looked at Jenson above the glass, and nodded a goodbye, as the truck started. He drove the semi-circle to the street. In that moment, he detested what he had done, and he loathed Jenson. As his eyes filled with tears, he drained the coke, crushed the can in his left hand, rolled the window down further, and threw it into the garbage can at the motel's entrance.

As he stopped at a red light, he heard the barking of a dog, a lazy, mournful, howling bark, as if the dog were barking for no reason other than to relieve his boredom. Neil wiped his eyes with his shirtsleeve, shivered and rubbed his arms, trying to erase the goose bumps. When the light changed to green, he quickly drove onto the highway heading north. It would appear to any passerby that the good-looking young man behind the wheel of a small truck was anticipating a great weekend somewhere. He thought, *Oh, man, what have I done, what have I done? God, please take care of Julie.* Then, with a shake of his head, he whispered, "Now to get back to the boat and wash it down."

On July 19th, 1983, Ron Larson and Allison Trent, each seventeen, were running on that portion of the beach near the water that was hard and smooth just after the tide had receded. With shoes tied together and slung over their shoulders, they ran seriously, taking long strides, enjoying the cool sensation of the damp sand beneath bare feet. It was one of those rare, magnificent summer evenings on Puget Sound. The bay reflected all the colors of a brilliant sunset, iridescent and glistening in shades from light pink to deep vermilion, azure, amethyst to deep purple.

The sun disappeared behind Whidbey Island, casting long shadows on the lush, green hills across the bay. The lean, athletic figures of the two young people projected elongated, gray images on the western shores of Camano Island. They raced their shadows, but could not pull away from them.

Allison, always watching for an interesting piece of driftwood on the beach, stopped short as she observed what appeared to be a mound of pale blue cloth. "Ron! Ron! Wait up!" she shouted.

Ron slackened his pace, turned, and glanced back, thinking that perhaps she had discovered an unusual piece of driftwood. He was astonished at her expression. She was staring at something. Jogging in place, eager to go on, he shouted impatiently, "C'mon, Al, we've got to get back!"

"Ron—wait! I—I—think it's a woman."

"A woman?" He stood still. "You've got to be kidding."

"Come here. Look." Allison bent to get a closer view. "Oh, Ron, it looks like she's dead. Her clothes are still wet—she must have washed up in the tide. There's seaweed all over her."

They each gaped at the lifeless form. As they stole a closer look, they noticed that she was wearing a pair of well-tailored blue slacks, a blue

T-shirt, and one blue sandal on her right foot. The other foot was bare. Her head was face down in the sand, and her thick, dark hair fell to the sides of her body.

"Shall we turn her over and look at her face?" Allison questioned.

Taking her arm, Ron gently pulled her away. "No, we mustn't touch her. C'mon, Al, we've got to run up to the cabin and call the police." Sitting on a nearby log, they quickly brushed the sand from their feet and put on their shoes, then headed for the path that led to the cabin above the beach.

Five minutes later, panting from the scurry up the hill, they were back in the cabin dialing 911. "Mom, Dad, it was awful. She was so blue. I've never seen a drowned person before."

"I know, Allison. It must have been a terrible shock to you. I wonder who she is and what happened," her mother said thoughtfully as she put her arm around her daughter.

Ron and Mr. Trent were talking quietly in a corner of the cabin. "I wonder who she is," Mr. Trent said, with a worried look on his face.

At 7:10 p.m. the troopers arrived. The young couple, along with the Trents, guided the officers hurriedly down the shaded, cool trail through the rust-colored madronas, and on to the beach where the body lay.

"Thanks for the lift, Harry. I'll see you in a couple days at school." Rafe jumped out of the blue Pontiac, opened the back door and grabbed his suit bag and briefcase. "Thanks again. Bye now!"

"Any time, Rafe. Remember, you're going to meet me next time. See you soon." Harry drove off.

Rafe ran up the steps to the front entrance of the two-story, old stone house. The door was locked. Strange, he thought. He groped in his pocket for his keys, unlocked the door, and walked into the front entrance hall. "Ann! I'm home, honey!" No answer. "Wonder where they could be," he whispered. "Ann! Julie! I'm home!" No answer. He ran hurriedly upstairs, shouting, "Ann! Julie!" Still no answer. Where could they be? He ran down the stairs and out the back door to the garage to see if the Bug was gone. No Bug. He assumed that Ann and Julie had gone to visit Aunt Laura, who lived out in the country in northern Washington State near the Canadian border. Many times, after a visit with Rafe's mother's sister, they would drive to Anacortes, over Deception Pass, then down Whidbey Island to the cabin. After a hurried call to Laura, he learned that she had not seen or heard from them in several days. "Okay, Laura, thanks a lot. I'll be in touch. Bye now." Perhaps they had gone to Seattle on a shopping spree. Julie would need new clothes for first grade. How excited she had been about going to school. Strange, nothing like this had ever happened in all the years of their marriage. It just wasn't like Ann, unless she had simply run over to the Ray's for a few minutes, or had popped in for a brief visit with Kim. When they had talked on the telephone, she had told him that she was eagerly anticipating his return, that she'd be anxiously waiting for him with open arms, but she hadn't mentioned anything about their plans to leave, or go over to the cabin. She knew the approximate time of his arrival. Perhaps, on impulse, they had decided to go to the island because the weather had been so ideal. It was bewildering indeed, and not at all like Ann.

Rafe reached for the phone and dialed Ray's number. "Hello, Mrs. Ray. How are you?"

"This is Rafe calling, isn't it?"

"Yes, it is, Mrs. Ray."

"Well, I really am feeling much better. How nice to hear from you, and thank you for asking."

"Say, Ann and Julie wouldn't happen to be there, would they?"

"No, they aren't here. Mr. Ray told me he saw them a few days ago driving down the road in the Bug. Neither of us has seen them since then."

"Okay, Mrs. Ray, thanks so much. We'll be in touch. Bye." He carefully hung up the phone and walked over to sit at the kitchen table. Head bent in concentration, he whispered, "Well, I'm sure they'll be home soon."

The piercing ring of the telephone startled him, and he jerked involuntarily. The phone rang again. He hesitated before going over to pick up it up. Premonition? Somehow he knew in his heart that the call would not be favorable, that something was amiss. He picked it up on the fourth ring. "Langley residence. Hello!"

"Is this is Rafe Langley?"

"Yes, yes it is. Who's calling, please?"

"This is the county sheriff, Mr. Langley."

"Who? The sheriff? Why? What's happened? Do you know where my wife and daughter are?"

"I don't want to discuss anything over the telephone, Mr. Langley. Could you please come down to our office?"

"Yes, yes, I'll be right down. Yes, thank you, I'll be right there." Rafe looked at the phone in his hand as if it were a person, held it momentarily to his chest, stared at the wall with a blank expression, then put the phone down intentionally. He broke out in a cold sweat. Grabbing a light sweater, he headed for the door.

"Mr. Langley, thank you for coming. Please come in. Have a seat. I must ask you a few questions."

Refusing the chair, Rafe asked, "What's this all about, sheriff?"

"Please—please, Mr. Langley, do sit down."

Rafe refused.

"Mr. Langley, when was the last time you saw your wife?"

Searching the sheriff's eyes for an answer—any answer, Rafe rubbed his chin, "Just before I went back to Chicago to a conference—about a week ago. I can't remember the exact date. I gave a paper there. What's this all about, anyway?"

"You are a professor at George College?"

"That's right. But, can you please tell me why I'm here?" Rafe was obviously getting extremely nervous and somewhat agitated.

"When did you get back home, Mr. Langley?"

"About an hour ago. My friend, Harry Lochrie, just dropped me off at the house. He met me at Sea/Tac and brought me home. He's also a professor at George." Rafe was still standing in front of the sheriff's desk.

"Yes, well, Mr. Langley, please sit down, will you? Please."

Bending over and placing both hands on the edge of the desk, he looked straight into the sheriff's eyes and said, "I don't want to sit down. Now, can you please tell me what this is all about?"

The officer continued, "I don't like being the bearer of sad news, Mr. Langley, but it is my responsibility to inform you that—that your wife is dead. Her body was found on the beach at Camano Island on July 19. She evidently drowned. We have tried repeatedly to get in touch with you."

"She *what*? She *drowned*? You must be mistaken, sir. My wife could not have drowned. She was an exceptionally good swimmer."

"I am sure she was. We are truly sorry, Mr. Langley. We are truly sorry, but I must tell you—" He hesitated. "Your wife's body is in the morgue. We would like to take you over there now."

"Ann *dead*? In the—in the morgue?" Rafe's tone was questioning, uncomprehending. "This can't be true—this can't be true," he whispered. He shook his head and repeated, "Ann dead?"

The sheriff rose and went around to put his hand on Rafe's arm. "I really am sorry, Mr. Langley."

"My little girl—Julie—do you know where she is?"

"No, we know nothing about your daughter, Mr. Langley. Come on, let's go over now. Dr. Henderson is waiting for us." Rafe began to shake. The officer took his arm and gently led him to the door.

The sheriff and Rafe walked into the morgue together. "Dr. Henderson, this is Mr. Langley. He has come to—to identify the body."

"Yes, hello, Mr. Langley. Please come this way, gentlemen." The graying, portly, gentle doctor led the way into an inner room. Ann's body lay on a cold slab. A white sheet was draped over the corpse. The pathologist carefully lifted the sheet to give Rafe a complete view. "Mr. Langley, is this your wife?" he questioned softly.

"Yes, yes it is," Rafe whispered in disbelief. His complexion faded to an ashen pallor.

Ann was lying on her back, clothed in her light blue Giovanni pants and blue T-shirt, which had perfectly matched the color of her eyes. Obviously, she had been in the water for a lengthy period of time. Her skin was blue and looked like that of a washerwoman. Rafe ran his fingers lightly over her arm. It felt cold, soft, bumpy. He noticed the outline of her panty brief and bra under the outer garments. There was one blue and white sandal on her right foot, but her left one was bare. Small pieces of flesh were gone from her arms, and there were little holes and tears in each pant leg, wounds and cuts on her left foot, and on her fingertips as well.

Rafe stood, staring down at Ann's corpse. She was a deathly blue color. He put his hand over his gaping mouth, and tears flooded his eyes. This couldn't be. It couldn't be Ann.

"This is not easy, Mr. Langley," the medical examiner sympathetically explained, "but we must substantiate her identity and get your authorization to perform an autopsy on the body."

"An autopsy? Why? Yes—yes—of course, I understand," Rafe answered incredulously, in total disbelief that this could actually be happening. "You have my permission to do the autopsy, doctor. You—you do believe that she drowned?"

"Yes, but you will notice, Mr. Langley, that there is a contusion on the left side of the neck. Do you see this?" He turned her head gently so that the darker spot could easily be seen. Turning her head again and touching her forehead, he continued, "There is also this dark bruise on her forehead. Of course, it would be difficult to determine just what caused the bruise."

Rafe was confused and bewildered. A wave of nausea swept over him. "This is terrible…terrible. How could it have happened, doctor?"

"I'm so sorry, Mr. Langley. I know this is a dreadful shock to you." He thoughtfully covered Ann's body and gently said, "Come with me, please." The older, gray-haired gentleman put his hand on Rafe's shoulder and guided him out of the room, away from the morose scene. "I'll be in touch, Mr. Langley. And again, I am so sorry, so very sorry.

Yes—yes, Dr. Henderson. It's just that I can't believe this has happened. And, where is my little girl? Where is Julie?"

"I am sure the authorities will do everything within their power to find your daughter, Mr. Langley. We will hope for the best, shall we?" The doctor took Rafe's hand and held it between his own. His thumb gently caressed the top of Rafe's hand. "Mr. Langley, will you please step over here for a moment to sign these papers?"

"Yes, yes, of course, and thank you—thank you, doctor."

The doctor led him to the door. "Goodbye, Mr. Langley. I will be in touch with you soon."


Later, Rafe could not recall when the sheriff left him, how he got into his own car, or remember any detail about how he got home. His eyes were blinded by the tears. A heavy mist was pouring in from the west, forms became indistinct, and everything was a blur. As he pulled off the main road, he drove carefully onto the small gravel driveway and, looking up at the house, noticed that it was enshrouded in a dense fog. The heat of the past few days inland was drawing the fog in off the water. Slowly he walked up the steps to the front entrance, unlocked the door, and stepped inside. It seemed so very cold, even though it was still the middle of the summer. It was an eerie day. A chill was in the air. He shivered and wrapped his arms around his body as he put the coffee on the stove. He moved about as though in a stupor, completely oblivious to his actions, in a state of total shock.

In a daze he walked slowly through the house on the main floor, from the kitchen into the dining area, then the living room. Slowly his fingers slid over the polished dining room table, pausing to lightly touch the floral arrangement in the center. He went into the study, touching the objects that had meant so much to Ann—the figurines, the pictures, the books. Papers referring to the Jam Jar were stacked neatly on one side of the desk. He noticed a manila folder labeled *Blackberries*. He picked it up. This was what she was referring to when they were driving down the highway to Portland, and he had completely forgotten to ask her to show him what she had found. That must have hurt her. She probably thought he wasn't interested. But, he was interested. It had simply slipped his mind. Oh, why had he forgotten?

Rafe opened the folder and glanced at her notes, notes written in small manuscript. He began to read:

> Blackberry—a member of the rose family, Rosacaea—Rubus genesis. A cluster of berries is called 'drupelets.' The U.S. is the world's leading producer. Blackberries have had innumerable medical uses. Pliny recommended them to counteract the venom of serpents and scorpions. The condensed juice of young stalks had several uses in Pliny's time—treatment of the eye and mouth, tonsillitis, spitting blood, troubles of the uterus and anus. Blackberry leaves were used as ointment for running sores, were applied near the left breast for heartburn, to the stomach for stomach ache, and for protruding eyes.

Rafe shook his head and whispered, "I can't believe this."

He turned to the next sheet of yellow, lined paper, and continued reading.

> English peasants believed that a salad made from the leaves of the plant would cure loose teeth, snake bites, rheumatism, and several other ailments.

Rafe thought, *Blackberries over in England, too.*

> They also applied the wet leaves to burns, to the accompaniment of a special prayer. The chewing of the leaves for bleeding gums goes back to the time of Christ. Blackberry leaves, roots, and berries contain astringents—Gallic acid and tannin, and these were used to cure diarrhea. A story is told about five hundred Oneida Indians in New York State, who cured themselves of dysentery with the blackberry plant, while the neighboring white settlers (from whom the Indians had contacted the disease) died.

The third sheet continued.

*Legends: The blackberry bush is reputed to be the "burning bush" in which God appeared to Moses. In the British Isles, the devil hated blackberries, and took delight in ending their growing season. In England he spat on all the berries that were left on October 10, in Ireland he stamped on them on October 28, and in Scotland he threw his cloak over them.*

Rafe did not want to read further so he closed the folder, and placed it carefully on the desk. *Well, darling, you were so right—these facts are interesting, and would have added a spicy, prickly, unique dimension to the Jam Jar. Ann, Ann, you had so much to give, so much to give.* Rafe inhaled deeply, expelling the air from his lungs slowly. The stillness in the house was maddening, gripping, holding him. He slumped into an easy chair, then, bending over, grasped his head with both hands, pressing until he began to feel pain, his hands like steel tongs. He wanted to hurt himself, to feel the pain. He deserved to feel pain. When they had needed him the most, he had not been there.

Climbing the stairway laboriously, he was drawn into Julie's room. Her twin bed was neatly made. Teddy, a gift from last Christmas, sat in the center of the pillows, surrounded by Snuggles, the wrinkly pup, and an array of stuffed animals and dolls. Ann had instilled the importance of neatness in their daughter from the time she was old enough to learn the difference between being neat and messy. When playing downstairs, it was Julie's responsibility to make sure that all of her toys were stored away in the big box in the closet every night before going to bed.

Rafe knelt at the side of her bed, and looked at the array—her special friends, just as he had done so often before. He reached over and picked up the stuffed bear, held it against his cheek, gave it a hug, and placed it tenderly back in the center of the other toys and dolls. Now, as he knelt beside her bed, the prayer he offered was different. He cried out for her safety. He pleaded with God. "I must know what has happened to her! I must know for sure! Please, God, let me know, and if she is alive—somewhere—keep her safe—watch over her." He stayed there on his knees, weeping, waiting for an answer. None came. The silence was overpowering.

Their bedroom was directly across the hall from Julie's. He slowly walked in. Everything in it reminded him of Ann. She had always been a bit eclectic in her tastes, and their bedroom reflected her character and personality—an antique or two, period furniture, a dash of the contemporary. How could he possibly stay there, sleep in that bed, without Ann? He picked up the photograph of their wedding. "Ann, Ann," he whispered, "You were so beautiful. I loved you so much. Why, oh why, did you leave me? I don't want to live without you. I need you, my darling, I need you." Still grasping the picture to his breast, he fell on the bed and began to sob.

Rafe had never felt so alone in his entire life. He made his way slowly back down the stairs and into the kitchen where he sat at the kitchen table, sipping a cup of black coffee, warming his hands on the heavy mug with the painted purple blackberries enveloping it, a gift from Ann last Christmas. If only he had not gone to that conference. He hadn't really wanted to go, but she had insisted. He had been asked to give a paper, so he couldn't have declined gracefully. *Honey, you must go,* Ann had said. *It will look good on your record. The college expects you to attend, and I want you to go. Julie and I will be just fine, and anyway, I have lots of work to do on the Jam Jar before opening day. You have a business gal on your hands now, you know. Rafe, you do want me to be a raging success, don't you?*

*Yes, yes, of course I want you to be a success—a raving success. He had kissed her on the forehead.*

Blackberries—jam—juice—pies. He noticed the seven jars of newly preserved blackberry jam on the kitchen counter. These were the last of the frozen berries from last year's crop. Ann had always insisted on filling the large deep freeze out in the garage, sufficient to last through the winter until the following August. There would always and forever be an abundance of blackberries. The pesky things. He had wanted to uproot them, burn them out completely, clear the mess away, but she had objected logically.

"Rafe, why should I have to leave our home and go and pick in the country when they are right here, within reach of the porch? Can't you see how convenient it is, my dear? And, you know that you just love to pick," she teased. "You don't want to waste your time driving around looking for berries, do you? You can pick right here at home, and Julie can help, and even Neil will give us a hand once in awhile. What more could we ask for, darling? Don't you dare take those berries out, Rafe!"

She had thrown her head back, and had laughed at him. Then, he had taken her in his arms, crushing her to himself. Even now he could smell her fragrance, could feel her breath on his neck.

*Ann, Julie, and Rafe made a game of picking. The ripe, luscious fruit grew profusely right in their own backyard. Those detestable thorns seemed to grab and hang on for dear life as one reached in for the ripest and largest berries. How well he recalled the time he was going to outsmart them and fill his bucket first with the largest, most succulent berries. He had placed a long plank out over the brambles in order to reach the elusive ones, but had slipped and fallen right into the patch. Every time he turned to grab the plank, the thorns tightened their grasp. It was like being entrapped in a steel vise. Ann finally had to seek help from the fire department to free him. Julie was crying, afraid that her daddy would never get out. Later, they had many a laugh over that incident, but at that moment it was traumatic, and Julie never thought it very humorous. Rafe always reasoned that it was worth the effort just to please Ann and make her happy. He liked the jam, juice, and pies, so he was willing to endure a few scratches, cuts, and bruises for the cause.*

*"Honey, we're going to have to buy another large deep freezer the end of the summer, just for the berries. Will there be room in the garage for another one?"*

*"Well, we can always park one of the cars outside, you know."*

*"Oh, Rafe, surely we can find room, can't we—if we clear some of that old furniture out that we were supposed to finish three years ago?"*

*"Sure, Ann. We'll find the room. We'll manage some way," he assured her.*

*Ann was forever planning, preserving, and creating. She was always willing to share her ideas, recipes, and expertise with friends, and once a week was invited as a guest on a local television station. How thrilled and ecstatic she had been with the prospect of opening her very own business. All of their friends had agreed that it was just what the area had needed. Hours and hours of planning, with Kim's assistance, had gone into the attractive shop. "We'll be fine!" The words kept reverberating in his ears.*

The incessant ringing of the phone brought him back to his senses. "Langley residence—Rafe speaking."

"Rafe, this is Kim. Is it really true? Ann? Ann drowned?"

"Yes, yes, it's true, Kim. They said that her body was found on the beach at Camano. I can't believe it, Kim! Why? What do you suppose happened? And, where in God's name, is Julie?"

"Oh, Rafe, you don't know how sorry we are. And no one seems to know anything about Julie. Shall we come over?"

"No, please don't come here. I'll come over there, if that's okay with you. I've got to get out of here."


Ken and Kim Ripley were the Langleys' best friends. They had grown up in the same locale, had attended the same schools, played and fought together when children, then Ken and Rafe had become close in their senior year of high school when they each played on the varsity basketball team. After graduation, they lived together in a small apartment in the University District in Seattle while attending the University of Washington. They shared living expenses, as well as an old jalopy that they drove back and forth on weekends. It was during these times together that they shared thoughts and ideas, and dreamed of the future. Their friendship was very special to each of them—the skiing at Snoqualmie and Stevens Pass in the winter months, the swimming and other outdoor activities during the summer months after work. It was only natural that they talked and dreamed of the future together, and that they double-dated. Ken received his Master's Degree in Psychology the same year that Rafe received his in Education with a science major.

Ken worked with several doctors in a clinic for a few years before opening his own practice with Doctor Jerome Casson, a psychiatrist. He worked primarily with disturbed and abused children in Snohomish County, and was, at the same time, pursuing his doctorate. Because of his credibility, he was often invited to lecture in the psychology department at George College, where Rafe was Chairman of the Science Department.

Ann and Kim had known each other casually in high school, but were not especially close until they began double-dating Ken and Rafe. Eventually, the four of them became inseparable. When Kim attended the University of Washington in her junior year, after two years at Seattle Pacific University, she had begun going with Ken, who was in his senior year. She was majoring in nursing, and they soon discovered that they shared much in common.

Ann attended Seattle Pacific, majoring in home economics. She and

Rafe had been good friends and had gone together in high school, but they didn't get serious about their relationship until he was in his senior year at the University. The foursome complimented each other quite well, and their friendships became solid and enduring. After Ken and Rafe received their Master's Degrees, the two couples married.

*"Ann, I'll be your maid of honor, and you can be mine. What say?"*

*Smiling, Ann looked at her best friend, "What else, Kim? I wouldn't have it any other way."*

*"Well, Ken, guess that means that we'll have to stand up for each other,"* *Rafe grinned.*

*"As Ann just said, Rafe, 'What else? I wouldn't have it any other way.'"*

It was understandable that Kim would be the first to call after hearing the news of Ann's death on the local television news broadcast. She was shattered. Her very best friend *dead?* She had so many questions, but knew that for now there were no answers. The first and most important thing for her and her husband to do was simply be strong for Rafe's sake. He would have to draw his strength from them, comfort from their love, understanding, and compassion. Clutching the phone in her right hand, she exclaimed, "I just can't believe it, I can't believe it, Rafe, and I am so sorry. It's absolutely devastating, and what am I going to do without Ann? I will miss her so much! Please hurry over. We want to be with you."

After placing the receiver down, she bent to gently stroke the dog's head. "Oh, Manley, how in the world could anything like this ever have happened?" The dog wagged his tail and licked her hand.

When Rafe arrived at the Ripley home, he was shaking visibly and violently. "Rafe, come in—come in." Kim gave him a big bear hug. " I just talked to Ken and he's on his way home right now. We can't believe what's happened, and we can't begin to tell you how we feel. We want to help. Here, please sit down. I'll get you a cup of coffee."

Rafe sank on the sofa. Manley, the cocker spaniel, was lying on the rug a few feet from him. The dog got up, shook himself, yawned, and stretched flat upon all fours. Then, as if sensing that his friend needed comfort, he padded noiselessly across the floor to Rafe. He rubbed his wet nose on Rafe's leg, seeming to recognize the pain Rafe was suffering. When Rafe stroked the rust-colored wavy coat and scratched his head, Manley licked his fingers, thumping the floor with his tail. Rafe picked up the old red sponge-rubber ball and tossed it across the floor. "Good boy," Rafe said. "Go get the ball, Manley." Manley padded across the room to retrieve the ball, returned, dropped it at Rafe's feet, stood, and waited patiently. Rafe threw Manley's ball across the room again. The dog compulsively chased it across the rug, retrieved it, and dropped it at Rafe's feet again, wagging his tail. Rafe played with his soft, floppy, silk-like ears, and the dog responded by licking his hand with his moist tongue. It was a reassuring and comforting act of love on the part of the dog. Rafe had always liked Manley. "Good ole boy. Thanks, Manley," and he continued rubbing and stroking the dog's head.

"Here, Rafe, have some coffee. Now, tell me what you know. Oh, wait a minute. I hear the car. Ken is home. He'll be here in a second." Kim was obviously shaken and extremely nervous.

Ken walked into the living room with long strides. He went directly to Rafe and gave him a hug. "Rafe, I'm so glad you came over." His voice was deep and resonant. Sitting on his haunches in front of his friend and placing his hands on Rafe's shoulders, he looked deeply into his friend's sad eyes. "You must know how we feel about this. Ann was like a sister—closer than a sister. What in the world happened anyway? Can you tell us what you know?" Rising, he sat on the edge of the chair opposite Rafe, waiting.

Rafe looked up with an emotionally exhausted facial expression. "Well, all I know at the present time is that her body was found by a couple of kids running on the beach over on Camano. Apparently she washed up with the tide. The medical examiner is going to perform an autopsy."

"An autopsy?" Ken questioned.

"Yes, they always do this to determine the cause of death." Rubbing the back of his neck, he continued, "There was a bruise on the left side of her neck—and on her forehead. I just don't know, Ken. I don't understand. I don't understand how this could have happened." He held his head in his hands.

Ken reached over to pat his shoulder in a comforting gesture. "You know we're going to be right here by your side through all of this, Rafe. You're not going to be alone. Do the authorities have any information about Julie yet?"

"No, they know nothing. I can't believe this has happened, Ken." Rafe broke, crying uncontrollably. He began to sob, "Poor Ann—poor Ann—she was always so good to everyone. Why Ann? We had a beautiful marriage. She was a wonderful wife and a good mother. And, what about Julie? We both loved her. Where is she? Is she dead, too? I should never have gone to that conference. None of this would have happened if I had stayed home. What am I going to do? What am I going to do?"

"Let it out, Rafe—have a good cry," Ken reassured him, placing his hands on his shoulders. Kim was expressing her own grief quietly, as she sat on the adjoining love seat. "We're just going to take one day at time, Buddy—work everything out. Say, why don't you consider moving in here with us? We have that extra room upstairs, you know, and it surely wouldn't be an imposition. You can't be alone at this time. You'll do that, won't you? We just won't accept no for an answer."

"That's really nice of you, but—but I—I can't impose like that. I'll be all right." As an after thought he added, "Mike and Erin don't need anyone else to share the bathroom with them."

"Hey, they won't mind. They think the world of you, Rafe! We insist!" Kim exclaimed. "Please, Rafe, stay with us for awhile. Don't stay alone in the house." Turning to her husband, she added, "Ken, why don't you go back with him so he can pick up the necessary things?"

"Sure, Kim, that's a good idea." Gently he spoke to his friend, "You're like family, Rafe. Your grief is our grief, too. You will move in for a while, won't you?"

"Well, I suppose I can. Yes—yes, I will. Thank you—thanks a lot. I'll go home and get some things." Rafe looked at Ken. "I'd appreciate it if you would come with me, Ken."

"Of course—c'mon, let's go."

The next evening, July 22, Gordon Ray was sitting in his comfortable lounge chair in the unpretentious family room off the kitchen, reading the evening newspaper as his wife, Emily, was clearing the dinner dishes from the table.

"Emily, look at these headlines in the second section. *'Ann Langley Found'*!"

"Found? Where has she been, Gordon?"

Gordon continued to read. "This is just dreadful, Emily. It says here that a couple of young people found her body on the beach over on Camano Island. I can't believe this! Why, I just saw her and Julie, that cute little girl of theirs, a few days ago. They were pulling out of their driveway, driving that little Volkswagen Bug of theirs as I was driving down the road, going to the store. You remember, don't you, Em? I had to go and get milk. I even honked the horn at them, and they waved back at me."

"Oh, my goodness, what in heaven's name happened?" Emily inquired, dinner dishes still in her hand.

"Just a minute. It says here that they think she probably drowned, and they haven't found the girl yet. It says that the green Volkswagen Bug was found over at the Langley cabin on Whidbey Island. Emily, this is just awful! Their dinghy had washed up on the beach—overturned, and articles of clothing that had evidently belonged to Mrs. Langley had also been found on the beach—her bag, and a sweater, and one sandal. It also says that Mr. Langley had been attending a conference in the east. He arrived home on the twenty-first. My, that must have been a terrible shock for Rafe, coming back home to find his wife had drowned." He patted his wife's hand, showing his affection and appreciation for her.

"Rafe called the day he got home, wondering if they could be over here. My, I wonder what in the world happened. What really happened,

Gordon? You know, I just loved that girl. She was one of the kindest, most considerate people I've ever known—always bringing us that delicious blackberry jam. I just can't believe it, I can't believe it!" Emily dabbed her eyes with her apron, obviously extremely distraught. "Does it say anything about that sweet little girl of theirs—Julie?"

Still holding the paper, Gordon continued, "It says here that an autopsy will be performed. No, it doesn't say anything more about Julie, only that she hasn't been found yet. I just wonder about her. Do you suppose she could have drowned, too?"

"I hope not—I hope they find her. That poor man. He's always been so kind to us, Gordon. Lance Olsen, Clara's son, is at George College now, and he said he was a terrific science teacher. It must be devastating for Rafe. I don't suppose he knows what in the world has hit him. I must see that he has enough to eat. I'll make something good for him tomorrow. My, my, I hope they find Julie, and that she will be all right."

"Well, the authorities evidently don't know anything about that yet—that's why they aren't saying very much, but it looks like she may have drowned, too. I don't know, Emily—I hope and pray they can find out what really happened."

"Poor Ann, poor Ann!" Emily lamented. "I'll never forget what a joy she was when she was a young girl. She was always happy and cheerful, and everyone loved her, and that wedding, Gordon, when she and Rafe were married—why, that was the nicest wedding I'd ever been to. You remember, their best friends, the Ripleys, stood up with them."

"Yes, I remember. She certainly was a beautiful bride all right," Gordon reflected. "Em, do you remember how solid she was when her folks were killed in that accident? She didn't hold it against that young man who ran into them. He'd been drinking, too."

"I know, I know, Gordon. She even visited him in jail and tried to help him. Say, when I was at the beauty shop the other day, the girls were talking about Ann's new business. She was going to open a little shop and call it The Jam Jar—sell pies, and jam, and juice. I sure thought that was a good idea—everyone did—using the blackberries, and not letting them go to waste."

"Yeah, I guess so," Gordon reflected, deep in thought. "My, my, what a tragedy. I do hope they find Julie—such a sweet, beautiful little girl. Sure strange to me though—finding Ann's body on Camano, yet her clothes washed ashore near their cabin on Whidbey. Doesn't that seem funny to you, Emily?"

"Yes, I suppose so. I don't know. You know I don't understand the tides and currents and all that stuff."

"I know, Em—I know," Gordon responded mindfully. "Here, give me that bowl. That top shelf is too much of a stretch for you. I'll just—I'll just put it up there for you, my love."

Dr. Henderson gave Rafe a copy of the autopsy report. He had never seen one before. As he glanced at it, it appeared that it would take someone in the medical profession to understand the jargon. Not actually reading, but turning the pages slowly, Dr. Henderson pointed out something that astonished him. "You see here, Mr. Langley—I want you to look at this page. We discovered a malignant mass in the frontal lobe of the brain. It would only have been a matter of time."

"What do you mean, doctor? Are you telling me that my wife had a tumor on her brain?" Rafe's hands were shaking; his lips were trembling. He accidentally dropped the report. Bending, he gathered the papers up carefully.

"That is correct, Mr. Langley. Here, let me help you." Stooping he reached for a sheet of paper that had slipped under a table and handed it to Rafe.

"Poor Ann. But—but, she never complained of a headache, or anything."

"No, I am sure she would not have complained, because she probably did not experience any discomfort. It's a type of cancer that frequently goes undetected, usually until it is too late for effective treatment."

Rafe was trembling. He was at a loss for words. He carefully placed the report into the large envelope, turned, and began walking slowly out of the doctor's office. "Mr. Langley, is there anything I can do to help? Are you going to be all right?"

"Thank you, doctor, there's really nothing you can do. You've been very kind, and I appreciate it." Later, he could not recall having left the office. Rafe drove slowly out of town, passed the high school, and turned right on the narrow road leading into Ferguson Park near Blackman's Lake. Many times he and Ann had come to this park. They had walked down to the lake when teenagers, had waded in water thick with black, slippery pollywogs, had watched with wonder when the pollywogs turned into little frogs, one leg at a time. It was here that he kissed her the first time, a simple, innocent kiss. It was in this park that they had their first picnic together, their lunch spread out on a large stump, a picnic they shared with several gray chipmunks.

How happy she had been. He could still hear her voice. *Look, Rafe, aren't they cute? Look how daintily they eat—holding that precious morsel of food with both hands.* He loved this place—always cool in the shade of the enormous trees even on the hottest summer day. How he loved the paths through the woods where they had strolled hand in hand.

He opened the car door, took the envelope, and began to walk on one of the shaded trails leading into the park. Unconsciously, he was searching for that same tree trunk, their old stump. He was almost sure that it was over to the right. Rafe discovered it at last, though it was somewhat hidden by the new growth enveloping it. He tossed the manila envelope on the smooth surface, and slumped on it, burying his head in his hands. *Ann—Ann—if only you were here.* Carefully he took the contents out of the large manila envelope and began to read.

After dinner that evening, he turned to his friend, "Ken, the doctor gave me the autopsy report. Would you like to see it?"

"Yes, yes, of course I would be very interested in seeing it, Rafe. C'mon, let's go into the living room for coffee."

Rafe followed him. "Just a minute, Ken, I'll run up and get it. Do you think Kim would like to read it, too?"

"I'll ask her. She probably would."

Rafe came back into the room with the large envelope in his hand. Kim drew up a nearby chair, an anxious expression crossing her lovely face.

Ken began to read aloud, then decided to read silently, handing each page to Kim as he finished. He paused and looked questioningly at Rafe, "A mass in the frontal lobe? What does that mean?"

"That's right. I wanted you to see that part specifically. Doctor Henderson said the growth was malignant, and it would have been only a matter of time. Can you believe that?"

Ken replied, "Rafe, this is really incredible. It surely makes one wonder, doesn't it?" Staring at the paper, he added, "I still can't believe it, Rafe. Is the doctor positive about this?"

"I'm sure he knows what he's doing. It has to be true, Ken."

Kim sat listening, not knowing what to say. In her mind's eye, she could see her best friend—so vivacious and vibrant, so full of energy. A malignancy on the frontal lobe? She faintly recalled studying about this type of cancer in class.

Rafe looked up, hands clasped tightly behind his neck, "She must have—well, maybe not—yes, well—she may have had to face a much worse death later—perhaps," he said mindfully.

## MICHAEL T. HENDERSON, M. D.

Clinical Pathology

Pathologic Anatomy

Forensic Pathology

NAME: Ann Sommerfield Langley AUTOPSY NO.789

## MICROSCOPIC DESCRIPTION:

Heart:    Unremarkable.

Lungs:    There is a pulmonary edema consistent with drowning.

Liver:    Unremarkable.

Kidneys: Unremarkable.

Adrenals: Unremarkable.

Brain:    There is a malignant tumor consistent with blastoma multiforme.

## TOXICOLOGY:

Blood: Alcohol:   None detected.

Urine: Alcohol:   None detected.

Drug Screen:    No drugs detected.

## FINAL DIAGNOSIS:

Asphyxia by drowning.

Malignant tumor, brain, consistent with glioblastome multi-forme.

Michael T. Henderson, M.D.

Forensic Pathologist

Medical Examiner

## OPINION:

Autopsy of this forty-year old female reveals that she died of drowning, and postmortem findings are consistent with her having been immersed for some three days after the drowning incident. An unexpected finding was the presence of a malignant brain tumor, which was apparently asymptomatic.

NAME: Ann Sommerfield Langley

## PRELIMINARY EXAMINATION:

The body is received in a green zip-up bag. Clothing consists of a light blue pair of pants with an elasticized waistband. There are three small tears on the right pant leg. There is a dark smudge on left pant leg. A matching blue cotton T-shirt covers the top of the torso. Synthetic undergarments consisting of panties and bra, both beige in color, are worn under the outer garments. There are no stockings. One blue and white sandal is on the left foot. The right foot is bare. A yellow metal chain is around the neck. On the left hand, there is a yellow metal wedding set, including a plain band and engagement ring with a multifaceted stone. There is a pair of pierced earrings containing multifaceted clear stones. There is a Bulova Accutron watch with a wide yellow metal band upon the left wrist.

## EXTERNAL EXAMINATION:

The remains are those of a Caucasian female, who has long black hair, and blue irides. The teeth, in both upper and lower jaws, are in excellent dental repair. The trachea is in the midline. The chest has normal anterioposterior diameter. The breasts have no masses. The abdomen is flat; no masses or organs are palpable. The external genitalia are those of an adult female. The extremities are intact and symmetrical, with no evidence of injury or deformity. There is diffuse immersion change, involving the hands and feet. There are abrasions on feet, hands, and arms. There is a slight contusion on the left side of the neck. There is early maceration of skin, notably hands, arms, and feet. There is a 3 ½" x 2 ½" contusion on left anterior shoulder.

## INTERNAL EXAMINATION:

SECTION: The body is opened with the traditional Y-shaped incision. Subcutaneous fat of the anterior abdominal wall measures up to one-quarter inch in thickness in the midline of the abdomen. The body's organs are present in their usual positions and occupy the usual relationships one to another.

CARDIOVASCULAR SYSTEM: The heart has normal contours and widely patent, coronary arteries. The myocardium of both right and left ventricles is normal in color and consistency. The endocardium and valves are unremarkable. The aorta and great veins are unremarkable.

RESPIRATORY SYSTEM: Lungs bilaterally, are hyperinflated, and diffusely weep frothy, pinkish-red, edema fluid. There are marked amounts of pulmonary adhesions, adhering the pleural surfaces, to the chest wall diffusely. The trachea and major bronchi contain diffuse amounts of a frothy pinkish-red fluid.

HEPATOBILIARY SYSTEM: The liver has a thin, gray capsule and reddish-purple parenchyma. The gallbladder and extra hepatic biliary duct systems are unremarkable.

GASTROINTESTINAL SYSTEM: The esophagus, stomach, and small and large intestine, each contain an intact mucose, having the usual pattern for the various segments. The stomach is distended from water, and contains partially digested food particles. The pancreas is unremarkable.

RETICULOENDOTHELIAL SYSTEM: The spleen and lymph nodes are unremarkable.

GENITOURINARY SYSTEM: The kidneys bilaterally have intact capsules, which strip with ease revealing smooth cortical surfaces. On cut section, each of the cortices are normal in thickness and well-demarcated from medullary regions. Calyces, pyramids, and ereters are unremarkable. The uterus and adnexal structures are unremarkable.

ENDOCRINE SYSTEM: The adrenals, thyroid, and pituitary are unremarkable.

CENTRAL NERVOUS SYSTEM: The reflected scalp and removed calvarium are unremarkable. The meninges are thin and transparent. Serial coronal sections of the cerebral hemispheres, reveal mild cerebral edema, as well. The cerebellum and brain stem reveal no focal lesions. There is a mass in frontal lobes, yellow-white, with firm outer cortex surrounding a necrotic middle. It measures one inch in diameter, and extends into surrounding white matter.

MICROSCOPIC FINDINGS:

Heart: Unremarkable

Lungs: There is a pulmonary edema consistent with drowning.

Liver: Unremarkable.

Kidneys: Unremarkable.

Adrenals: Unremarkable.

Brain: There is a malignant tumor consistent with glioblastoma multiforme.

TOXICOLOGY:

Blood: Alcohol: None detected.

Urine: Alcohol: None detected.

Drug screen: No drugs detected.

DIAGNOSIS:

1. Asphyxia by drowning.

2. Malignant tumor, brain, consistent with glioblastoma multi-forme.

Michael T. Henderson, M.D.
Forensic Pathologist

On July 24th, the evening paper headlined the story.

> The pathologist's report revealed few clues in the death of Ann Som-merfield Langley, wife of Professor Rafe Langley, head of the science department at George College. It has been determined that Mrs. Lang-ley's death was due to drowning. The medical examiner stated that no foreign bodies, other than what would be normal, were found on the body. Mrs. Langley had not been sexually assaulted. Julie Langley is still missing. Search parties are being organized to try to locate the girl. Anyone having any information which may lead the authorities to her discovery is requested to contact the local police department.

"Gordon, Gordon, I am just sick over this."

"I know, Emily. It is a terrible tragedy, and a great loss to this commu-nity. We will all miss Ann. I wonder if they will have a private funeral, or if we will be able to attend. You know, Em, I would very much like to go to a memorial service for her. She gave—she always gave so willingly."

"I will really miss that girl. I'm old and sick. It should have been me instead." Emily dabbed her eyes.

"Now, now Emily, don't you talk like that." Gordon held her, felt the hot tear on her cheek. "No, Em, it isn't your time yet. God knows. He knows," Gordon said knowingly and affectionately.

"Oh, Gordon, what would I do without you?"

"Quite well, my love, quite well, I am sure, Emily. Quite well."

After retirement from the Fire Department, Tim Pennington spent many hours at his church tending the landscape. He took great pride in maintaining the large lawn, pruning the trees, and caring for the rock and flower gardens surrounding the stately old white edifice. A skilled carpenter, adept at creating attractive, as well as useful objects, he was pleased with the benches he had constructed. He had painstakingly chosen precisely the right spots to place them—in the shade under the chestnut tree, near the rock gardens where the flowers could be appreciated, on a knoll offering a view of the valley.

While their parents stood around the entrance of the church after the conclusion of a Sunday morning service, visiting with the minister and complimenting him on his sermon, greeting friends, chatting with neighbors, the children delighted in playing in the lattice gazebo, the gazebo that their friend, Tim, had built.

There had never been a larger memorial service in this small, western Washington town in the Snohomish Valley. The sanctuary, surrounded by a lush carpet of grass, could not hold the capacity crowd. Brilliantly colored petunias in purple, fuchsia, pink, and white lined the walk leading up to the large double doors; the flower and rock gardens on each side of the walkway were resplendent with large white, pink, and purple dahlias in full bloom. Tall, straight stalks of bright gladioli complemented the dahlias, and yellow zinnias poked their heads out among the rocks.

A friend of Ann's remarked to her husband, "Brent, look—look at that lovely hydrangea bush. Somehow it reminds me of Ann—the delicate petals are turning from that soft blue color to a pale pink. And soon that dainty flowering leaf will drop."

"Yes, yes, I see what you mean, Doris. It is lovely."

The large overflow of friends and acquaintances sat solemnly on the benches and on the lawn near the rock gardens, outside the edifice. They could hear every word spoken from the pulpit. They could hear the sniffling and blowing of noses in the congregation.

The air was unmoving, calm. It was warm and humid, and though it was late June, the essence of an early fall day permeated the air. In the stillness of the air, the musical strains of the organ wafted out over the somber group of people, both young and old. Karen Logan sang Ann's favorite hymn, "How Great Thou Art." In a clear, bell-like voice, the words of the last verse resounded throughout the sanctuary and across the lawn: *When Christ shall come with shouts of acclamation, and take me home, what joy shall fill my heart! Then I shall bow in humble adoration, and there proclaim, My God how great thou art!*

Several in the congregation dabbed self-consciously at their eyes. The pastor stood behind the beautifully carved antique pulpit, and as the organ played softly in the background, he spoke in a strong, melodious voice. "I have known Ann Sommerfield Langley for many years. As a young, inexperienced pastor in this very church, I met Ann, at perhaps age thirteen, when she became a member of our youth group. There was never a more excited, spirited girl, and her involvement and enthusiasm caught on with the rest of the young people. Some of you will remember how the group grew in number from around eighteen, to between seventy-five and one hundred young people. She was the inspiration, the catalyst, the reactor that forged the group and gave it life.

"Then later, I remember her strength, her attitude, her acceptance and response, when both parents were taken tragically in an automobile accident—caused, my dear friends, by a driver under the influence of alcohol. It was Ann who went to visit that man in prison. It was Ann who showed compassion and sympathy for the accused. It was Ann who encouraged him to make the most of it, to take advantage of his situation, to study, to make his life worthwhile. She held no bitterness. She forgave willingly."

The pastor cleared his throat and continued, "I recall the weeks prior to her wedding day, when she and Rafe Langley came into my office for the required counseling. Many of you will remember that wedding—simple, but executed with exquisite taste, nothing detracting from the delicate beauty of the bride herself. It was Ann who always volunteered to bring blackberry pies for any and every function, and, without trying to offend any of the ladies present here today, it was her blackberry pie that disappeared first. How many of you have a small jar of blackberry jam from Ann's cupboard?" There were many smiles and nods among the congregation.

"Rafe and Ann waited about ten years before God blessed their home with a beautiful daughter whom they named Juliet. Today that little girl, Julie, is missing, and let us not forget to pray that she will be found— found unharmed.

"We are gathered here today, not to mourn Ann's death, but rather to celebrate her life and the legacy she left each of us, to keep deep within each of our hearts the abundant outpouring of love that she so willing gave. No, we are not here to mourn, for could we but fully understand and comprehend the beauty and joy of life in Christ, none of us would wish her back. In 2 Corinthians 5:8, we read, *'To be absent from the body is to be present with the Lord.'*"

The pastor opened the Bible to John 11:25-26, and read, *"Jesus said unto her,' he is speaking to Martha in this passage, 'I am the resurrection and the life; he that believeth in me, though he were dead, yet shall he live; and whosoever liveth and believeth in me shall never die.'"* He paused and bowed his head. "Shall we pray…"

Karen sang "O Love That Wilt Not Let Me Go" and the congregation filed out of the sanctuary into the sunshine.


Rafe was overwhelmed with the hundreds and hundreds of cards that filled his mailbox, both at home and at the college. Each expressed sympathy, solace, and an expression of love. A scholarship fund had been established in Ann's memory, and there were numerous checks and floral arrangements given as an act of commiseration for the tragic event that had shaken the community. His students, the faculty, and the administration of George College, had bonded together to support and uphold him. He had not realized that Ann had known so many people, had so many friends. The local television station had received hundreds of calls, cards, and letters, which were presented to him. He wanted to acknowledge every extended act of love and gratitude, and Ken and Kim stood by, assisting night after night into the wee hours of the morning, organizing lists, writing thank you notes, recognizing every contributor and each act of remembrance. Never had he appreciated their friendship as much, and over and over he repeated the words, "Thank you, thank you for your help and understanding. I don't know what I would have done without you."

"Rafe, we are so glad that we could be here with you—to help you in this small way," Kim said reassuringly.

"Yes," Ken added, "We know you would have done the same for us, Rafe."

"Well, you've done far more than I could have ever hoped for. You've just been wonderful. I love you guys."

"Let's take a break, shall we?" Kim reasoned. "What would you like? Coffee, tea, or hot chocolate?"

"Anything you make is fine with me, honey," Ken smiled.

"Me, too—anything. Surprise us, Kim," Rafe added.

After sipping the hot, spicy tea, Rafe turned to Ken, "You know, I can hardly think straight any more. My feelings are all bottled up inside, and sometimes I think I'm going to explode, Ken. And, I get mad. I really get angry. Would you believe I—I get angry at God?"

"Angry at God? Well, why not?" Ken placed his hands on Rafe's shoulder. "Listen, my friend, it's okay for you to be enraged. I'm mad, too. Let it out. Cry, yell, scream, if you want to."

"I just can't understand why—what good can ever come of it, from my losing Ann? Why did she have to die, Ken? And, what about Julie? Where is she? What has happened to her? Can there be any meaning in the stupidity of it all?"

"I don't know. I just don't have the answer, Rafe, and no one, I mean no one, really knows what you are experiencing." Ken continued, "But I do know that you can rise above this, and you'll be able to go on. In time the memories will heal, but just remember, it won't happen overnight. Give it time, my friend, and don't despair. Remember, it isn't going to hurt to have some good old-fashioned weeping jags. You don't have to be ashamed to cry, you know."

"I know, I know," Rafe said solemnly. "Thanks, Ken."

Kim piped up, changing the subject as she opened another envelope, "Well, what's say we get this show on the road? We don't have too many more to go now. We should be through in just a few more minutes."

"Okay, slave driver," Ken replied, his eyes full of love and appreciation. "When we get this all done, I'm treating to a night out—steaks at our favorite place."

"Really, darling? You mean, I don't have to slave in the kitchen and cook tomorrow night?"

"That's right, honey—we're going out for the best steaks in town."

Fall quarter would commence the middle of September, and hopefully, the administration would have sufficient time to find his replacement. Of course, they would understand why he wanted to get away. He would give notice immediately. The teaching position and the opportunity to do research in the field of microbiology at the small college near Brighton, England, was probably just what he needed, and too good an opportunity to pass up. He had made the telephone call to inquire. The position had not been filled. They still wanted him, and they offered to pay for the cost of his trip to England. After the initial invitation, which he had graciously declined, he simply erased the idea of a change from his mind. He had wanted Ann to succeed in her new business endeavor, and it was not the right time to chance such a move. Yes, he would be perfectly satisfied and happy to remain at George as head of the science department for a few more years. Julie was to have gone into first grade, an important occasion in her young life, and Rafe knew that it would be best for Julie to be in a familiar surrounding with friends.

Julie. Julie. If only he could know unequivocally that she were alive, or dead. It was terrifying, agonizing, not knowing the truth about her. Could she be lying in the woods, half buried under a pile of leaves and rubbish, murdered, a victim of child molestation? Or could she be wandering somewhere alone, not knowing who or where she was? Had she drowned, too? But, if she had drowned, why wasn't her body found on the beach, washed up in the tide? How he grieved for her. He could feel her slim little fingers wiggle as he protected them in his own hand. Could she still be alive somewhere, crying for her mother and father? Had she been abducted? If only he could know the truth, if only he could know.

The detective in charge of the investigation in the search for Julie had received numerous false leads, crank letters, and erroneous calls. Two calls came from psychics, there were several from kooks, and a handful of calls from people who said that they had dreamed of her. The days, the weeks, went by with no trace, no reliable clue as to her whereabouts. Investigative parties combed the beaches on Whidbey and Camano

Islands, searched the woods, and walked up and down the streets of every surrounding town and community. Neil had been extremely cooperative and useful. He had volunteered to organize and lead search parties, instructing each person to scan carefully the places that Julie had taken him. Nothing.

When the news first broke, Neil had gone to the authorities to explain that he had spent the day of the seventeenth with Ann and Julie on Whidbey Island. He told them that he had parked his truck on Camano, as he usually did, and had then gone across in the *Webfoot*. "Yes, we knew you had called their home that morning, Mr. Manning. We obtained this information at the telephone company. What time did you get there?"

"Oh, I think it was about ten—yes, about ten in the morning, sir."

"What did you do after your arrival?"

"Well, Ann had made sandwiches and drinks, and I took them out on the boat. It was just a perfect day."

"How long were you out on the water?" Sheriff Stevens inquired.

"Oh, a couple of hours I'd guess."

"What else?"

"Well, I wanted to ski, so Ann took over the controls and I jumped in and had some terrific skiing."

"Did Mrs. Langley ski?"

"No, she didn't. She's never tried, but she promised she was going to soon. She thought that she would love it."

"Then what?" Sheriff Stevens persisted.

"Well, I think they were getting a little tired and it was quite warm, so Ann suggested we go in and have our lunch on the deck," Neil lied. The officer looked at him, questioningly. Neil quickly remarked, "But, Julie and I couldn't wait. We were both hungry so we each had a sandwich and a drink. Ann said she wasn't really very hungry yet. She would eat later."

"Did you go out on the boat again?"

"No, Julie and I looked for agates and rocks, and I think Ann just rested. She was thinking a lot about the business she was going to start up soon—said she had a lot on her mind. I thought if we got out of her way for awhile she could get more done."

"So, Mr. Manning, how long did you remain at the cabin with them?"

"I wanted to go to Seattle to get some things for my boat, so I left about—oh, probably around 1:30—I think," Neil lied.

"And, did Mrs. Langley and Julie leave at the same time?" the sheriff probed.

"I don't know exactly what time they left. Ann told me that she and Julie were going to swim for awhile since it was such a great day, and that she thought they might go out a little way in the dinghy before starting back home. She said something about catching the 3:30 ferry—beat the traffic."

"And, you went back to Camano, loaded the boat on your truck, and then headed for Seattle?"

"Not exactly, sir. I didn't want to pull the boat to Seattle, so I decided to leave the boat on Camano and come back after it later—after I had gone to Seattle." That part of the fabricated story was true, true indeed.

"Okay, Mr. Manning, you have been a great help, and we appreciate all the work you're doing leading the search parties for Julie Langley," the sheriff acknowledged.

"You know, sir," Neil continued, "I am just devastated and shocked over what has happened. The Langleys have been so good to me, and I thought the world of Julie. I just wish that I could do more, Sheriff. If there is anything—anything at all that I can do to help, please let me know."

"Where can we reach you?"

"Well, I'll be staying here with a friend for another week or two, but then I have to go home and help my dad with the harvesting before fall semester. Here, I'll give you my phone number here as well as the one on the farm." Neil wrote the two numbers down on a slip of paper and handed it to the sheriff.

"Fine," the sheriff said as he took the slip of paper. "We will let you know if there is anything. Thank you for coming in. You did the right thing."

As Neil went out the door, the sheriff said to his deputy, "Seems like a very fine young man. Did you notice his eyes, Marv? Most unusual."

"Yeah, I did. He's a good-looking kid—clean-cut."

Rafe was in constant touch with the authorities. "But, Sheriff, have you done all within your power to find my daughter? It's driving me crazy not knowing what's happened to her."

"I know, I know, Mr. Langley, and we are doing everything within our jurisdiction to try to locate Julie. Her picture has been posted everywhere in the northwest. We have searched everywhere, and we will continue to search, and follow every lead that comes to our attention. We are not giving up—not yet. We will continue to give this situation first priority. You can be sure of that, sir."

"Thank you, thank you. I know you will."

"By the way, Mr. Langley, Neil Manning is a student of yours, a friend of the family?"

"Yes, yes, he is. He was also my assistant this past quarter at George—a really fine boy."

The sheriff continued, "Mr. Manning came in of his own volition to tell us that he had taken your wife and your daughter out on the boat on the seventeenth. He was quite helpful—explained everything they did that day."

"Neil spent a lot of time with us, Sheriff. Ann and Julie thought the world of him, as did I, and I understand he has gone out of his way leading search parties for Julie. He came by to see me the other evening and was so broken up about what has happened. Actually, I found myself comforting him."

"Well, Mr. Langley, I am really sorry to have to say that we have been unsuccessful in finding any clues to your little girl's disappearance, but we aren't giving up yet. We will continue to search."

Thoughtfully, Rafe remarked, "I think that by now Neil has probably gone back to eastern Washington to help his father with the harvesting. Guess there really isn't much more that he could do. I'll miss him."

It was Rafe's friends who kept him going, and who supported him encouragingly. Everyone seemed to suffer for him. Few knew what to say, and he appreciated those who simply listened, and who did not try to offer advice or suggestions as to what he should do.

Inevitably, the time came when he had to face reality. Ann was gone, gone forever. Julie was gone, only God knew where. His perspective had to change, and with it, his immediate environment. There were too many memories. He would never be able to concentrate on his work at George. He could not possibly be in their home alone, without them, at least not at this time.


"I've decided to accept that teaching position outside of Brighton after all," he announced one morning at breakfast. Ken and Kim looked at him simultaneously, questioning his statement.

"Really?" Kim's eyebrows lifted as she raised her cup of coffee.

"Rafe, that's a fantastic idea!" Ken assured him. "When will you be leaving? Fall quarter?"

"Classes don't begin until the end of September, and I don't have to be involved in registration. That gives me some extra time, and you know what I think I'll do?"

"What?" Ken questioned.

"I read that the QE2 is repositioning—sailing from New York City to London just about the time I want to leave, and I thought it would be a good opportunity for me to take advantage of it. They cut the fare, and what with the money the college is forwarding I can easily swing the cost. It will take a bit of doing to take care of everything out at the college, then there's the house—drain the pipes, lock it up."

"We'll check on the place, Rafe," Kim offered.

"Oh, I don't suppose it will be necessary for anyone to check on it very often—perhaps once in a while. I'll do what needs to be done and just lock it up tight, turn off the electricity, and so on. Let the old place have a good rest. She deserves one."

Ken and Kim both grinned, happy to see him more relaxed. Rafe continued, "Yes, I think this opportunity is a real godsend, and I think it will help me in my grief, though God knows I will never forget either of them." Glancing from one to the other, he added, "You both know what I mean, don't you?"

"Of course, you know that we understand, Rafe, and we'll be right here waiting for you when you decide to come back home." Kim was always so amiable.

The next morning Rafe slipped out of the house early and drove out to the cemetery. The ground was not yet settled over Ann's grave. The bumpy clumps of grass lay over the dark brown, moist, uneven soil, and as a reminder, someone had left a shovel resting on a tombstone a few feet away. The once beautiful fresh flower arrangements were now fading, the ribbons and bows streaked from the sun and rain. Rafe stood, looking down upon the scene, and in his thoughts he talked to Ann, asking her if it would be all right for him to leave, to go to England, to get away from his sorrow. No, he would not forget her. He would never forget her. He would always love her. No, he would never forget their precious child. He squatted, Indian style, and placed his hand upon the grave. "Ann, Ann, I loved you so much. Why? Why? I am lost without you."

After a few moments of silence, in the lonely solitude of the setting, his legs cramped, and he got up deliberately. Taking his handkerchief, he wiped his eyes, then his hands. He looked away to the east, to the Cascade Mountains, to Pilchuck, the mountain they had climbed together when in their teens. For a brief moment, an unexplained tranquility and peace came over him. In his heart he knew that a higher Power was in control. He walked slowly back to the wagon. *One day, one day at a time,* he thought.

In the second week of September, Rafe flew to New York from the Seattle/Tacoma Airport and boarded the Cunard QE2 bound for Southampton. He assumed a facade few detected as a cover-up for the pain and suffering within. Perhaps the time on board the ship would offer him an opportunity to reflect, to contemplate the future—alone. He needed this time to think. He wanted to think about Ann. He wanted to think about Julie. He wanted to think about his own career. Perhaps he would start working on a higher degree. He had always dreamed of receiving a doctorate, but the timing had not been right. Hmm, Dr. Langley—had a nice ring to it. The thought brightened his weary face, and he contemplated the possibility. It wouldn't take that long, actually—two years perhaps. All the hours he had earned beyond his master's would count.

When asked if he would prefer a table for four, six, or eight, Rafe replied, "I would prefer dining alone, if at all possible."

"Yes, sir, that can be arranged. One moment, please."

A handsome, young English waiter came up to Rafe, "Will you follow me, sir? You may have this table by the window."

Rafe followed and was pleased to find a small table with service for one by a large window. Turning to the waiter, he said, "This will be fine. Thank you very much." This was the first time he had ever traveled on a large ocean liner. He wanted to be alone with his thoughts, and he knew there would be too many questions, too much mindless chatter at the larger tables.

Rafe appreciated the unblemished, faultless magnificence of this elegant, floating hotel. There was little glass, and no chrome, but rather rich, lustrous, polished woods and burnished fine leather, splendid tapestries, select oil paintings, and luxurious furnishings. The ship was a true masterpiece of design and construction. This was not a fun ship, or a so-called Love Boat. He thought that Samuel Cunard must have been a true visionary. There were thirteen decks, a forty-car garage, a medical staff that even did surgery, a comprehensive foreign exchange service, and kennels with penthouses on the Signal Deck. Rafe did not have to go to London to shop Harrods. Harrods of London was on the ship. Rafe soon learned that he could get away from most of the tourists, especially those with whom he had no interest in conversing, and hide away in the British-type library. There he could sink into a comfortable lounge chair and read, or just sit and think. After luxuriating in one of the spas, every muscle in his body felt like warm liquid, and he found himself completely relaxed—relaxed for the first time in weeks. On two different occasions he attended films in the large movie theater, sitting quietly alone, a myriad of thoughts wandering aimlessly through his mind.

Rafe was more than content to retreat to his small, but quite elegant private cabin early, after the first dinner setting. It was not that he was unsociable, but he wanted no one to invade his privacy, nor did he want to have to clarify or justify his traveling solo. As he lay in bed, hands clasped behind his head, solutions to his life's problems seemed so clear during those moments just before sleep. Yet, in the morning he could never seem to recall the solutions.

During the night he would sleep intermittently, and dream. His dreams were always mixed up—a history class in high school with Ann two seats in front of him, Ann during their teen years, the times they spent at the park near Blackman's Lake, their college days in Seattle, their exquisite wedding, the reception, and the wedding night. He dreamed of the first years of their marriage, Ann in the hospital at Julie's birth, her rosebud, baby mouth searching for the nipple, gently biting, playing with her tiny toes while Ann recited, *This little pig went to market.* Julie's first step, her first word, her first tooth, helping to pick blackberries, Julie in a state of total despair when he fell into the blackberry briars. He dreamed of his embarrassment and chagrin when the fire department came to extricate him from the barbs that held him so securely. He dreamed of Neil in class, their conversation in the lab, Neil helping to pick berries,

Neil raving about Ann's blackberry pie, Neil reading books to Julie, the brown fleck in his one deeply set eye. Was it the right, or the left one?

Then, there was that incessant, recurring, repetitious, terrifying nightmare: Ann, Julie, Neil, Ken, Kim—all trapped in the blackberry briars. They would be struggling to get out, but the angry barbs, like sharp nails, would hold them as though they were caught in a gigantic barbed vise. Each time they moved, the vines would tighten their deadly grasp. The juice of the berries ran down their faces, mingled with their blood, and matted their hair. Their eyes would be wild with terror, and they would be crying out for help, but Rafe could not reach them, or set them free.

Their frightened cries would wake him, and he would sit straight up in bed, chilled from the perspiration that drenched his body. It was as though they were all caught in a web, a tangled web, a large, over-grown blackberry web!

Half awake, Rafe heard the soft, low sound of music from afar, from one of the lounges on the ship. He groaned, slowly slipped out of the narrow bed, and staggered to the sink. Turning on the cold water tap, he splashed the icy liquid on his face, and over his head. As a cut on the finger breaks open again and throbs at a hasty movement, memories of the past pierced his heart. He gazed at his image in the mirror, shook his head in disgust at the dark circles under his eyes, and reached for his comb. After running the comb through his hair, he filled a glass with clear, cold water, and sat down at the small round table. Pondering the dreams, the nightmares, he visualized the blackberry vines at home, those he had wanted to remove completely, but Ann had said, *"No! Not on your life, Rafe!"* They had needed pruning. He should have taken care of that before leaving.

Heavens, in a couple of years what would it look like? He speculated just how far they might get out of control. Well, he would worry about that after his return. Hmm, *pruning*—pruning was a strange word, an extraordinary word. What was its origin? He thought of his own life, the recent sorrows. Yes, perhaps that was it. He, Rafe Langley, was being pruned. He thought, *yes, it was the pruning of a soul—his soul. But, why? Why?* Hot tears began to fill his eyes, to spill over and slide silently down his cheeks.

On every floor of one of the largest hospitals in Stockholm, an announcement came over the intercom. "Doctor Sigurd Jenson, Doctor Sigurd Jenson, please report to the nurse's station on fifth floor."

Sigurd Jenson pealed off his rubber gloves and threw his bloodied white coat into the large receptacle. Looking at the young surgeon who had been assisting him, he said, "Take over, Doctor. Close."

A few minutes later Doctor Jenson came off the elevator on the fifth floor and walked briskly up to the counter.

"Yes, what is it?" His voice had the tensility of steel.

"It's a boy. A healthy, beautiful, eight-pound boy. Congratulations, Doctor Jenson!"

"My wife? Is she all right?" the doctor inquired.

"Dr. Userud said all went well, Doctor. He mentioned that it was a fast delivery. She's fine, just fine—no problems at all."

"Well, that's good. I'm pleased that everything went well. No complications. We were both a bit concerned as she had been having some problems. Cameron—Cameron will be his name," he whispered.

The nurses looked at each other. Brynn whispered, "Seems to me he could have been a little more excited at the birth of a son. I wonder if he ever smiles." Under her breath, she muttered. "Cold fish. That poor baby. I don't envy him his future. I can't stand that egotistical pill."

"What are you muttering about now, Brynn? Did you say something about a pill?" the nurse standing at the files questioned.

"Me? Oh, nothing, nothing at all, Kathleen."


Cameron Jenson was a happy, well-adjusted student in those first years of elementary school, and in his tenth year became an outstanding soccer player. "Dad, our team is having a game Saturday morning. Do you think you could make it this time?"

"Sorry, Cameron, can't do it. There's a meeting at the hospital on a new surgical procedure. I can't miss it. Maybe next time."

"I wish you could be there. Are you sure you can't come this time?"

"No, Cameron, I must be at the hospital. Your mother might like to go though. Have you asked her?"

"No, I haven't asked her. You know she's always too busy to go to anything I'm involved in. I heard her tell someone on the telephone that she had a club meeting of some kind Saturday morning. Oh, well, maybe next time then, Dad."

"Yes, yes, perhaps another time," the doctor replied.

Feeling completely neglected and dejected, as usual, the young man hung his head and walked down the richly carpeted hall to his bedroom. On the way, he jumped up and hit the Orrefors' chandelier. The beautiful bell-like, tinkling tone made by the cut crystal prisms reverberated down the hall. At least that was one happy sound in the house.

Many thoughts raced through his mind as he sat on the edge of the bed in his luxuriously furnished private sanctuary. *What was the use anyway? They never had time for him.* He couldn't wait to get out of there, to be on his own. He wished he could live at Peder's place. His best friend was always doing something with his parents—out on the boat, trips to the mountains for skiing. What difference did it make if his father didn't make as much money? Just what was important, anyway?


Elaine, several years Cameron's senior, had left home right after high school and had never returned. She had gone to the States to attend the University of Washington in Seattle. There she met and married Ralph Anderson; later they settled down in Ballard, a suburb in north Seattle. He missed his sister, who had been a bit reluctant to leave him.

"Cam, I just can't stand it around here any longer. Now that I'm through secondary school, I'm going to leave."

"When? Where are you going, Elaine? You mean you're going to leave me here alone with mom and dad?"

"You'll be okay, Cam. It won't be for much longer. Why don't you go to another school away from home for the last two years of high school? I'll bet dad and mom would let you. Why don't you suggest it?"

"Do you really think they'd agree to anything like that?" Cameron asked, dubiously.

"Yes, I'm sure they would agree. I'm sure," Elaine said emphatically. "Ask them. Promise me that you will, Cam."

"Okay, I will, I will," Cameron promised.

"You'll see, Cam. It will all work out."

"I'll sure miss you, sis. You won't forget me, will you?"

"Of course I won't forget you. I love you, little brother." Elaine put her arm around the young man's shoulder, and said reassuringly, "I'm really sorry, but I just have to leave. I will always keep in touch with you. You know that."

"Okay, Elaine. I understand. I really do. I sure don't blame you for wanting to leave."


Mrs. Jenson, not at all beautiful but striking and attractive in a sterile sort of way, was a woman of many talents. The statuesque, dignified matron had been a descendant of the aristocracy of Sweden. Her social life, her garden club, and the many organizations and societies to which she belonged were more important to her than anything in the world, including her two children. Climbing the rungs of the social ladder in Stockholm, presiding over fundraising functions, entertaining high society at their palatial home—these were the reasons for living.

Cameron's father, Doctor Sigurd Jenson, was too occupied with his profession, too engrossed in his work, to devote much time to either of his children—or his wife. Cameron enjoyed all the amenities a wealthy, prominent, urban family could afford, but he lacked the love, compassion, and closeness of a tightly knit family. There was no religious upbringing, so school and the activities it provided became his entire life.

Cameron's parents were very pleased when he asked permission to attend a prestigious boarding school the last two years of high school. His absence from the home would give them more freedom, and they would be under no obligation to attend any school functions. "Why, Cameron," his mother exclaimed, "that is simply a marvelous idea! Are you sure you want to leave home and live at the school? They have some pretty strict rules, you know."

"I know that, Mother, and yes, I do think I would enjoy it very much. I hear there is an excellent foreign language program there, and you know how interested I am in rugby. I'm sure I can make the team. Yes,

I would really like to go. I miss Elaine so much. It won't be as lonesome at a boarding school."

"Well, I think it is a splendid idea, Cameron. It's a wonder we didn't think of it first," his father acknowledged. He immediately picked up the newspaper and looked at the financial section.


Cameron's two years at boarding school were probably two of the happiest years in his young life. In his senior year he became captain of the rugby team and made some close friends from the continent.

After graduation two years later, Cameron chose to attend Aarhus University in Denmark, even farther away from Stockholm. He majored in foreign languages; when he earned his Master's Degree, he was fluent in four—English, French, Italian, and Spanish. It was also during those college years that he studied art history and became vitally interested in photography.

Cameron's father had wanted him to follow in his footsteps, to be a doctor, to pehaps one day become a famous surgeon. Cameron Jenson, however, had no inclination to study medicine, or human anatomy in any form that would relate to the medical profession. There were times when he thought that his father's mind must be about as cool as snake's blood. Cameron hated the sciences, could not stand the sight of blood, and wanted no part of his father's profession.


His telephone rang. He picked it up. "Hello. Cameron here."

"Cameron, this is your mother. How are you, dear?"

"Doing great, thank you, Mother. Why are you calling? Is anything wrong?"

"No, no, not all. Do you think you could come home for a few days now that the term is over and you have graduated? We would love to see you, and have a good visit. Could you?"

"Well, yes, I suppose so. Yes, I can make it. I could probably catch a flight on Wednesday. I'll call and let you know the flight number after I confirm. Okay?"

"Oh, that is wonderful, Cameron. We'll be looking forward to seeing you again. I'm going to have a few friends in to welcome you home. Is that all right with you?"

Hesitating, Cameron replied, "Well, yes, I suppose so. That would be nice. Will Peder be there?"

"I don't think Peder is in the city at this time, dear, but I will call and find out. That would be nice for you, wouldn't it?"

"Yes, I would really like to see him again. It's been a long time."

"All right then, we will be waiting for your call."

Cameron was stunned at the warmth his mother projected, and thought that there must be some reason. He hadn't planned to go back home, but a few days wouldn't matter all that much. At least, he would get some good meals again—that is, if Ingrid was still the cook.

Henry Samuelson, the new Minister of Education, and his wife, Ruth, had often played bridge with the Jensons. Their daughter, Sandra, was returning for a brief visit, after having completed her studies in Paris. Ruth Samuelson and Janelle Jenson had become good friends; they wanted Cameron and Sandra to meet and, hopefully, to fall in love so their families would be forever bonded. They plotted and schemed, and decided the children should meet at an informal dinner party in Cameron's honor.

Cameron and Sandra seemed to hit it off from the beginning. He was intrigued by her grace and her long, slender legs. She dressed casually, but with exquisite taste.

"Sandra, do you play tennis?" Cameron questioned, hopefully.

"Yes, I love tennis. Do you want to challenge me in a game or two?" she asked, with a twinkle in her eye.

"Tomorrow. I'll pick you up in the morning around ten. After the game, we can have lunch together. Okay?"

"Fine with me," she replied nonchalantly.

Janelle and Ruth looked at each other across the table. Ruth winked, and Janelle thought, *We're on our way.*

Sandra was tall, had a great figure, and was very athletic. She had no problem winning the tennis match. To Cameron, she was a real challenge, like an unbroken colt.

Three months after their first meeting, they were married in a small chapel adjacent to the large church Sandra's parents attended on Christmas morning and Easter Sunday. Sandra was lovely in a Chanel cream-colored suit. Her long, blond hair was fashioned in a French braid with fresh flowers woven in and out of the plaits.

Only close friends and family members were invited to the small exquisite wedding. Peder stood with his best friend, and Sandra's cousin was her maid of honor.

The marriage lasted exactly one week. Later, Cameron could never understand why he married Sandra in the first place. Their engagement had been too brief. They did not really know one another. He knew that their mothers did everything they could think of to bring them together. Perhaps he wanted to break Sandra, control her. It didn't work.

Sandra was short on patience; when her husband could not sexually perform to her liking and taste, she insisted the marriage a colossal blunder and, consequently, asked for an annulment of the marriage contract. Cameron was relieved, gratified that it was over, delighted that he could get on with his own life, pleased to be rid of the deceptive, hypocritical facade. He felt no remorse for Sandra, for her family, for himself, or his own family.

In subsequent years, he became somewhat of a drifter, traveling all over Europe, the United States, and Canada. Quite by accident, his favorite hobby, photography, became his profession when several pictures sold to a leading periodical. He earned a substantial living as a freelance photographer and enjoyed the freedom that such a profession offered. Along with his interest in photography, which he always insisted was a true art form, he developed a profound understanding of the fine arts. He was knowledgeable, proficient, acquainted with every important museum on the continent, and could converse judiciously on most artists of any period since the Renaissance. He seemed to have an uncanny sense and ability to be just at the right place at the right time for the right picture. He always carried a camera, his one constant companion.

Cameron Jenson never married again. His marriage had been a failure; and though he dated young women, he never found fulfillment in any relationship. He was content to be in the company of other young men who had like interests, and he soon accepted the fact that his sexual preference, leisure enjoyment even, was found in the company of younger boys. He felt no remorse, no compunction for his life style. He never forced his affections on anyone. He reasoned that the way in which he chose to live was his business, his alone. His lifestyle was nothing new. The custom of pederasty had gone back to the early Greeks where it was an accepted and socially sanctioned, approved relationship between an older man (the teacher) and the younger man (the listener.) It was even considered to be an enviable relationship, one that was adhered to by the greatest teachers, philosophers, moralists, and intellectuals of that day, among whom were Socrates and Plato. Cameron admired Socrates and felt akin to him and other great philosophers. For him, this chosen life style was the very essence of living, giving him satisfaction, comfort, and gratification. For the first time in his adult life, he knew true happiness and fulfillment.

Young men or boys willingly and voluntarily entered into a pederastic relationship with Jenson. He was always good to them, tender, loving. He did not malign them in any way, ever. In quiet, reflective moods, he thought about other pederasts, like Socrates. History had stated that this great philosopher was condemned to death on charges of impiety and corrupting the young by a jury of 2000 people! Socrates had even refused to try to escape the prison in which he was held. It was a known fact that he died by drinking hemlock. Well, Jenson would never go to extremes. He believed in moderation in all things. Yet, on quiet evenings, in his tastefully furnished apartment, alone and in a contemplative mood, he would fantasize about Socrates, dressed in a long white tunic, discussing the philosophies of the day. In his world of fantasy, they would lounge and young boys would run back and forth waiting upon their every need, serving them wine, cheese, and grapes. Then, the boys would gently massage their aching bodies.

About a week after the dissolution of his marriage to Sandra, Cameron was riding his mare across the fields and through the trees on the outskirts of Stockholm when a low hanging branch pierced his left eye. The injury was so severe that he lost the sight of that eye. Thereafter, he chose to wear a black patch over the disfigurement rather than a glass eye. The patch fascinated women and distinguished him among men.

Olaf and Greta Hansen drove their Volvo slowly by the high brick wall surrounding the Ensenborg Estate on the outskirts of Copenhagen. Passing the large black iron gates at the entrance, Greta looked at her husband and asked, "What in the world do you think the estate is being used for now, Olaf?"

"Oh, I don't really know, Greta. There is much speculation about it. Jens and Inga were talking about it one day, and they both thought that it may be an exclusive clinic for recovering addicts—you know, from drugs and alcohol. Many wealthy people become addicted, and perhaps they go there to get clean, kick the habit, and recuperate."

"*Ja*, that is so sad. It's becoming quite a problem, isn't it, Olaf? I just don't understand why so many people think they have to try drugs. God help them. It's a curse, that's what it is."

"Well, I suppose they have problems in their lives that they can't cope with and they turn to drugs and alcohol for comfort." Glancing her way he remarked with a grin, "They aren't happily married like we are, Greta." He reached over to pat her knee.

Greta looked lovingly at her husband, "You are so right, Olaf. We are so lucky to have each other. I really love you."

"*Ja*, my darling Greta," he acknowledged. "We have much for which to be thankful."

"Olaf, at our luncheon the other day several of the women were talking about the Ensenborg Estate, and I gathered from their conversation that some of them were wondering about it. As you say, there is much speculation. You know, when that wealthy family owned it, they opened it up on certain days, like Christmas, and they invited the people that lived nearby to come in for tea and cakes. I thought that was very nice of them. I wish I could have seen the inside. They say it is very elegant."

"*Ja*, that home has long been regarded as one of the show places in the country. You know, it was really unfortunate and sad that those dear people who owned it were killed in that accident. I think they were flying in a small plane, and it went down in the sea. Then, some young man from the continent inherited it. I think the owners were distant relatives of some kind. They didn't have any children of their own. I heard that this young man, a nephew I think, died, too. He wasn't at all well when he got the place. Too bad—young man like that. Seems to me there's been a lot of tragedy connected with it. I'll bet if those walls could talk they would have a good many tales to tell."

"*Ja*, that's for sure. Little do we know."

Olaf continued, "Well, just goes to show that money isn't the most important thing in life, is it, Greta?"

"No, Olaf, I would say it is much more important to have good health—and a good husband. And, you know, I wouldn't give up my cozy little cottage for all the castles in Denmark. I love my little home just the way it is."

"Except that you want me to add on a sun porch," Olaf teased.

"Well, *ja*—that, but don't you think it would be nice? We could have plants, and sit out there in our rocking chairs. Ah, it would be so lovely," Greta sighed.

"Well, I'll look into it next week. I promise."

"Thank you, Olaf, thank you. I know you will enjoy it as much as I." Greta was deep in thought, then said, "Getting back to the castle. I just can't help feeling sorry for that young man. He received such a wonderful gift, yet he never lived long enough to enjoy it."

"I heard a rumor among the men," Olaf said. "That the old manor had been sold to an affluent foreigner. I don't know if that's true or not. Perhaps someone from America purchased it. It would be interesting to know what really happened, and who bought it, but we may never know, we may never know.

"No, perhaps not, perhaps not," Greta agreed.


The walls of the late nineteenth century, two-story structure were constructed of brick, with sandstone ornamentations. Small rooms were located under the steeply pitched, hipped roof, which was punctuated by rhythms of elegant dormer windows. Strolling past the main gate, the inquisitive observer could catch a glimpse of the circular driveway leading up to the central entrance, accentuated with a Baroque-like pediment, finely carved in stone. An exquisitely designed wrought iron railing flanked the steps.

The probability that anyone in the near vicinity knew anything about the activities that went on behind the walls of the mansion were slight. Some insisted that it had become an exclusive, private school for wealthy children from the continent. Still others maintained that it had become a private clinic for affluent, recovering alcohol and drug addicts. Limousines—automobiles—had been observed going in and out of the gate. Yet, no one really knew why, and few cared.

In March 1983, Emol Rosenberg and his wife Hilda sat on the sofa in the spacious, handsomely furnished living room, sipping port and munching crackers with Brie as they watched the flames leap in the old stone fireplace. The glow from the fire caught the finely cut crystal goblets, bringing them to life, casting a warm glow on Hilda's plain face. Turning to his wife, Emol impatiently exclaimed, "I wonder what's keeping him. He should have been here a half hour ago."

"He will be along directly, Emol. Be—be patient. Something unexpected may have developed," Hilda explained in a thick Scandinavian accent.

Reaching for another cracker, Emol complained, "Well, you know how I dislike waiting for anyone."

"Yes, how well I know," Hilda agreed.

A few minutes later they heard the buzzer at the main gate. After a brief conversation between the driver of the car and the gatekeeper, the heavy iron doors swung open, allowing the long, black automobile to slowly advance. Its headlights flashed a light into the room as it rounded the curve to the front verandah. Emol and Hilda looked at each other with knowing glances as they heard the car door close. In a few moments, the front doorbell chimed. They each listened intently to the maid's voice as she opened the door. "Hello, may I help you?"

"Yes, is Mr. Rosenberg in, please? He is expecting me."

"May I tell him who is calling?"

"My name is Jenson—Cameron Jenson."

"Please come in, Mr. Jenson. I will tell Mr. Rosenberg that you are here." Mia turned and switched on the lights. The Waterford chandelier plunged the entrance into intense grandeur. Jenson waited, hat in hand, awed by the intricate splendor of the wood paneling, the exquisite Persian rug, the beautifully carved mirror over the narrow fruitwood table. As he waited, he ran his hand over the smooth marble top of the table, and noted that the scones on each side of the mirror matched the chandelier. Mia returned quietly and smiled. "Will you please follow me, sir?" The tall, distinguished gentleman with a patch over his left eye followed the maid into the living room. Emol rose to greet him with an extended hand.

"Mr. Jenson, how nice to finally make your acquaintance. We have been waiting for you. Mia, please take the gentleman's coat and hat."

Jenson observed the deep lines in Emol's face, a face that looked like it had been chiseled from granite. The light blue eyes were piercing and cold—like cracked ice. He removed his coat, and handed it to the maid. Bowing slightly, Mia withdrew with the light raincoat over her arm. Motioning to a comfortable lounge chair, Emol invited Jenson to sit down. "Please have a seat. And, will you join us with a glass of wine?" Turning to Hilda, he exclaimed, "Oh, please forgive me, Mr. Jenson— my wife, Hilda Rosenberg."

"I am very happy to meet you, Mrs. Rosenberg," Jenson bowed slightly. "Yes, thank you, a glass of wine would be quite enjoyable." Rather than selecting the soft lounge chair, he sat down cautiously in the rosewood antique straight back. Jenson's glance swept the room, "This is very lovely, very lovely indeed." He held the wine glass to the light, turning it casually, admiring the exquisite Waterford cut crystal goblet. "Beautiful, just beautiful." Smiling at the couple sitting on the sofa across from him, he raised the glass, "My friends, shall we toast the future?"

Together they raised their glasses, and in unison said, *"Skol."*

"Yes—well, let's get right down to business, shall we?" Rosenberg looked directly at Jenson.

"By all means," Jenson coolly replied.

Assertively, Emol explained, "Mr. Jenson, my wife works closely with me, so we can talk candidly about everything in her presence. You will meet Miss Astrid Skagen later. She is the expert on passports and the proper papers.

"Yes, they praised her attributes. I know about her fine work and have perceived that she is quite exceptional," Jenson acknowledged.

"Astrid will be of great assistance to you in your travels, and after the children are settled in, she will have classes for them—teach them English, as well as the basic skills. There is a room set aside for their schooling. You see, we do want to keep the children healthy and happy, and we feel that their education is vital. That is the least we can do for them, do you not agree, Mr. Jenson?"

Jenson nodded in agreement. "By all means, by all means. We want to keep them happy."

"You realize, Mr. Jenson," Emol continued. "They can't possibly be in production all of the time, and we need to keep them busy and out of mischief."

"Absolutely. I am in full agreement," Jenson replied.

"We will be delighted to show you all of the properties later, Mr. Jenson. Your given name is Cameron?"

"That is correct."

"Well, let us not be so formal with each other. May I call you Cameron?"

"Of course, and with your permission, I will call you Emol and Hilda," Jenson smiled.

"Yes, yes, by all means." Emol continued. "I am confident that you will be very satisfied, comfortable, pleased, yes, even delighted with what we have here at the estate. There is a beautifully furnished, decorated room with extensive props and sets, just for the film making, as well as for still photographs."

"Wonderful," Cameron replied.

"Cameron, I have seen some of your still photographs, and I must say that they are absolutely unique. I have marveled at the various angles and configurations, and the lighting you used with the silhouettes is absolutely fascinating."

"I loved the silhouettes," Hilda interjected. "I've never seen anything like that before. Exquisite, absolutely exquisite."

Emol continued, "There is an adjacent room, a bit smaller, for developing, editing, viewing, and packaging the films. These rooms are all located on the first floor in the right wing, just opposite the servant's quarters. We will be the only ones who will be using these particular rooms, so do not be concerned about anyone coming in unexpectedly."

"That's good, very good," Cameron interjected with a smile.

"There are several small bedrooms on the third floor with adjoining baths for the children," Emol added. "Each room has a dormer window and opens to a long common sitting room with a fireplace and library. There are cook and maid's quarters on the first floor in the left wing of the house, with an apartment over the four-car garage for the gardener-chauffeur and his wife. Our bedrooms are all located on the second floor, and each has a private bath and sitting room, beautifully furnished.

"Well, I must say it appears to be more than adequate, Mr. Rosenberg…Emol. You have surely done an excellent job thus far. The Cartel will be more than gratified with your work. They certainly did make the right decision when they purchased this property."

Emol responded, "Yes, they surely did. It is perfect for the operation."

"Perhaps, some day, I could learn about the details of the purchase," Jenson added.

"Yes, well, it is very interesting—very interesting, indeed. I will tell you about it later." Emol continued, "Cameron, how long a period of time will you require in order to arrange to have all the children here? How long before production commences?"

"How many children are we talking about?"

Hilda interjected, "We were thinking of three boys and three girls. Of course, we want beautiful children, and they must all be foreigners."

"What ages?" Jenson inquired.

Rosenberg, one hand cupping his chin, replied, "Well, we thought perhaps between the ages of six and twelve, or thirteen years, no older. What do you think?"

"That should pose no problem, no problem at all. That's entirely agreeable with me. And, when do you want to start production?" Jenson asked.

"We still must do a great deal of work here in the estate—security, organizational, contacts to make, some hiring of employees. Hilda will be sending sophisticated news letters to several organizations with whom we have had contact in the past, annotating our holdings after production commences." As an afterthought, Emol glanced at his wife and added, "My, my, this operation is going to be quite different than the last one, isn't it, Hilda?"

"Yes, yes, indeed—I would say that this operation will be, will be…" Hilda searched for the right word. "Yes, will be—cosmopolitan. It will be chic, and very, very—what is the word I want—sophisticated? Yes, sophisticated. That is it."

Cameron nodded in agreement, but said nothing, somewhat amused at her groping for the right word.

"Well," Emol continued. "Let's see, when should the children be here? I would like to assume that all six children will be here no later than July. Will this allow you sufficient time?" Extending his hand in an affirmative gesture, he added, "Remember, we do not want just ordinary children. Each one must be, shall we say, exceptional? Unique? Our productions will be, without a doubt, the very best of their kind in the world, Mr. Jenson…Cameron. With your expertise and exquisite taste for the finest quality, no other similar operation will eclipse the distinction of our films. Having seen your work, I am anticipating even greater accomplishments in the future. Style, illustrative quality—ah, it is just going to be wonderful working with you."

"Thank you, thank you kindly. I am sure that you will not be disappointed," Jenson replied, smiling in agreement.

Rosenberg continued, "Each child must be of a different nationality, if at all possible. This will necessitate your traveling, Cameron. Search carefully, scrupulously, and be extremely discriminating and selective."

"Of course. I understand absolutely. Please do not be concerned, Emol. It will be a flawless operation, I assure you." Jenson paused, then continued, "There is a matter, however, which I must discuss with you first. I am obliged to travel to the United States, to Seattle, to visit my sister because of an illness in the family. I must go and lend them my support at this time. They are expecting me this month. In fact, I have made arrangements to leave by the end of the week. Immediately afterward, I will give the situation my undivided attention. Say, would you by any chance have the video, the one you made in the last operation, that I could take with me? I would be very pleased if I could get an idea of the kind of work you have done in the past."

"Yes, we can supply you with several, if you wish, and, Cameron, it will be all right if you must go to the States, but before you go we would like to introduce you to Astrid. As I explained earlier, she will be working closely with you, and together you can collaborate regarding every detail of every situation."

"And, when will I have the pleasure of making her acquaintance?" Jenson inquired.

"She will be here the day after tomorrow. When can you move your belongings in, Cameron?"

"I'll go back to the hotel tonight and check out in the morning, if that arrangement is acceptable."

"That will be fine, but you will probably want to take most of your meals out. We have not, as yet, employed a cook, and probably won't hire one until the first of June. You may take your meals with us whenever you wish, however. Between my wife and Astrid, we should have some pretty fine fare. Isn't that right, my dear?"

Hilda responded with a smile, "Perhaps, Emol. You know, I really do enjoy cooking once in awhile, and I wouldn't mind for just the four of us."

"And, I may even have the courage to make a meal on occasion," Jenson grinned. "Now, my dear friends, if you will excuse me?" Jenson rose. "I must return to the hotel. I will be here tomorrow, late morning. Let us not be concerned about the meals. I am easy to please." Jenson extended his hand, first to Hilda Rosenberg, then to Emol, and continued, "I shall be looking forward to tomorrow, and thank you, thank you very much. Be assured that we are going to be very successful. The four of us will make an exceptional team. This operation will be unequaled."

Thus was the genesis, the birth, of the most sensuous, hedonistic, artistic child pornographic ring in the Scandinavian Connection.

## Hans

Hannah Reiman was the eldest daughter of Rudolph and Inga Reiman. Hannah had two older brothers, and two younger sisters. Her brothers had both abandoned the family nest to live independently, leaving their parents with three girls to raise, a task Rudolph and Inga Reiman tried heroically to accomplish, but with minimal success. Inga insisted that the girls attend school regularly and, though the headaches persisted almost daily, made sure that every morning each had a good breakfast and a substantial sack lunch to take to school.

Hannah accompanied Renate and Elsa to school, but would often sneak away, wondering around the streets of Frankfurt, gazing wide-eyed at the enticing window displays and the beautifully dressed mannequins in the shop windows, dreaming of an unrealistic future. One day she would be a famous dancer, another day an accomplished teacher. Some day she would fly off to America to attend a large university. She would get a good position in New York City and send money to her parents. They had never had much as far as worldly goods were concerned, and she wanted to give them happiness. She would buy lovely clothes for Renate and Elsa.

Hannah lived in a world of fantasy and illusion. Her parents could not begin to perceive the secret world she guarded so scrupulously. They did the best they could. They made rules, and Hannah honored and respected their wishes. That she could not date until she was sixteen, and then only in the company of others, was understood unconditionally.

A short time after her sixteenth birthday, a momentous occasion, Hannah asked her parents if she could attend a dance with her girl friends.

"Hannah, where is the dance to be held?" her father inquired.

"It is going to be at the American Air Force Base, Daddy," she answered hopefully. "Please—please let me go."

"Well, I don't know. Who will you be going with?"

"My girl friends. You don't really know them, but they are all nice girls—Greta is Mr. Kohl's daughter. You know him, don't you?"

"Mr. Kohl? Of course. Fine man, fine man," he acknowledged.

"Then, there's Helen and Susan." Glancing at her mother, she continued, "You know their mothers, don't you, Mom?"

"Yes, I know them very well. They are in my ladies' group at church. I like them both."

"Well, Inga, what do you think?" Hannah's father questioned as he glanced at his wife.

"I think Hannah should be able to go with the girls, Rudolph. She is sixteen now, you know."

"Yes, yes, I know." Rudolph appraised his eldest daughter. "I can hardly believe that you are already sixteen, Hannah."

Hannah held her breath as her parents debated the question. Her father finally conceded, "All right, Hannah, you may go, but remember the rules. We expect you to be home no later than midnight, and we are counting on you to act like a lady."

"Yes, I know, I know. Thank you, Daddy. I will be home by twelve, I promise." Turning to her mother, she added, "Thanks, Mom."

It was at the dance that she met Richard Stanford, who seemed to be the answer to her longings. They talked and danced, danced and talked. Richard was a wonderful dancer, smooth, light on his feet, as he glided her around the floor. Later, in the ladies' room, Hannah grabbed Susan's shoulders, "Oh, Susan, isn't he the most terrific dancer you've ever seen?"

"Yes, you've lucked out, Hannah. Wish Jim were as good. He's forever stepping on my feet. Seems you always get the breaks."

Richard bragged about America and asked if he could see her again. She invited him home to meet her parents, and they liked him. He was polite, sociable, and reserved in their presence. That night, after the two young people had gone to meet their friends, Rudolph glanced up from reading the paper, "Inga, now I would say that this Richard is one fine young man, wouldn't you? I am really impressed with him."

"Yes, I do like him. Hannah knows what she's doing. He seems to be a very nice young man—attentive and kind."

After several "group" dates, her parents allowed her to go out with him alone to movies, to dances, and on picnics, and Hannah had never known such happiness. It was Richard whom she trusted explicitly, whom she thought she loved, who made many promises to her—and it was Richard who took her virginity. How disillusioned and mistaken she had been! She became pregnant, and brought shame to her family.

In 1971, on a cold, bitter night in the middle of the winter, at 1:30 a.m. in Frankfurt, West Germany, Hannah Reiman gave birth to a son. He weighed exactly eight pounds. She called him Hans. Hans never knew his biological father, who had been a corporal in the American Air Force. His mother had given her heart and soul to the dashing young serviceman she thought was the answer to her dreams, the man who would bring her joy and true happiness, the man who would take her to the United States. She never dreamed that the handsome, seductive, persistent, fast-talking air force corporal was already married, with a wife and child in Joplin, Missouri.

Hans came into the world rejected by a disconsolate mother who was much too puerile to accept the responsibilities of motherhood. She treated the baby boy like a doll, a plaything, loving him when she fancied, rejecting him when more important subjects vied for her attention. Hans was passed from one to another of the immediate family for care, what care he received—his ailing, unforgiving grandmother, his mother's two younger sisters, friends, and finally, neighbors. Little Hans, reaching out for love and affection, seemed to be a happy, healthy baby, with a ready smile, especially when someone took the time to play with him. His development was normal, and he grew into a tough little boy, worldly wise at a young age.

Hans was more at home on the streets than in school (which he attended rarely) or in his mother's apartment, where men would come and go frequently. His mother would often say, "Hans, some day we are going to leave this place, and we shall have a beautiful cottage in the country with a white fence around it, and chickens in the yard, and a dog for you. You will see." Hannah Reiman had good intentions, but of course, it never happened, and life for Hans became extremely difficult. His mother appeased him with some money, sufficient for his immediate needs, but spent little quality time with her son. Though Hans put on a callous, inflexible facade, the muscles in his stomach tightened from the pain he hid, from the lack of love and affection he craved, and this incessant gnawing rarely left him.

It was May 1983. Cameron Jenson had an unnatural affection for handsome, young, blond boys. As he sat at a sidewalk cafe in Frankfurt, sipping coffee, he noticed Hans Reiman sauntering by with two other boys. Intuitively, he knew that he wanted that particular boy, the blond, for himself, as well as for the organization. Quickly, he reached in his pocket for some marks, placed them on the table, and rose to go. He walked with accelerated steps until he was within a few yards of the boys. After following them for approximately three blocks, one boy waved a good-bye as he turned the corner. "Don't forget, I'll meet you by the statue at seven tonight," Otto said.

"We'll be there, you can be sure of that," Hans replied.

Just around the corner, Otto turned into the entrance of a dilapidated apartment building. The other two boys sauntered along, kicking whatever object they saw on the sidewalk. Two blocks down the side street, Hans, the handsomer of the two, slapped his friend's shoulder, "I'll pick you up on the way tonight, Rudy—before we meet Otto. Okay?"

"Great! I'll see you!" Rudy exclaimed. "See you a little before seven."

Hans continued down the street, and turned to go down a narrow walkway to a side door leading into what appeared to be some kind of apartment building or rooming house. Jenson made a note of the address, turned, and began to retrace his footsteps. He wouldn't rush it.

For the next three days, Jenson watched the action surrounding that side door. It didn't take long for him to determine the type of business activity the blond boy's mother, or guardian, was engaged in. One day, as he walked by the entrance, Hans came out of the building and almost collided with Jenson. "Oh, excuse me, I didn't know you were there!" Hans exclaimed apologetically in his best English.

Jenson smiled, "No harm done, young man—sorry, it was really my fault."

"No, I shouldn't have come out so fast. I'm sorry, Mister."

"Well, I don't think that it was your fault at all. Say, why don't you let me buy you an ice cream, or a soda? That should square things up between us. What do you say?"

"You mean it? Gee, that would be great, Mister!"

"Let's go to that cafe in the next block. Will that be satisfactory?"

"Sure! Thank you, thank you very much! They have good ice cream."

Politely, Hans tried to make light conversation as they walked along. "Do you live here in Frankfurt, sir?"

"No, I'm visiting here from Denmark. Maybe you could tell me what to see around here, or where to go. Have you lived here for a long time?"

"Yes, I was born here," Hans replied with a hint of disgust in his voice.

"How old are you?"

"I am twelve years."

"What is your name?"

"Hans. Hans Reiman."

"Do you live with your mother and father?"

"I live with my mother. I don't know my father, or where he lives." Hans hung his head and kicked a stone on the sidewalk.

Jenson thought, *Perfect.* They came to the small sidewalk cafe. He continued, "Well, here we are, Hans. Come, let's sit at this table." He led him to a small round table by a planter filled with red azaleas. The waiter came to take the order. "What will you have, Hans?" Jenson inquired.

"Oh, I don't care. What will you be having, sir?" he asked politely, in a thick German accent.

"Well, I think I'll have coffee and a cake, but you can have whatever you want," Jenson replied.

"Beer?" Hans grinned and winked, as he warmed up to the kindly gentleman.

Jenson exclaimed, "Hans, I thought you wanted ice cream."

"I do! I just wanted to see what you would say if I asked for beer. Don't worry, Mister, I really don't like beer. I would like to drink a Coca-Cola though," he grinned.

Jenson thought, *Hmm, a real sense of humor. I like that.* The waiter stood, waiting patiently. "Coffee and a sweet cake for me, and a big dish of ice cream with hot chocolate for my young friend here. Oh, yes, and a coke, too, please."

They enjoyed the treat together and Jenson noted that Hans ate slowly, relishing every bite. "Well, Hans, what shall I do while I'm here in your fair city? What should I see before I leave Frankfurt?"

"Well, it's fun to go down to the river, the Main River, you know. My friends and I go there a lot. It's really busy at the harbors—lots of activity." Hans took a deep breath and continued. "There's a trade fair going on right now. You might like that. Do you like museums, Mister?" Jenson nodded with a smile. "Our class had to go to Johann Wolfgang von Goethe's home. It's a museum now. It was boring, though. I didn't like it very much myself, but adults do, you know." Hans paused to glance up at Jenson, who looked at him with sincere interest.

"Go on, Hans." Jenson repressed a smile, enjoying the chatter.

Confidently, the boy continued, "Have you been to the Romer Town Hall?"

"No, no, I haven't been there. Is it worth seeing?"

"I think so. It's neat. Real old building, but nice. The Rhein-Main Air Base is not far from town, too. I think my dad used to be there." Hans stopped abruptly, looking at the red azaleas, yet not seeing them. Jenson noted the thick blond lashes, the strong profile.

They finished their snack, and the older gentleman rose to go. "Thank you, Hans, thank you very much for all of this information. You have been a great help. Say, would you like to meet me here again tomorrow, say about four in the afternoon, right after school? Then, I can tell you what I did. I'm planning to get up early in the morning to see all the sights you've mentioned."

"Yes, sir! But, I don't even know your name. What is it?"

"Jenson—Mr. Cameron Jenson. Okay, then, I'll meet you here tomorrow. Let's make it at four o'clock, shall we?"

"I'll be here—for sure, Mr.—Mr. Jenson."

"I'll bring you up-to-date on all I've done between now and then."

"Yes, sir—Mr. Jenson!" Hans grinned. "Thanks for the ice cream." Hans ran down the street, skipping, hopping, kicking rocks, thinking that Mr. Jenson must be very rich. He wondered why he wore a black patch over his eye, but he didn't dare ask. Sure was funny.

Jenson met with Hans on several occasions, gaining his respect and confidence with each meeting. He wanted him to think of him as a friend. The time would come, the right time to make his move. He would be his participant, not his victim.

"Hans, I have something I must take care of back in Copenhagen tomorrow. How would you like to come with me? You will have private lessons, and there'll be other boys there. What do you say? Do you think that your mother would allow you to go?"

"Copenhagen? Really? Man, I would really like to go there. I'll ask my mother, Mr. Jenson. I bet she'd be glad to have me out of her way for a time. Shall I tell her that I'm going to be working for you? Will I need money?"

"No, you won't need money. Just tell her that you are going to work in a private school out in the country near Copenhagen, and that you will not need any clothes or money, that the school will provide that. Also, that you will be tutored. Hans, you will love it there, and the work won't be difficult. You will have a good time. Ask your mother and see what she says."


"Tutored? You mean you won't have to attend school with other kids?" Hannah Reiman was impressed. Well, why not let her son go? He was old enough to leave home, to be on his own. It would mean just that much more for her. She did not see very much of Hans anyway, and sometimes he could get in the way.

"You really like this man, this Mr. Jenson, Hans?"

"Yes, Mama, he is a very nice man. I like him."

"Well, I can't see any reason why you can't go to Denmark for a time, but you have to promise to write to me once in awhile. You will, won't you?" In her heart she knew that she had not done much for her only son, but she did love him in her own peculiar way. She could be much freer without him to worry about, and it would mean more money to spend on herself.

"Of course, Mama." Hans put his arms around her. "I'll write letters to you—always." He was excited about the whole idea—the adventure, the mystery, the unknown. He had never been to Copenhagen. He wondered if he would ever get to see the Little Mermaid.

Hans Reiman was the first boy to come to the private estate on the outskirts of Copenhagen—blond, blue-eyed, personable, fun-loving. When he saw the large iron gate and the entrance to what was to become his home, his mouth gaped in astonishment. He had never seen anything so magnificent in his entire life.

Hans soon came to realize that it was a good life, and the work required of him was not difficult. He helped with some of the chores around the estate, had his own room and bath, and excellent food. Mr. Jenson explained to him that other children would be coming to live there, and they would all be involved in making films. Hans thought he was the luckiest boy in the world. He and Mr. Jenson became very close, and Hans would do anything to please him. For the very first time in his life, he felt important, wanted, and loved. At last Hans Reiman was a somebody, and the gnawing in his stomach had completely vanished. He wondered what his mother would think about his new life.

### Monique

Cameron Jenson wasted little time finding a suitable girl in Paris. As he walked slowly down the street in front of the Moulin Rouge, several girls approached him. An old, heavily made-up hag, a derelict, desperate for a few coins, had the audacity to come right up to him, to whisper in his ear, to proposition him. Without acknowledging her, he turned away in disgust. A tall, slender brunette in a tight mini-skirt and low-cut blouse walked by him like a panther in estrus, swaying her derriere. Jenson grinned. Not bad, but too old. Then there was the little redhead— demure, shy, hesitant. She appeared nervous and out of place, insecure, glancing here, glancing there, frightened as a young puppy searching for a loving hand. Cameron followed her for a block, crossed the street, then catching up with her, walked by her side, gently taking her arm. "May I walk along with you?"

"Yes, Monsieur—yes, yes, of course."

Monique accompanied the man with a patch over his eye of her own volition. Never had she been treated with such respect, such gentleness. The street in front of the famous Moulin Rouge was not her territory. The older, more sophisticated girls had cautioned her before, explaining emphatically that she was not welcome there. Humiliated, with head bowed in shame, she had been minding her own business when the kindly gentleman caught up with her. Jenson had fallen in step with her, walking by her side, talking in a courteous manner, like a father would talk to a daughter. Monique kept looking back, back to the other girls who gave her dirty looks, but was intrigued by this gentleman and will-ingly allowed him to guide her down the street. They walked for several blocks to one of the finer hotels in the area. This was not a sleaze pot of infestation.

As she sat on the edge of the bed, with one leg tucked under her slight, fragile body, Jenson pulled up a chair in front of her, and placed a hand on her knee. Monique wondered if he could be one of the really strange ones, and became suddenly suspicious of this kindly gentleman.

"What is your name, my little redhead?"

"Monique—Monique Marchant," she answered demurely.

"Where do you live, Monique?"

"Here and there, Monsieur. I used to live with my grandmother, but she died a little over a year ago. I have a friend. At times I go to her place. She is very kind to me."

"How old are you, Monique?"

"Sixteen, Monsieur," Monique replied abruptly, with a twinkle in her eye. Jenson said nothing, but raised his right eyebrow, questioning her reply.

"Well, not really," she responded sheepishly. "I am twelve—I just turned twelve. But, everyone thinks that I am much older, Monsieur! Don't you think that I look older? My friend helped me with make-up to make me look older." Monique was heavily made up with a cake-like covering on her face, rouged cheeks, black-rimmed eyes, thick mascara on her false eyelashes, and dark-blue eye shadow. It was quite difficult for Jenson to guess her correct age. He thought, however, that he could distinguish a pretty face beneath the masquerade.

"How would you like to leave Paris, and go and live in a lovely, large home, Monique?"

"Oh, Monsieur, that sounds too good to be true, but how? How could I ever do that? What must I do?" She looked down at her hands and ran her thumbs over the bright red finger nail polish. Her lower lip extended. "Do you not want me?" she pouted.

"My dear little Monique, just a moment, please. Look—look at me."

"Yes, Monsieur," she said sadly, as she raised her head and looked directly into Jenson's eye.

"Listen, and I will explain what I want you to do. I am going to leave you here alone for a short time, and I am wondering if you would do something for me?"

"Yes, Monsieur," she nodded somberly.

Jenson continued, "I want you to undress and take a good, long, hot bath. I want you to wash your face, shampoo your hair until it squeaks, and soak yourself. You do not have to hurry. Just relax in the bathtub, and get very, very clean. Do not dress again. Wrap up in one those big, yellow bath towels. Do you understand?"

"Oh, yes, I do! I do understand!" She gave the man with a patch over his eye a knowing wink and a big wide smile. She thought, *This is really different. Now he's going to leave me and go out, probably to bring back a couple more girls. I wonder why he wants me to take a bath. I just had one three days ago. Maybe I stink. Maybe he doesn't like my smell. I need some more perfume.*

During the hour that Jenson was gone, Monique drew a sumptuous bath, filling the largest bathtub she had ever seen almost to the brim. Submerging her entire body in its steamy depths, she took in deep breaths of air and ducked. With eyes tightly closed under the water she imagined she was a mermaid. She immersed again and again, splashed about, and bent her head down to blow bubbles in the warm, sudsy water.

As she luxuriated in the most wonderful bath she had ever had, she rested her head on the edge of the tub. Her mind drifted back to another bath, a bath in a much smaller tub. Her grandmother was bending over the lithe body of a girl of five. *"My darling Monique, let granny wash your back now. You get your little fingers in those ears. Here, use this thin washcloth, and I'll use the big one."* How she had loved her dear granny! How happy they had been together!

Monique could still remember her mother and father. They had been tragically killed in an automobile accident while vacationing in Austria. She did not know what really happened, but her grandmother had said that it was in the Dolomite Mountains; the road was very narrow with many sharp curves, and another car was involved. Her grandmother cried a lot after the accident. Monique could still remember the funeral, though she was only four at the time. Her grandmother was always at her side, loving her, comforting her, helping her with her prayers, promising to take care of her. She hugged her several times during the day. When she was old enough to go to school, she walked with her, shielding her from any harm. Monique always had sufficient food, and wore simple little dresses her grandmother had made. Granny had taken in sewing for a living, and many times she would allow her to pin and baste.

Monique recalled when granny became ill, coughing incessantly, her gnarled fingers still stitching. Most of the miserly income she earned was spent for medicine. Consequently, little by little, old family possessions were sold for food. It was bitterly cold that winter. Granny was so thin, and after school one day in February, when Monique was ten, she entered the bare flat to find her grandmother in bed, covered by her ragged coat.

*"My medicine is all gone, Monique. I don't know what else we can sell, or how we are going to get food. My darling little girl, granny is so sorry. I wish I didn't have this terrible cough."*

*"Don't worry,* Grandmere, *I will take care of you. There must be some way we can get your medicine."* Monique searched the room for something to sell, but there was nothing left, except the clock that had been in the family for years, a prized possession that would some day be hers. *"*Grandmere, *we don't really need the clock any more, do we? I think that I will take it to an antique store to see how much I can get for it. Will that be alright with you?"*

*"Yes, Monique. Take the clock. Oh, I am so sorry that I can't help you."*

*"Don't worry,* Grandmere. *I will get medicine for you. You will get better; I just know it. Do you think you will be all right alone?"*

*"Yes, my sweet little girl. I will be fine."* She went into a frightful fit of coughing.

Monique warmed the broth and helped her sip it slowly. *"I'll be right back,* Grandmere. *Just try to stay warm,"* she said tenderly as she kissed her on the forehead. She must get medicine; she must get food; yes, she would take the clock to an antique dealer. It was valuable and they needed the money.

The clock was cumbersome and heavy, but Monique carried it down the street to the first antique dealer. *"No, no,* fille, *the clock is worthless. Can't you see that it does not work any more?"*

*"But, Monsieur, surely it is worth something. It is very old, and someone could fix it."*

*"I am sorry. I cannot give you anything for it."*

Dejected and discouraged, Monique carried the clock back to the flat. *"*Grandmere, *I am so sorry, but the clock does not work, and the antique dealer could not give me any money for it. I am so sorry."*

*"That is alright, my darling. You tried. Oh, I am so tired. I think I will just try to sleep for awhile."*

Monique struggled with her thoughts. There was nothing else to sell now—except—except herself. I will just slip out while Grandmere is sleeping. I will get money.

Walking hesitantly out into the cold streets of Paris, she shivered and flipped the collar of her thin coat up around her ears. Approaching a well-dressed *man, she pulled on his coat and whispered, "Monsieur, I'm a virgin—will you, will you buy?"*

*"No, my child. Get on with you now." The gentleman hurried down the street.*

*In her shame, she approached a man who was standing on a corner in front of a restaurant. "Monsieur, Monsieur, I—I am a virgin. Will you buy? Will you give me money?"*

*"Sure, kid! Just come with me."*

*Later, she went to the pharmacist with her money. She could still hear the druggist's harsh, cynical remark, 'This is worthless, fille—counterfeit—* fake—money is no good. Go back home and bring good money, then I will give you the medicine."

*Uncomprehending, Monique questioned, "My money is not good, Monsieur?"*

*"No, it is worthless. It has no value. I am sorry, but I cannot give you medicine in exchange for this."*

*"But, sir, I need the medicine for my grandmother. She coughs—she coughs all the time. She is very sick."*

*"I am sorry, fille. I cannot do that."*

*Crushed, she walked slowly out the door. How could that man have been so cruel, so ruthless? She had been cheated. She had been deceived. She was defeated, her body ached, and she felt so dirty. It had hurt so much, so very very much. At that moment she hated all men.*

*Downcast, she reached their meager flat, opened the door gently, and crept softly to the bedside. Her grandmother appeared to be sound asleep. She had such a peaceful look on her serene face. She whispered, "Grandmere, Grand-*mere!" There was no response. "Oh, dear Grandmere, I tried, I tried!" she cried. She felt her grandmother's head, gently smoothing the gray, thinning hair back from her brow. There was no answer. She laid her head on her breast to see if she could hear the heart beat. She felt her wrist. There was no pulse. "No, Grandmere! No! Don't leave me! Please don't leave me! *I tried, but the money was no good! It was worthless!" She gently stroked her arm and rubbed her gnarled, bony hand. She was cold, so very cold.*

*Never in all her life had she felt so alone, so sick, so utterly helpless. She laid her head on her grandmother's breast and wept, wept as though her heart would break. "Grandmere! Grandmere! Oh, Grandmere, I love you! I* tried so hard! Please don't leave me! Don't leave me!"

The realization of her grandmother's death stunned her, leaving her numb and in a total state of shock. She lost track of time as she lay by her side, not moving, barely breathing. Her beloved grandmere *was dead. She was gone, gone forever. It had all been to no avail.* "Dear God, is Grandmere *with you? Is she safe now? Is she warm?" She must tell someone—she must go immediately and tell someone, but who? To whom could she go? She thought of Mrs. Goullet. Her grandmother had sewn for her because Mrs. Goullet had difficulty finding dresses that would fit. She was a large woman—much too fat, but Mrs. Goullet had been kind, often bringing a bread or cake when she came for a fitting. Yes, she would hurriedly go and tell her. Mrs. Goullet would know what to do. She would help.*

Lying in the large bathtub, Monique allowed the tears to flow down her shiny face and mingle with the water. She lay there a long time thinking, thinking, playing with the soap suds, swirling them around and around into abstract designs, remembering, remembering. In the suds she saw a rabbit, its two ears sticking straight up. There was a fat, smiling teddy bear. *"Grandmere,"* she whispered, "if only you were here with me, if only you were here with me. I miss you so much. You would love this big tub!" *I must get out now,* she thought.

Jenson returned, his arms full of packages. Monique, wrapped in the oversized yellow towel as he had requested, sat in a chair by the window, the sunlight silhouetting the lovely head of curls. *What an exquisite picture.* Her naturally curly, shortly cropped hair was a mass of unmanageable ringlets. A soft glow seemed to radiate from her translucent, slightly freckled face, with its small turned-up nose. She was fresh, clean, and vibrant without the heavy make-up. The transformation was remarkable, like a beautiful butterfly emerging the imprisonment of a painted cocoon.

"I'm clean, Monsieur!" she smiled, coquettishly.

Jenson gazed at her in wonderment, and with approval. "Yes, I can see that you are just sparkling, Monique. You look radiant and lovely. Here, I brought you some new clothes. Put them on."

"But, Monsieur! I—I—do not understand! Do you not want me?" She was embarrassed, sad, and somewhat confused.

Jenson picked up the pile of cast-off clothing, and threw them into the wastebasket. Turning to the child, he explained, "My dear little Monique, I do not want your—your body. Just get dressed. We shall be leaving in a few minutes. Are you hungry?"

"Monsieur, my clothes! They are all I have! Please do not throw them away!"

"But, you will not need them any more, Monique. Do you not see that I have brought you new clothes? Everything is here that you will need. Hurry now, get dressed—then we will go out to eat."

Unwrapping the packages, she exclaimed, "Oh, Monsieur, this is such a fine dress, so very, very fine, and I just love pink!" She ran her fingers over the material. "And, this slip and these panties are so pretty, and you even brought new shoes and stockings. I have never, never had anything so lovely. Do you mean that it is all really mine? To keep?"

"Yes, Monique, it is all yours. Hurry now. Get dressed. We're going out for a good dinner." Jenson walked away and stood in front of the window, arms crossed, gazing out at the city. He mused, pondering how this lovely child ever ended up on the streets of Paris. He shrugged and thought, *Well, that is no concern of mine.*

"First, I shall go into the bathroom and put on my makeup," Monique declared.

"No, Monique, do not put on any makeup. You do not need it. Your lovely hair with those bronze curls and ringlets escaping deliberately are the best decoration you have." Jenson smiled as he lightly touched a curl, ran the back of his hand down her silky smooth face, and tilted her chin so that he could look down into her questioning eyes. "Just get dressed, and leave your face exactly as it is now, shiny and clean."

"Yes, Monsieur, I will do as you say. It will take me just a few moments to dress." She wondered what kind of man this could be.

A distinguished looking gentleman with a patch over his left eye and a young, freckled-face, well-dressed, redheaded girl ate together in one of Paris' finest restaurants. Never had Monique enjoyed a meal as much. She had not known that such food existed on the face of the earth.

"David, David, look at that beautiful little girl sitting with that man with a patch over his eye—over by the window. Did you ever see such gorgeous red hair? Those curls! Isn't she a lovely child? Her mother must have had red hair. She didn't get it from her father."

Glancing toward the man and the child, then looking across the table at his wife, he said, "Yes, she's lovely, Simone—very lovely, indeed. Her hair is beautiful, a mass of ringlets. Her father must be very proud of her."

Simone reached across the table to touch her husband's hand. "David,

I still want to adopt. If we can't have our own child, please, darling, let us find a beautiful little baby girl. There are so many unwanted children. Surely, we can find just the right baby."

"Are you sure you want a girl?"

"It really doesn't matter—boy or girl—just so the baby is healthy."

"We'll start the proceedings Monday."

"David, you're wonderful! I love you."

An hour later Simone exclaimed, "Look, David, they are leaving now. She is *so* pretty—so sparkling. My, her father is caring. You can be sure he won't let anything happen to her."

Astrid had the necessary papers, and the three boarded the plane for Copenhagen at 11:00 p.m. that same night.

Life was much more pleasant for Monique at the estate. She had a lovely room, a bath of her very own, clean clothes, and all the good food she wanted, including fruits and vegetables. She liked Hans, the boy from Germany, and they played table games together. Later, she would discover that the work required of her was not as distasteful, nor as difficult, as that which she had been forced to do on the streets of Paris. She actually enjoyed the photography sessions with Hans, who insisted that Mr. Jenson was a great photographer. Mr. Jenson was always kind and patient with each of them, explaining fully what he expected them to do. Using light and shadow, directing their every move, he would often exclaim, "Hold that! Perfect! Perfect!" Monique was a natural when it came to posing. Her body did not embarrass her, and it pleased her to know that her pictures would go all over the world.

Monique began to realize how fortunate she was to have been invited to this wonderful place. She was required to study several subjects, and was learning to speak fluent English. Because Monique was the eldest, she became a mother figure to the younger children who later came to live in the home. Her heart went out to them because they were so fearful, so innocent. Monique longed to comfort and protect them, and in her motherly, sympathetic way, she would hold and hug them, and whisper in their ear, "Don't be afraid. I love you, and I care. No one will hurt you."

*Alberto*

A freshness was in the morning air. It had rained during the night, and small puddles collected in the narrow streets of Florence, as well as a modest amount along the curbsides. A bird enjoyed his morning bath, dipping his head in the clean water, and fluttering his outer feathers, revealing bits of bright color underneath.

The fourth year class was walking in pairs across the Ponte de Vecchio, the only bridge in Florence to have survived World War II. The children chattered, skipped, and hopped along, much like a flock of birds, splashing in the puddles when their teacher was looking elsewhere, pointing at objects that caught their attention, delighted at catching glimpses of the colorful displays in the windows of the various shops. Some of the students stopped briefly to watch an employee busily prepare for the tourists.

The class, on a walking tour of Florence, was headed for the Uffizi Gallery. "Everyone stay together! Remember, walk in pairs!" the teacher admonished.

Inside the museum, they paused in front of Botticelli's *Adoration of the Magi*, and the teacher lectured, "Class, let us all gather around as close as possible, please. I want to tell you about the painting." The children pushed and shoved, and stood demurely in front of the work of art. The teacher continued, "You will notice that the Virgin is robed in red and blue, and she is sitting in a rough shelter which looks like a Roman ruin. Look at the stylish, important-looking people standing around her. They are models that the artist used." She added disdainfully, "I'm afraid that they are more conscious of being painted than of being in the presence of the Holy Child."

"Miss Ciulla, did the models get paid for being in the picture?" Maria inquired. The other children looked up with admiration at their teacher, waiting for her reply.

"Yes, I suppose they received something, but I don't really know. Perhaps just having the honor of posing for Botticelli was all they wanted."

"Look, Miss Ciulla," Samuel exclaimed. "Look at that old man, who is kneeling before the Child offering his gifts. He looks just like an old man I know by the name of Glaviano that comes to church and sits in the front row every Sunday."

"Yes, I know, Samuel. The models all look just like many people that we know today. But, class—quiet, please! Shh, Alisaria! Everyone pay attention, please! That man, the one kneeling before the Christ Child, is actually the greatest of the Medici, Cosimo the Elder, the Father of his country."

The children gazed in awe at the painting. One chubby, dark-haired girl spoke up, "Miss Ciulla, why was he called a Father? Did he have many children? Was he extremely rich?"

"Yes, he was very rich, Lenora. The Medici Family was the ruling family. Right now I can't recall how many children he had, but I am sure he had many. Yes, Lenora, they were very, very wealthy. They sponsored the artists of the day."

"What does sponsored mean, Miss Ciulla?" Romano inquired.

"Well, it means that they paid the artists for the work they did. When an artist is sponsored, he doesn't have to worry about anything."

"You mean they gave him everything he wanted—like food even?" Antonio asked.

The teacher smiled. "Yes, Antonio, I suppose they received everything they needed, even food. Artists didn't have very much money in those days. I suppose the artists would not have had enough to eat if the Medicis had not given them money—had not supported them."

"Well, didn't the artists have parents who could help them, Miss Ciulla?" Sophia inquired.

"Of course they had parents, Sophia, but you must remember, they were not children. They were on their own, and they needed to make some money to live."

Every child in Florence had learned about the Medicis as far back as their first year class, and many of their parents had discussed the history of the Medici family at home around the dinner table. Children were fascinated with the stories about the rulers of their country. The teacher continued, "This family was the most important one in Italy's history, class, and especially in our own city of Florence."

"We know that, Miss Ciulla," Alberto said quietly. The teacher thought Alberto was such an observant, sincere, gentle boy. The group of children continued from one room to another.

The class stopped in front of the four-foot-high painting of Venus by Botticelli, awed by its beauty, by the shadows and tones of its colors. The teacher spoke to the class again, "Venus was a goddess, and the model was the most beautiful woman in Florence in 1470..." her voice droned on and on.

Alberto Giovani Lento was so engrossed in his own dream world that he dropped the hand of his companion, Marco, and stood alone, gazing up at the painting. "If only I could paint like Botticelli and become famous some day," he whispered. He studied the work of art for a long time, then realized that the class had gone on without him. "Oh, , which way did they go?" he exclaimed, as he looked, first one way, then the other.

Alberto was bright, artistic, and sensitive. He possessed a bell-like soprano voice, and was a member of the boys' choir that sang for early mass each Sunday morning in his church. He loved to sing, and when he sang, he knew that God was there with him. He was always the happiest when in church singing about God.

Alberto was delicately built for a boy, tall for his age, thin and angular. His wavy, black hair grew into a perfect hairline at the nape of his neck, his ears were small and hugged his head. His dark brown eyes were rimmed by thick, black eyelashes. Alberto was somewhat reticent, but was a superior student. Though serious, he possessed a delightful sense of humor, and took great joy in teasing his older sister, Carmela.

The Lentos were a respected family in Florence, well liked by their immediate neighbors. Carlo Lento was an artist, a gentle-mannered, considerate husband and father, who made a substantial living as a sculptor. Angela, his wife, gave private piano and voice lessons to students in their modest home.

Carmela, two years older than her brother, was outgoing, happy, and cheerful, always sharing amusing, lively incidents that happened at school with the quieter, more serious Alberto, who looked up to her in amazement and wonder. She was a bit plump, but that did not concern her. She gave Alberto a deep sense of security, and they shared an exceptional rapport few brothers and sisters could ever realize.

There wasn't a city in all of Italy that the Lento family would exchange for their beloved Florence with its rich art history.

Alberto stood scratching his head, looking to the left, then to the right. A tall man with a patch over his left eye approached him and inquired in perfect Italian, "Are you lost, young man?"

"No, no, not really, sir. I am with the class from my school. They are in another room, and I must find them, or—or..." his words trailed off.

"Perhaps I can help you find them," the kindly gentleman offered.

"Oh, would you? Thank you! Thank you!" Alberto was anxious, and trusting.

Jenson had been observing the group from the time they had crossed over the Ponte Vecchio. He followed them from room to room, with an uncanny sense that one of the number would become separated from the rest of the children. He waited patiently, as a hunter would stock his prey. "Perfect," he whispered.

Jenson guided the youngster in just the opposite direction. Alberto became disconcerted. "Where are they, sir? I don't think they went this way."

"Don't worry, young man. We'll find them."

"My teacher will be very angry with me if I don't catch up!" He was becoming extremely nervous, and quickly glanced one way, then the other.

"We'll catch up with them," the gentleman assured him. He caressed his shoulder in a comforting gesture, and took his hand. They walked out of the side entrance, and looked in both directions. The class was nowhere in sight. "What is your name, young man?"

"Alberto—Alberto Giovani Lento. I wonder where they are," he said anxiously.

"Where do you live, Alberto?"

"About six or seven kilometers from the school, on the other side of the Ponte Vecchio."

"Well, why don't we just drive you on home? My car is right over there. Later, your mother can call the teacher and explain everything to her."

"I—I—don't know, sir. I should find the class here and go back to school with them." Big tears filled the boy's eyes and ran down his cheeks.

Jenson thought, *What beautiful, large brown eyes.* "Don't cry, Alberto—perhaps the class has already returned to the school. Would you rather go there?"

Alberto withdrew his hand from Jenson's clasp, and wiped the tears that trickled down his face with his sweater sleeve. He took a white handkerchief from his pant pocket and blew his nose. "That might be better—maybe I'll get there about the same time—yes, that would be better, I think. Thank—thank you, sir."

A bit reluctantly, Alberto took the extended hand of the man with the patch over his eye, fearful, yet hoping it was all right to go with him.

"Here's the car, Alberto. Let me get the door." He unlocked the passenger side of the blue Fiat and opened the door. "There you are, young man." Alberto got in. Then, Jenson walked nonchalantly around the rear of the car, and got in on the driver's side. "All right, Alberto, where do we go? Where is your school?"

Pointing, he said, "Drive the car over there, and I will explain which way to go."

Jenson drove slowly out of the exit, and Alberto pointed in the direction of the school. Turning to Alberto, Jenson held out a white sack of chocolates. "Here, have a candy. Now don't worry, Alberto, everything will be just fine. We'll get you there in no time at all." Without thinking Alberto accepted the chocolate from the small white sack, and slowly put it in his mouth. Jenson thought, *such lovely manners.*

In just a few moments, the drugged chocolate took effect, and Alberto's eyes closed. His head fell forward on his chest. Jenson accelerated the engine, circled around several blocks, and drove down the narrow street, turning the next corner in the direction of the Donatello Hotel. Alberto would be semi-drugged, and in a few hours they would be on the flight to Copenhagen. Astrid would be waiting with the proper papers. Jenson mused, *That was easy. Three down and three to go. Right on schedule! Emol and Hilda are going to be so very pleased, to say nothing of the praise I will receive from the Cartel. Now, another girl—or boy—whichever.*

"Yes, thank you very much. We would appreciate getting on the plane first. Our son is quite ill as you can see. His medication has made him very drowsy," Jenson explained to the airline attendant.

As Jenson carried the child down the ramp, Astrid held on to his arm, comforting the frail child whose eyes were half closed, expressionless.

## Kari

Jenson always enjoyed the 1,600 feet ride to the top of the Tryvann Hill, just outside the city of Oslo, Norway. The scenery was magnificent, and from that position, one had a fabulous panoramic view of the city. He had taken the Holmenkillen rail ride to the end, and had walked up to the tower in twenty minutes. He felt in top physical condition. Astrid had chosen to linger in the Scandinavian Hotel where she could freshen up before going to the performance at the Norwegian Folk Museum. Jenson promised to return around four in the afternoon, in sufficient time to accompany her there for the 5:00 p.m. presentation in the open-air theater.

It was a lovely, clear, fresh summer day in June 1983. The sky was a vivid blue, and fluffy, white cumulus clouds turned into a menagerie of sheep, poodles, and bears. There was ample to do, considerable to see in Oslo, but Cameron Jenson and Astrid Skagen were not there on a sightseeing trip. It would be Jenson's responsibility to find a girl, the right girl, blond, blue-eyed, flaxen hair, around seven or eight years old.

Sitting in the hotel coffee shop, Cameron turned to his companion and said, "There is an indoor ice-skating rink in a lovely residential district about twenty minutes from here, Astrid. I think I'll go out there and look around. So many of these Norwegian youngsters take skating lessons. This may be the place to find our girl."

"Ja, that sounds good. I won't expect you until later this afternoon then." She admired Jenson, and thought she could be romantically interested in him, but he was all business in his interactions with her. She wondered if, perhaps, he had a special friend, what he was really like under the facade, what life would be like if she were his sweetheart—or his wife.

Kari Johanssen, who had just completed her second year in school, was an exemplary student, who brought home the highest marks. Her father, Professor Johanssen, had agreed that she would be allowed to take ice-skating lessons three days a week during the summer months, if she would agree to practice piano an hour each day. Kari's skating lessons were on Monday, Wednesday, and Friday after lunch. They shook hands on the agreement. "I promise, Daddy."

"Okay, Kari, now remember—an hour a day at the piano." He gave her a big hug. "I love you."

"I love you, too, Daddy, and thank you, thank you for letting me skate."

Lenna Johanssen, an elementary teacher, would often take her class on field trips. If at all possible, she would arrange for Kari to accompany the class, especially if the trip involved an overnight stay. In the fall, after the beginning of school, she was planning a five-day outing by ferry, bus, and train into the fjord country. Of course, several parents had already volunteered to chaperone and assist.

"Do you think you should take Kari out of her class for that length of time, Lenna?" Nels inquired. "Think she'd be fine here with me while you're away."

"Yes, Nels, I do think that she should go along. You can't be here when she comes home from school, and I don't want her to be here in the house alone. I've already spoken to her teacher, and she thinks it would be wonderful for her to go with us. She's even offered to give her lessons to take along."

"Okay, but it'll surely be lonesome around here without my two girls," Nels smiled. "When school starts, do you think she should continue the skating lessons? You'd think she was training as a future Olympian. Who knows? Maybe she is, and Oslo may even host the Olympic Games again by the time she's ready to perform."

"Well, I think it's wonderful that she wants to be a figure skater, Nels. And remember, she is practicing her piano every day."

"Yes, she promised, you know."

Jenson sat by the window in a restaurant adjacent to the skating rink, sipping the sweet, strong coffee slowly, carefully observing the children and young people going in and out of the rink.

A pretty young girl, with thick, blond, plaited hair, dressed in a pair of red slacks, a white turtleneck sweater, and a windbreaker, romped gaily by the restaurant. It was obvious from the outline of the skate guards at the bottom of the bag that her figure skates were in the Scandinavian Airline canvas tote bag she had slung over her right shoulder. She half skipped, half ran, her blond braids bouncing carelessly in the air, until she arrived at the entrance of the rink. Jenson admired her pure Scandinavian beauty—the thick, blond hair, the fair complexion, the high cheekbones, and thought she would be exactly right for the project.

He ordered another cup of coffee, and some Norwegian *lefse* with butter and sugar. He loved the *lefse*, and who could make better coffee than the Norwegians? He relished every bite. "More coffee, sir?" the waitress inquired.

"Yes, please—it is delicious." He sat quietly, thinking, pondering, planning, but his thoughts were racing. *I wonder if she comes every day at the same time.* He thought he'd take a brisk walk while she was skating, then return to the cafe for another cup of coffee. He'd sit at one of the small tables out on the verandah where nothing could obstruct the view of the children coming out of the skating rink.

Later, Kari and her friend, Siri, were walking past the restaurant together after their skating lesson. While Jenson sipped the coffee and enjoyed the sunshine, he listened carefully to their conversation.

"Siri, I just love skating, don't you?"

*"Ja,* I love it, Kari. Do you think we will ever be good enough to compete in the contest by September?"

"I don't know about that, but I hope so. Perhaps, if we practice long and hard we'll make it," Kari said confidently.

"Race you to the corner!" Siri shouted as she bounded down the street.

"Not fair—you had a head start!" Kari shouted as she ran after her friend.

For the next few days Jenson made it a point of being in the same restaurant at the same time. With a knowing smile, the waitress brought the coffee and *lefse*. The object of his attention did not come on Tuesday, but she appeared again on Wednesday. She did not come on Thursday, so he assumed that perhaps she would come on Friday. That would be the day that he and Astrid would make their move.

Jenson was friendly, but not companionable as far as Astrid was concerned. Their relationship was purely business, but when he arrived at the hotel Thursday afternoon, and met her in the lobby, he announced, "Tomorrow we make our move. Tonight we are going to dine out,

Astrid—in style—at the *Frognersaeteren*. I will explain everything to you then. Could you be ready to go at 6:30?"

*"Ja*, that would be fine. Thank you, thank you very much, Mr. Jenson." He wished Astrid could learn to say "yes" instead of *"ja."* It was so uncouth, so rather contemptuous. These Scandinavians! Course, he was Swedish too, but he didn't go around saying *"ja"* all the time.

They took the tram up the mountain to a restaurant that had a magnificent panoramic view of the Oslofjord. The sunset was spectacular, the sky, a canopy of color in shades of pink, yellow, gold, fuchsia, changing gradually into the deeper magenta hues, outlined by azure blues and achromatic greens. The air was crisp and clear, and after twilight a full moon and a myriad of stars burst forth to lighten the darker, deep blue of the sky. They could still view the magnificent scenery at least ten miles down the fjord. The restaurant, noted for its excellent food, was located in an authentic Norwegian log house, with an interesting décor. Unfortunately, the dining area was crowded with tourists. At a small table in the corner near the fireplace, Jenson and Astrid relished the wonderful meal.

After dessert, they sipped espresso together and talked like two normal people. Astrid was surprised at how gracious and considerate Jenson could be. For those few moments, he was almost jovial, even charming. Why couldn't he be like this more often? Then, his personality changed. He became serious, explaining in minute detail how the abduction would be handled on the following day. *All business*, Astrid thought.

On Friday they sat in the restaurant adjacent to the rink. Jenson glanced down at his watch. "She will be coming out in about fifteen minutes, Astrid. Go get the car now. She may be with her friend, but her friend will turn east, and she will continue around the corner to the west. I will be just behind her at the time you are driving next to the curb. Do not be concerned. It will be uncomplicated." It had all been carefully calculated. He would accidentally bump into the child, catch her, and when Astrid opened the car door, Jenson would push her into the front seat between them.

The scheme was accomplished exactly as planned. Before the girl could utter a scream, Jenson quickly injected the needle, right through the lightweight sweater, and in a few moments, the drug took effect.

Jenson put out his hand toward Astrid, who handed him the phony passport. The reservations had been confirmed earlier, and soon the "parents" and the sick "daughter" were in the sky headed for Copenhagen. Jenson reflected with amazement how easy it was to abduct a child.

### Alexander

The Sunday edition of the London Times was later than usual. Abigail Lancaster and Charity Kendall were sipping tea at the small table in the cook's quarters of the stately old home in Brighton, England. "I wonder what in the world is keeping that delivery boy today!" Mrs. Lancaster inquired of Charity, as she raised the cup of tea to her lips.

"I can't imagine, Abigail. Timothy is usually so prompt."

"Well, Charity, I have a matter to attend upstairs. Call me when the paper arrives, will you, old girl?" Mrs. Lancaster got up laboriously and slowly walked out of the room. Piping hot tea and the morning paper had become a ritual, enjoyed by the two elderly women each Sunday morning. The problems of the world had all been resolved over their teatime. Had the Royal Family listened to their counseling, they would have maintained the dignity of the throne. As it was…

About an hour later, Timothy knocked hurriedly on the back door. "Here's your paper, Mrs. Kendall!" he shouted. "Sorry, Mum, that it's so late today. Guess there was some kind of problem at the plant. Personal delivery service today—right to the door! Well, you have a good day, Mum," he grinned.

"Here, laddie, take these biscuits with you. You are a good boy. Get on with you now!" Mrs. Kendall nodded in approval.

"Thanks, Mrs. Kendall! Tell Mrs. Lancaster that I'm sorry the paper is late, and thank her for the treat. Good day, Mum!" He popped a biscuit into his mouth, and skipped down the steps.

"That is one nice boy," she mumbled as she turned away from the back door. She walked to the bell ringer, gave it two short pulls, and sat down at the table. Mrs. Lancaster soon appeared.

"It's about time! What in the world happened with that boy today anyway, Charity?"

"It wasn't his fault, Abigail—something at the plant went wrong. Have another bit of tea?"

"Yes, thank you, Charity. Say, are there any more crumpets? I think I'll just have one more. They are so good."

"Yes, I believe there are just a few left. I must make some biscuits soon. We're getting low."

Taking the second section of the paper, Abigail facetiously remarked, "Well, I wonder what's new today with our dear House of Windsor."

"Abigail, do you think that Charles and Diana are ever going to be really happy? When you see pictures of her she usually looks beautiful, but you know, there is a sadness about her, and she is so thin. I wonder if she is well. Do you think it's true that Charles may have another woman in his life?"

"Oh, who knows the answer to that, Charity? I do know that this Camilla went with him several years ago, and I heard that she fell madly in love with him. Some think that he loves her, too, so how can he honestly love two women at the same time? She's married to one of his best friends, but I wouldn't be at all surprised if they meet secretly. Diana must know about this, and this is probably why she looks sad. Anyway, I think that this marriage was simply a partnership".

"What do you mean—a partnership?"

"Well, Charity, she married, not the man, but a way of life. Charles had an obligation to the family, and to the nation, to marry and produce an heir to the throne, and he wasn't getting any younger. She's an attractive little thing, quite a bit younger than he, but she was a good catch as far as I'm concerned. I feel sorry for any commoner that would marry into that family. It must be a very difficult and unhappy life."

"Now she has William, though, and he's a beautiful child. I heard that she was very devoted to him—plays with him, loves him a lot. He's really a darling child, and I suppose he will be the future king."

"Yes, if all goes well, if all goes well," Abigail responded doubtfully. "Anyway, we can't always believe what we read in the papers. But, I get so disgusted with Charles. He seems to be jealous of Diana, and even in public he shows little concern or love as far as she is concerned. Just between you and me I think he's a poor excuse of a man, and I hope the Queen can see through him and keep him off the throne. You know, I'm just about ready to give up on the whole family, and I wonder at times just how long this country will put up with the monarchy and the disgraceful things they do. Why do we have to continue to support their lavish lifestyles? Some of them are a disgrace. My heart goes out to that girl, though. Imagine what she has to go through to please the Queen and the rest of the family. She'll never have any kind of life of her own." Abigail declared.

Each of the women was engrossed in reading when Abigail, looking at the front page of the second section, exclaimed, "Can you imagine? Listen to this, Charity."

## PARENTS PLEA FOR MISSING CHILD

Thomas and Marjorie Blenheim reported that their five-year-old son, Alexander, was playing with friends at St. James Park, on Saturday. Alexander's nanny, twenty-one year old Sarah Long, had been sitting on a bench with Leah Cook, nanny to Alexander's friend, Jonathan Ames. Ms. Long glanced over at the swings and realized that Alexander was no longer swinging. She ran over to the group of children and asked if anyone had seen Alexander. No one had seen him leave the scene.

Abigail continued to read.

Alexander Blenheim is a charming little boy with brown hair and brown eyes. There is a mole over his right eye near the hairline. He was wearing beige shorts and a green T-shirt. His father is in the shipping business, and is offering a big reward for information leading to his return.

"What in the world happens to all of these missing children, Charity?"

"Well, Mum, I just don't know. I just don't know. It is a sick world out there these days, and people are doing all kinds of crazy things. God help them." Charity shook her head in dismay.

"Those poor parents. Can you imagine what it would be like to have your own child missing? I'll wager they're just worried to death, wondering where he is, or what's happened to him—whether he is alive—or dead. Do you suppose he could have been kidnapped? His people must be wealthy. Oh dear, perhaps they will receive a note demanding a large sum of money for his safe return."

"I wonder. I feel so sorry for them," Mrs. Lancaster replied. "No one deserves to lose a child. The dear people. I'd like to get my hands on the person that took him. I'd show him a thing or two."

"Abigail, it may not have been a him. It may have been a her. There are many women who just go out and steal a child because they can't have one of their own."

"Yes, I know, I know. You're right, Charity. Well, anyway, I hope they find little Alexander, and that he's all right."


Marjorie Blenheim went into the study and picked up the phone. She waited patiently after dialing—three, four, five rings. "Eleanor, Eleanor, this is Marjorie. Could you please come over for awhile? I am beside myself and I really need you! What? No, I'm alright. That isn't it. No, No, El—Alexander is missing! Yes, yes, he was playing in the park and he just disappeared! No, Sarah *was* there–sitting on a bench with her friend Leah. She's in tears—doesn't know how he could disappear so quickly. She had been watching him swing and there were other children around, and a lot of adults, too. I don't know what we're going to do. What? Yes, Thomas is working with the authorities. He's down there now. No, he didn't want me to come. Oh, thank God he happened to be home now. I can't believe this! Could you please come right away? No, come by yourself. Thomas and Jack can get together later. Yes—yes—I'll be all right. Just hurry."

Eleanor was at her best friend's home in fifteen minutes. Taking her hands in her own, she exclaimed, "Oh, Marj, I am just so sorry." Holding Marjorie close, she spoke with assurance, "I am sure Alex will be found. Come on. Let's go into the kitchen and have a cup of tea. You know I'm going to be right here by your side and I'll do anything—anything to help."

Marjorie's eyes filled with tears, and she sobbed, "I know that, and you don't know how much I appreciate your coming." She dabbed her tear-streaked face. "You've always come through for me. When Alex was sick with pneumonia and we thought we would lose him you were the one who would not give up. He's frail, El, and he needs me. I know that we have probably spoiled him, but he's needed more from us than either Gloria or Josh. They're both shocked—going to put posters with Alex's picture all over town. Oh, why—why did this have to happen? I fear for him, El."

"Don't give up, my dear. He isn't as frail as you think. I was just watching him the other day out in the back yard—running like a deer, and I thought then that he was really getting stronger—such a handsome little boy. The authorities will find him. We'll trust God, Marj. He's still in control, you know."

It was the last Saturday of June 1983. A tall man with a patch over his eye and a short, blond woman escorted a small boy through the gate to the plane that would fly to Copenhagen at 10:30 p.m. The boy seemed to be ill, so his father was carrying him. His parents were so concerned, so loving, so compassionate, giving the child their undivided attention. It was a joy to see such a caring family.

Jenson received a call from Seattle in July. It was his sister. "Cameron?"

"Yes, Elaine? This is Cameron. Are you all right?"

"No, Cameron," she sobbed.

"Elaine, Elaine, what's the matter? What's happened?"

"Could you please come right away? Eric passed away. You know, he hasn't been at all well, and he died suddenly—in his sleep."

"You don't mean it! I am so sorry, Elaine. How did it happen? I thought he was getting better. Did the old problem come back?" Jenson inquired with genuine concern.

"No, he had been feeling really quite well. I just don't know. It happened so quickly. We don't really know the cause of death yet. There will be an autopsy. Cameron, what am I going to do? I loved him so much," she cried. "Would it be possible for you to come—right away?"

"Yes! I will be there tomorrow if I can get on Scandinavian Air. Please, Elaine, control yourself, and don't worry. You'll become ill. Hang in there. You will, won't you?"

"I'll try, Cameron, but do hurry, please," Elaine replied quietly, but emphatically.

"I will, Elaine. Just don't worry. You know I'll do anything I can to help. Are his folks around?"

"Yes, but they are devastated. His mother is in a state of shock. They're wonderful people, Cam, but I do need you."

"I'll be in touch right away regarding my schedule."

"Thank you. You are such a dear."

Elaine knew that her brother would never say no to her. Though she was older, he had always treated her as though she were his responsibility. She wouldn't call her parents until it was all over. She did not want them to come, to offer any sympathy. It was too late, yes, it was too late for that. They had never cared about anything in the past. Why would they be concerned now? No, but she could always depend on Cameron. No matter where he was, no matter what he was involved in, he would drop it all and come to her aid, and give her support and advice.

It was so sad. Eric had been such a fine man, still quite young. He had been a great provider, and they had a wonderful life together. He had been so thrilled with his new boat, and they had been anticipating great outings on Puget Sound, exploring the San Juan Islands, going up the Canadian coast.

Eric's parents were caring people, always there for you in any circumstance. They couldn't understand why this had to happen, and they were brokenhearted over his death. Why, oh why? Elaine wept openly.


"Emol, my sister's husband has passed away in Seattle. I must go and be with her at this time. I think Astrid should probably accompany me. Perhaps we will be able to wind things up there. Will this be all right with you?"

"Fine, Cameron. I'll speak to Astrid about it. I am sorry about your brother-in-law. I recall that you said there was an illness in the family the last time you went to Seattle. Was this the cause of his death?"

"I don't really know. My sister said that he had been feeling quite well. It happened suddenly. Well, thank you. Tell Astrid I'll be ready to leave tomorrow morning on the first flight out," Jenson said.

"I am sure that will be fine with her. She always has a bag ready to go."

After the memorial service, Jenson would remain in Seattle two more weeks. He would help his sister, and more importantly, he and Astrid would try to complete the group with an American girl. Then, the real work would begin in Copenhagen, the kind of work that he thoroughly enjoyed and excelled at, the work that was more like play, like one grand performance. How he looked forward to the acclaim and praise he would undoubtedly receive from the Cartel.

The funeral was held on July 16 in a large Lutheran Church in Ballard. Jenson did not know exactly how he and Astrid would accomplish their task, but during the service, he contemplated the many possibilities. Perhaps they could take in a movie, one that had great appeal to children. Or, they could go to a baseball game. Children always had to go to the restroom, and sometimes parents were too interested in the game to accompany them, to make certain their little darlings were all right. He and Astrid could visit the zoo at Woodland Park, or go to Green Lake, or down to the beach. And, there were always the fast-food restaurants, brimming with children and lazy mothers who did not want to stay home and cook a nourishing meal. The possibilities were endless.

Little did Cameron Jenson realize at that moment, sitting with the family in the first pew of the sanctuary, how absolutely faultless and uncomplicated the abduction would be. He held his sister's hand and looked mindlessly toward the gray casket. A large floral arrangement of carnations covered the lower half of the coffin, and the corpse held one red carnation in its cold, hard hand. Jenson looked at the face of his departed brother-in-law, not seeing. His thoughts were not of Eric, no, not even of Elaine and her sorrow. The empty socket where his eye had once been began to throb and burn.

Telephone calls, notices to the military, to social security and insurance companies, burial plans, accounts to take care of, death certificates, acknowledgments, correspondence—there were so many things to do. Cameron was at Elaine's side, helping in every conceivable way, day after day, night after night.

A day after the memorial service, the telephone rang. Elaine picked up the phone. "This is the Anderson residence. May I help you? Who? Who did you say this was? Neil Manning? Oh, yes—yes, I do remember. You came here with Bill—from the college. Mr. Jenson? Yes, he just happens to be here. Would you like to speak to him? Yes, yes, he's on the deck. I'll tell him you're calling."

"Cameron, it's for you. Neil Manning. You met him when the boys came down with Bill from George College last spring. Remember?"

"Neil Manning," he said thoughtfully. "Ah, yes, I recall having had quite a conversation with him. He was a nice looking chap—blond, had very unusual eyes, deeply set, blue-gray. Yes, I do remember." Jenson also recalled having had a feeling that perhaps they would meet again some day.

"Hello, Jenson here. Mr. Manning, I believe? What can I do for you?"

Monique sat at the window of her small bedroom, gazing out at the green, deciduous trees and the sweeping landscape, and smiled sweetly as she looked up at the soft blue of the morning sky. She was happy at the estate, so thoroughly content. For the first time in her life she felt important, and pleased that she no longer had to work the streets of Paris in order to survive. Her sensitive, sympathetic heart went out to Kari and to Alberto, who cried most of the time, and she tried desperately to comfort them. Hans was amicable and good-natured, and he, too, tried to help by playing games with the younger children, but he disappeared for long periods of time when Mr. Jenson was at the estate. Monique wondered why, but had learned at an early age not to ask too many questions.

"Alberto, I'll play checkers with you if you would like," Monique said.

"No thank you, Monique. I don't feel like playing," Alberto replied somberly.

Hans looked at Kari, who was aimlessly leafing through a book, yet not reading it. "Hey, I have a good idea, Kari! Alberto and I will be partners and we will take on you and Monique. How about it?"

"That is a splendid idea, Hans. What's say, Kari? We can beat them. I know we can," Monique declared with enthusiasm.

Kari looked at Alberto, "I will try, if you will, Alberto," she said.

"All right. I will try. Hans, you sit here next to me, will you please?" Alberto said doubtfully.

The next morning a dark blue Volvo pulled up to the front verandah, directly beneath Monique's room. She could not see who got out of the car, but she heard the door slam. She quickly slipped into her robe, and went out into the sitting room adjacent to the other bedrooms. She knocked gently on Kari's door and cried, "Kari! Kari! Come out! Someone is coming!"

Kari opened her door, and rubbed the sleep from her eyes. "Who is coming, Monique?"

"I don't know. Maybe it's Astrid, and we can have our English lessons again. Perhaps she is bringing another girl, Kari!"

Kari stared past Monique, a blank look in her large, blue eyes. "I am going to dress now, Monique," she quietly announced, as she closed the door. She wondered if there would be another girl. There were still two small, empty bedrooms, with a twin bed in each one. They had peeked in one day. *"Oh, Mama. og Pappa, jeg lengter hjem, nor kommer di og henter meg?"* (Oh, Mother and Father, I long for home, when are you coming for me?)

A few minutes later, Hans, Monique, Kari, and Alberto sat at the round oak table in the small dining area off the kitchen. Their breakfast had been prepared by Mrs. Wickstrom, the Swedish cook, who was plump and pink, and always smelled good. Her kitchen was spotless, a happy place, and she always welcomed them with open arms. How they loved Mrs. Wickstrom.

"I have a very special treat for you this morning after you finish your breakfast," she said with a smile.

"What is it, Mrs. Wickstrom? What is it?" Hans asked.

"Abelskivers!" she said, with a broad grin.

"You mean those little cakes like we had once before?" Monique said. "Mmm, they are so good. I just love them."

"That's right, Monique. Now, let me get them and the lingonberries and powdered sugar."

"Thank you, Mrs. Wickstrom," Alberto said politely. "You are very kind to us. Thank you."

Hans and Monique chattered as they ate the abelskivers, and they were giggling over a story Hans had related, when Astrid walked into the room with a boy about five years old. He was a handsome child, with dark brown hair and large brown eyes. Kari noticed the mole over his eye near his hairline. His eyes were not focusing, and Astrid supported him, as he looked at the other children in a confused manner. They each stopped eating, and looked up at Astrid.

"Good morning, everyone," she said with a smile. "This is Alexander. Alex, this is Monique—Hans—Kari—and Alberto." Astrid introduced him to each of the other children. Then, turning to Mrs. Wickstrom, she continued, "And, Alex, this is Mrs. Wickstrom. She is a wonderful cook."

Mrs. Wickstrom smiled and, bending over, picked up the boy's limp hand. "I am pleased to know you, Alex. I hope you will like it here." There was an inexplicable sadness in her eyes.

Hans spoke up, "Here, Alex, sit down. Sit here and have an abelskiver. They are delicious! You can have them with lingonberries and powdered sugar. Mrs. Wickstrom made them for us."

Alex sat down willingly, and took one of the muffin-like cakes. Hans continued, "Do you like milk, Alex?"

"Yes, I like milk," he replied in a weak whisper.

"Here, I'll pour you a glass," Hans said politely.

"Thank you," Alex murmured. He took a long drink of the milk, and carefully picked up the fork.

Hans continued, "Where are you from, Alex?"

"From London," Alex replied in a weak voice. "I liked it there. My father went across the ocean in a big ship, and my mother always stayed home with me and my brother and sister. They are older than me, and their names are Gloria and Josh."

Monique asked, "Did you go to school, Alex?"

"I went to preschool and I played in the park with my friends. I had pneumonia." A tear fell on his plate. "I miss my mother."

Monique put her hand on his shoulder. "I'm sorry, Alex. You must have been very sick, Here, have another *abelskiver*."

"Thank you," Alex replied politely.


On July 20, late in the evening, Monique heard an automobile drive up to the front verandah. "Someone's coming! Someone's coming!" she announced to the other children, who were watching television.

"You really have good ears, Monique," Hans teased.

"I wonder who's coming this time. Perhaps it will be another girl," Kari said solemnly.

"Well, I hope Mr. Jenson is back so we can begin making movies. You knew we were going to make movies, didn't you, Alex?"

"No, I didn't know. What kind of movies?" Alex asked meekly. "I like cartoons the best."

"We don't know yet. Mr. Jenson is nice to us. He explains everything he wants us to do very carefully when he takes our pictures. He uses all kinds of lights, but sometimes it is quite dark," Monique explained.

"Oh," Alex said timidly, not comprehending.

In a few minutes, Astrid walked into the room with a lovely, raven-haired girl, who appeared to be about five or six years old. "Hello, everyone! This is Julie. Monique, will you please introduce her to the other children, and make her feel at home? I believe that her room is ready. You may explain things to her. I have to go now to meet with the staff. Goodnight!" She smiled, closed the door gently, and walked down the hall.

Julie stood with downcast eyes, not knowing what to expect or say. Monique went to her, and put her arm around her narrow shoulders. "We are here with you, Julie. We are your friends." Julie sniffed, raised her head, and gazed into Monique's eyes. Her lips began to quiver like the leaves of an aspen in a gentle wind, her eyes filled with tears, and her body began to shake. A large tear trickled down her cheek and made a dark spot on her blue blouse. "Oh, you dear little thing! I will help you! Don't cry, Julie!" Monique exclaimed as she gently held her, and stroked her head.

"But, why am I here? Why am I here?" she cried. "What are they going to do to me?" A bewildering cacophony of thoughts shouted in her head. She began to cry uncontrollably.

Hans spoke up enthusiastically, "We're going to be in movies, Julie! Mr. Jenson told me they were going to make movies, and we would act in them. Isn't that right, Monique?"

"Yes, that is correct. We are going to pose for them, and they will take all kinds of pictures, and the pictures will be sent all over the world. That is right, Hans. I have already had my picture taken many times. Mr. Jenson uses all kinds of things to make the pictures pretty. And, there are lots of lights and—"

"We study together, too. Astrid teaches us. She is nice. I like it a lot better than going to school," Hans interrupted.

"I miss my family," Alberto said. "So does Alex. Don't you, Alex?"

"Yes," Alex replied solemnly. "I want to go home now."

"I want to go back to Oslo," Kari added. "I miss my mother and father, and I am sure they are worried about me. And, I miss my ice skating lessons, too." As an afterthought, she whispered, "I wonder if Siri is skating."

Hans asked, "Who is Siri, Kari?"

"She is my best friend. We did everything together. We were in the same class at school."

"Oh," Hans replied with a nod.

Julie, eyes red and swollen, looked at them in astonishment. "I need a tissue, please," she said somberly.

"Here, here is a tissue," Monique offered.

Julie blew her nose and sniffed. "But, when will I see my mother and father again? Where am I? When can I go back home?"

As Kari and Alberto looked at her in silence, Monique tried to be optimistic, "I don't know—I don't know. Maybe we will all stay here and work for a long time." Defiantly, she stood up straight, threw her shoulders back, and in her best English, the freckled-face, lithe girl declared, "I don't care, though—I really don't care. I would rather stay here than go back to Paris again. I never want to go back there again—never!"

"Why?" Alberto asked.

"Just because—just because I don't want to. That's all."

"I'd rather stay here, too," Hans agreed. "I don't want to go back to Frankfurt for a long time. Course I miss my mom, but I like it here, and I just love the food. Mr. Jenson has given me these nice clothes, too. No, I want to stay here."

"Where are we?" Julie inquired in a weak voice.

"We are in Copenhagen, Julie—in Denmark. Where are you from?" Hans inquired.

Julie hesitated, then tried to explain, "I am from near Snohomish."

"Snohomish? That's a strange sounding place." Monique exclaimed. "Where is Snohomish?"

"In Washington—in Washington State. We live close to the bay—to Puget Sound." She added, as an afterthought, "We have a cabin on Whidbey Island." None of the children seemed to understand what she was talking about, but they shook their heads in agreement.

"Oh," Hans said thoughtfully. He had never heard of Snohomish, or Puget Sound, or an island called Whidbey.

Alberto, who had been unusually quiet and contemplative, asked in a weak little voice, "When are we going to start working? When are we going to make the movies? I've never made any movies before."

"I don't know for sure, but now that Astrid and Mr. Jenson are back, I think it will be soon—very soon," Hans declared.

"I can hardly wait," Monique said.

Rafe actually found himself relaxing and enjoying the train excursion from Southampton to Brighton. The busy port was located on the English Channel about an hour from London. Upon his arrival, he took a room at the Old Ship Hotel. The brochure he picked up in the station declared the Old Ship to have extraordinary character and an accommodating staff. It sounded good to Rafe. The character part offered a bit of intrigue. Anything would be all right with him. But, what did it really matter? He had no one to share it with.

Arising early the next morning, Rafe learned that Carlisle College was located out of the city on King Edward's Parade Road, approximately five miles from Sussex Square Annex. He soon discovered that Brighton was, indeed, a charming town, with its very own cosmopolitan style. The many fine squares and terraces made it unique. The Royal Pavilion, one of Britain's most exotic and beautiful buildings, dominated the town square. The Lanes, famous for its shops, was a hub of activity and drew many tourists and shoppers. Rafe felt at ease and comfortable. The atmosphere appealed to him; he looked forward to roaming around the city and taking long walks into the country. He simply wanted to melt into the crowds, explore, discover, and visit the Dome and the Theater Royal.

"Are you finding everything you need, Mr. Langley?" Is your room satisfactory?" Vernon, the desk attendant, inquired.

"Yes, actually everything is quite pleasant, Vernon. Thank you for asking."

"Mr. Langley, do you like theater? Concerts?"

"Yes, yes, I do, though I haven't had much of an opportunity to take in the finer things of life it seems," Rafe said cordially.

"Well, you can look forward to some excellent musical concerts and great theater here in Brighton, Mr. Langley."

"Really? That sounds good—something to look forward to after I get settled into something more permanent than a hotel. Say, Vernon, could you recommend a good place for an evening meal?"

"Yes, Sir! I am especially fond of Midhurst's Spread Eagle. It has great atmosphere—and good food. Why don't you give it a try?"

"Thanks for the tip, Vernon. I will—tonight."

So, Rafe's first evening meal was at Midhurst's Spread Eagle, an attractive old inn with tapestries and archaic copper pans hanging on the walls. It was all that Vernon had said, and the food was excellent. He must remember to express his thanks for the tip.

Residing in the Old Ship Hotel for a few days gave him the opportunity to become acquainted with the city, and to determine exactly where he would like to live. He found the Gardener Arts Centre, with its wonderful selection of fine restaurants. The Brighton marina was the largest in Europe, a spectacular setting for sea sports and leisure. He wondered if he could arrange a fishing trip out into the channel. One day he must ask about that. The countryside offered the quiet he craved, and the blackberry bushes along the side of the road reminded him of home. How he longed for Ann and Julie. They would have loved it. If he had only decided to come before.

Rafe was offered housing at the college, a small, modest apartment in a complex set aside for visiting professors. He felt, however, that he would rather not be concerned with the preparation of meals and the mundane tasks of housekeeping, nor would he want to eat in the cafeteria all the time, so he inquired about the possibility of a rooming house. The young secretary at the college told him about a lovely, old estate that had been transformed into a boarding home. At the present time, it was being managed by an older woman, a widow, whose husband had passed away the year before. Her name was Abigail Lancaster.

"Mr. Langley, would you like to have me call Mrs. Lancaster to see if she has an opening?"

"By all means. Thank you. Thank you so much, Miss…"

"Mrs. Bristol, sir." She smiled.

"Mrs. Bristol—yes, well, what else do you know about it? Can you tell me anything more?"

"The estate was once the home of an early Lord Mayor of York many years ago. The heirs didn't want to sell. It is very lovely, Mr. Langley. So they hired Mrs. Lancaster to administer it. I guess they all agreed to turn it into a rooming house—for a time, at any rate. They didn't want to leave it empty." She talked with a decided, but delightful British clip.

"Sounds ideal. Please go ahead and call, Mrs. Bristol. I have some other matters to attend, so I'll check back with you in about an hour, or an hour and a half. Will that be all right?" he grinned.

"That will be just fine, Mr. Langley. I'll get on the phone right away."

An hour later, after speaking to the secretary again, Rafe hiked out to the given address. He walked up to the iron gate, opened it, and sauntered up the walkway. The sweeping lawn was well manicured, the walk bordered by chrysanthemums of all colors. Clusters of gladioli and dahlias were in full bloom in flower gardens, the bright colors a striking contrast to the dark green shrubs. He stopped briefly to admire, to lightly touch a deep purple dahlia.

Rafe bounded up the flight of steps leading to the front entrance. He admired the carved double doors with the oval, stained glass windows. He touched one of the large white post supports, which reminded him of his own home. His eyes swept down the wide verandah, with its lounge chairs. He rang the doorbell, and stepped back. A friendly, matronly woman opened the door.

"Mrs. Lancaster?" he questioned.

"Yes, and you are Mr. Langley?" The smile revealed a deep dimple in the left cheek. Abigail Lancaster was sixty-two years young, with silver gray hair, sharp, keen blue eyes, and a peaches and cream complexion. She was pleasingly plump and smelled of Yardley's soap or bath powder. Instantly Rafe liked this person who greeted him so cordially.

"Yes, I am Rafe Langley, visiting professor at Carlisle College. I understand that you have a room for rent?"

"Mr. Langley, how nice to meet you." She extended her soft, warm hand. "Yes—yes—of course. Do come in, please." She led him into a small sitting room adjacent to the front entrance hall. "Please sit down, Mr. Langley. Would you like a cup of tea?"

"No, thank you anyway." Rafe sat on the edge of an old-fashioned straight back chair.

"The room that is available at this time has a lovely view of the English Channel, Mr. Langley. There are six other tenants in the home with whom you would share your meals. Breakfast is served at 7:00 a.m., except on Saturdays and Sundays, and then it is served at 9:00 a.m.

We do not serve lunch, but you may have a sack lunch, if you wish. Just remember to let Mrs. Kendall know the night before if you want one. Dinner is served at 7:00 p.m., except on Saturdays and Sundays when it is served at 3:00 p.m. in the afternoon. Again, if you have other plans for dining out, you must tell Mrs. Kendall ahead of time."

Rafe interrupted the chatter, "May I please see the room, Mrs. Lancaster?"

"Oh dear, I'm sorry, Mr. Langley. Here I am, assuming that you want it, and you haven't even seen it! Of course, you must see it first. Come, follow me, please."

She led Rafe back into the main entrance hall, with its strikingly elegant fruitwood paneling, toward the wide, circular staircase leading up to the first floor. Breathing rapidly, Mrs. Lancaster stopped near the first floor landing. "Mr. Langley, I do have one room on the second floor with dormer windows, which you might take a fancy to—it is a bit smaller than the one which is available on this floor. Do you think you'd be interested?"

"I'd like to see them both, if you don't mind."

"Well, let's stop here and take a look at this one first, shall we? Then, I can catch my breath." She opened the door to a spacious room, tastefully furnished—a double bed, dresser, chest of drawers, desk and chair, two lounge chairs, a sink, an ample closet, and windows with draw drapes, facing south. "That door is to the bath, Mr. Langley. You would share with Mr. Horton, the gentleman in the adjacent room."

"Very nice," Rafe smiled. "Could we see the other one?"

"All right, Mr. Langley. We'll go on up to the second floor." Mrs. Lancaster smiled her cheery smile, and they continued walking the stairs to the second floor landing. Mrs. Lancaster's hand slid up the polished banister as she laboriously progressed to the second floor.

"Here we are! Oh, I'm—I'm really—winded. Phew! Good thing that my room is on the ground floor isn't it, Mr. Langley?" She laughed, unaware of the deep dimple that Rafe found extraordinarily fascinating and pleasant.

Rafe followed the friendly woman into a room that immediately suited him. The dormers made it unique; it was light, airy, and furnished in good taste—a firm, single bed, flanked by a dark mahogany head and foot board, a large matching chest of drawers, a mahogany desk and cushioned chair, a small sofa, much like an American love seat (he thought of Ann who had always wanted a love seat), and, by the side of the bed, a round fruitwood table, polished to a high lustrous sheen. There was an exquisite Tiffany lamp sitting on a crocheted doily on the table, a floor lamp by the love seat, and a good reading lamp on the desk. He appreciated the excellent lighting. Mrs. Lancaster opened a door to an ample closet, which had a private, connecting bath. "I think I prefer this one, Mrs. Lancaster. I'll take it."

"Good decision! Most of the gentlemen I show it to feel it is too difficult to climb the stairs. But, you're young, and in good condition, I might add. I just hope you won't invite me up often, Mr. Langley—the stairs are almost too much for me. I suppose I should take off a few pounds," she smiled. "Well, shall we go back downstairs to the office? You will lease it for at least a year, Mr. Langley?"

"By all means—a year—perhaps two."

The next afternoon, Rafe checked out of the Old Ship, gave Vernon a handsome tip, and moved into his new home.

Carlisle College was located about five miles from York Estate. Rafe would decide later if he needed to buy a small European car. For the present, a bicycle would have first priority, and it would offer an excellent workout. Rafe began to thoroughly enjoy the ride, or walk, back and forth from his new home to the college. There was just one problem— the rain—very much like the Pacific Northwest. He recalled, with a grin, what his grandmother had often told him as a child when he complained about the rain in Washington. "Just remember, Rafe, you're not made of sugar, or salt, so you won't melt!" Many times, however, by the time he arrived at his destination, he would be drenched. In many ways, Mrs. Lancaster reminded him of his grandmother. He really liked her.

The primary emphasis at Carlisle College was in the sciences, specifically microbiology. Besides teaching two classes, Rafe was involved in a research project with another professor, Dr. Alan Strickland. He poured all his energy into his work. He and Alan became congenial friends, but Alan frowned on too much leisure time. He was thoroughly involved in the research project, the true perfectionist. "Yes, Alan, I know—I know. I've worked and shared with a perfectionist before, believe me. I know all about it. Now, will you please forget about this experiment for the time being and come with me? We're going to have a night out on the town. My treat, and I won't take no for an answer." Rafe was good for Alan, and Alan helped to ease the pain, the loneliness in Rafe's new life.

In time, the deep wounds began to heal, the despairing darkness began to lift. His classes, his research, and his new friendships with Alan Strickland and the beloved Abigail Lancaster became his existence. At the dining table with the other guests he was amiable, but quiet. He acquired a restricted social life, attending college functions only when required to do so. Occasionally, he and Alan would go into Brighton, attend the theater, enjoy a play, listen to a concert, get lost in the crowds, walk around viewing the landmarks, watch the people, and stroll around the marina. They walked miles. Physically, Rafe was in top condition.

Besides the lab, his room on the second floor became a refuge. He loved it—the light, the comfortable furnishings, and he would stand for long periods of time, gazing out the windows toward the English Channel. In his mind, he saw Puget Sound. He thought about the waters that separated the islands, Camano from Whidbey, Whidbey from Hat, Hat from the mainland. His mind drifted back to that day in the college lab when he drew the map for Neil, showing him how to come across from Camano to Whidbey. He could almost hear the voices of his friends, of Ann, of the children, running up and down the beach in a game of tag. He thought of Ann and Julie, sitting by his side in front of the fireplace in their cozy cabin, the rain pouring down outside. He could hear the *crunch, crunch, crunch* as they took large bites of hard delicious apples. "Mommy, will you please make some more popcorn? Daddy has eaten most of it, and I'm not full yet!"

"Of course, honey. Rafe, how could you?" she teased.

Rafe became extremely fond of the motherly, protective Mrs. Lancaster, and would often take tea with her in the parlor—or in the kitchen, where Mrs. Kendall would also join them in conversation. Sipping tea, quietly listening, he learned a great deal about life in Great Britain, about Parliament, about the House of Windsor, about the problems of today's world. If only these two could be in government service, he mused. Together they would put the country back in shape.

"Abigail, do you remember that little boy who was abducted in St. James Park awhile back?"

"Yes, Charity. Did they find him?"

"No, I don't think so. There's a little article here in the paper about it. See, it's right here."

Abigail took the paper from her friend and began to read. "Hmm, it just says that they have found no trace of him and that the father is offering three hundred pounds for information which will lead to his safe return."

"I feel so sorry for those dear people—all of these children missing. I'm glad my children are all raised." Charity shook her head. "Mr. Langley, what do you think about it, anyway?"

Rafe sat there for a long moment, staring—staring into some closed dark recess in his own mind, and then he looked at Charity, "I don't know—I just don't know—I don't understand—I don't..." his words trailed off. "Ladies, please excuse me!" Rafe rose. "Thank you—thank you for the tea."

After Rafe left the room, Abigail looked at Charity and exclaimed, "Did you see the sad look in his eyes, Charity?"

"Yes, yes I did. Oh, dear, he looked so disheartened. I wonder why, I wonder why. That article really upset him, didn't it? There's something behind that look, I just know it. Abigail, are there any more crumpets?"


During the night, toward the early morning hours, Rafe had the same nightmare, the recurring dream that was beginning to haunt him: *Ann, Julie, Neil, and others—caught in the blackberry briars, each crying for help, their eyes wild with fear and agony, the vines as thick as none he had ever seen before, the barbs like sharp knives piercing the flesh on their faces and their body extremities—the blood and juice intermingling, and slowly running down their faces—every move making their escape more impossible. The barbs held them as though they were caught in a vise.* Their screams awakened him. He sat straight up in bed, drenched with perspiration. "Why? Oh, my God—why?"


"Rafe," Mrs. Lancaster said one day after tea, "Don't you think you're working too hard? I think you need a rest, perhaps a change of climate. Why don't you consider going to the continent, perhaps to Spain for a week or two? Could you get away?"

"You know, I think you're absolutely right, Mrs. Lancaster. I've been thinking the same thing. Spring quarter will be over in a few days, and I could surely use a couple of weeks to unwind—get away from my work for a while. You really think that Spain is the answer?"

"I love Spain, Rafe. It would be a wonderful change for you—warm ocean water, sunshine, cool nights. You'll come back feeling like a new man. I guarantee it. Get on with you, my dear man, and make arrangements right away," she said enthusiastically.

Rafe's body cried out for relaxation, a white sandy beach, a swim in the tepid ocean water. His mind cried out for the luxury of a good book. He had almost forgotten how to read for the pure enjoyment of a good story.

After checking into the hotel at Barcelona, and taking his bags to the room, Rafe decided to meander down to the lobby, and perhaps go out for a stroll to acquaint himself with the immediate surroundings. It couldn't be! It was pouring buckets outside! Was he back in England? As he stood gazing at the deluge, he overheard a woman's voice exclaim, "I can't believe it—such lousy weather."

He glanced in her direction. She was standing about ten feet from him, gazing out the window. Rafe casually remarked, "Yes, it is, isn't it? Lousy weather, I mean."

She turned to him and smiled. Rafe, standing with his hands in his pockets, glancing out the window, continued, "Well, we surely can't venture out in this, can we? It's really coming down out there."

"No, I guess not, and to think I left my umbrella home and I forgot to bring a rain coat."

Hesitantly, he asked, "Say, would you like to join me for a cup of coffee?"

She wavered momentarily, then replied with a smile, "Why not?"

He took her arm and gently guided her into the small restaurant. "My name is Rafe—Rafe Langley. And yours?"

"Amanda—Amanda Cates." He led her to a small, round table by the window, and graciously pulled out a chair for her before sitting down himself.

"Well, Miss Cates, would you like anything with your coffee?"

"No, I don't think so. On the other hand, well, let's see—I shouldn't, but yes, I'll have something. Perhaps a brownie—if they have one. I'm a bit of a chocoholic. Will you join me?"

"Well, why not? I'm not on a diet, and this is a vacation. Guess we need to splurge once in awhile, don't we?" He smiled.

The waiter came. Rafe ordered. "We'll have coffee, and two brownies, please."

"Sir, we do not have brownies, as you call them. May I suggest a pastry from the dessert tray instead?"

Rafe's eyebrows rose questioningly at Amanda, and she smiled, "That would be fine." She questioned the waiter, "Ah, Spanish pastry, a tarta, right?"

"Yes, Madam. I will bring the dessert tray."

Rafe noticed her lovely smile. He found himself comparing her with Ann—not as beautiful, but surely attractive and fresh looking. Her hair was thick and shiny, cut in a short wedge, her eyes reflective, straightforward, pleasant, a soft brown, almost hazel in color, and she had a lovely olive complexion. He liked her, the soft voice, the encouraging smile. She reminded him of someone, but he couldn't think who it was. Perhaps it would come to him.

"What brings you to Spain, Amanda? You don't mind if I call you by your first name?"

"No, of course not. Well, I just decided it would be good to take a little time off from my assignment, and I thought it would be relaxing and fun to come down here for a few days. Why are you here? Pleasure? Business?"

"For more or less the same reason you're here, I guess. I'm on a little holiday, as they say on the continent. I've been in England at a small college in Brighton this past year—teaching—and—doing a bit of research."

"Oh? That sounds interesting. In what field?"

"Well, I'm teaching a couple of science classes, but I'm doing the research in microbiology. It has to do with water pollution—using microbes to clean up oil deposits in the English Channel, and in Puget Sound, the area I'm from in the States." With a twinkle in his eye, he added, "Sounds intriguing, wouldn't you say?"

"Yes—yes, it does—very interesting. You said Puget Sound. Just where are you from, Rafe?

"Near Snohomish, Washington. Ever hear of it? It's a small town about eight miles east of Everett, about twenty-eight miles north of Seattle."

"Yes, I do know it. In fact, I've been there quite a few times. I really enjoyed the antique shops. Found a unique thimble in one of them. It's a habit of mine, looking for thimbles. It's a picturesque old town, isn't it?"

"Well, yes, I guess it is. They call it the Antique Capital of the Northwest, and there are some beautiful old homes there. And, what is your work, Amanda? You—you do work, don't you?"

"Yes, I'm a writer—well, a reporter, really. I just completed some articles on the educational systems in the Scandinavian countries. I'm on the staff of *Today's World*. Do you ever read it?"

"Of course! Amanda Cates! I knew I had heard that name before! I've read a lot of your articles, as far back as the Vietnam War, and didn't you report from Afghanistan and India? And then, didn't you go to China for a while? Amanda, I'm impressed! Hey, are you sure you have time for this?"

"Don't be ridiculous. Of course, I have time. Nothing like a cup of coffee and good conversation. As far as my work is concerned, I've been very fortunate, Rafe—seems I'm almost always at the right place at the right time. And I have a terrific boss."

"Then, what brings you here? Are you on an assignment? Are you writing about Spain—covering a big story?"

"No, I'm working in Copenhagen. I've completed the education reports, and now I'm going to start a series of articles on child abuse." Looking down at her plate, and tapping the plate with her fork, Amanda added, "I have a difficult time controlling my emotions when it comes to this subject."

The waiter came with the coffee, and filled their cups. He set the tray of pastries on a side table.

"Cream and sugar, Madam?"

Amanda shook her head. "No—no, neither. Thank you."

"Sir?"

Rafe answered, "No thank you." The waiter held the tray of pastries, and they each chose one. Amanda took one that was covered in chocolate, while Rafe chose a small white cake. The waiter glanced at Rafe. "That will be all for now, thank you," Rafe said.

Amanda took a sip of the coffee. "Whew!" she exclaimed, "This will make the hair cells stand at attention! I think I will have a bit of cream. This is really potent." She reached for the silver pitcher.

They sat there in companionable silence for a while, two strangers, sipping coffee and enjoying pastries, each wondering about the other.

"Where is your home in the States, Amanda?"

"I'm from Oregon, but I'm gone most of the time. My mother lives there yet, and of course, I always look forward to going back home. Still have a lot of friends in the area, and I have a sister in Portland."

"Well, isn't it a small world? We're each from the same part of the country."

"Quite a coincidence, isn't it? Yes, it is a small world. Would you believe that one time I was coming out of an elevator in a hotel in Taipei and I ran right into a girl I had known from Seattle?"

"You did? Amazing. I suppose these things happen all the time. Unfortunately, I haven't seen anyone I know from the States over here."

"Well, hang in there. Your day will come, you can be sure," she said with a smile.

Rafe broke the silence, "How long do you plan to stay here in Barcelona?"

Pausing to swallow a bite, then dabbing her mouth with the napkin, Amanda replied, "There's nothing definite about my plans. I thought I'd like to look around and see some of the sights here, then perhaps go farther south to Majorca before flying back to Copenhagen. How about you?"

"Well—a—my plans are really indefinite, too. I did want to get to a good beach, soak up the sun, swim, read, and just plain relax." He noticed the ring on her right hand. It was white gold, exquisitely cast in the form of an open rose with a diamond in the center, and two smaller diamonds on the petals. "I've been admiring your ring. It's lovely."

"Thank you," she smiled as she held it up in admiration. "I think it's beautiful, too. A friend, who is in the jewelry business, designed it for me. I receive many compliments on the design."

Rafe wondered about the diamond. Had it been an engagement stone? She wore the ring on her right hand. Was she, had she been married?

Amanda glanced at his left hand, at the plain gold band on his left ring finger. Candidly she asked, "Is your wife back in the States?"

He paused, the cup near his lips. Placing the cup on the saucer, his fingers tightened around the handle. He looked away, hesitated, then said, "My wife—my wife is dead, Amanda. It happened last summer—in July—probably a boating accident of some kind—they discovered her body on the beach on Camano Island. I wasn't home at the time." Rafe spoke softly, a faraway look in his eyes. He lifted the cup to his lips again.

"Oh, I'm so sorry. It must have been terrible for you. I shouldn't have asked."

"No, no, that's all right. It's just one of those things, but it's been so difficult to accept the fact that she's gone. Her name was Ann—Ann—and she was a wonderful person. We had a great marriage." He added gently, "She was one terrific girl." Smiling, trying to erase the memories of the past, Rafe asked, "What about yourself, Amanda? Are you married?" Then, glancing at her right hand, he added, "Was the diamond an engagement ring?"

"No—no, I'm not married, Rafe. I was engaged a couple of times, but none of the relationships lasted. I don't blame anyone except myself. It's just that I've been so busy with my work." After a brief silence, she smiled and murmured, "And perhaps too particular." On a lighter note, she added, "I haven't found the right one yet, though I must admit that I haven't been looking very hard." She sighed as she held her right hand up to admire the ring. "No, the ring is just a gift, a gift to me—from myself."

"Well, there's nothing wrong with that!"

They finished the coffee and pastry, and Amanda, pushing the chair back, rose. "I've really enjoyed our little visit, Rafe, and thanks so much for the treat."

"Oh, do you have to go?"

"Well, I noticed they're trying to prepare the tables for the evening meal. I think they'd appreciate it if we'd clear out."

Pushing his own chair back, Rafe rose and walked around the table to her side. Lightly touching her arm, he asked, "Amanda, would you like to have dinner with me tonight? Here?"

She walked ahead of him out into the lobby. The rain was still coming down. She turned to him to extend her hand. "I'd like that very much. Shall we say about eight? I'll meet you here in the lobby."

His eyes followed her to the elevator. He walked over to the gift shop and bought the latest edition of *Today's World. Hmm, Amanda Cates—wonder if she has an article in this copy.* There was a faint smile on his face.

During the last week of March in 1983, Amanda let an apartment in a lovely old home near Tivoli Gardens in Copenhagen. After an exhausting bike ride around the city, she sank into the leather recliner and closed her eyes. *Dear Lord, why am I here? Why am I here? Please lead, direct, and guide me.* The silence was comforting. She closed her eyes. Her thoughts drifted like autumn leaves down a tranquil stream—back to her high school days, working on the school paper, the high acclaim she received in her senior year reporting on the great 9.2 Alaskan Earthquake; the four-year journalism scholarship from Ashland, the reporting, her German and French classes; her Master's in '69 from the University of Oregon; the job offer from Charlie Moore, editor of *Today's World*.

*Charlie, Charlie, you're the one, you're responsible for my successes. You never gave up on me. Thank you, thank you, Charlie, for the wonderful experiences—the trips, your confidence in me.*

Vietnam was forever imbedded in her thoughts, and in her mind's eye she was at the airport, arriving just two hours after Agnew. She couldn't erase the images—a child's face, thin arms extended in cries for help, her comfort and words of encouragement to the wounded in the hospital, and the statistics–the statistics that staggered the imagination: 46,000 American lives obliterated, over 184,000 South Vietnamese gone, 5,000 people or more lost, six million displaced refugees, and her appeal to the American public for help. *Was it Pluto who said, "Only the dead have seen the end of war?"*

*Oh, Charlie, you kept me so busy.* The months, the years sped by in her mind's eye like the fluttering wings of a butterfly: Patty Hearst in trial; James Earl Ray and Doctor Martin Luther King; assignments in Japan, China, Kabul, and the kidnapping-murder of Dubs, the American Ambassador; India and the death of Mrs. Ghandi's son in a plane crash; the Gulf War, Afghanistan—the Soviet advisers, the children being trained in guerilla warfare. *Afghanistan, a powder keg. Wake up, World! And now this, Charlie? After Pakistan, Bangladesh, Sri Lanka, Nepal? I won't let you down, but how shall I make this interesting—a comparison of the educational systems in the Scandinavian countries with those in the United States? Can't help it. Feels a bit like a let down, but I'll give it my best shot!*

*Help me, Lord, help me. Direct my paths...*she drifted off into a deep sleep.

Upon awakening she was content to snuggle in her down comforter and contemplate her assignment. *Hmm, a comparison of the educational systems in Norway, Sweden, Denmark, and the United States.* Where would she start? How could she make it interesting? Reclining, she glanced up at the painting hanging on the wall over her dresser, a painting of a lovely child stooping to smell yellow and white wildflowers in a meadow. She studied the print, and an inspirational thought came to mind. Of course, the children. She would start by talking to the children and young people. She would get their views.

Amanda sought interviews with the Minister of Education, and was given permission to sit in on education classes at the University. She talked to professors and teachers, and visited high schools, as well as elementary schools. She strolled in the park, and as often as possible, would stop to chat with young people and children, as well as with their parents.

Thoughts and ideas were slowly born, and she pounded away on the typewriter into the wee hours of the morning. Surprisingly, the comparisons were interesting. Perhaps her readers at home could gain some insight into a few practical changes, and come up with some suggestions that might make the American educational system more meaningful and significant.


Rafe and Amanda, as fate destined, were both staying in a moderately priced, old-fashioned hotel, the Gotico, in the heart of the Gothic Quarter, just down from the Plaza San Jaime. It had been several hours since his eyes followed the attractive American writer as she walked to the elevator, since he had purchased the latest copy of *Today's World.*

Rafe was sitting in the lobby reading an old copy of *The Wall Street Journal* when Amanda walked up to him. She was attractive in an aqua-colored ultra suede skirt with a matching blouse, piped in a darker shade of ultra suede fabric. A wide matching belt emphasized her narrow waist. She carried a black patent leather clutch bag, and wore black patent leather pumps. Rafe rose and touched her arm, "How lovely you look, Miss Cates."

"Thank you, kind sir," Amanda smiled.

Since the rain had stopped, Rafe suggested that they venture out of the hotel to a restaurant. "Have you eaten escargot?"

"Yes, and I love them. But where? Do you know of a good place?" Her hands raised in question.

"Well, I hear there's a great place not far from here that specializes in escargot—has a lot of atmosphere. I think it's called Caracoles. Are you willing to take a chance?"

"Sure! Could we walk?"

"Hold on—I'll ask." Rafe walked over to the young man behind the desk and conversed with him for a few minutes. The clerk was drawing a map and explaining directions in broken English.

"Okay, Miss Cates, I know the way. Let's go."

"Rafe, give me a minute, please. I'd like to run up and get a sweater."

For the first time in many months, Rafe was happy–happy in the company of a woman. As they strolled down the boulevard together he took her arm. He sensed that she was relaxed and content in his company. The dinner was delightful and it was a pleasure to watch her relish the food. He couldn't recall when he had enjoyed an evening as much. "What's on your agenda tomorrow, Amanda?"

"Oh, I don't have any specific plans—sightseeing around here, I guess."

"Amanda, I don't want to impose, or appear presumptuous, but would you like some company? I'd love to see the sights with you. There are so many interesting places to explore, and it's really more fun not having to go alone."

"Of course, I'd like that, Rafe. Since tomorrow is Wednesday, however, there is one thing I just must do, and you may not relish the idea."

"What's that?"

"Well, there's a flea market, and they tell me it's very interesting. The vendors have stuff from all over the Scandinavian countries, as well as the continent. I'm sure we can find something we can't live without—a book, a picture, an antique. And you can't beat the prices!" It's open tomorrow in the Plaza de las Glorias Catalanas. Do you think you'd like to go? Now be truthful. Don't say yes if you don't mean it."

Rafe thought, *just like a woman*. "That sounds terrific to me. I've been to only one flea market in my entire life—Ann and Julie begged me to take them once so, after much begging, I finally gave in and went along with them."

"Julie?" Amanda questioned.

"Yes, my daughter. She would be almost seven now." Rafe looked down at his plate, and tapped the edge with his fork. "She was presumed drowned the same time they found Ann. They just never found her body."

Amanda, listening intently, felt deep sympathy for him. "I'm so sorry, Rafe. It must be very painful for you."

"That's all right, Amanda. It's just that—well, you know. I really don't know what happened to Julie. I can't help thinking at times that she may still be alive—somewhere."

"I'm so sorry, Rafe. Perhaps some day you'll know for sure."

The meal was delicious, and they sat for a couple of hours sipping espresso, sharing, laughing. After a leisurely stroll back to the hotel, Rafe told her how much he had enjoyed the evening. They agreed to go to the flea market immediately after eating a continental breakfast in the hotel coffee shop, perhaps around nine or nine-thirty. As they said good night in the lobby, Rafe brushed his lips against her cheek and turned to go. "Thanks, new friend, for a marvelous evening."

Amanda looked up at him, smiling, "I enjoyed it, too, Rafe. Good night. See you in the morning in the coffee shop."

Rafe walked away slowly, pondering who in the world it was that she reminded him of—someone, someone.

The flea market was great fun. "Rafe, look! That woman is showing all kinds of thimbles. I must look."

"Okay, while you look them over I'm going over to that antique booth. They may have a book I can't resist."

Ann bent over to scrutinize every thimble, picked out a couple, tried them on, and then said, "I'll take this one." She gave a bill to the old woman, received change, smiles and nods and many thanks, and walked over to stand by Rafe's side. He was thumbing through an old, weather-worn edition of Browning. "Are you a fan?" she asked.

"Yes, I am. I've always loved her work. Here take a look. Don't you think I should have it?"

"By all means, Rafe. You can tell it's gone through a lot of reading. Go ahead. Buy it."

After Rafe paid the gentleman, he suggested that they find the metro and do a bit of exploring. "Let's see if we can't find a good restaurant for lunch." He grabbed her hand and they ran to the station.

The next morning they went up Mount Tibidabo, and with their maps, charted sightseeing ventures to museums and other tourist attractions. They intermingled with other tourists and foreigners in the elegant shops along the Paseo de Gracia and the Diagonal around the Plaza Francesc Marcia, and discovered that the rabbit warren of narrow streets in the Gothic Quarter between the Ramlas and Via Layetena was extremely fascinating. On Friday, they enjoyed the antique market in the cathedral square.

"Why don't we check out in the morning, and go to Port Bou, Amanda? It must be something like Waikiki—the growth of its popularity in the past twenty years has been phenomenal. There are literally thousands of hotels, and the beaches are terrific. At least, that's what Roaldo tells me," Rafe chatted on, reflecting his good mood. "You know, that fellow is a walking encyclopedia—full of information and suggestions for the tourist."

"Every hotel should have as good a desk clerk. Rafe, I'll go only if we can find a really good beach. I don't have much more time, and I would love to spend the last part of my vacation just relaxing, swimming, and sunning."

"That's exactly what I want, too," he agreed.


The weather was perfect, and the fantastically brilliant blue of the sea was a beautiful contrast to the redish-brown headlands and cliffs along the shoreline. On the way, they agreed that they would rather stay in an older hotel, so they chose the Palamos in Gerona, which had a pool and very attractive gardens. While dining near the beach that evening, they could see the distant lights of the sardine fishing fleet reflecting across the wine-colored waters at dusk. It was lovely, but they both felt hemmed in from the many tourists everywhere. "Rafe, this is very lovely, but it is so crowded—just too many people." Hesitating, she continued, "I don't know if I mentioned it or not, but I really had my heart set on Majorca."

"Yes, you did talk about it—the first day we met."

"Are you willing to go there? It's only about 120 miles south of Barcelona. It takes less than an hour to fly down. What do you think?"

"Well, I've always wanted to see that place. Sure, let's go. I'm all for it. One night here is enough. As you say, it is too crowded. Let me do some inquiring as to flights and hotels. It may not be easy to find a reservation, but we'll see."

The next morning, as they were on the plane heading south, Amanda exclaimed, "You know, this is just wonderful! Listen to this: It says here that Hercules found the Golden Apples of the Hesperides in the mythical times of the Greek Argonauts on Majorca. Did you know that? It's steeped in legend. Here, look at this brochure."

"Nope, didn't know that," Rafe mused. "But, I did do a bit of research as to where we should stay, and ended up reserving rooms at a tiny hotel in a picturesque spot which was highly recommended. It's called the Banalburfar. I liked the name. I trust that it meets with your approval."

"I think you know by now that I'm not very fussy as long as it's clean. I've been in some pretty disreputable places in my travels. Anyway, how much time does one spend in a hotel room? I want to be on the beach as much as possible, don't you?"

"Yes, yes, I do." Rafe appreciated her attitude and that she put him perfectly at ease. "I agree."

The small, unobtrusive hotel was all they imagined. They walked on the beach, and sat on a bleached log to watch the sun disappear behind the horizon. They took off their shoes and walked down to the water's edge. The gentle waves ebbed and flowed, the warm foam lapped around their feet, and the coarse granules of sand played hide-and-seek between their toes. Sea gulls swooped around them, talking incessantly among themselves like a bunch of women at a tea party. The moon came up. Rafe turned to her, "Thank you, Amanda—this was a great idea. It's really been wonderful. I haven't been this relaxed in ages. Say, wouldn't you agree that those gulls are having some kind of political meeting?"

"Surely sounds like it. Rafe, I'm enjoying it just as much as you are. It's been fantastic." The waves chased each other, licking the rocks as they rolled in on the white sands of the beach like folds of silk satin. "I just hate to leave, Rafe. It's so peaceful here. Thank you, thank you so much for the wonderful time. I've enjoyed every moment of the time I've spent with you. Look, look way out there. The water looks like it's covered with millions of diamonds. It's so beautiful, and such a lovely night."

"Yes, yes it is." He squeezed her arm. "It's just about perfect, and I can't begin to tell you how much I've enjoyed the time spent with you, Amanda."

They went back to sit on the log. They sat, their toes digging into the cool, damp sand, drinking in the beauty of the scene. No words were spoken for several minutes. They simply enjoyed each other's company, the peace, the tranquility. Rafe finally spoke, "Are you getting a little hungry? I am. Do you think we should go in and see what they have on the menu for dinner?"

As Amanda reached down to brush the sand from her feet and to put on her sandals, she looked at him and smiled, "Good idea. I'm ready for something. Better put your shoes back on."


Rafe was awakened again in the middle of the night by the haunting nightmare, the same dream. Would he ever get over it? Would it hover in his sub-consciousness forever? Why did he keep dreaming the dreaded fantasy over and over? Ann was still alive in the dream. Could it have been one terrible mistake? Was it really Ann lying on that cold slab? *Ann, you are alive, aren't you? You are alive! You aren't dead. You're still warm and vibrant! Oh, God, why is she gone? I know I'm not supposed to ask why, but I loved her so much. What about Julie, Lord? You must know where she is—if she is still alive. Please, if she is still alive, keep her safe until I can find her. What shall I do? How can I find her? How can I find out, once and for all, if she is still alive, or if she is dead? Must I always keep searching, searching, searching? I must know the truth in order to have peace of mind. If only I had not felt compelled to go to that stupid conference. Dear God, I can't get them out of my mind, and I keep dreaming about them—caught in the blackberry vines. They are screaming for help, but I can't reach them. It's all my fault, all my fault. How can I be forgiven? My beautiful wife, and my darling little girl. It never would have happened had I been home.* Sobbing,

Rafe finally fell into a deep, fitful sleep. He dreamed again—this time about Amanda. His emotions had not withered completely.

Their days and nights together on Majorca were unforgettable, and went all too quickly. They strolled leisurely, and talked by the hour—about their childhood antics, their high school and college days, their families, their likes and dislikes, friendships, and loves. They laughed together, and were rarely at a loss for words, each interrupting the other when a similar thought or story popped into their minds. Neither tired of the other.

Amanda wanted him to take her in his arms, kiss her, hold her close, but he kept his distance, except on two different occasions. One afternoon, as they were out on the beach, Amanda suggested they try to make a sand castle. Rafe laughed, "Okay, you make the castle, and I'll make the dragon that lives in the moat, ready to attack."

They worked diligently, and laughed and frolicked as two children, until the project was completed, completed just in time for a high wave to destroy their work of art. Rafe was covered with sand, and Amanda's nose and forehead were streaked. She grabbed a handful of wet sand and covered his face with it, laughing and jumping around as a child. Delighted by her hilarious, smudged face, and her funny expression, he grabbed her, and together they went down in the wet sand, right on top of the castle, crushing it along with the infamous dragon. He pinned her shoulders and grinned, "Have you had enough, Amanda Cates?" She shook her head. Then, he bent over her and kissed her lightly, tenderly on the lips. When he released her, he remarked, "Well, that's just about the sandiest kiss I've ever had." They both laughed.

Their last night together was unforgettable. After dinner by candlelight, they walked barefoot on the beach. The moon was full, the night air balmy. "Mandy," Rafe said, "It's been a wonderful vacation—all because of you."

Reaching for his hand, she smiled, "And, you have made my holiday very happy and pleasant, Rafe. I can't imagine how it might have been had we not met—no doubt it would have been a real exercise in boredom."

"I know." After a time of silence, he continued, "Do you suppose I could see you again sometime? Somewhere?"

"Of course! I'd love to see you again."

"I don't know when, but let's keep in touch, and perhaps we could work something out. Brighton and Copenhagen aren't that far apart, are they?"

"No—really—it's about like going from one state to another. We'll see each other again, Rafe. I'm sure."

"I hope so—I sincerely hope so." He stopped, placed his hands on her shoulders, and turned her so that the moon was shining on her face. In a fervent, innocent embrace, he held her, lifted her chin and kissed her, softly, tenderly. This was the second time he kissed her in this manner, and she had never been so ecstatically happy.

Later, as Rafe lay in bed reflecting, his thoughts turned again to Ann. Until now he had no interest in meeting women. It seemed a betrayal to Ann for him to even think about dating. He had lost her, but slowly, slowly, the pain and emptiness were beginning to regress. He had found satisfaction and contentment in new friends, in his teaching assignment, in his research. For him, the act of love was not only physical, but more importantly, emotional. When looking at other women he never had even a slight desire to be intimate. It had always been Ann—Ann and Ann alone. From their first date, from their first kiss at Ferguson Park, he had never loved anyone else. But now he had met Amanda.

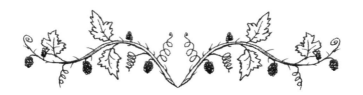

Back in her modest third-story apartment in Copenhagen, Amanda began to delve into her writing project on child abuse. She thought that she would much rather be writing about the Viking expeditions to this part of the world, or perhaps about the history of Hans Christian Andersen's "Little Mermaid." Anything but this! The subject depressed her, and a deep heaviness came over her every time she thought about it. The more she read, the more she researched; the more disheartened she became, the more resentment she felt. Children were such innocent victims. Why did they have to suffer needlessly for the greed and sins of man?

Amanda wired Charlie a few articles covering various aspects of abuse—the neglect of children in the home, encompassing shelter and nutritional neglect; emotional abuse; educational and medical neglect. She wrote an extensive article on the characteristics of abusive families—about parents who lacked any knowledge of childrearing practices. She wondered why some people ever got married, why they brought children into the world in the first place. Such couples did not deserve the blessing of children. She thought, *well, leave it to an old maid to grumble and complain about something over which she has absolutely no control.*

It was now the middle of August, and she was going to delve into researching the most abhorrent of all abuses concerning children—sexual abuse. To exploit a child in this manner was the most degrading, detestable, and loathsome of all abuses, especially if the child were used for monetary gain. A business? A profitable scheme? It really infuriated, repelled, and repulsed her.

Amanda knew that sexual abuse in all of the fifty states, as well as in Washington D.C., was against the law; yet the laws in Denmark were very lax regarding the subject. There was a thriving pornography business between her own country and Denmark. Pornographic pictures in this historic, beautiful city were displayed in public places for any and all to view. Children could be seen standing in groups talking, giggling, and pointing to the lewd pictures on display. When Amanda went to look, her face turned crimson from embarrassment. Sexual paraphernalia was readily available in stores. She hardly knew where to begin. The problem was extremely difficult for her to accept in the first place, let alone write in detail about it.

It didn't take long to discover that there were no reliable statistics available reflecting the incidences of sexual abuse against children. There seemed to be a secrecy involving the offense, and the majority of cases were never even reported. How could she be factual, give her story credibility, if she could not obtain the true facts? Factual information, data, and information were unknown, unavailable; she could only draw conclusions.

Amanda began to gather information and statistics from educators, child abuse centers, street people, and from hours and hours of research in public and college libraries. She learned that there was a vast difference of opinion as to what constituted sexual molestation in the first place. Though thousands of incidents had been reported, it was believed that even more were not reported. And, what about the thousands and thousands of children included in the business of prostitution? Were they reported? What about the children who were the victims of pornographic exploitation? It simply boggled her mind.

In her first article of this particular series, she concluded that the incidents of sexual abuse committed against children were infinitely higher than anyone would dare believe, perhaps in the millions in just one year.

In her probe, she learned that sexual abuse occurred more frequently within a family unit, or that the offense was committed by a relative or a close friend of the family, someone who would never be suspect. Incest occurred among all kinds of people, not just the poor, but in all educational and socioeconomic levels. Sexual offenders were not usually prosecuted, or convicted, because the crime was difficult to prove, and a trial could be a traumatic experience for a child. A child could easily be manipulated by a brilliant defense attorney. Amanda learned that all children were susceptible.

Amanda was beginning to think that she was most fortunate not to have married, not to have had her own children. She asked herself the question, *"What would I do if I were a parent, and someone had sexually molested my child?"* Her heart went out to the parents of the millions of children that had been abused in one way or another.

Amanda tried to discover if there had been any studies on the harm a child would suffer from this type of abuse. Surely, she reasoned, there would be physical, as well as emotional and mental harm, which would, without a doubt, persist throughout the victim's life. Again, statistics were vague, and little research had been done on the subject. She held her head in her hands—running her hands through her thick, glossy hair—and closed her eyes. Her obligation was to inform the world, to reach out and help, to support the victims, the children.

The second article in the series was not written to her satisfaction, but she decided to send it anyway. Charlie could edit it himself. He would probably wonder about her writing and communicative skills. She concluded the article with a statement.

> Most people do not want to discuss the subject, or even believe that it is happening, but the public must become aware of the problem. Nothing will ever be done if the populace is not informed, if they do not realize the seriousness of this ugly enigma. Educational programs must be emphasized; the victims must be vindicated; the perpetrators must seek help. Society must deal with the problem in a realistic, open manner.

Was she becoming too didactic?

Elbows on the table, her hands holding her head, she thought about Rafe. She could not get him out of her mind. As she recalled his gestures, his eyes, the lock of uncontrollable hair that persisted in falling over his left brow, she smiled. She remembered so vividly the light tender touch on her arm, his old-fashioned gesture of a kiss on the hand, the night he brought her one red rose and the light-colored chocolate creams.

In the third article of the series, Amanda tried to explain the behavioral indicators of molested children.

> Younger children withdraw into worlds of fantasy, older teenagers often run away from home. Some of the older boys and girls turn to a life of prostitution. Children react differently. Some become hostile

and infuriated, others become promiscuous. Abused children usually develop an extremely poor self-image, and are unwilling to participate in school activities and functions. Some experiment with alcohol and drugs, withdrawing from normal social relationships. Others become loners and are unable to develop friendships with their peers. They become distant and isolated from former friends.

The telephone rang. Who could be calling her at this time of night? Wrong number!

Again, her thoughts reverted to Rafe. *What is he doing? Is he giving me any thought at all? Does he like me? Could he ever love me? Had something happened? Why hadn't he called? Had something gone wrong? Was it because of Ann?* He seemed always to be in her subconscious, and it was difficult to concentrate on her work. She relived those wonderful two weeks in Spain, and especially the last few days on Majorca. *Am I in love?* She had never felt quite like this before. But his hurt, the loss of his wife and daughter, had been so troublesome, so difficult to overcome. It would take time for the wounds to heal. *Does he compare me with Ann? No, he would not do that, not deliberately. He is too honorable, too admirable. He possesses an inner quality that I've never found in any of my former relationships. He has integrity and esteem, and seems incapable of using profanity. I've never heard him utter a curse word, or tell an offensive story.*

The telephone rang again. "Hello, this is Amanda Cates speaking. Yes! Oh, hi, Rafe! How wonderful to hear from you! Yes—I'm just great—thank you! Did you know that I was just sitting here—thinking about you?"

Faintly, the reply came over the wire, "You were thinking about me? At this very moment? C'mon, Amanda—are you sure you're not just pulling my leg?"

"Honestly, Rafe. You know that I always tell it like it is. I was thinking about you. How are you anyway?"

"I'm doing great, Amanda. Say, summer session will be over toward the end of the month, and fall term starts the tenth of September. Registration begins then, and I would have to be here for that, but do you think we could meet somewhere? How about Amsterdam?"

Amanda's heart was pounding. Providential guidance? Mental telepathy? She didn't want to sound too thrilled, too excited, too enthusiastic. "Well—ah—yes—maybe we could meet. Perhaps it could be arranged. Let's see—I wonder if I could do a little work there on my research."

"What's the current subject of your research, Amanda?"

"What is it? Oh, I'll tell you all about it when I see you. Rafe, did you have a good summer term?"

"Yes, I did—really interesting. Dr. Strickland and I have pretty much completed the research project I mentioned to you. Did you know that microbes are the answer?" he chuckled. "Say, they have invited me to stay on and teach next term, so I'm pretty excited and pleased about that. I don't think I'll have to work as hard, and I'll have more free time, though Alan is mentioning that he would like to have me work with him on a new project—something to do with plastics. I have really learned to appreciate that fellow. He's absolutely brilliant."

"A plastic project?" Amanda questioned. "What do you mean?"

"Yes, plastic. I'll explain when I see you, Amanda. Hey, I can hardly wait. By the way, my friend, Brighton is a terrific place in the summer. It's quite the resort. You must come for a visit some day."

"I'd rove it!"

"Okay then, when shall we meet?"

"Well, let me look at my calendar. Rafe, I'll drop a note—or call. Okay?"

"That will be fine. You'd better call, Amanda. Don' t keep me waiting too long, will you? Bye then!"

"Bye! Goodbye, Rafe!" Her face was radiant. She carefully placed the phone on the receiver, and picked up the calendar, scanning the dates. *Let's see—summer term would be over the end of August, but he didn't say the exact date. I suppose he would have exams to grade, and grades to record. Oh, why not just set a date—August 31—I'll meet him August 31.* She reasoned with herself that she definitely needed a respite from the sexual abuse research.

The telephone rang again. Could it be Rafe? Something he had forgotten to tell her? "Hello—Amanda Cates speaking."

"Amanda, this is Charlie!"

"Charlie, where are you?"

"Where else? San Francisco, of course. How you doing, Angel?"

"Oh, fine—just fine, I guess. Charlie, have the articles been okay?"

"Yes, yes, Amanda. They are good, very good. But, I want you to lay off for awhile with the porn business, and go on a special assignment."

Amanda thought, *Oh, no—now I won't be able to meet Rafe.*

"I want you to go down to Hamburg, and cover the trial on the forged Hitler diaries. You speak and understand German. It will be an easy assignment and very interesting."

"You mean it? When?" She tried to sound enthusiastic.

"Well, I think you should plan to be there around the fifteenth of September. Will that work out for you?"

Relieved, she said, "Yes, Charlie, yes, that will be fine. I had planned on a trip to the Netherlands—Amsterdam, August 31 for about eight days. Yes, I can be there the fifteenth."

"I have great confidence in you, Amanda. You've been doing a terrific job on the child abuse stuff, and I want you to know that I understand that it can't be an easy assignment."

"Thanks for your vote of confidence. Well, you're the boss."

"I'll be making the reservations for you from here. I'll let you know."

"Okay, Charlie. I'll do my best. Thanks."


After several telephone conversations between Copenhagen and Brighton, Rafe and Amanda agreed on a place and time to meet in Amsterdam. He was standing by the concourse as she walked through the entrance into the terminal. The smile was genuine. He held out his arms for her. "I've missed you, Amanda Cates," he whispered in her ear, as he gave her a bear hug.

"I've missed you, too, Rafe." She responded affirmatively to his touch. How wonderful, how secure were his arms. Rafe released her, and held her at arm's length. With his hand, he cupped her chin, and gently raised her head until their eyes met. Each searched for the right response, a suitable remark. He kissed her lightly on the forehead, and then exclaimed, "C'mon, Mandy, wait 'til you see the lovely rooms I've reserved."

The Pulitzer was a unique hotel, a row of undersized, attractive medieval houses, each exclusive, each different and distinct. Rafe had chosen small, single rooms, with a private bath in each one. He remarked, "I've been told that the food isn't anything to rave about here, but there are so many interesting places close by. You won't mind that, will you?"

"Silly question. Of course I won't mind, Rafe. We'll want to explore, see the sights, and it'll be fun running around, trying different restaurants, and unusual sidewalk cafes," she smiled. "Rafe," she continued, "Let me change into something more comfortable, then let's go walking. I need some brisk exercise after sitting on the plane."

"Okay, that's a great idea." He squeezed her hand, and went into his own room to change into walking shoes. It was early—they could stroll around for several hours before the evening meal.

Amsterdam was built on a latticework of concentric canals, which were bordered by delightful, picturesque houses. The city seemed like a museum in itself with all the fine architecture, monuments, and statues. As they walked, hand in hand, Rafe remarked, "Amanda, they're very relaxed about the drug issue here, you know. Pornography, too, I guess."

"From what I understand, it's almost as bad as Denmark," Amanda replied. "You know, that seems so strange to me, Rafe—I have always felt the Dutch were such a straight-laced people—religious, family-oriented."

"And, I am sure they are. You can't judge the people because of that problem. I understand that in the 60s and 70s this place was a haven for drug users, but the authorities claim that the crime rate has dropped since then. Drugs are illegal here, though."

"Yes, I know, but I'm afraid the disgusting business of the distribution of pornographic materials is alive and well. Rafe, for now, let's not be concerned with any of that, please," she pleaded.

"I agree." They strolled hand in hand around the Royal Palace on Damsquare and the Tower of Tears, from which Henry Hudson set sail when he discovered New York. They chatted as they sauntered through the older parts of the town, stopping at a sidewalk cafe for coffee. It was a gloriously beautiful, clear day, the kind of day that revitalizes the body. Rafe reached for her hand. "How would you like to visit a diamond factory, Mandy?"

"Oh, I'd love that! I've never been to one." She wondered if he could be thinking what she was thinking. No, it couldn't be. That would be too presumptuous on her part. Not yet. Not yet. It was too soon. The timing wasn't right—not yet.

They didn't bother to change for dinner that first night. Instead, they went into one of the Brown Cafes, which was more like a British pub—dark, with a great deal of atmosphere. Their meal was excellent and they determined, as they walked out the door, to return at least one more time before their holiday ended.

After leaving the cafe, Rafe took her hand and remarked, "Just look at the hundreds of brick houses. They are so narrow. Can you believe it? Have you ever seen so many stepped gables?"

"Never. And, Rafe, look at the lights—so lovely—like rows of candles glittering in a cathedral. It's simply exquisite. I love it! I'm so glad we came. Aren't you?"

"You know I am," Rafe grinned, and squeezed her arm.

It was a few minutes before nine o'clock, when Amanda remarked, "I realize it's early yet, but I'm really tired, Rafe. Could we go back to the hotel now? I'd like to call it a day, and get a good rest tonight. Do you mind?"

"Of course not—that's okay with me, too. Perhaps we can get up early, well, not too early—and act like a couple of genuine tourists in the morning. I'll meet you in the hotel coffee shop about nine. How does that sound?"

"Super! And, thanks—thanks so much for a perfectly wonderful day," Amanda smiled. She stood on her tiptoes, lifted her face to his, and kissed him ever so gently on the lips. "See you in the morning, friend."

Rafe lay on his back, arms folded behind his head, wide-eyed. He was still conscious of the warm, gentle touch of her full lips. His hand touched his own lips and he smiled. Almost immediately after snuggling in his down comforter, he fell into a deep slumber. He dreamed—the same dream that had haunted him repeatedly the past year—*Julie, Ann, Neil—the blackberries twining and intertwining around their bodies, the thorns pricking their flesh—their cries—the blackberries like ripe purple plums. He tried in vain to reach them—he stretched out over the brambles as far as he could possibly reach, as far as he dared—to no avail. He kept hearing their cries, "Daddy! Rafe! Daddy! Help me! Help us!" The cries faded into oblivion, into total darkness, into an abyss of despair.* He awakened with a start, and sat up in bed. "Oh, my God, not again. Not again!" He held his head in his hands. Would it ever cease? Would it ever cease?

Amanda slept like a baby, the smile on her face revealing happy thoughts, pleasant dreams. Yes, she was in love—unequivocally in love at last. It was the real thing this time. She wanted him more than anyone in the world, but she knew that she must not be too anxious. Ah,

Rafe Langley—Mrs. Rafe Langley—Amanda Langley. Nice—very, very nice.

✳   ✳   ✳

"Rafe, guess what," Amanda glanced up from her breakfast plate. "What?"

"I want to go to the flea market."

"Oh, no—not again, Mandy. Do you mean to tell me that they have flea markets here, too?" He questioned in disbelief.

"You really don't mind, do you? You know that I have this thing about flea markets, Rafe." she teased. "You will go with me, won't you? Please!" She pleaded as a small child, begging for a parental favor.

"Sure, I'll go with you, my dear. Where is it?"

"It's on Waterlooplein. Would you like to go to a book market over by the University, while I snoop around the flea market?" She thought that he might enjoy that more.

"No, no, the flea market will be fine, but one day I would like to have you accompany me to a cheese market." He added, with raised eyebrows, "Since we seem to be into marketing so much."

It took the entire first morning to cover the flea market. "Why do you suppose they call these things 'flea markets' anyway, Mandy?"

"I don't know—perhaps in the beginning they all got together to sell fleas." She was engrossed, looking again at thimbles—thimbles, of all things. Rafe just shook his head, and looked around for something that might be of interest. It wasn't easy. Everything seemed to be pure junk.

Later, at a snack bar, or *broodjeswinkel*, as they called them in Holland, they munched on soft buns stuffed with eggs, crab, cheese, and ham. "Rafe, listen," she said quietly as she touched his arm. "Do you hear that music? That's Willie Nelson singing 'On the Road Again.' I love his voice and that song, but honestly, I do think he sometimes looks like a perfect mess—different, at any rate—that long hair with that headband and all."

"What difference does it make, Mandy, the way he dresses? He couldn't make it in a business suit, you know. When he wore one, he wasn't accepted. After he changed his image, he became a big hit. I really like his music, too, and I do love that song." Rafe began to hum along with the recording, singing some of the words.

"Tell me about your research with Dr. Strickland."

"Do you really want to know about it?"

"Of course I want to know, Rafe. C'mon, what were your findings?"

"Well, Mandy, it's a bit difficult to explain in a nutshell, but it has to do with pollution—pollution in the English Channel, and pollution in Puget Sound in Washington State. You see, it's become a real problem disposing of the accumulated wastes of industry and the refuse from a growing population in the surrounding areas. All the waste flows down the rivers and into these bodies of water. The governments have frowned upon using microbe power to dispense with the problem, but Alan and I have concluded from our research that the microbe could convert the pollutants into harmless substances. They can purify the river waters, which flow into the Channel and into Puget Sound, and use up the inorganic chemicals, which cause the problem."

Amanda looked intently. "As simple as that? That's good, Rafe. Really, really good!"

"It's so simple, it's remedial. You see, Mandy," Rafe continued, "There have been so many new housing projects that the sewage systems can't handle the overload from the increased population. When it rains, as it does in England, and in the Pacific Northwest, raw sewage dumps into the rivers, compounding the problem."

"Go on," Amanda looked at him with genuine interest.

"Well, the microbes recycle the pollutants. They provide a cleansing system so the fish can live—humans, too, for that matter. We refer to some of this as microbe mining, because the microbes separate the metallic residue from the other components in a sludge. Actually, they consume it as food, keeping the water pure. The pollutants are broken down by the microbes to form harmless materials. They metabolize the sewage, degrading the toxic molecules to harmless substances."

"Rafe, I am so impressed. It sounds so logical. Nature takes care of a lot of it, doesn't it? Those little armies go to work for everyone, and without compensation, too."

"How right you are." Rafe smiled, pleased that she showed genuine interest in the subject.

"So, what are you going to be working on now? I think you said something about—about plastics?"

"Yeah, plastics. Alan wants me to collaborate with him this term, but it won't be as time consuming—something to do with discovering a new plasticide additive that can be infused in the material to make the plastic biodegradable. Microbes will attack like an army ready for combat!"

Thoughtfully, he added, "It seems that nature has the answer to a lot of the world's problems."

"I read somewhere that there is a possibility that microbes could actually control oil spills," Amanda reflected. "Do you know anything about that?"

"Well, not much—it has something to do with the combination of sand, ash, and trapped oxygen. I guess the sand and ash would make the oil sink, and then microbes would degrade the oil. Not many people realize that without microbes, our beaches would have been long gone—they all work to keep them clean. Hey, listen, that's enough about my work. What's next on your agenda, Amanda? Something to do with children and pornography?"

"After your first call suggesting we meet here, my boss called. He asked me to go down to Hamburg to cover those Hitler diary forgeries. I guess he thought I needed a change from this child abuse mess."

"Gee, that should be interesting. I've been reading a little about it. Seems quite absurd to me."

"Yes, I know. Well, the child abuse research was getting to me. I needed a diversion for a time, Rafe. You can't believe what I've learned about the sexual abuse of children. I've almost completed that part of it, but still have this porn business to delve into. Haven't you noticed the openness of this sort of thing here, too? It really blows my mind."

Rafe saw the look of complete and utter disgust on her face, and changed the subject. "Has it been proven that the Hitler diaries are forgeries?"

"Well, not yet—the case is still going on. Charlie wants me to try to get interviews with the two men and the girlfriend, too, if I can. Guess I'll be sitting in on the trial, and sending my observations to him. It will be a different kind of assignment for me. I'm looking forward to it."

"Do you understand German?"

"Yes, I speak it, too."

"I didn't know that. Smart gal," Rafe smiled.

They finished their lunch, and had another cup of coffee. Time had a way of slipping by too quickly. Rafe, a twinkle in his eye, reached across the table and took both her hands in his, "What say we go over to visit the Van Hoppes diamond factory now?"

They were escorted, step by step, through the entire process of diamond cutting, polishing, faceting, and grading. Most of the diamonds had come from South America. Amanda was entranced with the entire procedure. "Isn't that exquisite, Rafe? How beautiful. I didn't realize there were so many colored stones—yellow, pink, blue. And there—there is the smallest diamond in the world, perfectly cut. Isn't it amazing?"

"Yes, it's a miracle that the artisan could work on a diamond of that dimension."

"You know, I guess I didn't realize there are so many cuts. Look at that one. It has so much life. It's just brilliant."

"Yes, it is. It's really a beautiful stone." Turning to the gentleman behind the counter, Rafe pointed to it, "May we see that one, please?"

"Yes, sir—it is one of our finest stones in that size." The clerk handed the diamond to Rafe, who scrutinized it carefully, turning it round and round, and holding it up to the light.

"This diamond has a total carat weight of ninety-eight points, which is just under a carat. It is flawless, and the color is clear and brilliant," the clerk explained.

Rafe was amused at Amanda. "You have good taste, my dear." The stone was set in a simple, white gold mounting, which showed off its beauty to perfection. "Here, Mandy, try it on." Rafe slipped it over her ring finger. It was too large. "Too bad—it doesn't fit. Well, perhaps we'll have better luck next time," he chuckled.

Discreetly, he handed the ring back to the clerk. "Thank you. It is very lovely."

The clerk observed the wink.

During that week, Rafe and Amanda were inseparable, except for the afternoon when she did some research in the library, and he was out exploring on his own. They probably saw more of Amsterdam in one week than most tourists see in a month. Having had several courses of art history in college, Amanda especially enjoyed the Rembrandt museum.

When they visited the Van Gogh Museum and observed his works, Amanda remarked, somewhat sadly, "He was always seeking, seeking for light. His paintings show this so clearly. Look at that one with all the suns. I do hope that he found peace in the end. He died a pauper, you know, and now his paintings are worth millions. I've always been fascinated with the painting called *The Potato Eaters*. Those poor people almost look like potatoes. He was really a great artist."

"He was the artist who cut off his ear, wrapped it up, and presented it to a lady of ill repute, wasn't he?" Rafe recalled how that story had fascinated him as a youngster.

"That's right, Rafe—such a sad life. Seems most of the impressionists died poor. Too bad they couldn't have realized a bit of the wealth when they were living. Today some of their works are worth millions—prize possessions—and sought after all over the world."

They took the evening boat trip on the canal, and were amazed when the guide pointed out the catboat, where animal lovers fed the city's strays. They floated down the Brewery Canal and the Singel Canal. In certain places the canal was so narrow that the boat smashed repeatedly into the walls. "Mandy, that's the Europa Hotel over there—very formal, high class."

The guide mentioned that soon they would be passing through the Red Light District, the safest place in Amsterdam. Everyone on the boat chuckled—and stared.

"No street crime here," the guide laughed. The boat pulled up opposite the Central train station, a Dutch Gothic marvel in brick, with its cupolas, turrets, and towers.

So, here they were—two Americans, no longer strangers, usually holding hands as they walked or strolled arm in arm through the streets of Amsterdam. They were the epitome of pure contentment and happiness. They spent one entire afternoon at the Arts and Craft's Center, both intrigued with the pottery shop, the Delftware, and the china painting. They watched the silversmiths and the goldsmiths at their craft, and marveled at their intricate works. "Well, Amanda, tomorrow we have to part again. What a week it's been. I'll never forget it."

"Nor will I. It's been absolutely wonderful," she smiled.

Amanda knew that she had fallen in love with him; but though he was warm, tender, and caring, he had never verbally expressed his love for her. He was unlike most men she had known—gentle, not at all aggressive, so considerate, and gracious. His eyes twinkled when he was amused, and yet, there were times when there was a faraway expression, an inexplicable sadness in his blue eyes. Her heart cried out to hold him close, to comfort him, to say, "I know, my darling—I do know how you are hurting, but it will be all right some day."

They had kissed each other good night every night, affectionately, but never passionately. She wondered if she appealed to him romantically, or if their relationship was more like a deep friendship. Perhaps he could never forget Ann. Perhaps he would never consider marriage again. Well, she would not invade his privacy, intrude into his world—until she was invited. He would have to take the initiative, show her how much he wanted her—if, indeed, he did. She knew, without the slightest doubt, that her love for him was genuine, and that she wanted nothing more than to share her life with him.

Rafe selected De Dikkert, quite an expensive restaurant in an old converted windmill in the suburbs, for their last evening meal together. How handsome he was in his gray slacks and navy blue blazer. She chose to wear a peach-colored, ultra suede jumper with a matching long, full-sleeved blouse. The angel-skin coral pin and earrings enhanced the costume. "You are lovely, my dear—your costume, your jewelry—so perfect for your coloring."

"Thank you, kind sir. You look pretty handsome yourself."

It was a quiet dinner, and a certain sadness came between them. Again, he took both of her hands in his, and searched her eyes. In the flickering light her eyes were like liquid pools, the iris a deeper, darker color. He seemed to sense her feelings, though she tried to hide her emotions. She glanced down at her plate. "Amanda, how can I tell you how much this week has meant to me? It has been one of the happiest times of my life, believe me. You do believe me, don't you? I just don't know how to say what I feel, but you have," he paused. "You have come to mean so much to me. I just hate to leave you. I wish you could come back to England with me. But, I know that this isn't possible—not now."

She could hardly look him in the eye. She thought, why don't you come right out and say it—say that you love me. He continued, "Mandy, after you've been to Hamburg, and after you begin researching this child porn business again, do you think you could take time to come to Brighton—say, for Christmas? I would drive up to London to meet you. Would you like that? Please tell me you can make it. I really want you to come to Brighton, see the college, meet Mrs. Lancaster and Alan Strickland—yes, and Mrs. Kendall, too. Could you? Could you, Mandy?"

"Well, yes," she hesitated, "Yes, I suppose I could arrange it." She wondered if her disappointment were showing. And yet—yet—there was hope. It wasn't over. He was inviting her to England. She looked at him and, after pulling her hands from his grasp, touched the top of one of his hands, "Yes, I'm quite certain now that I could come." Raising her eyebrows, she continued, "Charlie may have other plans for me, however.

We'll have to wait and see. But, no—I'm sure now that I could make it, Rafe."

"That's wonderful. You don't know how happy that would make me. I hate the thought of going through another Christmas without Ann— ah—I mean—without someone who means something special to me." He had not wanted to say her name, but it had slipped out.

In that one infinitesimal moment she felt an indescribable twinge in the pit of her stomach. It sent a signal to her brain. She wanted desperately to reach out to him, to touch him. She held back. So, he could not forget her. He could not forget Ann. They must have had a beautiful marriage. Well, Ann was gone, and she could be patient. Amanda Cates could be very understanding and long-suffering. Some day he would need her. Some day he would want her.

Charlie had made a reservation for Amanda at a moderately priced hotel in the suburb of Billstadt. The Apart-Hotel Panorama was, in fact, a small apartment where she could prepare light meals if she wished. He knew how she detested going out to dine alone in a strange city, and how much she enjoyed making her own coffee. The accommodations suited her. It was absolutely amazing how Charlie could always manage just the perfect place. There was a diminutive, but effectual kitchen supplied with the bare necessities, a small sitting room, which contained a sofa bed of sorts, a rectangular table for dining and writing, and a private bath. The lighting was good. She laughed when she saw the size of the tub, deep, but extremely short. After the attendant left, she flippantly said, "Well, my thanks to you, Charlie. This will be ideal for a few weeks."

Amanda had no difficulty discovering room eleven of Hamburg's century-old civil court building. It was here that she witnessed a fascinating real-life drama, one full of spice and intrigue, a ridiculous pageantry of ludicrous exaggerations and misinformation.

Day after day she sat, listening painstakingly to testimonies, jotting down facts, doodling, drawing caricatures of the judges and the defendants. The sketches were unique. She thought of her eccentric art teacher in high school. He would have appreciated her undertaking, and probably would have given her at least a B- for effort. She could hear his voice, "There is some doubt in my mind, Amanda, that you could make it as a courtroom artist. Better think of another career option."

It was only natural that one judge resembled Rafe. He was the most handsome of the group. Another was the spitting image of Alfred Hitchcock. Oh, the story he could have contrived from these proceedings. Then, there was the old goat who looked like Ichabod Crane, an exaggeration of course. One judge resembled her father. The judge on the far right of the panel reminded her of Agnew. Right on his trail when he went to Vietnam. Vietnam—she shook her head to erase the memories. Amanda found herself comparing the German courtroom with those in the United States. She missed the American flag, the individual state seals. Procedures were strangely different.

On September 19th, one poor official, who was sitting as a judge in the case, happened to doze off. A rude individual, in the back of the courtroom, spoke up in a loud voice, "Wake up!" The errant man (Ichabod) was later replaced by another judge. His alternate bit his fingernails and, because of his slicked down hair and meager black mustache, reminded Amanda of Charlie Chaplin. Preposterous! She quickly sketched on the long yellow legal pad. Amanda thought the entire fiasco more interesting, more intriguing, than any stage play she had ever attended.

The first defendant, Gerd Heidemann, had worked for thirty years as a reporter, and was nicknamed "Die Nose" by Stern personnel because of his inexplicable ability to scoop the unnatural, the bizarre, the sensational. Now he was involved in one of the biggest Hitler hoaxes in history—the selling of the so-called Hitler Diaries to Stern Magazine. Ironically, historians knew that Hitler dictated rather than wrote by hand—perhaps, because he suffered from palsy, which always made him shake and tremble. The handwriting in the diaries, on the other hand, was firm and unwavering. Did Heidemann actually believe that Hitler had written the diaries?

Konrad Kujau was a Stuttgart dealer in Nazi memorabilia, who began forging the diaries in 1978. He was the second defendant in the case. Not only did the two defendants fight the prosecution, but they argued with each other. Heidemann stated that Kujau had deceived him, but Kujau contended that Heidemann knew it was a scheme, a plan to make them both very wealthy."

Amanda conceded that one of them had to be lying, but which one? Her pencil made a slight scratching sound as she wrote rapidly, and her mind began to wander—to Spain, to a sandy beach, to Rafe. She was back on Majorca. They were sitting on a large piece of driftwood, playing in the sand with their bare feet. His foot had touched hers. She could hear the sea gulls screeching, could see them dive bomb for food, fight with each other over the precious morsel. Momentarily, she sensed the gentle touch of his hand on the side of her cheek. There were no emotional complications between them—not yet, but his very presence had offered her encompassing warmth. As her mind drifted, she could feel his hand around her waist, his gentle kiss, and when she did not resist, the second, lingering kiss. At times, however, he seemed to retreat into another world, and she knew instinctively that his thoughts were with *her*—with Ann.

"Prosecutor Klein is invading the privacy of my client!" the defense protested in a booming voice. Amanda's head jerked to attention. "Now if I may have the courts indulgence, I would like to show some slides. These are from Mr. Heidemann's personal collection of trophies."

The slide projector was set up, and the pictures were projected so that everyone could view the screen. There were murmurs and chuckles among the onlookers when one slide showed a picture of underpants—underpants that had belonged to the former Ugandan dictator, Idi Amin. Amanda whispered, "I can't believe this. Bizarre?" It appeared that Heidemann had retrieved the picture when he was on a special assignment in Africa, after the dictator's removal from office in 1979. And to top it off, the framed picture had hung on his apartment wall! What in the world did this have to do with anything relating to the case? "This is really good," Amanda whispered. A man sitting next to her reprimanded her with a cool stare.

She continued jotting notes.

Heidemann admits he has an obsession with Hitler, and has a good collection of artifacts from the Nazi regime."

Amanda watched more of the slide presentation, and kept writing in the semidarkness, hoping it would be legible enough to read later.

Stern embarrassed when officials claimed diaries were forgeries. Stern fires Heidemann.

Cambridge University historian, Hugh Trevor Roper, a Nazi specialist and so-called expert, who had said the diaries were authentic, admitted later that he was wrong. Stern lost four million dollars, which included the amount paid for the bogus diaries, and another two million in payoffs. Its circulation dropped to one and a half million copies from 1.6 million.

Amanda recalled that the German department in her high school had subscribed to the periodical. At one time, the school librarian had questioned its value, but the German teacher insisted the publication well worth the cost, and especially significant for her advanced German classes. The kids used to snicker over the risqué photographs and pictures. Little did Amanda dream then that one day she would be involved in a trial pertaining to *Stern*—in Germany—and in a court of law.

The trial went on incessantly for days and days. Amanda was completely engrossed in the project, writing copious notes, interjecting her own observations. Yet, at the same time her thoughts would wonder—wonder about nonsensical things—why men with beards continually pulled and played with the hairs on their faces, why that one judge constantly bit his fingernails. Over, and over, she heard the words, "Your Honor, I submit!..." "I submit..." "Objection!" or, "I contend, I contend that..." and their words trailed off. "Your Honor, may we approach the bench?" She wondered how many times she heard these statements repeated—submit, contend, objection, sustained—over and over, words taught in law school.

Spectators were yawning, a man burped, a woman choked and began to cough. With her hand over her mouth, her face beet red, she almost ran out of the room. Amanda fought sleep, closed her eyes, and fantasized an interview with Heidemann.

*"Mr. Heidemann, what was your salary for Stern?"*

*"Oh, about $3000 a month."*

*"Do you, at the present time, have any outstanding debts?"*

*"Yes, I owe about $130,000."*

In her fantasy, she gave him a stumper.

*"How then, Mr. Heidemann, could you afford to buy two holiday homes in Spain and, at the same time, rent a luxury apartment in the Poeseldorf district, a district which probably has the highest rent in the city?"*

*"No comment," he replied.*

Her imagination ran wild.

*"Did you, indeed, keep more money from Stern than the $690,000 bonus paid to you for finding the diaries?"*

*"I don't know anything about that, Miss Cates."*

Back in her unpretentious flat, the courtroom scene played over and over again, like a broken record. The montage of faces—the judges, the attorneys—the conversations, the testimonies, constantly ran through her subconscious mind.

Amanda sat, hour after hour, day after day in room eleven, trying to focus, trying to give her undivided attention to every detail of the trial. She soon discovered that she could not always master her thought processes, that at times she simply lost it. He would be there at her side. They would be back in Amsterdam—at the diamond factory, at a restaurant, strolling along the canals, his hand clasping hers in a firm grasp. It was difficult to concentrate. Would she be able to sort out fact from fiction later? Her articles must not be a figment of her imagination. They had to be factual.

The trial continued, and Amanda kept taking notes from which to reconstruct her own articles for *Today's World* in the privacy of her room. She hoped that Charlie would not be disappointed in her efforts. Amanda filled several legal pads.

Heidemann appears very drawn—has lost weight. It appears that Kujau enjoys his celebrity. Kujau collected information from historical and other sources, always scribbling down notes, then going to his room above the store to produce the forgeries. One slip-up that almost no one had noticed, was that he reversed the order of the Gothic letters denoting Hitler's initials on the diaries' covers.

After transcribing long into the night, Amanda finally took a hot bath and went to bed, but she couldn't get the facts of the case out of her mind. She dreamed of an interview with Kujau.

*"Mr. Kujau, will you please give me a copy of Hitler's autograph?"*

*He amicably showed her his skill at the signature. "Not bad is it? You're an American, aren't you?"*

*"Yes, I am. Mr. Kujau, how did this all start anyway?"*

*"Well, Miss, it really started back in 1978 when I wrote the first volume as a joke."*

*"A joke? Surely you do not mean that, Mr. Kujau."*

*"Yes, a joke, Miss Cates, and it just went on from there."*

*"What happened next?"*

*"Well, I agreed to produce twenty-seven more volumes in exchange for $900,000, and one of Heidemann's prized possessions, a uniform that former Luftwaffe Chief Herman Goring once owned."*

*"A uniform? But, why would you want Goring's uniform?"*

Amanda awakened.

There was no answer. She, Amanda Cates, was the prosecutor in the dream, and it was so undeniably real. Amanda had heard most of the conversation in the dream on the witness stand the day before. Kujau had testified that he had promised to write up to fifty volumes after Heidemann told him that a larger number of the forgeries would lessen the chances of discovery.

The day after the realistic dream, the sky darkened as she walked hurriedly to the civil court building. Upon entering the building she encountered one of the prosecutors. "Sir, sir, may I speak with you for a moment please?"

The short, portly, bald-headed gentleman looked up. "What is it? What is it?" he asked in German.

"My name is Amanda Cates. I am a reporter on the staff of *Today's World*. It is based in San Francisco. I'm here covering the trial. Would it be possible to have a few words with you when the trial is over?"

"Miss Cates, my office is in room twenty-nine. Please make the necessary arrangements with my secretary. Yes, I will be happy to have a short meeting with you—when the trial is over. Good day. I must hurry along now."

Amanda was elated. She had thought it next to impossible to talk to any of the prosecutors.

As the day progressed, Amanda began to get writer's cramp, but she continued on her yellow pad.

Stern editors told of Heidemann's cloak-and-dagger methods, how he had met secretly with former Nazi officers, making payoffs to generals and others in East Germany. Meeting secretly, along highways, he had exchanged books for a lot of cash.

Amanda wondered how *Stern* could ever have fallen for the charade. Why hadn't they taken more precautions? Heidemann had tried to explain his obsession by saying that he wanted to understand how good and evil lie so closely side-by-side. Amanda thought of a research paper she had done in college as an undergraduate student on the subject of insanity. She had titled it, "Where Tragedy and Humor Walk Hand in Hand." It seemed to be more or less the same thing.

Amanda continued taking notes.

Heidemann was on the witness stand.

The diaries were found by farmers out in a field, where a plane had crashed in World War II, near Dresden.

Amanda wondered how he had thought that one up.

Kujau found most of the information for the diaries in history books, and in his own imagination. One 1936 entry read, "Must not forget to get tickets for the Olympic Games for Eva Braun." The Fuhrer complained in another, "On my feet all day long—must close now."

Amanda concluded that Kujau had one terrific imagination, and that both men were visionaries.

Other testimony revealed that the publishers had overlooked inaccuracies. When polyester fibers, and other postwar materials, turned up in a chemical analysis of the booklets immediately after the *Stern* announcement, there was no doubt of the hoax.

Just before drifting off to sleep, exhausted after a full day in the courtroom with Kujau on the witness stand, Amanda fantasized again.

*"Mr. Kujau, I understand that you are quite an artist. Are you painting here in prison?"*

*"Yes, Miss Cates, I do paint. I am very good. I've been doing quite a few portraits of Hitler for my fellow inmates. They think that I am really outstanding. Would you like a sketch for yourself?"*

*"Yes, I would. Thank you very much. Charlie would appreciate that for the magazine."*

Then she awakened. She groaned, "What's happening to me anyway? My imagination is about as absurd as Kujau's or Heidemann's."

She was almost at the end of the yellow legal tablet.

Kujau has a certain touch of class, and a good sense of humor.

She noted that the final paragraph of his written confession was executed in perfect Hitlerian script.

"I admit having written the Hitler Diaries. It took me two years to perfect my handwriting." He signed it Adolph Hitler.

The words, "Beyond a reasonable doubt—guilty beyond a reasonable doubt," kept ringing in her ears.

Many questions remained unanswered. Amanda was troubled in her thinking. Where was the more than three million dollars *Stern* paid for the diaries? The thoughts ran rampant in her mind. Ten or more years in jail isn't such a long period of time to serve. Hmm—what about Edith Liebland, Kujau's girlfriend? How does she figure in the case? What important part does she play in the scenario? Amanda would try for an interview with Edith. She just might be successful. She would try to get the reactions of the family members. She would talk to the people on the streets. She would frequent popular restaurants, ask questions, observe reactions, interview that chubby little prosecutor, and write, write, write. Charlie would be pleased.

After almost two months in Hamburg, Amanda returned to Copenhagen. Charlie wired from San Francisco, "I like your human touch, Mandy. You did an absolutely fantastic job! Articles are excellent. Good comments from readers. Bigger sales. Much interest. You may not be Farrah, Amanda, but you're Charlie's Angel. Hang in there."

"I love you, too, Charlie Moore." she exclaimed, with a big smile.


Amanda felt rested, pleased, and happy—happy because Charlie was elated with her coverage of the Hitler forgeries, happy because she was going to be seeing Rafe again in approximately five more weeks, happy because—because she was in love. Should she confide in Charlie? She decided to wait. After all, what would she tell him?

She was reluctant to return to the business at hand—the scum and smut, the obscenity and filth of pornography. She began.

Few readers realize that there is a worldwide network of dealers in child pornography, and that it is a business that generates billions and billions of dollars annually. There are few government sanctions to stop them. Denmark and the Netherlands are responsible for most of the child pornography entering the United States. Only recently have the governments of these two countries taken any action to restrain this lucrative, loathsome business. Prime Minister Raud Lubbers of the Netherlands stated that the Dutch government had proposed making it a crime to manufacture, distribute, import, transport, or export child pornography. Yet, today business goes on as usual. This year in California the Queen of Kiddie Porn admitted that most of the material she received and distributed was Scandinavian made.

There was a knock on Amanda's door. Strange, who could it be at this hour? Amanda called out, "Who is it?"

"Cable for Miss Amanda Cates," came the reply.

"Just a moment, please." She supposed it must be from Charlie. The cable read, "Indictment of four in Popieluszko death. Warsaw November 27. Want you there. Recap story. Charlie."

"That man!" Amanda exclaimed. "Well, I guess it won't take many days to get a recap for the old boy." She couldn't help grinning when she turned her thoughts to Charlie. He knew exactly what he was doing when he sent her off to Europe. He knew that she would never let him down.

As usual, he had made all of the arrangements prior to her arrival. She wanted desperately to please him. A recap. She decided on a bit of history first.

Poland is about the size of the state of New Mexico. It has one of the most youthful populations in Europe, primarily due to the loss of some six million people, half of whom were Jews, during World War II. This was followed by a baby boom. Most major cities have been restored, or rebuilt, since the war. Western companies have erected several impressive looking new hotels in the major cities.

Poland has experienced a consumer boom since its takeover by Communist rule. There are thriving private enterprises such as shops, restaurants, and small industry, but living standards are lower than in the United States. Many people have two jobs in order to care for family needs. A foreigner can mingle freely with Polish residents in restaurants, cafes, and nightclubs. Rural life is centered on the home and work done out in the fields. Formation of the free trade union, Solidarity, in August, 1980, made world headlines, and illustrates Poland's desire for independence. Martial law was imposed by the government in late 1981, but suspended later.

The murder of a Polish Catholic priest caught the attention of the world, so Amanda researched his life.

Father Popieluszko, an affectionate, young, caring, frail man, was born in 1947 in Okopy, a poor village in eastern Poland, located about twenty miles from the Soviet border. His parents were peasant farmers, and he, one of four children, had been frequently ill. Father Popieluszko was selfless, always doing for others, and as a young man served as an altar boy, waking at five in the morning and walking three miles to the church.

Father Popieluszko had been a loner, so he was called The Philosopher. He was influenced by Maximilian Kolbe, a priest who had given his life to save a prisoner at Auschwitz. His days in the seminary—days of difficult labor and hard beatings, isolation, threats, and torture—did not thwart his determination to become a priest. Because of the brutality, his health was threatened, and his heart and kidneys were weakened. He developed a serious blood disorder, yet he continued to work until he was totally exhausted.

The outspoken priest became the first chaplain to the factory workers, and an honorary member of Solidarity. He was constantly shadowed by the secret police, but he continued to stand by his people through trial and triumph, through sickness, despair, and finally death. Though his delicate frame was racked with pain, he disregarded his own suffering, and cared only for others, often mistaken for a pauper because of his appearance. Those who worked with him—students, attorneys, and doctors, were also persecuted by the secret police. His apartment and car were bugged. His soft-spoken message to the steelworkers was, "Overcome evil with good."

Father Popieluszko was perplexed and astonished at the hatred in men's hearts. He was falsely and unjustly imprisoned without cause.

Numerous priests and lay people had been murdered, or were missing, and he felt it was all an offense against their religion.

It is believed that Father Popieluszko, tortured beyond recognition, was murdered October 19 because of his outspoken stand against the government. His face was deformed, his hands broken and cut, his jaw, nose, mouth, and skull were crushed, and part of his scalp and large pieces, or strips of skin on his legs, had been torn off. He had sustained a brain concussion, as well as a damaged spinal cord. It was said that no one—no one had ever been mutilated so brutally. His tongue was like mush, and his teeth were smashed. It was an ugly picture.

Amanda continued with the background of the arrests that had been made.

Three officers had been arrested in connection with the murder. Colonel Adam Pietruszka, a fourth security police officer, and a suspect in the crime, was detained November 2 for aiding and abetting the murderer. General Zenon Platek, his immediate supervisor, was suspended for lack of sufficient supervision. A Lieutenant Colonel in the municipal department of internal affairs was also detained, but later, charges against him were dismissed.

On November 6, the Politburo authorized Jaruzelski to take over Communist Party supervision of the cabinet department responsible for the security police, to assume direct personal control of them. Some analysts felt his actions were an attempt to counter opponents within the regime, who wanted a firmer stand against dissent.

Jerzy Urban, a spokesman for the government, said that by November 7 they were almost certain the crime had been committed by the three original suspects. Father Popieluszko had been strangled. Urban denied that there were broken bones and disfigurement. One suspect had claimed that the officers had only acted out of personal anger over the government's leniency toward the priest's open dissent.

It is unusual for a Polish head of state to appear at a press conference, but Jaruzelski did remark that the government would continue to investigate the party, or parties, who allegedly incited the murder. He further stated, "All people, who have a bit of common sense and goodwill have noticed how, in a firm and unequivocal way, the Polish authorities have responded to this shameful act, and with what energy and firmness we have carried out the whole operation of discovering the culprits." When Jaruzelski was asked who might have instigated the murder, he replied, "We don't know; we don't know them. We would like to find them."

Amanda continued writing.

The Politburo blamed the murder on opponents of government policies, declaring that the instigators had "cherished hopes of using the crime as a detonator of internal disturbances, with the aim of canceling the rights of the beneficial prisoners, as well as developing favorable relations with foreign countries."

Shaking her head in weariness, her mind began to wander. What was Rafe doing? Would he be happy to see her again? Her thoughts went back to the trial in Hamburg. She must discipline her thoughts—and her writing.

The government issued a warning to civil rights groups, who monitored police brutality, and stated that they would take legal action against them, if they continued their cause. KOPP, a citizen's committee against force, was organized by workers and intellectuals because of Popieluszko's murder. The government stated, "Civil rights committees were seeking to open the way to anarchy, and warned that legal steps would be taken to their actions." In Warsaw, the committee was told that they would be sent to jail if they continued their activities. Reporters were told not to cover any part of their actions.

Amanda wrote without stopping until 2:00 a.m.—she could not quit until everything was finally out of her head, and down on paper.

An impassioned crowd of mourners, probably 200,000 to 250,000 strong, attended the burial ceremony for Father Popieluszko at St. Stanislaw Kostka, the Warsaw church he had served. Solidarity leaders, Lech Walesa, and Jozef Cardinal Glemp, the Roman Catholic Primate, spoke at the ceremony. Afterward, about 10,000 mourners marched through the city's center, closely watched by police with water cannons and militia vans. There were no incidents.

There was a Mass for the Fatherland, a tradition begun by Father Popieluszko, on November 25 at his Warsaw parish church. A pro-solidarity priest, Father Malkowski, was banned from preaching because his sermon was anti-government and "alien to the Spirit of the Gospel."

The regime of Premier Wojeciech Jaruzelski moved to assert control over the security police, and curb opponents of the government. On November 27th, the government announced that the four officers of the state security police would be indicted for the murder of Father Jerzy Popieluszko.

Ironically, it has been said that Father Popieluszko's last words were, "Most of all, may we be free from the desire for violence and vengeance."

Amanda sent the articles off to Charlie, and made reservations to fly back to Denmark. It was Sunday, December 2, and an icy bitter wind swept down from the north. Shivering, she pulled the parka hood over her head, and with head bent, walked back to her hotel.

With three weeks remaining before Christmas, Amanda launched into a whirlwind of activity—shopping, wrapping, writing to family and friends, mailing cards and gifts—trusting all would arrive before Christmas Eve. After her father died, her mother decided to spend the holidays with her sister in Portland, Oregon, so this would make it somewhat less complicated, since all the family would be in one place. Christmas had always been a happy, fun celebration in the Cates family, and she didn't want to disappoint any of them. Each received a special gift. Oh, if only she could be there with them. After an exhausting day, a hot relaxing bath, and a mug of hot chocolate, she went to bed early and snuggled in her down comforter. Just as she was dozing off, the telephone rang. Now, who could that be at this hour? Fumbling for the receiver, she whispered reluctantly, "Amanda Cates speaking. May I help you?"

"Charlie here, Angel."

"Charlie! Why are you calling me at this hour? Did you get the Warsaw stuff? Was it all right? What's up now? Is everything okay?"

"Hold on—hold on, Amanda! Yes, I got everything and I was really impressed with the story about the Catholic priest. I'm confident that reader-interest will be high. The whole shebang was terrific, Amanda—exactly what I wanted—the old human touch, along with the facts. Say, I want you to make a little trip again to cover another story."

"Now? What? Where?"

"I'd like you to go up to Oslo on December 10—"

She interrupted, "December 10? Why?"

"The Nobel Peace Prize presentation—Bishop Tutu—do you think you could go? Try for an interview with him—write a little recap. It's just a short assignment."

"Okay, Charlie. I'll be there."

"Knew you would. Can always count on you, Amanda. Have a good time in Oslo. Hey, maybe you could buy my Christmas present there. I sure do like those Norwegian sweaters." Charlie chuckled.

Amanda's mind was going in circles. She was wide-awake. She would have to accomplish all of her personal obligations in a rush—before her trip to Oslo. Would Charlie really like one of those heavy sweaters? What would she buy Rafe? Would he give her a gift? Tutu—strange name—it would be an honor to meet him, that is, if she could arrange for an interview. She would put the porn articles aside for now. Good. She wouldn't have to think of it during the Holy Season, not until after the holidays. She finally drifted off to sleep.

On December 9, Amanda checked into the Carlton Rica Hotel in Oslo,

Norway. After a recent snowfall, it had become bitterly cold. The snow had been cleared, leaving the ground wet and icy, and stinging wind gusts from the north penetrated her coat. She shivered, flipped the collar of the coat up around her ears, and walked hurriedly into the hotel lobby. She smiled at the young blond man behind the reservation desk. "Hello, I believe there is a reservation for Amanda Cates?"

Glancing at the list, he said, "Ah, yes, Miss Cates. Your room will be number 542. Would you like some assistance with your bag?"

"Thank you, no. Do you have a local paper written in English?"

"Yes, we do." Pointing, he said, "You'll find several right over there."

Amanda found just what she thought she wanted and went back to the desk to pay for it. Then, picking up her bag, she headed for the elevator and the fifth floor. Her modest room was tastefully furnished, and the first thing she did was sit on the bed and bounce up and down. Then, she took off her coat and sank into the large leather chair to remove her boots. With her feet up on the coffee table, she turned on the lamp and began to skim the front page of the paper. Bishop Tutu made the headlines, then world news, local news, the usual. There was a brief history about the Nobel Peace Prize, continued on page eight. As she turned to page eight to finish the article, another feature caught her attention. A local professor, Doctor Nels Johanssen, had been interviewed again regarding the disappearance of his young daughter, Kari Johanssen. She had vanished from Oslo over a year ago, leaving no trace. Kari had gone to take ice skating lessons and had never returned home. Her skating instructor said that she had completed her lesson, and he was positive that she left the rink with her friend, Siri Sorrensen. Siri later confirmed this, and said that after she turned the corner, she saw no more of her friend. No one knew what had happened to her. The Johanssens were making another plea for help, offering a large reward for information leading to her safe return. The authorities had no clues whatsoever regarding her disappearance. The Johanssens were heart-broken and were desperate to have their daughter home for Christmas. Amanda's thoughts went back to Copenhagen and the series on child pornography. A nauseous feeling enveloped her, and she wondered what happened to Kari Johanssen.

On the evening of December 10, after a good dinner alone in her room, she wrote the recap.

An African Anglican clergyman, Bishop Desmond Tutu, the head of the South African Council of Churches, was chosen to receive the Nobel Peace Prize for his role as a "unifying figure in the campaign to resolve the problem of apartheid in South Africa."

Since 1978, Bishop Tutu, who was fifty-three years old, had been secretary general of the church council, the first Black African to hold that position. Bishop Tutu was a supporter of the outlawed African National Congress, the country's chief black underground organization. At the same time, he was committed to a non-violent struggle for change in South Africa. In the West, Bishop Tutu was regarded as the most respected voice for Black Nationalism in South Africa.

The award was announced when Bishop Tutu was a visiting professor at a seminary in New York City. On October 18, he hurriedly returned to South Africa. He celebrated and took advantage of the publicity to speak out on apartheid and the plight of the majority of South African citizens. He attacked President Reagan's policy of "constructive engagement" with the South African government, and declared it to be an "unmitigated disaster." He also stated that during the Reagan administration, the apartheid system had become much worse.

The Nobel Committee said that the peace award should be seen as a renewed recognition of the courage and heroism shown by black South Africans in their use of peaceful methods in the struggle against apartheid. A Norwegian bishop, and friend of Bishop Tutu, stated that "it would now be difficult for the government of South Africa to do anything to him, or to the council."

On December 10, 1984, the day the prize was to have been awarded in Oslo, Norway, someone tried to interrupt the acceptance ceremony with an anonymous telephone call claiming that a bomb had been planted in the building.

Amanda was unsuccessful in her bid for a private interview with Bishop Tutu. Charlie would understand.

After an exhilarating ten-mile ride on her bike, Amanda ran up both flights of stairs, and walking into the kitchen, clutched hard at the small sink with both hands. She turned on the tap and let the water run until it was cold, filled a glass with the clear liquid, and drank greedily, quenching her thirst. She thought of the task before her. But first, she would have scrambled eggs and toast with a piping cup of hot, spicy tea. And a bath, yes a bubble bath. Refreshed, she would launch into a typing frenzy on the old portable. Reclining in the short, deep tub, she almost fell asleep. Her thick, yellow terry-cloth robe hung on the hook behind the door. After a brisk rubdown, she wrapped the oversized robe around her slim body and walked back into the small sitting room. Sitting at the table, which also served as a desk, she reached for a piece of paper and inserted it into the typewriter.

How did it all start? No one really knows. In 1977, the United States Congress outlawed the production (but not the distribution) of child pornography in the United States. In 1980, both Denmark and Sweden followed suit. In the United States, Congress passed the Child Protection Act, creating the toughest anti-pornography ordinance in the history of the United States. What has happened since 1977? In the following six years, only twenty-three child pornographers were convicted of federal crimes in the United States.

This information Amanda had discovered in the public library in Copenhagen, only a few blocks from her apartment!

Little did she dream just how much she would accomplish in that short time before Christmas. She wanted to finish the whole business, be done with it, so she wrote copiously.

Many incidents of sexual abuse of children by children have been fueled by pornographic literature, easily obtainable by these children. Hundreds of cases have been reported of children—ages eight, nine, ten, and eleven years old—abusing younger peers. One case had been reported of a five-year-old boy sexually assaulting a three-year-old girl. Invariably, pornographic literature was involved in every occurrence; in some instances the children had seen pornographic films. Child sexual abuse is becoming a horrendous problem, an international disgrace.

On May 21, 1984, President Reagan signed the Child Protection Act of l984, and in so doing, stated "we have taken some other initiatives in the anti-pornography effort. Last year, the Customs Service increased its seizures of obscene materials coming in across our borders by over 200 hundred percent. Sixty percent of the material was child pornography."

Amanda continued.

Justice Department studies indicate that "Thousands of children under eighteen years old are killed annually by repeat murderers, who prey sexually on children, and by adults involved in child prostitution and pornography." It is not known how many male and female prostitutes there are under the ages of sixteen in the world, but the estimated numbers stagger the mind—hundreds and hundreds of thousands. Children are being exploited in almost every nation of the world. There are organizations that openly advocate sexual abuse of children. In California, the Rene Guyon Society boasts a membership of over 8500 members. Their motto is, "Sex by eight or it's too late." NAMBLA (North American Man/Boy Love Association) is based in the eastern section of the United States, as well as in the Midwest. They recommend total abolition of the Age of Consent laws relating to sexual intercourse between adult and child (mostly males).

The Pedophiliac Information Exchange in Great Britain suggests that age four be the age of consent. Some of these organizations have gained credibility through the media.

Dr. Shirley O'Brien, author of Child Pornography, states, "Pornographic exploitation of children makes people react in one of five different ways. The first has never heard of it, the second says live and let live, the third becomes sick, angry, and motivated to action, the fourth pofiteers from it, and the fifth is sexually excited by it."

Amanda stretched, threw her shoulders back, rotated her aching arms, and yawned. Walking into the small kitchen, she made a fresh pot of coffee. Standing in front of the stove, one hand cupping her chin, she contemplated the research she had done. She looked up, closed her eyes, and shook her head. Walking slowly back to her desk, she sat down with a sigh and began to type again.

Two decades ago "Kiddie Porn" was virtually unknown, yet, today there are literally hundreds of magazines on the market, each full of child pornography, many of which are published monthly. Unscrupulous, corrupt suppliers advertise openly in these periodicals. Large quantities of pornographic literature and film are confiscated during child molestation arrests, and law enforcement agencies state that there is a direct relationship between the porno material and sexual molestation. Child sexual abuse has increased as the distribution of child pornography has increased.

Testimony was given in the United States Senate that a worldwide network of child pornographers exists, who engage in sex tours and auctions. Few governments make an effort to stop these activities and children, as young as eighteen months, have been sodomized, bought, sold, swapped, and photographed in obscene sexual acts.

Amanda stopped to open a new ream of typing paper. She inserted another sheet in the typewriter, and continued pounding away on the keys.

The Scandinavian Connection imports volumes and volumes of child pornography to the United States. The ring, based primarily in Denmark and the Netherlands, also distributes videos around the world. The postal authorities, as well as United States Customs, confiscate thousands of pornographic materials, half of which involve children. The United States government has pressured foreign capitals in the Netherlands, Denmark, and Sweden to make an international effort to stem the flow of these materials to America, but in Denmark the law covers only the sale of materials, not the production designed for export. The producers get the materials into the United States by using a variety of false shipping labels, mostly from fictitious businesses.

The lurid world of child pornography exists because of greed and the sickness of seriously disturbed minds. Profits are never reported, so the business becomes the perfect tax shelter. Those in the business in the United States utilize the Scandinavian Connection, and in so doing, evade the more stringent United States laws that cover areas untouched by foreign law. The new laws and court rulings have driven the business underground. Parents make a lucrative living by selling pictures through the underground network in classified ads of their own children engaging in sexual acts with each other and with adults. It has become a very serious social disease. There is no such thing as a consenting child—it is an act of exploitation, unjustified. The child is the victim, and society itself is a victim, as long as it allows such a crime to exist. Child pornography is nothing but child abuse in its vilest, most insidious form.

Amanda sent the articles to Charlie, and breathed a big sigh of relief.

The strong, steady beat of his heart began to accelerate as Rafe hastened to meet the attractive woman walking to the baggage claim area. Grinning from ear to ear, he lifted her off her feet and swung her around. Then, holding her at arm's length, he exclaimed, "Amanda, you look positively marvelous!"

"Rafe!" He took her completely by surprise.

Taking her arm, he led her away from the crowd. "C'mon, Miss Cates, let's hurry and get your luggage. So, how've you been?" He hardly gave her a chance to catch her breath.

"I've been fine, just fine, Rafe." Walking along briskly, she asked, "And you? Been working hard?"

"I'm feeling great, Mandy, even more so now that you're here. My Fiat is in the parking garage. I'll get it, while you wait for your luggage. I'll pull up right out there in front. Watch for me, then I'll help you with the bags, and we'll be on our way."

"I can handle the luggage, Rafe. Go on—just get the car." She thought, *"He's surely in a jovial mood."*

As they were crossing over the River Thames, they had an exceptional view of the Tower of London. "There she is, Mandy. If she could but speak, what stories she could tell."

"Yes, I know. Steeped in history, isn't it?"

Rafe drove in and out between the traffic, circling several blocks, down narrow streets. Amanda remarked, "What a maze—these streets—seems there's no logic at all in the planning. Well, glad I'm not the postman—post woman, I mean."

"How right you are, my dear. Say, did you know that the Tower is almost a thousand years old? She's the real foundation of London's history. We must come back and see it at night—pretty impressive with the floodlights shining on it. Do you see that white tower in the center, Mandy?" He pointed in the direction.

"Yes, I see it."

"Well, that's the oldest part of the fortress. But, the Bloody Tower is the most infamous—that's where they confined and tortured the prisoners. There's a small cell in there they call Little Ease and, Mandy, it's so tiny, that the unfortunate inmate couldn't lie down, stand up straight, or even sit down in it. A few years ago they found a well in the lower part of the tower filled almost to the top with human bones. Nasty, huh? Sometimes I wonder about these Brits!"

"Pretty gruesome—but—fascinating," Amanda replied. She was pleased that he seemed to enjoy playing the part of a knowledgeable guide. "How many smaller towers are there, anyway?" Amanda asked, genuinely interested.

"I think that there are fifteen, and they each have their own name. We'll come back tomorrow, or day after, and spend a few hours here. It's full of historical facts."

"I'd love that," she said.

Rafe continued, "Will you look at those ravens! See! Over there, Mandy!"

"So many of them."

"You know what they say?"

"No, not really. You mean that the ravens actually talk?" she asked facetiously.

"Funny, funny. No, they say that if the ravens ever leave, the Tower will fall apart. Maybe even England will fall. There's probably more truth than fiction in that remark since the raven's wings are all clipped." They both laughed.

"Aren't the crown jewels here somewhere?" Amanda asked.

"Yes, we'll see them, too. We need a month!" Rafe looked over at her and gave her a wink. At that moment, he wanted to hold her, kiss her lovely lips, tell her how much he cared. Yet, there was something—something that kept a distance between them. Ann? "By the way, I booked rooms for us at the Goring. This challenge seems to be my lot in life— always finding just the right hotel, huh?"

"You're very good at it, Rafe."

"Well, anyway, it's a family hotel, small, comfortable, unpretentious. It's known for its hospitable staff—personal, friendly. I thought you'd like it—not at all high class—not like the luxury hotels, but we're not going to be spending all of our time in our rooms anyway, are we?" He seemed to be having a hard time explaining. He grinned at her, and felt foolish. Why was he trying so hard?

"It sounds lovely, Rafe. I like a smaller hotel." She smiled and looked over at him, "Anything you choose will be fine with me—you know that."

Rafe went on, "If it's okay with you, we'll stay here in London until Christmas Day—see the sights, explore, shop a little, look around the city, and then we'll drive down to Brighton for Christmas dinner in the evening. If you would help me find gifts for Mrs. Lancaster and Mrs. Kendall I'd really appreciate it. Need to get something for Alan, too—perhaps something made out of plastic—remind him of our project, you know. Mrs. Lancaster will be expecting us, and she'll have a nice room ready for you on the second floor. I've really learned to love Brighton and my friends there, Mandy. Mrs. Lancaster is a dear lady—has been very kind to me—acts like my mother, reminds me of my grandmother a lot. She is really anxious to meet you." He touched her arm. Whenever he wanted to get a point across, he would touch her, or hold her hands, or look into her eyes, all signs of some kind of reassurance. She loved these features about him. He exuded warmth and understanding. *Oh, how I love him. But, does he love me in the same way? Could he love another woman as he had loved Ann? No, I would never expect that of him. No one could possibly love two people in the same way. Each individual is different.*

"It sounds just perfect to me, Rafe. I'm sure I'll just love Brighton—and Mrs. Lancaster."

Rafe liked this vivacious, intelligent American woman. He had been commanded by God to love, but had not been commanded to like. He mused how important it was to like another person. He was always thinking about the difference between loving and liking. Could one love another individual, yet not like him? Yes, he thought so. It was probably more difficult to like people than to love them. He knew couples who loved one another, yet, they didn't seem to like each other very much. He wondered how Amanda would feel about his philosophy. He'd ask her some time. Not now.

Rafe slowed down, and pulled up in front of a remodeled Edwardian hotel. "Here we are. You go in, and I'll park the car. They're expecting you. I'm in the room right next to yours. I'll bring your bag."

They acted like a couple of teenagers, excited, thrilled with each new discovery—shopping, riding the tubes, laughing, joking, walking hand in hand. "Rafe, I'd love to go to Madame Tussaud's Wax Museum again—saw it several years ago, and I was so impressed. I couldn't believe how small some of the members of the Royal Family were. Have you ever been there?"

"No, but I've gone to the Planetarium right next door. Tell you what, Mandy—we'll go to both places."

"That would be great, and don't forget, I want to see the jewel house, too. I suppose we could spend a full day at the Towers, huh?"

"We'll go there tomorrow."

Each day was an adventure, each evening distinctive—dining by candlelight, going to the theater, attending a Christmas concert, sitting and talking by the hour in little out-of-the way nooks. They spent hours talking about themselves, their work, their likes and dislikes, their families, the sports they enjoyed, the foods, their religious beliefs. Amanda told him all about the absurd Hitler Forgery trial, the sad story of Father Popieluszko, her trip to Oslo and the bomb scare. Would they ever be at a loss for words? No, theirs was a comfortable, compatible relationship—a perfect harmonious duet.

Rafe wanted Christmas Eve, their last night in London, to be unique, intimate, and a time they would forever cherish. Sitting together on a leather sofa in the small lobby of the hotel, Rafe took her hand. "Mandy, let me tell you about St. Paul's Cathedral. You know, the church was built after the great fire in London, and was the masterpiece of Sir Christopher Wren. Well, on Christmas Eve there is a special service in the memorial chapel in the cathedral to honor the American forces in Britain. Wouldn't it be nice to go?" Before Amanda could answer, he continued, "After the service, we can go to a nice restaurant for our Christmas Eve dinner. How does that sound?"

"I can't think of anything I'd rather do on Christmas Eve, Rafe, but, will you let me choose a place for dinner?"

Rafe smiled, "Of course, I'd be delighted if you would make the arrangements. I'm really not so hard to get along with."

As they sat in the chapel, his arm nudged hers, and he reached over to take her hand. Amanda thought, *What God hath joined together, let no man...*

She chose the English House for dinner, a charming dining room in a private home that served traditional English meals. Soft Christmas music played in the background, and the old-fashioned Christmas tree sparkled in the dimly lit room. The light of the candle on the white linen tablecloth softened their facial features, and as the light flickered, Amanda's eyes glistened. She wore a beautiful, loose-fitting blouse, with full dolman sleeves, over a dark green narrowly cut skirt. The blouse had threads of silver woven into the dark green and royal blue fabric, which also picked up the lights. "You look absolutely beautiful tonight, Amanda," Rafe whispered. Was it the light, or was it because her face radiated her love for him? They spoke in hushed tones as they enjoyed the roast beef dinner with all the trimmings, and the Yorkshire pudding, accompanied by a cup of strong coffee for dessert. As they sipped the coffee, Rafe looked intently into her eyes and whispered, "Amanda, I would like to give you a little present tonight."

"Really?" Her eyebrows raised in question and surprise.

"Yes, really." He reached in his blazer pocket, and brought out a small box wrapped in silver paper with a matching silver bow. There was a small white angel in the center. Looking directly into her expectant eyes, he grinned, "Here you are, Miss Cates. Go ahead. Open it."

"I don't have to wait until tomorrow?" she teased.

"Nope, you don't have to wait. Go on, darling, open it."

He called her *darling*. Could it be a ring? Meticulously, she removed the bow, and with her fingernail, loosened the tape. She opened the small white box, only to discover a black velvet one inside. Carefully, she raised the top, and there discovered a pair of diamond earrings. "Oh, Rafe, they're absolutely gorgeous! But, but it's too much—way too much! Thank you, thank you! Oh, I can't believe this! I'm going to put them on right now."

She struggled to remove the white gold loops in her ears, and placed them on the table. Then, with some maneuvering, put the solitaires in each lobe. Each diamond was about a third of a carat, round, and brilliantly cut. Her eyes were watery. Was it because of her happiness, or was it because of her disappointment? Turning her head from side to side, she asked, "Do you like them on me, Rafe?"

"They just suit you—absolutely perfect—for a very special person," he smiled.

Amanda exclaimed, "Well, Mr. Langley, I have a gift for you, too, but you will have to wait until tomorrow to receive it!"

"Now, how could you do that to me?" he teased. "Do you think you're playing fair?"

"Can't help it—you have to wait," she teased.

The night closed about them as they walked down the street and into the hotel, arm in arm. It was late. Amanda felt exhilarated, but tired. "It's been such a wonderful day, Rafe. I've loved every minute of it—the chapel service, the dinner, the company—and, my magnificent gift." She had always had endless reserves of stamina; yet, now she felt completely drained, as withered as an orchid corsage two days after the dance.

Sensitive to her feelings, Rafe suggested that they turn in early. "We have another big day tomorrow, Mandy." In front of her room, he put his arms around her, and held her close. Then, he took both of her hands and slowly moved them around himself, loosened them, and moved his hands up between her shoulders. She rested her head on his chest, and listened to the steady, strong beat of his heart. "Mandy, I want to tell you something." Amanda raised her head and looked into his eyes. He continued, "When Ann died it seemed that everything I'd ever hoped for in the future died, too. And not knowing what happened to my little girl just added to the heartache. Now I am trying desperately to move on, to accept all of it and believe that God is still in control. I really didn't know if I could ever be interested in another woman, and now you have come into my life. I know that my attitude has caused a distance between us, but now I want to tell you that I have fallen in love with you." He buried his face in her hair, drinking in her fragrance. His lips touched her ears, "Amanda Cates, I love you—I love you with all my heart."

"Oh, Rafe," came the muffled cry, "I love you, too!" He cupped her chin, tilted her head, then slowly bent his head until their lips met. When he released her, he looked down at her and smiled, kissed her lightly on the tip of her nose, and whispered, "Good night, my darling. Sleep well, and I'll see you in the morning." With that, he turned and walked to his room.

Amanda stood in the doorway, watching him walk to the room next-door, wondering why he left so abruptly. She closed the door softly, deliberately, and leaned against it. She was elated, excited, too stimulated to go to bed immediately, so she decided to take a long bubble bath. She had proven that she could survive in a man's world, but now she was willing, ready, and even glad to relinquish her independence—at least to a certain degree—to this wonderful man. She thought of the past and the abandoned opportunities—men who were bright, intelligent, fun to be with, but who wanted no permanence; many of the relationships and special friendships had ended in disappointment. Rafe was different; he wanted stability. For some reason, nothing had ever worked out in the past for her. She had been engaged three times, none of which broke her heart when they were called off. Perhaps she rebuffed some men. Perhaps she did receive her high in life by working hard, by pouring all of her energy into her work. She played in the water, swirling her hands around and around in the warm liquid, making whimsical, uncanny, priceless abstracts in the sudsy water. Lifting the bubbles out of the water carefully, she blew them off her hands, and smiling, mused, *"Mrs. Langley—Mrs. Rafe Langley—Amanda Langley."* But, he hadn't given her a ring. Could he be teasing her? She recalled his words, his phrases, his tone of voice. *He was sincere, but are his thoughts still with her? With Ann?*

Rafe tossed and turned throughout the night, conflicting emotions filling his very being. His thoughts were of Ann. Was it unjust, unfair to her memory to fall in love with Amanda? What would she have done if the tables had been turned, if she had been left alone? He had loved her as much as any man could love a woman. *Oh, Ann, what would you have done? Why did you leave me? I loved you. I loved you with all my heart.* He struggled to erase the troubling thoughts from his mind. He did love Amanda. *Could we be happy together?* His thoughts went from one to the other. *I loved them both. Yes, I loved each of them. God, help me not to compare them. It isn't fair. It isn't fair.*

About three in the morning, he was awakened again. *Blackberry brambles choking, grasping, clutching—Ann, Julie, Neil, Ken, and Kim. He tried so desperately to reach them, but they were beyond his grasp, and the vines were enormous, winding around and around their bodies, holding them securely. He heard Julie's cry, "Daddy! Daddy! Help us! Help me! I'm choking, Daddy!"* He awakened with a start. His body was shaking. *Oh, no, not again—not tonight, dear God—not tonight.* He lay back, exhausted, depleted. He could not stop shaking. He got up and took a drink of water. At four o'clock in the morning, he finally drifted off again. His thoughts were of Amanda.


They met in the coffee shop on Christmas morning for a light breakfast.

"Can you be ready to leave about eleven, Mandy?" Rafe asked. Amanda noticed the dark circles under his eyes.

"Of course, Rafe. How are you this morning? Oh, by the way, Merry Christmas! A very, very Merry Christmas, Rafe."

"Oh, I'm so sorry. For a moment I forgot. Merry Christmas to you, too, my darling. I'm okay—just woke up in the middle of the night, and couldn't get back to sleep." He decided not to tell her about the perpetual nightmare. "Listen, after we finish here, get your bag packed, and I'll take it down for you. In the meantime, I'll get the car and park it out front. Okay?"

"Oh, Rafe, I can manage the bag by myself. I'll meet you in the lobby."

"Okay, that will be fine."

They were each unusually quiet on the drive heading south. Amanda's thoughts ran rampant. *He declared his love for me, but is he on the rebound? Does he really love me? Could he be happy with me? Does he compare me with Ann? Does he love me enough to ask me to marry him? If we were married, where would we live? Would he want to return to their home? How would I feel in Ann's home?* "You're so pensive this morning, Rafe," she remarked.

"Just thinking—thinking about what a terrific time we've had in London, and how happy I am that you're here. And, Amanda, to be honest with you, I have to admit that I have been thinking about Ann—and Julie. I know that Ann is gone—gone forever, but I still wonder about Julie—where she is—if she could be alive. If only I could know what really happened to her."

"I'm sure that this is a very difficult time for you, Rafe. We're supposed to be happy at Christmas, but for many it can be such a distressing, sad time. We tend to reminisce—think about our parents and the wonderful Christmas celebrations when we were kids. It's hard for those who have lost loved ones, or who are far away from family and friends, alone in a strange place. I'm trying to understand, but I realize that one can't possibly know what another individual is going through unless that person has experienced the same thing, the same loss." She touched his arm, consoling him.

"I'm sorry, Amanda, but I just can't help it."

"I know, I know, Rafe. Please don't worry about it. Try to be happy, and just take one day at a time. Everything will work out. You will see. Now, not to change the subject, but when can I give you your present?"

"My present? Oh, I almost forgot. Well, I think we'll stop at a high grassy knoll overlooking the Channel just before we get to Brighton. It's one of my favorite spots. It would be a perfect place for you to give it to me there. Okay?"

"Sounds wonderful," she smiled.

The view was more spectacular than she had anticipated. "I just love it!" she exclaimed. "It's a beautiful place."

He drove the car close to the bluff and turned off the ignition. Turning to her with a grin he said, "I knew you'd like it. After I discovered it, I would come up often, sit in the car and think and reminisce. Even rode the bike up a few times when it wasn't raining. Just look at that view—reminds me of Puget Sound in so many ways."

"Yes, I see what you mean."

"I'm ready!"

"Ready for what?" she teased.

"My present! C'mon, you don't expect me to wait any longer, do you? This *is* Christmas you know."

Amanda opened her bag and took out a shiny, long box, wrapped in green metallic paper with a red bow. Smiling, she said, "Well, here you are, Rafe Langley—Merry Christmas!"

"Well, isn't that pretty! Shall I open it now?"

"Of course. Go on. Open it." Her eyes were gleaming with delight. She felt like a little kid giving her first special gift.

He tore the ribbon off, and ripped the paper from the box. "Shall I close my eyes?"

"Yes, close them after you remove the wrapping. Open the box and then look."

The cover snapped open and, at the same instant, he opened his eyes. "A watch? Mandy, it's beautiful, just beautiful. A real dress watch, so thin and elegant, gold. Thank you, darling. I love it. But, Mandy, it's much too nice for me. I'm used to these big, heavy ones like this," he exclaimed, as he pulled his sleeve back and held up his arm.

"No, it's not too nice for you. You need a dress watch, Rafe."

"Yes, I believe I do—I really do. I've never had one like this. Thank you, Mandy. And, now I have one more little gift for you." Reaching behind the driver's seat, he grabbed a large box and handed it to her. "Here, just a little something in addition to yesterday's gift."

"Another one? Oh, Rafe, you shouldn't—the earrings…" She couldn't imagine what could possibly be wrapped in such a large box. A purse perhaps? She tore the wrapping off—more paper, tissue, and more tissue. Another box and more paper. Her fingers finally found a small, white, velvet box. "Oh, Rafe, now what have you done?"

"Open it."

Amanda opened it gently, and her eyes widened. It was the ring—the same ring she had tried on in the diamond factory in Amsterdam. She was speechless, and ecstatically happy. Rafe took the ring out of the box and held her left hand. "Amanda Cates, will you—will you marry me?"

"Oh, Rafe! Yes! Yes! Of course, I'll marry you! I love you so much, but how, when did you get the ring?" She hugged and kissed him. Her eyes filled with tears, tears of joy and happiness.

"Hey, just a minute. Let's do this thing right, shall we? I want to see if it fits." Rafe slipped the ring on her finger.

"You had it sized! Remember, it was too large before? Aren't you the clever one though," she teased.

Rafe took her in his arms, crushing her to him. Longingly, she looked into his eyes. Her hands caressed his face, gently pulling it down to her own until their lips met. "I love you, my darling Mandy," he whispered between kisses. Amanda's stomach fluttered as though a myriad of butterflies were trying to escape.


The wedding date was set for April 5, Good Friday. The marriage would take place in Brighton, and Abigail Lancaster and Dr. Alan Strickland would be their attendants. Charity Kendall would be in charge of the reception at the estate. "Oh, Abigail, I am so happy for Rafe. Did you see the look on his face when he told us that they were getting married? He really loves her, and I do too. She is a very special girl, a very special girl, indeed."

"Yes, she is, Charity, and just think, she has asked me—me of all people—Abigail Lancaster, to stand up for her. Do you know I have never, never in all my life, stood up with anyone before? I am so thrilled. I can't believe it."

"Now, Abigail, it doesn't mean that you are going to get out of helping me with the reception. I will do most of the baking and fixin', but you are going to have to help me decide what to prepare. You will, won't you?" Charity asked with a look of concern on her plain face.

"Oh, Charity, don't be ridiculous. Of course I will help you with all the preparation. You know I want to be a part of everything. This is going to be the nicest reception imaginable," Abigail declared emphatically. "Amanda asked me to try to find a pretty dress in a watermelon color, or a salmon color—you know, like king salmon. Oh, I just love those colors. You will have to help me shop, Charity."

"I will, and I want a new dress for the occasion, too. Oh, it is going to be so much fun. Just wait 'til my Edna hears about this. Say, maybe we could run up to London and have a look around. Edna has room for us, you know."

"Yes, that's a good idea—a very good idea. We'll work it out. We have plenty of time, you know."

On the way to the airport Rafe looked at Amanda with a big grin. "Those two women will have the time of their lives planning and preparing for this wedding. You know, honey, that was really nice of you to ask Abigail to stand up with you. Did you see her face light up when you asked her? She's really a great person. Thank you for that, Amanda."

"It's what I want, Rafe."

They held each other a long time before Amanda reluctantly boarded the flight back to Copenhagen. Could anyone be any happier? On the plane she reclined in her seat, eyes closed, and reminisced. Thoughts, ideas, images ran rampant in her head. In her mind's eye she visualized the wedding. She would walk gracefully down the long flight of stairs. Rafe would be waiting at the bottom to greet her with an outstretched hand. She would place her hand gently in his, and he would give it a squeeze. What would she wear? Well, she had time to decide that. Her wedding. Could it really be true? What would her mother say? Would she and her sister come for the big event? They had given up hope that she would ever get married. There was really no reason why they couldn't arrange to come. Neither of them had ever been to England. She would invite Charlie and Jean, too, though she knew they would probably not accept the invitation. Charlie rarely took a vacation. Yet, for her? Perhaps! She would probably wear a white, or off-white Chanel suit or dress. She didn't want anything too ostentatious—she wasn't the type. Oh dear, if Debbie came, she would have to be her Matron of Honor. With Abigail? Of course, that would work out. They could both stand up with her.

Glancing out the window, she noticed the billowing cumulus clouds—such a thrill to be above them, looking down. What an absolutely perfect flight. She was happier than she had ever been in her entire life. It was so wonderful to be in love, to be loved by such an incredible, caring man.

Late that night, after dinner and a hot bath, she was sitting in her robe, going through the mail. The telephone rang, and in a melodious voice she answered, "Hello! Amanda Cates speaking."

"Amanda, this is Charlie. How are you?"

"Hi, Charlie! Fine. I'm fine—just got back from a little trip to England."

"Did you have a good vacation? A happy Christmas?"

"Oh, yes! It was absolutely marvelous!" Should she tell him about her engagement? Not yet—not quite yet.

"Listen, Amanda, the trial on the Popieluszko murder started today. I'd really appreciate it if you'd go back to Warsaw. Stay with it until it's over. It shouldn't take very much longer. What's say, Angel?"

"I'm rested, Charlie. Sure—I'll do it. Same hotel?"

"Yes, I've already made the reservation for you. Your visa is still valid, isn't it?"

"Yes, of course."

"Okay then, if you can get ready, go back tomorrow. You did such a superb job before—I would like to have you complete the story. We can't leave our readers hanging, can we?"

"No, of course not. They deserve to hear 'the rest of the story!' as Paul Harvey would say, and I'll fill them in on all the details. Oh, and Charlie—thanks so much for the Christmas present. I'll buy something very special with the check. How was your Christmas?"

"Just super, as usual. Whole family got together and we had a great time."

"Anything else?"

"No, not for now. Good luck, Angel, and bye!"

She placed the phone back on the receiver. A feeling of excitement coursed through her body. Charlie was the most considerate boss in the world.

Amanda wondered what Charlie would say if he knew that she was planning to be married. Maybe he just might come for the wedding. She was confident that he and Jean, that her mom and Debbie and her family would all love Rafe. Who wouldn't? Marriage would no doubt change her lifestyle considerably, in more ways than one, but surely, she could still pursue her writing career. Perhaps she and Rafe would be returning to the States to live—Washington state. The thought intrigued her. She smiled as she put the kettle on for tea, and began to sing, "The skies are always blue in Seattle." What a joke that is. Hands on waist, standing like a model, she smiled at her reflection in the mirror, and was pleased with the mirrored image. She held out her hand to admire the diamond engagement ring. Would he take her to their home? Would she like that? Ann's home?

Amanda, now fully involved with the case back in Warsaw, wrote non-stop. Little did she dream that she would be there for a month or more, sending day-by-day write-ups to Charlie. She concluded the articles late into the night of February 7.

> Today the court found the security police officer, and the three former officers, guilty of murder in Father Jerzy Popieluszko's death. The ringleader, Piotrowski, was sentenced to twenty-five years in prison. Pekala received fifteen years. Officials of the Roman Catholic Church in Poland claimed that the murder had been treated as a secondary matter. An attorney for the priest's family implied that the Soviet Union had been linked to the crime. The lawyer stated that the murder had been staged to create a "spiral of mutual terror," as tensions between the dissidents and the government increased. He also stated, "Every school child knows who would profit from a weak Poland! I am afraid to think about it further."

Amanda added a postscript to the concluding article.

*Charlie, please don't ask me to return to Poland again. I am sick to death of this business. What does it look like to you? Can't you read between the lines? We're not so dumb, are we? Love, Amanda.*

❋　　❋　　❋

Amanda's mother's doctor thought it unwise for her mother to travel at the time of the wedding because of a chest congestion, so she called and talked to each of them, wishing them all the happiness in the world. She was thrilled that Amanda had found such a wonderful husband. Debbie's family was involved in a big Easter production at their church and could not come, but she and her mother promised another reception upon their return to the states. Charlie and Jean were entertaining their grandchildren over the spring vacation. Charlie had sent congratulations and a generous check along with instructions to have a great honeymoon. The wedding was all that Amanda and Rafe had anticipated. She was radiant in an off-white tailored Chanel suit, complemented by a small bouquet of Talisman rosebuds on a white Bible. The Bible was old, borrowed from Charity, and Abigail gave her a large blue garter to wear high on her thigh. She wore a choker of Mikimoto pearls and matching earrings, a gift from her father upon her graduation from college many years before. Alan heard a gasp from his friend as she walked gracefully down the winding stairway. Grinning from ear to ear, he took her hand at the landing and led her to the minister. A beaming Abigail, lovely in a salmon-colored dress, stood at Amanda's side, and Alan, casually dressed in a navy suit, a light blush-colored shirt, and peach-colored tie, stood next to Rafe. Rafe was handsome in a black suit, a white shirt, and a salmon-colored tie. They repeated their personal marriage vows as several chuckles were heard among the small gathering of friends, and kissed tenderly when the minister pronounced them man and wife. The guests enjoyed a wonderful time of fellowship, delicious tea, small heart-shaped sandwiches, crumpets with cheese, wedding cake, candy kisses, mints, and nuts. For the groom's cake, Charity had baked tiny fruitcakes and wrapped them individually for each guest. After the gifts were opened, the bride and groom mingled among the guests, thanking each one for coming. Then, holding hands, they said goodbye to everyone and went out the door. As they walked hurriedly down the steps, several of Rafe's students threw rice, and Alan Strickland shouted after them, "Be good, and don't do anything I wouldn't do!" Everyone clapped and cheered them on, and Abigail dabbed the tears falling down her rouged cheeks.

The first weeks of their marriage were painfully complex because they were apart most of the time. Rafe was obligated to the college, and Amanda had received several assignments on the continent, each time putting aside the final phase of the sexual child abuse business—pictorial pornography in various forms. They were together whenever possible, but traveling back and forth was expensive, and their schedules would not allow that precious time together.

On Mother's Day weekend, May 10, Rafe flew to Copenhagen to be with his cherished bride. It would be approximately three more weeks before the end of the spring term, before they could be together *"for as long as you both shall live."* Many decisions had to be made—planning for the future—where to live, what to do.

"Rafe, I'm almost through with these articles on child pornography, and I want to wind it up this next week, but I have these two videos from the authorities here in Copenhagen that I must preview. I was fortunate to even get them. I'm quite certain they will give us a good idea of just what these perverts are producing and sending all over the world. Will you please watch them with me? They're not very long."

"Come on, Mandy, do I have to? I hate that sort of thing. I'd really rather not. You go ahead, and I'll just read until you're through. I won't mind at all."

"But, Rafe, please! Please watch them with me—then, you can help with the evaluation." She implored so diligently that he finally conceded.

"Okay then, but let's get it over with right away, shall we?"

Amanda hurriedly placed the video cassette into the player, and they sat together on the sofa, holding hands, watching the monitor. "This is the one that is called, *Ring around the Rosy*," Amanda explained. "Can you believe they even give titles to these things?"

In the film there were four children, three boys and one girl, a freckled-faced, redhaired beauty in the early stages of puberty. She was the "Rosy" in the center, dressed in a beautiful pink ruffled dress. She held a pink rose in one hand. The young boys, each naked, formed a ring around her, and slowly circled her. As she undressed, deliberately, garment by garment, piece by piece, each of the boys performed various sexual acts with her and—with each other.

"I can't believe this! They're just children! Amanda, do you mean to tell me that this—this is available to the public? To anyone?"

"Yes, Rafe, I'm afraid it is—readily available. You can get just about anything if you want it badly enough. You know, this is a multi-billion dollar business, and the biggest market for this rubbish is in our own United States."

"I can't believe it! It's sick—sick, I tell you! Why doesn't the government put a stop to it?" Rafe was becoming infuriated. He hadn't known it was so disgusting, so degrading and offensive.

"Our government has passed legislation, but it's difficult to control, Rafe."

"What's the world coming to anyway? This is the most disgusting thing I've ever seen. I never dreamed…"

Amanda interrupted, "I don't know what the world's coming to, Rafe, but you know that we've always had child molestation in one form or another. It's just within the past few years that it's come out of the closet, so to speak. I just can't conceive the type of individual that would get a kick out of watching children engage in sexual acts though. It makes me nauseous. It makes me furious!"

Amanda pushed the reject button, removed the cassette, and Rafe rose. "Honey, wait, there's one more. Please watch it with me. This one is entitled *Ripe Red Apples.*"

"*Ripe Red Apples?* Shall I get the popcorn?" he asked facetiously.

"Be serious, Rafe, please. It won't last long. C'mon, sit down." She pushed the second cassette into the player. The video was even more demoralizing than the first one. Rafe sat, hunched over, holding his head in his hands, his arms propped on his knees. Two boys and two girls engaged in devious sexual acts with each other, using little red apples that had been cored. Rafe was absolutely dumbfounded. There was a close-up shot of a lovely blond girl, about eight years old, with long, heavy braids, and blue eyes, such sad eyes. Then, there were two small boys, both handsome little fellows, the same ones from the other film, and a tall, slight, raven-haired girl with cobalt blue eyes. She had a fixed, hapless smile, and as she slowly turned around in full view, Rafe stared at the girl. It couldn't be! It couldn't be! He jumped up and shouted, "Amanda, stop it! Stop it!" Amanda was startled. She stared at her husband's ashen face.

Amanda jumped up. "What is it, Rafe? Are you ill?"

Rafe was shaking. "Rewind! Rewind! Oh, my God, it can't be! That dark-haired girl looked like Julie!"

"Julie? Your Julie? Oh, Rafe, it couldn't be."

"Please, Amanda. Rewind. Go back again. She'll turn around in full view. When she does, freeze the picture. You can do that, can't you?"

"Yes, yes, of course."

"Just as soon as the girl turns completely around, and is in full view, stop it."

Amanda rewound the film, then pushed the play button. "Stop! Stop it there!" Rafe shouted. She pushed the pause button. Rafe bent over and stared at the monitor. "It *is* Julie! I am sure of it. It's Julie! I can even see the little mole above her right eye. But, look at her eyes, look at her eyes! She looks so gaunt. She's sick, she's sick, Mandy!" There were dark rings under the big blue eyes and the pupils gazed out, wide and coal black. "But, where is she? Where was this thing made?"

"I don't know, Rafe, but we'll find out. We'll find out—we'll find her. Are you sure it's Julie? I promise, we'll find her!"

Rafe was shaking uncontrollably. "I—I—can't believe it! Oh, my God—my baby—my little girl! What have they done to her? Did you see her eyes? They looked—they looked so blank—so sad—just like the other girl's eyes. And, she is so gaunt and thin, Amanda."

"Please try to control yourself, sweetheart. We'll go to the FBI—Interpol—the local authorities—they'll…"

Rafe raved on, "We have to find her! Those perverts! I can't believe anyone could do a thing like this. Why, Mandy? Why, in God's name, do they abuse innocent little children? Why, Mandy? Why? How did they ever get Julie?"

"I don't know. I don't know, but it's all for money, Rafe, for the love of money. Some people will do anything for money."

"If I ever get my hands on the person responsible for this, I'll kill him. I'll kill him! I swear, I'll kill him!"

"Oh, Rafe, please, I know you're upset. So am I, but try to control yourself. You'll have a heart attack, or make yourself ill. We can't do anything tonight—it's too late, but tomorrow we'll go to the authorities. My dear, please try to get some rest now—please, Rafe."

"I can't sleep, Mandy. I can't get that video out of my mind. How can I rest, knowing that Julie is alive, that they are exploiting her in this manner?"

"Try, Rafe, please try. Will you take one of these sleeping pills? It will help you relax, and maybe you can get to sleep."

"I feel guilty sleeping when Julie is alive somewhere—out there with those corrupt panders. Oh, dear God, we've got to find her." Rafe was shaking uncontrollably.

"We will, Rafe. I know we will. Please take one of these pills. You'll need your strength."

"But, tomorrow is Sunday, and I have to go back to Brighton! If only I could resign right now, but I can't do that, Mandy. There are just a few more weeks of this term."

"I know you can't quit your work now, but Rafe, I'm here. Think about it. I promise to begin working on it right away. I have good connections, and I've met a lot of people through my research that will help. The authorities know much more about what's going on than they have begun to tell me. They have their sources, Rafe. We will find Julie. I just know it!"

"Okay, okay. I'm so tired—so tired. All of a sudden I—I feel completely drained. I can't think straight. I'm sick. I think I'm going to throw up." Rafe walked into the bathroom and shut the door.

"Oh, Rafe, come out! You've had a terrible shock, darling." She spoke in words that resonated with the pain in his heart. When he opened the door slowly, she put her arms around him, and held him close. "C'mon, let's get you to bed." Amanda led him into the bedroom, and helped him undress. He seemed to be in a daze, stumbling and weaving as he walked. With arms outstretched, he seemed to have difficulty focusing. As he sat on the edge of the bed, she brought him a glass of water, and gave him one of the pale blue pills, which would help him relax and eventually make him drowsy.

Rafe lay with his hands clasped under his head, wide-eyed, staring at the ceiling. "I can't believe it. I can't believe it," he kept muttering. "Oh, how terrible, how degrading. Julie! My little girl! My little girl." Amanda sat beside him, stroking his forehead, gently running her fingers through the unruly lock of hair, trying to comfort him.

In his subconscious, there were little knots of children huddled together, unedited snippets of video, and a montage of strange, distorted, opaque faces of children. He groaned in a fitful sleep.

Amanda didn't sleep much that night, either. What if she had not insisted that he look at the videos? She would never have known the raven-haired beauty was his child, his Julie. Fate? Perhaps. Divine intervention? Yes, surely it was. My, the child was a pretty little thing. Poor Rafe. Her heart went out to him. For an infinitesimal moment, she almost felt like an outsider, someone else looking in upon a family affair from which she was completely detached. How she loved him, how she longed to comfort him.

Around three in the morning Rafe began to moan, groan, and thrash in his sleep. He startled Amanda from her restless sleep. At first, she couldn't recall. Then, everything came back to her—the video, his reaction to seeing Julie. He moaned and murmured, "No, no, no. I'll help you. But, I—I can't—I can't reach you!"

Amanda began to shake him, "Rafe, darling, wake up, wake up! You're dreaming. You're having a nightmare."

He awakened with a start, and sat upright in bed. His body shook and he stared straight ahead. Then, he covered his face with his hands. "Oh, no, not again. Not again. It's the same nightmare, the same one all the time." Tears filled his eyes, and he cried, "Why am I so weak? Why am I so weak?"

"Oh, Rafe, you're not weak—you're the strongest man I've ever known. Crying is not a weakness. It's a strength. Don't talk like that, Rafe. What do you mean—the same nightmare? Can you tell me?"

"It's the blackberries."

"The blackberries? Why would you dream about blackberries?"

"I keep dreaming this same frightening nightmare all the time, Mandy. It haunts me. In it I see Ann, Julie, some of my friends—Ken and Kim—they're all trapped—trapped in the blackberry vines! The vines are enormous, and some of the berries are as big as plums. The vines are winding around them, round and round, crushing them. The berries are oozing juice, like blood. It's in their hair, and all over their bodies and they are held fast, and their faces are grotesque, and they can't get out. They're all crying for help, and Ann's cry is way off and very weak, and Julie is crying, 'Daddy! Daddy! Help me! Help me! Daddy, they're choking me! They're crushing me! Help! Help me!' And, I try to reach for them, but I can't get to them. I can't! The vines are holding them fast. I can't help them, Mandy. It's driving me crazy!"

"You poor darling—how terrible. Did you say you dream this same thing all the time?" She put her arms around him.

"Yes, I keep dreaming this same nightmare over, and over, and over."

"When did it all start?"

"Right after I came to Brighton—no, coming across on the ship, I think. No, I dreamed it when I was staying with Ken and Kim. I don't know. I can't remember now when it started. It obsesses me, and it's about to drive me completely out of my mind."

"But, Rafe, why blackberries?"

"I don't know. I don't know. We picked them often. Ann made terrific pies, and jam, and juice. She was planning to open her own business featuring blackberry pies and jams. She was going to call it the Jam Jar."

"The Jam Jar," Amanda reflected.

"But, Mandy, why would I keep on dreaming this crazy dream all the time, hearing Julie cry? Blackberries, for heaven's sake." Quietly reflecting, he continued, "One time I fell into a growth myself, and though it was a bit humorous at the time, it really wasn't that funny when I couldn't get out of my own volition. When I made a move, the vines just tightened their grasp. I was helpless. You should have seen me—cuts all over. The fire department had to finally come and get me out. It was really frightening. You can't imagine how big those vines can get, Mandy. I've seen them envelop buildings. Did I ever take a razzing over that incident."

Amanda mused, "How could anything so delicious be so treacherous?"

"I don't know. I just don't know. But, think of all the things in this world that have their own defense—artichokes—various fruits and berries—they each have a form of defense, and that defense becomes our irritation. Funny, isn't it? And, I really like artichokes."

"So do I, and don't forget, my dear, that some irritants cause beauty. Look at the pearl."

"I know. I know. Let's just hope and pray that something—something beautiful comes out of this. But why are we talking like this? Blackberries—artichokes—pearls—I should be out hunting for Julie, for my little girl."

She cuddled up close, and hugged him, and kissed his neck. "We'll find her, darling, just be patient. It will all work out. You'll see. I love you," she whispered into his ear.

"I love you, too, and you know, I would be lost without you now." He turned, and lay there for what seemed like hours, with his eyes wide open, staring into the darkness. He couldn't get the video out of his mind. He cried, "Oh, my God! Apples? Blackberries? Please help us find her, please help us find her."

After a long talk with Amanda, Rafe was convinced that there was nothing he could possibly do in such a short period of time, so he agreed to leave for the time being, convinced that Amanda would do everything within her power to meet and work with the authorities regarding the search for Julie. On Sunday evening he took a seven o'clock flight back to London. Early Monday morning Amanda walked into the Interpol office with the two videos in her brown leather briefcase.

"Yes, yes, Mrs. Langley. Are you positive that one of the children in this pornographic film is an American citizen?"

"Yes, I know she's an American. Her father saw the film. He recognized her."

"Her father saw this film? Where is he now? Why isn't he with you?"

"He had to return to Brighton to conclude his teaching assignment. His name is Rafe—Rafe Langley. He is a visiting professor in a college in Brighton. I am his wife. We were married just a few weeks ago—on Good Friday. I am not the girl's mother."

"Is the girl's mother in the states?"

"Her mother is dead, sir."

"I see." The officer reflected thoughtfully, and looked down at his yellow tablet. Glancing up at Amanda, he asked, "Mrs. Langley, how did you get this film? Why were you viewing it?"

"I am a reporter, a writer, Mr. a…a…"

"My name is Sommers, Mrs. Langley."

"Yes, well, Mr. Sommers," Amanda continued her explanation, "I am a reporter on assignment with *Today's World* to write a series of articles on various kinds of child abuse, child molestation, and children who are being exploited in pornography. I had gone to the local authorities to ask if they had any videos that I might preview, and they gave me these two. I don't know how they acquired them. I didn't ask. They also showed me some still photographs of children in pornographic poses. I don't know where the authorities obtained the films."

"I see," Mr. Sommers replied thoughtfully.

Amanda continued, "I asked Mr. Langley to watch them with me. In fact, I implored him to watch with me. Believe me, Mr. Sommers, he objected. He hates this kind of thing, and when he viewed it he was shocked and extremely distraught. Then, when he looked at the second video he shouted, 'Stop it! Stop it! Rewind!' He thought one of the children in the film was his missing daughter. I rewound the film and froze the frame. He recognized his daughter, Julie, and he was beside himself—intensely upset, as you can well imagine."

"Yes, it must have been a dreadful shock, a dreadful shock."

"He was stunned, bewildered, and he became extremely disoriented and incoherent. He couldn't believe that it was actually his daughter, his little Julie in the video. You see, when her mother drowned almost two years ago in Washington State, they discovered her body on the beach, but the girl, who was with her at the time, was never found. I think it's a miracle, Mr. Sommers, an act of divine intervention that I obtained this particular video, that he viewed it with me, and that he recognized her in the film."

"Yes, Mrs. Langley, I would have to agree with you there. This is hard to believe. It's a chance in a million that this would ever happen. Yes, it is truly amazing, truly amazing." Mr. Sommers rubbed his chin.

"I assured him that she would be found," Amanda said emphatically. "I didn't know exactly where to begin, Mr. Sommers. I came here because I thought you could help. I promised him that I would find the source of the film. I assured him that we—you—you would find his daughter. You will help, won't you?"

"Yes, yes, of course, we will do everything within our jurisdiction to help, but if you are certain that this is an American child, you will also have to go to LEGAT, the American emissary, or deputy, of the FBI in Copenhagen. I will contact the Embassy for you, and explain the situation. The consulate will contact us and the local authorities, and we will work together on the case. You see, it appears that the crime may also involve kidnapping and slavery. I am confident that the producers are not utilizing local children. They are probably all foreigners. How many different children did you observe in the films? Do you recall?"

Amanda looked down thoughtfully. "Let me think. Yes, I do remember. In the first film, there was one redheaded girl, who I would judge to be about thirteen, and three younger boys. Then, in the second one there was a lovely blond girl, perhaps six or seven years old, Julie, and the same two smaller boys that were in the first video. Six different children I believe."

"Julie? Julie Langley?" The investigator hurriedly scribbled notes on the yellow pad.

"Yes, Mr. Sommers."

"Were there any adults in the films—in either of the productions?"

"No, not in either video—only children, beautiful children. A handsome blond boy and the redheaded girl appeared to be in their early teens. The other children were younger, probably from six to eight years old. It was repulsive and abhorrent."

"Yes, yes, I am sure that it was. I believe that individuals involved in exploiting children in this manner possess the same mentality as the people who lived in Sodom and Gomorrah, Mrs. Langley. They have reprobate minds." He shook his head slowly, then added remorsefully, "And, it's all for money."

"Do you want me to take the videos to LEGAT, Mr. Sommers?" Amanda inquired.

"Yes, you may take them with you. I will call to inform them that you are coming. Just explain everything—tell them exactly what you have told me. We will be in touch with them, as well as with the local authorities."

"Where is their office?" Amanda asked.

"One moment, please." Mr. Sommers picked up the phone and said, "Lorraine, please ask Mr. Dahlberg to come in for a moment."

A young man with a slight limp entered the office. "Mrs. Langley, this is Mr. Dahlberg. He will drive you over. Now don't worry, Mrs. Langley, we'll find the girl if she's in this country, but it may take considerable time. And, when you speak to Mr. Langley tell him not to feel guilty about having to return to Brighton because at the present time there would be really nothing that he could do here—except wait. Just tell him to be patient and assure him that we will do everything within our jurisdiction to crack the case." The investigator rose, clenched his right fist, and hit the palm of his open left hand over and over. "This may be just what we've been looking for—a part of a very large, active porn ring." Extending his hand, he said, "Thank you, Mrs. Langley, for coming to us. You did the right thing, and we will be in touch." Mr. Sommers picked up the phone and began to dial.

Amanda went out with Mr. Dahlberg, the two videos in her brief case. That evening she wired Charlie, "May have big scoop to wind up porn subject. Amanda."

Rafe wasn't sure how he completed the last three weeks of the spring term. Classes were dismissed on May 31, but he could not leave Brighton until the sixth of June. During those three weeks, he explained everything to Alan Strickland, Mrs. Lancaster, and Charity.

"Charity, do you remember the day we read in the paper about that little boy who was missing, and Rafe excused himself and left? He had such a sad look. Now we know why. Oh, that dear man has been through so much—his first wife drowning—his daughter missing. I just hope he finds his little girl."

"Yes, I remember, Abigail, but isn't it wonderful that he now has Amanda to help him? It's a miracle that she got that video and he saw his daughter in it. I can't believe it."

"I am sure it will all work out. The authorities know what they're doing," Abigail replied softly.

"Well, we'll just have to pray and have faith."

"Yes, yes, that's the least we can do," Abigail agreed.

Amanda ran into his arms as he walked through the passageway from the plane. "Oh, darling, I'm so glad to see you again, and I have good news—good news, Rafe!"

"Julie? Have they found Julie yet?"

"No, not yet. Nothing new since I talked to you on the phone day before yesterday, but I have been in constant contact, Rafe, and they have all been wonderful. Just this morning they gave me such an encouraging report. They think they're winding up their investigation. It all takes so much time. They have to be sure, you know."

She linked her arm through his, as they began to walk down the corridor. Though she felt his weariness, and noticed the deepened lines in his face, the dark circles under his eyes, he was still good looking. She thought he was the most handsome man in the world.

"Mandy, what have they found? Do they know where Julie is?" He asked the questions in almost a whisper.

"They're not sure yet, but they think they're close, Rafe. I don't think they tell me everything, you know. They just say that they're on to something, and it looks positive. You know, they view the films over and over, and examine the background very carefully. They look at the lighting switches, the type of electrical outlets, the height of the doorknobs, the controls on the television sets, the type of woodwork, the wallpaper, every minute detail in the film. It helps them determine where the film was made. I think this whole business is bigger than any of us can imagine, Rafe, involving many different people. We just have to be patient."

"But, do they think that Julie is here—in Copenhagen?"

"They won't say definitely, one way or the other, but it indicates that this may be the case. This business involves other children, too, and they did tell me that they feel the children are all from foreign countries. That means that other governments will be involved as well."

"Oh, I hope they crack it soon, Mandy." Rafe shook his head sorrowfully. "I've had a terrible time getting through the end of the term at school—couldn't concentrate at all. The only thing I could think of was Julie, and the degradation they've put her through." Disdainfully, he added, "Perverts."

"How are the ladies—Abigail and Charity? And, Alan?"

"They're all fine, just fine. I told them the whole story—about Ann's death, Julie missing, and they were so concerned and understanding. Talk about support! One could never find nicer friends."

"Well, it will soon be over, darling, and she will be with us. I know it. Trust me, Rafe, and trust the authorities. They are doing everything within their power to find her, and they'll know when to make their move. Please, just wait here for your luggage. I'll get the car and pick you up out in front."

"Okay." Rafe thought how intuitive Amanda was, and yes, often dogmatic. He was so thankful for her help, her concern, for her love. Oh, the questions, the unanswered questions, questions crowding his mind in a contest to escape.

Early in the morning, on Saturday, June 16, 1985, the lovely country estate on the outskirts of Copenhagen that many assumed was an exclusive private school for wealthy children from foreign countries, was surrounded by the local authorities, FBI agents from the United States, and officers from Interpol. The men, stationed within view of the front verandah, watched as the chauffeur-driven long, black limousine stopped at the entrance. Right on time. The chauffeur got out of the limousine, and walked around to open the door for the gentleman seated in the back. The man, dressed in a gray business suit, walked up the steps to the front door and rang the bell. He turned and looked at the surroundings. Mia, dressed in a black dress with a white voile apron, opened the door. "Yes? May I help you, sir?"

"My name is Mr. Green. I have an appointment with Mr. Rosenberg."

"Just a moment, Mr. Green. Please, come in and wait here." She closed the door behind him and said, "I will be back in a minute."

The gentleman in the gray business suit stood in the hall, admiring the mahogany woodwork, and the elegant furnishings. In a few moments, Mia returned, "Please follow me, Mr. Green." Mr. Green was ushered into the parlor. Mr. Rosenberg rose to greet him with an extended hand.

"It's nice to meet you, Mr. Green. You had no problem finding the estate?"

"Not at all. The directions were excellent."

Taking Green's arm, Emol led him to a comfortable chair. "Here, won't you please sit down? And, may I offer you a cup of coffee?"

"Yes, thank you. I only had time for one cup this morning, but my time is limited, Mr. Rosenberg. I must catch my plane in just three hours, and you know how traffic can be at this time of day." Mia poured the coffee, and handed the fine china cup to Mr. Green.

Smiling at Mia, he said politely, "Thank you, young lady. Thank you very much."

Emol turned to the maid, "That will be all for now, Mia. Thank you." She bowed slightly and left the room.

Emol continued, "You said on the telephone that you were on your way to New York?"

"Yes, that is correct. I will be flying to New York first, then to Los Angeles."

The two men engaged in pleasantries as they sipped the coffee. Draining the cup, and setting it on the coffee table, Mr. Green rose to go. "Well, thank you for the coffee, Mr. Rosenberg. You do have an exquisite place here, I must say."

"Yes, it is very lovely, and perfect for our operation. We have had marvelous success since we located here. Business has been unbelievable, and I am confident that you will be very pleased with all of the productions in the package," Emol assured him.

Reaching into his inside pocket, Green pulled out a white envelope. "Here is the money—I'd suggest you count it just to make sure it is the correct amount."

Rosenberg took the envelope, opened it, leafed through the bills, and smiled, "Yes, well, it appears that it contains the exact amount. Thank you."

"Now, the films?"

"They have been brought to the entrance hall. Come with me, Mr. Green." Emol put his hand on Green's shoulder and added, "By the way, I do hope that we shall meet again. I assure you—you will be delighted with the films. The photography is absolutely superb, and we will keep you posted on the latest productions in the future. It's really been a pleasure meeting you."

As Emol walked, he gently, but nervously slapped the envelope of bills repeatedly on his left hand. "Yes, well, here we are, and here are the videos. There are twelve in the package, exquisitely executed—nothing cheap or inferior about the quality." He stooped to pick up the package and handed it to Mr. Green. "Here, allow me to get the door for you." Emol opened the door, and followed him out onto the verandah.

Green put the box down, and reached in his pocket for his card. He quietly showed the Interpol card to Rosenberg and announced in a firm statement, "Mr. Rosenberg, you are under arrest. It will do you no good to protest, or give warning to anyone in the house. The place is surrounded. Your game is over, Rosenberg." At that moment, two officers ran up on the verandah, turned Rosenberg around, and handcuffed him.

Green continued, "And, now let us go back inside and take a good look at what we have in this magnificent estate, Rosenberg. I'd be interested in meeting the entire staff, especially your photographer, in seeing the production room, the props, and of course, all the stars in the productions you have sold to me, especially those who receive no pay for their performances."

Emol looked disdainfully at Green, turned, and walked slowly back into the entrance hall without saying a word. Green followed him, with two police officers at each side.

It was Monday, June 17, the day after Father's Day. Rafe's heart beat began to accelerate like the pistons in the old jalopy he and Ken shared when they were students. Not knowing what to expect, he simply stood on the opposite side of the room and waited—waited patiently for Julie to walk through the door and into his arms.

When the door opened slowly and she walked hesitantly into the room, he thought his heart would burst. Thoughts flew through his mind like leaves flying through the air on a windy day. What a lovely child—tall for her age, perhaps a bit too thin and lanky, standing with shoulders straight, but with downcast eyes. She bit her lip nervously.

The motherly looking matron, her hand on Julie's shoulder, bent over and said softly, "Julie, your father is here." Her bowed head slowly raised, and those beautiful sad eyes in the pale, opaque, expressionless face searched his for answers. Her tongue, small and pink, rolled to lick her lips, which parted in a faint cry, "Daddy! Oh, Daddy—is it really you?"

Rafe held out his arms toward her, and she ran into his warm embrace, her small arms reaching around his body, holding him fast. Her body was shaking, and great sobs came from her throat. "Daddy! Daddy! You found me! Oh, please let me come home! Please don't leave me!" Large tears rolled down her face.

"Julie—Julie—there, there, honey—I'm here, and I'm not going to leave you. You're going to be all right, sweetheart. Please don't cry any more. You're safe now, and you're going to be all right. Everything is going to be fine now." He held her, comforting her with warmth and love, and for the moment, his closeness did console her. Yes, for that moment, at that given place in time, his presence, his closeness, his strength were all sufficient. Large tears rolled down his face, falling on her dark hair.

Amanda, standing near the wall, remained silent, her eyes brimming with tears. She turned to the matron and the gentleman in attendance, "Thank you, thank you—you've been very kind." They shook hands, acknowledging her appreciation. "We'll be going now," Amanda said. Rafe thanked them, put his arm around Julie's slim shoulder, and they went out the door. Amanda followed, closing the door softly behind her. Each was so overcome with emotion they could say nothing.

On the way down the long flight of stairs, Rafe, his right arm around Julie, his left hand clasping Amanda's hand, said, "Honey, I want you to meet a very special friend of mine." They all stopped at the landing. Rafe continued, "This is Amanda, Julie. She helped me find you."

Julie's deep blue eyes turned slowly toward Amanda, not seeing, as though a darkened veil covered them. She said nothing.

Rafe was at a loss to know what to say or do next. "Well, let's go to Amanda's apartment, shall we? Honey, are you tired? Are you hungry?"

Julie simply nodded in the affirmative. They continued walking down the steps. Julie paused, and looked up at her father, "Daddy, where's mommy?" she asked.

The direct question stunned him momentarily, then he stepped down two steps in front of her, bent down, took her hands in his, looked directly into her eyes, and said, with deep compassion and sympathy, "Julie, your mother is gone. She—she died." There was a long pause before he continued, "You have a new mother now—Amanda—and I know that you are going to love her. We'll all talk about it later, after we get home, shall we?" He paused to see what her reaction would be, but her eyes were expressionless. She scrutinized him without saying a word. They continued walking down the long flight of stairs, down the street, hand in hand, with Julie in the middle. Her hand was limp in Amanda's hand, but Amanda clasped it firmly. She thought, *Julie was a gorgeous child. Ann must have been a real beauty.*

Rafe's thoughts were running rampant. She wasn't the little girl he had left in Washington state. She wasn't the same. She had changed. *What had they done to her? I'd like to get my hands on them.*

As they neared Amanda's apartment, Rafe said, "Well, Julie, we're just about there." He was obviously extremely nervous.

Amanda didn't know what to say. "Here, I'll get the key." She fumbled in her purse for the key and unlocked the door. She tenderly took Julie's coat off, and asked, "Honey, are you hungry?" Julie shook her head. "Wouldn't you like to have a cup of hot chocolate?"

Her blue eyes were expressionless. She gazed, but did not see. "Yes, thank you," came the weakly whispered reply.

Amanda prepared the hot chocolate while Rafe and Julie sat at the table. Rafe took her hands again, and spoke in almost a whisper, "Honey, we're so glad we've found you—you're going to be all right, everything is going to be all right now that you're here with us." Julie said nothing, but nodded her head ever so slightly in agreement.

After they finished drinking the hot chocolate, Amanda asked, "Julie, would you like to take a little nap for awhile?" Julie nodded her head. "C'mon, honey, let's go into the bedroom and tuck you in." Julie followed Amanda into the bedroom, sat on the bed, and bent over to untie her shoes. She lay on top of the bed, and Amanda covered her lovingly with an afghan, tucking it in around her frail body. Rafe stood, watching in the doorway.

"You have a good rest, Julie," Rafe said, "and maybe tomorrow we can go on a sightseeing trip around Copenhagen. Would you like to see Hans Christian Andersen's "Little Mermaid"?"

"Is he the same one who wrote the fairy tales, Daddy?" Julie inquired in a whisper.

"Yes, sweetheart, he's the very same man. Okay, you try to get some sleep, and we'll be in the next room." He bent over her, kissed her on the forehead, and pressed his cheek lightly against her own. Whispering in her ear, he said, "Have a good nap, Julie. I love you—I love you so much." He straightened, turned, and walked out of the bedroom.

Rafe and Amanda sat at the kitchen table, talking for hours. "Oh, Mandy, what are we going to do—what's it going to take? She isn't the same girl. Can't you see the sadness in her eyes? I just can't believe this has happened to her, and I still can't understand why. Where is the fairness? What meaning can ever come from all of this anyway?"

"Rafe, darling, you know that suffering is a stubborn fact of life, and it comes to all of us, to everyone, without discrimination. No one is immune. Each of us must face some form of suffering in this life whether it be war, death, famine, disasters, defeats of all kinds in our lives, in our jobs, in our relationships, and you have suffered so much from all of this. Losing Ann was devastating, then not knowing what had happened to Julie was the last straw. But, just remember, my darling, that suffering does not last. It won't go on forever. Just think, we found Julie! We found her, and she is with us. It's really a miracle. She's with us now, and she will be all right, eventually. Have faith, Rafe! God will show us how we can help her."

"You know, Amanda, I have sometimes felt like the psalmist in the Bible when he thought God had thrown him away. I kind of thought that God had thrown me away. I have had a terrible time accepting all that has happened, yet I know in my heart that He hasn't thrown me away."

"Of course He hasn't, my dear. God is still in control."

At midnight, Julie was still sound asleep. Amanda made a bed for her on the sofa, and Rafe picked her up tenderly, and carried her into the living room. She didn't awaken. "Do you think she'll be all right here, Mandy?"

"Of course. C'mon, it's been an exhausting day. You need some rest, and so do I."


At eight o'clock in the morning Julie was still sound asleep. Amanda looked down at her, and smiled, "She was simply exhausted, Rafe. Do you know, she's slept twelve hours or more? Poor little thing. She's so lovely, Rafe."

"Yes, she is. She's a beautiful child—takes after her mother. Sometimes I think she just can't be mine." Rafe and Amanda waited patiently for Julie to awaken. They spoke in hushed tones so that she could sleep as long as possible. Finally, a few minutes before nine o'clock, Julie opened her eyes and looked around the room.

"Good morning, sweetheart! You've really had a good long sleep, do you know that? I'll bet you're ready to have breakfast now, and a bath, and then go with us to see the Little Mermaid." Rafe spoke enthusiastically. He went over to give her a big hug, and her little arms reached around his neck. She squeezed him as hard as she could.

Julie yawned, rubbed the sleep from her eyes, and whispered simply, "Daddy."

"Julie, breakfast first, or your bath?" Amanda asked.

"I'd like my bath first, please, Amanda," Julie replied politely.

After breakfast, Julie looked sadly at her father, and asked meekly, "Daddy, why did mommy die? How did she die?"

Rafe set his coffee cup down, and reached over to take her hands in his own. "Honey, I don't know why. No one knows why she had to die, but we all know that she's in heaven—with Jesus—and she's happy, Julie. Your mommy drowned. They found her on the beach."

"At our cabin, Daddy?"

"No, Julie, over on Camano Island."

"Camano Island?" Julie's voice quivered.

"Yes, sweetheart, but, let's not talk about it now, shall we?"

Julie was persistent. "But, who found her? Why did she drown, Daddy? She was a good swimmer."

"I know, I know, Julie. A couple of nice young people, who were running on the beach, found her, and they reported it to the authorities. Let's not talk about it now, shall we?" Rafe pleaded.

"All right, Daddy." With her fork, Julie played with the hardened yellow egg yolk on her plate. She dabbed her eyes with her napkin, as one big teardrop landed on the plate. Amanda stood by the sink, shaking her head, thinking, *Poor child*. Julie slowly got out of her chair, and looked sadly at her father. "I'm going to brush my teeth now, Daddy. Do you have a toothbrush for me?"

"I have a new one for you, Julie," Amanda explained. "I'll get it for you."

"That's a good girl. You brush your hair and get ready, then we'll go." Rafe thought his heart would burst with sympathy for his little girl. "Say, sometime today we're going shopping, too—just for you. You have to have some new clothes. Would you like that?"

"Yes, I'd like that. I haven't been to a store since I was in Washington. Amanda, will you help me?"

"Just try to leave me out of it! Of course, I would love to help you. I probably like shopping much more than your father does. Maybe we should leave him at home. What do you say about that?"

"I think Daddy should come, too, Amanda."

There was a big grin on Rafe's face as he looked first at Julie, then at her new mother.

❈    ❈    ❈

For the next five days, they went on a whirlwind tour of the so-called happy city. Rafe rented a tandem bicycle, put Julie in front, and they joined the throngs of men, women, and children peddling down the flat, bustling thoroughfares of Copenhagen.

"I can't believe all these people on bikes," Rafe exclaimed. "Good that there aren't many hills. Really makes sense to me. We should utilize this mode of transportation more in the states—everywhere. Save on gas."

"If you think there are a lot of bicycles here, Rafe, you should see China. It is absolutely unbelievable. One million people in a city, and nine hundred ninety nine thousands bicycles!" Amanda laughed.

They visited the zoo, ate lunch at the Familiehaverne, and spent hours in the Garden of Tivoli and the amusement park, Bakken.

"Come on," Rafe exclaimed, "We're all going on the rollercoaster. Julie, you can sit in the middle."

"I don't know, Rafe. I don't think so. I'm not too good on those things," Amanda argued.

"Oh, come on, Mandy. I'll hang on to both of you. Okay, I'll sit in the middle. You want to go, don't you, Julie?"

"Yes, Daddy, I'll go with you."

"No, no, I've got to think about this—I've got to think about this, Rafe," Amanda pulled his arm in protest.

"Amanda, there's nothing to be afraid of. You'll be okay. Come on. Julie and I won't let anything happen to you. You'll love it."

"All right, but hang on to me. You will, won't you?"

"Promise," Rafe said.

The attendant buckled them in. "Rafe, do we have to sit in this one, the front seat?"

"I guess so, Mandy. Now, don't worry. You'll be just fine," Rafe grinned.

Amanda and Julie screamed as the roller coaster took the first big drop. It went so fast, and they were visibly shaken when the ride was over. "Everyone okay?" Rafe asked.

"Never again, Rafe! Never again! I...I can hardly catch my breath. Do you realize that there was air between our rumps and the seat? What if the straps had broken?"

"But, they didn't, did they? You'll be okay, Mandy. Knees a bit wobbly, huh?" Rafe teased. "Say, Julie, see those little antique cars over there? I think you would enjoy driving one. We'll watch, and while you drive, maybe Amanda can catch her breath." Rafe arranged for the ride, then joined Amanda to watch as the car went around on the fixed track. They thought that Julie would enjoy the fun and excitement, but she rarely smiled. She simply accommodated them, following like a frightened, chained puppy in a new family.

"Let's walk over by that small lake. The gardens are so lovely," Amanda said.

Julie took her father's hand and when they walked near the merry-go-round, she exclaimed, "Oh, Daddy, look! I just love a merry-go-round. Do you remember the time you took me in Snohomish? Could we all ride on it? Please? I've never seen one as pretty as this one. I'd like to get on that beautiful horse over there."

"Sure, honey. We'll all go. Come on, Mandy—promise, you'll like this better than the roller coaster." Rafe thought, *this is the only indication she has shown all day that she may be experiencing a shred of happiness, a ray of sunshine in her troubled life.* Rafe was more than pleased to accommodate her.

"Rafe, did you realize that there is a Tussaud wax museum here? It probably isn't as large as the one in London, but I'm sure it's good. Let's go in, shall we? I'll bet that Julie would like it, too."

"That's a terrific idea, Amanda. Julie, you've never seen people formed in wax, have you?"

"No, Daddy."

"Well, we must go then," Rafe declared.

The world's biggest yacht race, the Round Zealand Race, was in full swing at the June water carnival. They watched that, as well as the Midsummer Eve on June 23rd, a night of outdoor dancing, singing, feasting, bonfires, and fireworks, like an immense carnival. Julie was wide-eyed, and seemed to enjoy the festivities, but rarely commented or smiled.

The next day they went to the High Bridge, which offered them a great view of many important historical buildings. Rafe played the part of the most knowledgeable guide in Copenhagen, pointing out the round tower, the astronomical observatory built by Christian IV, and numerous other landmarks. Julie politely obliged her father with an occasional, "Yes, Daddy, that is very nice."

They watched the changing of the guard, and visited the Rosenborg Palace. They admired the Dutch crown jewels, and Rafe especially enjoyed seeing the pearl-studded saddle that had belonged to Christian

IV. "That saddle is probably one of the greatest tourist attractions in Copenhagen," he said.

"Well, I can think of a lot of other ways to put those lovely pearls to use!" Amanda laughed.

"Where did they get all of those pearls, Daddy?" Julie inquired.

"From oysters. That's where they come from, Julie. A little piece of sand works its way into the oyster, and the oyster builds that beautiful protection around it, and that becomes a pearl." Rafe added, "Of course, those in the business plant that tiny bit of irritation inside the oyster. It's a big business, especially in the Orient."

"Do you mean in Japan or China? Do pearls cost a lot of money, Daddy?"

"Yes, good ones do—they can be pretty costly. There are all kinds, grades, and colors, but the fine ones are very, very expensive. I think most pearls come from Japan. If you ever hear the name Mikimoto, you know it's a good pearl. In fact, Amanda has a strand of Mikimoto pearls, and I know she would love to show them to you." Rafe was happy and pleased that Julie was showing some interest.

"Rafe, did you know that Victor Borge was born in Copenhagen? I really enjoy him. Have you ever been to one of his performances?"

"No, I haven't, but I've seen him on television. He's really funny, isn't he? Very clever man."

"Who is Victor Borge, Daddy?"

"He's an excellent pianist, and a great entertainer, Julie. Perhaps some time we can go to one of his concerts. You would like him."

"Is he young?" Julie inquired.

"No, I wouldn't say he is very young. I think he'd be in his late 70s now, but you'd like him, anyway."

"Like Mr. Ray," Julie commented in a whisper.

"Yes, about like Mr. Ray, though I don't think Mr. Ray is quite as old, Julie. Mr. Ray must still be in his sixties, I'd say." *So, she's thinking about home. Funny that she should bring up Mr. Ray.*

To keep the conversation going Amanda said, "I was reading a brochure about the city, and it said that the Royal Danish Ballet is one of the oldest major ballet companies in the world. I love ballet, but I certainly haven't had much of an opportunity to attend. Have always wanted to see *Swan Lake*, and every Christmas I say I'm going to *The Nutcracker*, but something always comes up and I've yet to see it."

"Well, I know that Julie would enjoy that, too, and when we get back home, I promise I will take both of you to see *The Nutcracker* before Christmas. Now, don't let me forget," Rafe smiled.

"We'll remind you, won't we Julie?" Amanda affirmed with a smile.

"Yes, Amanda, we won't let daddy forget."

"Know what?" Rafe questioned them both. "One more day of sightseeing in this fair city, and we're going to Switzerland—to Lucerne for about a week. How does that sound? Would you like that, Julie? Amanda, how about you? The Alps are beautiful in the winter, but they're also spectacular in summer."

Amanda replied, "I just love Lucerne. What do you say, Julie?" Anything to break the monotony of sightseeing in Copenhagen. Poor Rafe—he was trying so hard.

"Well," Rafe continued, "Tomorrow, which is our last day here, I'd like to take the electric train out to Sorgenfri. We'll go early in the morning, see the sights, have lunch, and get back to the apartment late in the afternoon. There is an open-air museum there, which covers about forty acres. It's a collection of Danish farms, windmills, and country homes from all over Denmark—all outfitted with authentic furnishings. It's a must for tourists." There was no comment from either Amanda or Julie.

Rafe wondered if he was pushing too hard—too fast. How could he show Julie how much he loved and cared for her? Wasn't it better to keep her busy, to keep her mind off of the past two years?

"And, when will we be leaving for Lucerne?" Amanda asked.

"The reservations still have to be confirmed, but if all goes well we should be on the plane first thing the next morning—about eight at the airport. Think you two can make it that early?"

"Of course, but let me make a suggestion, Rafe. You and Julie go out to Sorgenfri without me tomorrow. It will give me a chance to catch my breath, and put things in order in the apartment. Okay?"

"Is that all right with you, Julie?"

"Sure, Dad," she sighed.

Amanda was relieved to learn that there would be a change of pace, a change of place. Was he trying too hard and pushing too fast? Was he expecting a miracle overnight? Poor dear. Her heart went out to him, and to Julie. She wondered how long it would be before they would learn the truth about the whole sordid affair.

✳ ✳ ✳

During the next week in Lucerne, Rafe and Amanda did all within their power to make Julie feel comfortable and at ease. The three of them, hand in hand, wandered through the picturesque old quarters on the west bank, crossing and re-crossing the centuries-old wooden bridges. They toured the Glacier Gardens, which were full of potholes created during the Ice Age. They saw the famous Lion of Lucerne, a stone carving executed in the early 1800s. The trio took a boat tour of the lake, stopping at many small resorts along the way. Julie seemed to particularly enjoy the tram ride to the top of Mt. Pilatus. How fitting to hear a recording of Rossini's "William Tell Overture," while they enjoyed a marvelous meal in a restaurant high on top of the mountain.

That evening the sun set in a brilliant display of rainbow colors—at first, light shades of blue and pink, then darkening into deeper shades, with streaks of red interrupting the more tranquil, subtle colors. Soon, dark clouds began to gather, and claps of thunder resounded in the distance, each clap louder and louder. Julie hovered close to Rafe. The winds came with interminable force, and lightning crackled across the horizon. It began to rain, gently at first, then in a deluge, giving much needed nourishment to the flora, the tall green grass, and the wild flowers growing on the steep hillsides. They were content and comfortable to be inside. Slowly, the rain subsided, and the moon and one lone star appeared in the heavens.

"Well, that was some cloudburst," Rafe said. "I think it's time to go back down the mountain now that the storm is over. Are you girls ready?" The ride was pleasant, the air refreshing, and a peace and calm settled over the mountain. Rafe looked at Amanda's serene face. Julie was staring out of the window, and though he could not see her face, he sensed that she was smiling—faintly.

The next morning, after a good breakfast, Amanda whispered to Julie, "Would you like to go out for a little walk with me after we do the dishes? This will give your father time to write his letters."

"Sure, Amanda, I will go with you," Julie replied somberly.

"Rafe, Julie and I are going for a hike while you finish your letter-writing. Okay?"

"Fine, that will be fine. You two enjoy yourself."

Julie took Amanda's hand, and the child responded with a firm clasp of her own volition. They walked nonchalantly down the street, picking up their pace as they headed out of the city. Amanda had learned from her research in Denmark about a hospital on the outskirts of Lucerne that treated abused children, and she thought that perhaps they could walk by it. If only she could think of a way to take Julie in.

After they had been walking about half an hour, chitchatting, exchanging pleasantries, Amanda asked, "Julie, do you remember the last day you were with your mother?"

"Yes, I remember, Amanda—we were out in the boat with Neil."

"Who's Neil?"

"Neil was our friend. He was in daddy's class at the college. He came to sit with me, and he would read books to me."

"Do you remember what happened in the boat, Julie?"

At first Julie did not respond. Then she stopped abruptly and looked up at Amanda with tears in her eyes. "Neil was doing something to me that mommy didn't like and she got real mad and came back and grabbed me away from Neil. Then, everything went black. I don't remember what happened after that."

Amanda got down in a crouching position, and put her arms around Julie, "Oh, Julie, I am so sorry, so sorry." *How was she going to handle this? How?*

They walked along in silence for a few minutes. Pointing to some attractive, cottage-like buildings, which were set back from the main road, Amanda spoke, "Julie, do you see those buildings over there?"

"Yes."

"Well, they are really a clinic, a hospital for children, and there are some very nice people in there who would like to help you. I learned all about it when I was in Copenhagen. Do you think you would you like to go in there with me and talk to someone about what happened to you?"

"I don't know, Amanda. I don't know. I suppose I could," she replied reluctantly.

Amanda gently caressed her cheek. It was a maternal gesture, spontaneous and affectionate. "Okay, let's go in and see what it's like, shall we?"


"Well, did you two have a good walk? Your cheeks look like red apples. Come here, Julie, and give your dad a big hug. I've really missed you two, you know—even though you've only been gone a few hours," Rafe exclaimed.

"It was a great walk, Rafe. It is so beautiful here. Now, what are we going to do this afternoon?"

Julie piped up, "Zug is a funny name, Daddy. Did you say we were going there this afternoon?"

"Yes, and we'll take the train. I think you'll both like it very much. We'll go just as soon as we've had a bite to eat." Picking up the letters, he added, "I'll find the post office and get these in the mail right away."

Zug was an ancient walled city, which had an interesting museum of gold and silver works, and crafts of all descriptions. Occasionally, Julie seemed to be genuinely interested. At other times she acted like a frightened kitten, pensive, as if living in another world. Rarely did she smile or laugh. Rafe bought each of them an ornate silver bracelet. "Thank you, Daddy, it is very nice," was her only remark. Her mind seemed to be elsewhere.

One night, alone in their bedroom, four days after their arrival, Rafe, with a dismal look of concern, remarked, "Amanda, we're never going to know the hell that child went through. She's been violated. How long is it going to take for her to get over this anyway? Those poor kids—six of them, all stars in a lurid play, a play with no beginning, no end, no plot, no characterization. And, to think that their pictures have been distributed all over the world, even in the United States!"

"I know, Rafe—I know."

"Isn't it amazing how they hit on the location of the videos? I just can't get over the fact that they knew no other building in Denmark had that particular kind of woodwork." Rafe cupped his chin, deep in thought. "The light fixtures and...and even the door knobs and wallpaper were dead give away. These things actually cracked the case. You know, I'm really frightened," Rafe continued, "and I'm sick to death with all this European liberation in matters of pornography and sex." Amanda put her arms around him and held him close. "Will Julie ever be normal again? How long is it going to take, Mandy?"

"Well, all I can say is that I know it's going to take time, but, I am sure—I just know that she will be all right eventually."

"What do you think we should do, Mandy? I really should get back to Washington. We should, I mean."

"Rafe," Amanda interrupted, "I've been doing a lot of thinking about

Julie, and what would be best for her, and I really feel that you should consider admitting her to that hospital here, the one I mentioned that we had visited briefly the day we were out walking. Remember I told you that I had read about their work when I was researching child abuse in Denmark? Well, when we were out there I felt impressed to go in and have a look around, get a first-hand picture of just what it was really like. At first I wondered how you would feel about it, and I didn't know exactly how to tell you..."

Rafe interrupted, "You actually went in—with Julie? Did you talk to anyone?"

"Yes, we met Doctor Berne, a wonderful, understanding man, and I had a little private conversation with him, while a nurse took Julie out to meet some children. The doctor talked to Julie for just a few minutes, and I felt that she sensed that he wanted to help her. It's not like an ordinary hospital, more like a private estate out in the country. The doctors and staff are wonderful. They understand this type of problem, and they will know how to help her, Rafe. I'm sure that eventually she'll open up, talk about her experiences, and tell us everything. First, however, we have to gain her complete confidence."

Rafe listened intently. "But how in the world can I go back to the states and leave you both here alone? What would you do, Mandy? How long do you think she'll have to stay in the hospital? I can't stand the thought, even for a couple of months, or whatever length of time it would take."

"Rafe, I can assure you that it isn't going to happen overnight. You must not forget that she was in that environment almost two years. The doctors will know, but I'm sure she will need additional therapy for years, Rafe. Didn't you tell me that your friend, Ken, was a psychiatrist or psychologist, who worked with abused children in Washington? Perhaps he will be able to help her."

Thoughtfully, running his hands through his graying hair, Rafe responded, "Yes, Ken's in his own clinic now. Terrific fellow, and a great friend—my best friend, Mandy. Julie loved him, too."

Amanda went on, "Let her stay here for awhile with me, Rafe. Don't you know what they say about Switzerland? Things work here. Everything runs on time—the trains, the boats, the watches. Things rarely get stuck. There's order, Rafe, and people are practical. For the time being I think this is the best place in the world for Julie, and it won't be forever.

She'll have time to adjust—she needs that, and when the doctors feel she's well enough to go back home she can receive additional therapy from Ken and his associates. I'm confident that this would be the best thing for her . . begin her rehabilitation right here...as soon as possible."

Amanda continued as Rafe sat listening intently, deep in thought, "I'll get a room, or an apartment, near the hospital, and continue my writing, but I promise that I'll spend as much time with Julie as they will allow. I'm confident we will get to be good friends—I just know it, Rafe. I think she has accepted me, and I do think she likes me."

"I know that she likes you, Amanda. Perhaps this would be the right thing to do. Yes, I think you're probably right. I'll make the necessary arrangements, and I only hope that Julie will understand and accept the fact that I have to leave without her—for a time. I must go back to Brighton before I leave for the states, and I want to have a long talk with this Doctor Berne before I go. There is so much I don't understand, and I want to know just how they deal with this sort of thing."

"I think that Julie realizes that she needs special help, Rafe. She isn't completely at ease, even with us—yet. It's difficult for her to trust an adult. I'm confident that she will want to stay—if we explain everything to her, and both of us are with her when she has her initial interview. Those doctors will know just what to say, and how to deal with her emotions. Please don't worry, darling, because I know it's going to work out. It will, Rafe!" Amanda touched his arm and looked directly into his eyes, "And, listen, there is something I must tell you before you leave—something Julie told me when we were out walking."

"What? What did she say?"

"Well, as we walked along near the hospital, we were chatting casually, and I asked her if she could recall the last time she and her mother were together. She stopped suddenly. Silence. I waited. I gave her time. I knew she was reluctant to talk, but I was patient and didn't push her. Then she looked up at me with a glimpse of sadness in those gorgeous blue eyes, and she told me that she and Ann were out in the boat with Neil. Do you know a Neil?"

"Yes, yes, of course! He was one of my students. He was a good friend of the family—and he especially loved Julie."

Amanda went on, "Well, she said that Neil and her mother were fighting in the boat. The last thing she remembered was her mom lunging at her and Neil. She reluctantly told me that Neil was doing something to her that made her mother mad. She was ashamed, and all she could do was just bow her head. Rafe, I could have cried. She has such a guilt complex. Then, we stopped and I bent down and put my hands on her shoulders, caressed her cheek, and kissed her on the forehead, and assured her that she would feel better if she could confide in me. I explained about the hospital, that they wanted to help children, and asked her if she would like to go in and see it. She didn't know at first if she would want to do that, but then she agreed to go in. It wasn't until after we had been in the clinic and she had talked to Doctor Berne that she hesitantly told me, in a manner I shall never forget as long as I live, what Neil was doing to her. It wasn't pleasant. It was that which made Ann so angry. Rafe, your friend Neil must be a pedophile."

"A pedophile? Oh, my Lord! No! No! It couldn't be! Neil? He was so fond of Julie. He was one of my best students. He was at our place all the time. He was the best sitter we had." Rafe held his bowed head in both his hands, rubbed his temples. Shivers ran up his spine. "Oh, Amanda, I just can't believe it. How could I have been so stupid, so blind? I was too trusting and I should have known. I'm an idiot!"

Amanda put her hands on his shoulders. "Honey, I asked her why she didn't tell you, and she said she was afraid to tell you because he was your friend, and her mommy liked him, too. That's all she would tell me for now, but she will be able to talk more and more about this as time passes. She has to understand that what happened to her as a little girl was not her fault—not her fault, Rafe. She must accept that fact. She thinks that she is the one who is responsible for what happened between Neil and herself, for having been brought to Copenhagen. I am sure that she feels that she did something very, very bad. That's why she can't talk, not yet. Oh, Rafe, think of what's going through her mind. She must have professional help."

"Yes, yes, I know. You're right, Mandy. Neil—I can't believe it. But now that I think of it, I'm sure Ann had some doubts about their relationship. Oh, I've been so stupid." Rafe talked quietly, as though in another world. His thoughts went back to Ann, to their conversation in the car when they were on the way to Portland, when they trustingly left Julie with Neil for the weekend.

"Rafe, if the doctors can get Julie to talk, to bring everything out into the open, they will be able to help her deal with her fears, and it will no doubt reduce any harm in the future that this terrible experience may have on her. She must be assured, and reassured, that none of this was her fault."

"If only I could get through to her. If only I had stayed home. If only I had not gone to that stupid conference. I've been so blind, so trusting, so foolish. Neil threw Julie to the lions, Amanda! It all makes me so angry! I'd like to throw him into the lion's den. I'd like to get my hands on his throat, and choke the very life out of him."

"Now, Rafe you must not blame yourself for this. Do you understand? It isn't your fault. Don't ever think that. It's so easy to trust those that are close to us. You didn't have a clue that he was that kind of person." Amanda continued, her hand resting on his arm, "Honey, we'll find out what really happened. In the meantime, I think you can put two and two together. Your friend, Neil, must have been responsible for Ann's death. She caught him doing something to Julie in the boat. She must have been furious. Don't you see, Rafe? Julie can't remember clearly much of anything after the fight, until she was on an airplane with a blond lady called Astrid, who was very nice to her. She had given Julie new clothes and she kept telling her not to worry—she would be all right—they were going to a beautiful place to live for a while. And, Rafe, she kept repeating, 'It's all my fault.' Honey, she doesn't know how to tell you, not yet, but she will—someday. Be glad, Rafe, that she's opening up to me. This is the best thing for her. At least, she's beginning to communicate. Please be patient. Try to understand. It's probably easier for her to talk to me—woman to woman, you know."

Rafe ran his fingers through his hair, bit his lower lip, muttered to himself. "How could I ever have been so trusting, so stupid? I put all my trust in Neil, and he betrayed me—betrayed all of us, and especially Julie. I am the one at fault, Amanda. Really—it's all my fault."

"No, no, you must guard against guilt, and your memories of the past have to heal also. They will in time, Rafe," she emphasized.

"Yes, I know—I know you're right, Amanda

"Mr. Langley, thank you for coming. I'm chief of staff, Dr. Berne, and this is my assistant, Miss Lewis." Looking directly at Amanda, he continued, "Mrs. Langley, how are you today? And, Julie?"

"Fine, thank you, Doctor Berne," Amanda replied. Julie said nothing.

The first thing one noticed about Doctor Berne was the fine shape of the head, in spite of the fact that he was bald, except for a dark rim of hair just above the ears. His eyes were dark brown, penetrating, yet kind. He was short in stature, but trim. He was in constant motion, putting his horn-rimmed glasses on when in conversation, taking them off to look at the family, putting them back on when jotting down notes. The doctor walked over to Rafe and extended his hand. "Mr. Langley, let's go into the inner office where we can talk privately. Miss Lewis will show your wife and daughter around the hospital and the grounds." Glancing at Julie, and smiling kindly, he added, "Perhaps Miss Lewis can find an ice cream cone for Julie."

Rafe followed the doctor into an inner office. "I am so happy you called for an appointment, Mr. Langley. Here, please have a seat. I want to have a long talk with you, so that you will better understand what we do here."

Rafe sat in a leather armchair opposite the doctor. "There is so much that I don't understand, Doctor Berne. I really appreciate your time…"

"Not at all, Mr. Langley," the doctor interrupted. That's why we're here. We want to help in any way we can. We want to help Julie."

Rafe immediately felt at ease with Dr. Berne. He liked him, and felt that his concern for Julie was genuine. He liked the way he looked directly into his own eyes.

"Child pornography, Mr. Langley, is one of the worst kinds of child abuse—because the rights of the child are abused. Since it has only recently come to the fore, there is some speculation about therapy for the victims. You know, there is a question today as to whether or not pornography has an affect on children." He sighed deeply and shook his head slowly. "That anyone would even question this is a mystery to me. Wouldn't it be just common sense to assume that the effect is bound to be negative, abusive, and harmful?"

"Yes, I would assume so," Rafe agreed.

"This is going to be difficult for you to accept and understand, Mr. Langley," the doctor continued. "From what I understand about this case, Julie, your daughter, was a prisoner in a estate in Copenhagen. No doubt, they kept her mildly sedated. She was like a captive, and the perpetrators used her as a pawn in a pornographic game of chess. She had always relied on adults for truth—now they were betraying her. Where were her parents? Why didn't they find her?"

"Believe me, Doctor, I tried. I tried. I didn't know which way to turn."

"Yes, I am sure you did. I am sure you did all within your power to try to find her," the doctor acknowledged. "Julie, however, finally accepted her fate, and did exactly what they wanted her to do, because she thought she was being punished for a wrong that she had committed. No doubt, after almost two years, her hope was completely gone. Her life was filled with terror, and yet, in the beginning, perhaps contained an element of mystery to her."

Rafe interjected, "But, Doctor, she was only six years old!"

"I know, I know, Mr. Langley, but even at that age, she may have had mixed feelings. I understand they actually treated her quite well, excluding the acts they forced her to do. For that you can be most grateful."

"Yes, I appreciate that fact. She had good food, was cared for, and— and thankfully, she wasn't beaten. Compassionate pornographers. Now that's what you would call a real oxymoron, isn't it, Doctor?"

"Yes, I suppose you're right. That's a good point."

"Please go on, Doctor Berne."

"Mr. Langley, Julie will have to be rehabilitated, brought back into the world slowly. It will take her a long time to recover completely, but first she must begin to realize that she is important. She must gain back her self-respect. She must be able to trust others again, especially adults. There may always be an expectation of betrayal. She may exhibit traits of behavior unfamiliar to you, her father. She may have nightmares, and when she is older she may experience sexual difficulties. She may never choose to marry. One thing is in her favor, however. She is still very young, so she has a better chance of rehabilitation. She may have horrifying memories, and confusing emotions, such as guilt. She may even miss her abductors at times, and this will trouble her."

"You mean to tell me that she will actually miss those that abused her, Doctor?"

"Yes, in a case such as this, this may be true. Her situation was most unusual, Mr. Langley. The arrangement became a surrogate family to her. She will definitely miss the other children, especially the girls."

"I see," Rafe said quietly.

"Let us just hope and pray that she becomes a fighter, Mr. Langley, not just a survivor of this terrible atrocity."

Rafe sat there, entranced, seemingly in another world, in another timeframe. He visualized the two videos he had seen. He glanced down at his shoes, and shook his head, not knowing what to say.

The doctor went on, "Mr. Langley, I know this is very difficult for you. You are having trouble accepting the fact that this actually happened to your little girl."

"You're so right."

"You will have to work hard at instilling new values in Julie's life after she goes home with you. Remember, her intellect has been violated. She has been exposed to acts of sexual perversion that neither of us could dream possible. You must sympathize with her, try to imagine what she has gone through, but please, please do not pity her. That would make her feel guilty."

Rafe interrupted, "How in God's name could anyone in his right mind be involved in such a thing—with children?"

The doctor shook his head, "I don't know, I can't begin to answer that question, but I'm afraid that today there is a big racket in pornography in all forms, both print and film. Organized crime may be behind much of it, but from what I have read, this is usually not the case. It's a billion dollar business, Mr. Langley. Some people are getting extremely rich exploiting these children. We must rise up in arms and fight it, for the sake of our children, our young people, and our society."

"I find it hard to believe that men could stoop so low, Doctor. What kind of mentality do they have anyway?"

"These men had no feelings as to how Julie might have felt during these lascivious acts. They, no doubt, complimented her with sweet talk. They may have given her lovely gifts to compensate and keep her happy. I don't believe that, in her case, the men or women physically abused your daughter themselves. It was probably always a case of children with children. I believe the oldest boy was thirteen. We must believe that the damage can be repaired. You will have to understand they required them to perform all types and forms of sexual perversion—all done to arouse the adult as he views the picture or the film. Those who see these callisthenic copulations—performed without a sense of respect, beauty, or any kind of affection—may find the promiscuity attractive. They are reprobate, Mr. Langley."

"It's hard for me to believe that there are actually people out there who pay for this kind of thing. It's absolutely sick—money-mad reprobates that's what they are."

"Well," Dr. Berne continued, "the whole thing boils down to this: exploitation of a child for the sexual gratification of an adult. It's as simple as that. The child is used. In my very brief encounter with Julie the other day, I gathered there was probably group sexual activities, but I do not believe she was ever tortured, as is sometimes the case. In some circumstances, Mr. Langley, there have been instances where a child has actually been offered as a sacrifice to Satan after lewd sexual acts. These people did have a certain amount of caring, shall we say?"

Rafe said nothing, but thought, *Caring? Another oxymoron.*

Doctor Berne continued, "Had Julie never been found, sooner or later those in the business would determine that she would not be needed any longer, and at this juncture she would no doubt become a prostitute. This is what happens to most children who have been caught in this web. Thank God she was found."

Rafe shook his head in disbelief. "What a shame. What a filthy shame. Our most important natural resource is our children. They need protection—just like the rivers, the mountains, the trees, and—and all of creation."

"Yes, that is so true. By the way, Mr. Langley, your wife had mentioned to me before, outside of your daughter's presence, that she thought perhaps Julie had had some kind of sexual encounter with a young man, a friend of yours—a student? I believe she said his name was Neil."

"Yes, I'm afraid that's true, Doctor—Neil—Neil Manning—and—and it's really hard for me to accept. You see, he was my student, my assistant, a friend of the family. I trusted him explicitly." Shaking his head in disgust and looking up at the ceiling, he added, "I was so blind, so stupid."

"Your feeling that way is understandable, Mr. Langley."

"Yes, but don't you see? I should have known, I should have known."

The doctor continued, "This Neil, probably through some subtle power, confused Julie when she was very young by telling her over and over that what they did should remain a secret, just between the two of them. It was intellectually impossible for Julie to have assimilated the reality, and the repercussions, of what this young man did to her when she was four or five years old. He no doubt told her that he loved her very much, and was her very best friend. Where is this young man now?"

"I'm not sure, Doctor, but I believe that he may be teaching school by now—probably high school."

"And, I would venture to say, also, that your friend was probably abused in some way himself when he was a child—perhaps emotionally and sexually. Neil was conceivably like a child himself. He was more comfortable with Julie than with an adult relationship. He received too little gratification at his early age of development. He probably dreamed and fantasized about her. Mr. Langley, it was a play, and he was rehearsing, preparing himself for stardom at a later date when he would be happily married himself. He was sexually and socially immature, and very naive."

Rafe simply shook his head in agreement.

The doctor continued, "God help you, Mr. Langley. I hope you can bring him to justice, but let me warn you that it is extremely difficult to prove in a court of law that this Neil committed a sexual offense against your daughter. I hope that eventually everything involving the death of your first wife, Julie's kidnapping, Neil's involvement—all of it will be unveiled, and that justice will be served."

"Yes, I hope so. I truly hope so, Doctor."

"If you will agree to allow Julie to remain here with us we will work with her, and do our very best for her. Her normal behavioral attitudes have been reversed, you know. Her mind has even been affected to some degree. Natural love and affection have been repressed. She doesn't completely trust anyone anymore. My staff and I will have to first gain her confidence, and then let her know that we love and care for her. We will try to instill the correct values, Mr. Langley. It will take time, but let me assure you that those that work here are dedicated; this is one of the finest facilities of its kind in the world. We only ask that you will be patient and give us the support we need. And when we feel she is ready for the next step, we will suggest that she remain here for a time as an outpatient."

"Thank you, Doctor, thank you. I have every confidence that you will be able to help her."

"I understand that your new wife will remain here in Lucerne?"

"Yes, that is correct. She will be available to help whenever you need her. Perhaps Julie will be able to stay with her on weekends, or at least see her...."

The doctor interrupted, "Yes, we want her to have a close contact with her family. She needs a supportive environment. Perhaps Julie could take ice skating lessons with other children her age. I imagine that she could live with your wife, eventually, and be an outpatient, coming here for treatment a number of times a week."

"I would like that very much," Rafe interjected.

"Your wife is a lovely woman, Mr. Langley—extremely understanding and kind. I sensed that Julie liked her and I do believe that she trusts her. Their relationship is vitally important in her rehabilitation."

"Yes, I am really happy about that. Amanda is a wonderful person. I don't know what I would have done without her, Doctor. It was she who really found Julie in Copenhagen, you know. It was she who insisted that we come here."

"Yes, yes, I assumed as much. And you, Mr. Langley? What are your immediate plans?"

"Well, as much as I hate to say this, and as much as I dread leaving, it is imperative that I go back to Brighton for a week or two before returning to the States. I have a lot of work to do, but, I feel so guilty leaving. I'm not sure that I'm doing the right thing."

"This may be best for Julie, Mr. Langley. You may as well take care of your business in Brighton, and go on to Washington to get everything ready for them because we would like to work with her for a time without any family intervention. I don't mean to sound harsh, but we have discovered that it is sometimes better if immediate members of the family—those the child shares a history with—are not in close contact in the beginning of her treatment and rehabilitation. Do you understand?"

"Yes, I guess so. I understand—but it's hard to accept." Rafe smiled.

It was the first time he smiled since he began his conversation with the doctor. His thoughts turned to Neil, and the smile faded away.

The doctor rose, ending the conversation, "God go with you, Mr. Langley. I'm sure you will make the correct decisions. And, remember, your daughter cannot be expected to instantly reintegrate. Time, Mr. Langley, time—give her that."

"Yes, Doctor, I will. Thank you very much. You have been very kind, and I think I understand the situation much better now."

"All right then. Let us go into the outer office where my secretary will draw up the necessary documents for you to sign." The doctor put his hand on Rafe's shoulder. "Come this way, Mr. Langley."


It was Monday, July 22, 1985. Rafe, determined to take Amanda and Julie out for a very special evening, decided on a picturesque Swiss restaurant. They sat by the fireplace at a heavy oak table, dipping chunks of French bread into the delicious cheese fondue. Singers in authentic Swiss costumes stood by their table and yodeled. Julie was especially captivated by the young man who played the accordion. She was delighted when he came right over to their table, and stood in front of her, his eyes twinkling, a big grin on his robust face. And, there, just for Julie, he sang.

"I like it here, Daddy. I love the music."

"I'm glad, Julie." Rafe was pleased.

"Mm, this is good," Julie exclaimed, as a drop of the melted cheese landed on her chin.

"You really like the fondue, Julie?" Rafe responded with a twinkle in his eye.

"Yes, Daddy. I've never had this before."

Their meal was superbly prepared, and served by a colorfully costumed waitress. They ate amid splendidly carved wood decor, with large brass kettles and pots hanging on the walls and from the ceiling.

Amanda glanced up while holding the long fork in the fondue pot. "Rafe, do you remember my assignment on the *Hitler Diaries* in Hamburg? Well, I heard that Kujau, Heidemann, and Edith Liebland were all convicted and sentenced. I tried to interview them last September, remember?"

"Yes, I remember, Amanda. It was a most bizarre intriguing case. What's happened now?"

"Woops! I lost my bread." She took another piece and carefully ran the long fork through it. "Well, I heard that Kujau got four-and-a-half years, and the *Stern* reporter, Heidemann, received four years and eight months for fraud in procuring the sixty volumes for the periodical. Kujau's girlfriend got eight months probation for receiving stolen property—some of his earnings from the forgeries."

"Amanda, what's a forgery?" Julie was listening intently.

"Honey, it's a fraudulent imitation of the real thing. In other words, this man who wrote the diaries, supposedly another person's—Hitler—made it all up. He was pretending to be Hitler. The diaries were fakes—they weren't real."

"But why would they do that?" Julie inquired.

"Well, to make a lot of money, I guess. You see, they sold these diaries to a German magazine called *Stern* for over three million dollars. And, it was all phony–not true—fake."

"That's a lot of money, isn't it?"

"It surely is, Julie—a lot of money." Amanda smiled at her, pleased that she was interested.

Rafe asked, "How many judges were on that panel, Mandy? Do you remember?"

"Five, I believe," Amanda replied. "Of course, each of the defendants claimed he had been deceived by the other about the origin of the volumes."

"Will there be an appeal?"

"I think the attorneys said they would appeal the sentences. I did hear that Heidemann would be allowed to go free, pending his appeal, but that Kujau would probably have to stay in jail because of an arrest warrant for tax evasion against him in Stuttgart." Amanda continued, "I guess Edith Liebland is so sick and tired of the whole mess she wants to just forget about it. However, she did comment that her boyfriend admitted that he did write the diaries, so he knew he would have to serve some time. Kujau claims that he did not know that *Stern* was buying the forgeries, and that Heidemann always did know who had actually written them."

"What's happened with *Stern*?" Rafe inquired.

"Oh, they're still publishing, of course, but they fired Heidemann two weeks after the government declared that the diaries were fraudulent. Kujau has already written a book about it, *I Was Hitler*, and now he says he's going to write another one about what really happened. Can you believe it? He got so involved in this whole thing that he almost thought he was Hitler! I can't imagine such a thing."

"Well, they say that if you hear something long enough, or if you're told a particular thing over and over, you actually begin to believe it. I suppose it would be the same way with this forgery business. He did such a good job on it, and put so much into it, that he actually began to believe it was all for real. Crazy, isn't it?" Rafe shook his head.

"Yes, and now Heidemann is going to write a book, too. He maintains that important information was withheld in the trial. Honestly, it seems to me that so many criminals have a way of making still more money—from books, interviews, movies. Can you imagine how many books have been written in prison?"

"You're so right, Mandy, and I suppose if they do write books, that they'll be bestsellers. The public eats up this sort of garbage. Then, after their books are published, they'll sell them to some big producers in Hollywood, who will in turn make another bundle—for themselves and the crooks."

"Unfortunately, that's about the way things go in this day and age," Amanda agreed. "Heidemann says," Amanda continued, "that West German intelligence agents, who were also involved in the hoax, got off scot-free. He tried to tell them this in the trial. I actually heard him say it, but, naturally, no one would listen."

"Have they found all the money yet?" Rafe was genuinely interested.

"No, but I guess *Stern* has reporters trying to trace it. They have leads pointing to South America and Spain. The court believed, but had no evidence to show, that Heidemann had kept almost half the money. I guess the judge really reprimanded *Stern* in no uncertain terms for printing their so-called scoop without first making sure the diaries were authentic. I'm sure Charlie would think that pretty stupid business."

"Well, it is pretty stupid, " Rafe agreed.

"It seems to me that South American countries are forever in the news when it comes to hiding some criminal, or their money."

"Yeah, and I'll warrant that each of the defendants in the case will emerge and still make a lot of money," Rafe laughed. "It's all so ridiculous, so ludicrous."

Amanda and Rafe glanced over at Julie, who had been listening intently, quietly, deep in thought. Rafe rose, "Well, are you two gals ready to go?"

"Yes, Daddy, I'm ready," Julie said somberly.

Amanda was lying on Rafe's arm in bed. "Honey, when Julie goes into the hospital, I'm going to fly back to Copenhagen and take care of some business, wrap things up, and give up the apartment. Dr. Berne indicated that he felt it would be for the best if neither of us was around Julie too much in the beginning. Then, later, she'll be with me more and more—maybe become an outpatient. Do you think it will be okay if I leave for a few days?"

"Yes, I've been wanting to talk to you about that. Do you think you'll have a problem finding a little place here for a couple of months? I can hardly stand the thought of leaving you and Julie behind. I hope that it's no longer than that."

"It will only take me a few days, and I'll be back. I've already done some inquiring, and I think I can get a small apartment about a mile from the hospital. I can walk back and forth, and if the doctors will allow Julie to leave, she could spend time with me there. Say, maybe I'll bring my bike here. I could ride back and forth to the hospital."

"That's a great idea. Doctor Berne explained to me that it would be for the best if neither of us is around in the beginning of her rehabilitation, and then later she could be with you. It will be hard to leave her with them, but I do think she will understand, and it will give both of us time to do what has to be done."

"It sounds encouraging, Rafe. I have every confidence in their work."

"What will you do here, Mandy?"

"Well, I think that Charlie wants me to write some articles about the Swiss government—how the twenty cantons work, and he mentioned that I could look into the country's defense system, point out the differences in their educational system and the judicial system—just whatever I might find interesting. It won't be difficult. Might be a bit boring, so it will be a challenge to make it interesting to our readers. I'll have to think of some way to spice it up a bit," she laughed. Amanda continued, "One thing I thought I might do is write a follow-up on the porn business, without mentioning names or places. Perhaps I could use Julie as an example—talk to the doctors and counselors at the hospital, the nurses, some of the patients. That is, if they would allow it."

"Do you really feel that would be wise, Amanda?"

"Honey, Julie would never be implicated."

"Well, I suppose it would be all right, if nothing is written specifically about her." Rafe kissed her over and over, as if he would never again have the opportunity. He held her close, and Amanda had never known such happiness, such complete fulfillment.

"I love you, Rafe," she whispered in his ear.

"I love you, too, darling—more than you will ever know."


The day before Rafe was to leave for the States, he and Julie went for a long walk together. As he held her hand firmly in his own, he asked, "Julie, honey, do you think you could tell me a little bit about that place you lived in when you were in Copenhagen? Before we found you?"

"What, Daddy?"

"Well, how many kids did you live with in the estate?"

"There were two other girls and three boys," Julie replied hesitantly.

"Did you like the other kids? Were you all friends?"

"Yes, Monique was always very nice to Kari and me. She was the oldest girl. We studied English together, and I used to even help her, and we studied numbers, too. Monique was from Paris. She had freckles and red curly hair, Daddy."

"Who were your teachers?" Rafe inquired.

"We just had one teacher—Astrid."

"Did you like Astrid?"

"Yes, she was on the plane with me. Mr. Jenson was there, too."

"Mr. Jenson?"

"Yes, he told us what to do, and took pictures of us, and made movies, too."

"Julie, did Mr. Jenson ever hurt you?"

"No, Daddy, he never hurt any of us. He just told us what to do and took pictures, and he had a black patch over his eye."

"A patch? Why?"

"I don't know. He just had a patch on it. Maybe he didn't have an eye there. I don't know for sure."

"Did Kari tell you where she was from?"

"She told us that she lived in Oslo, Norway, and that she was taking skating lessons. Her father was a professor, and her mother was a school teacher, and she was going to go on a field trip on a boat with her mother's class after school started."

"Did you like Kari?"

"Oh, yes, we were best friends. We played together whenever we could. I really liked Kari."

"What about the boys, Julie?"

"Well, there was Hans. He was the oldest boy, and then there were Alex and Alberto. They cried a lot, and so did Kari, and so did I. But, I think that Hans liked being there. So did Monique. One time they said that they would never want to go back to Frankfurt and Paris. Maybe they didn't have a nice mommy or daddy. I don't know why."

"Honey, did you always have enough to eat? Did you have to sleep together?"

"We always had lots of food, and we could eat all we wanted. I liked the food, Daddy. Mrs. Wickstrom was the cook, and sometimes she would make cookies for us. We could go into the kitchen and have cookies and milk. And, she made good homemade bread, and abelskivers. Do you like abelskivers, Daddy? Do you know what they are?"

"No, I don't think I do. Well, on the other hand, maybe I have eaten them. I think your mother made them once, and we put blackberry jam on them. What were yours like?"

"Well, they were cute, little, round cakes—like muffins—you know—and we ate them with lingonberries. Daddy, I just loved Mrs. Wickstrom. She was so nice and round, and she smelled good, and her skin was so soft and pink. One time she hugged me, and my cheek touched hers. That's how I know she was smooth. She didn't speak very much English, though. Only Kari could really understand her very well. We all liked Mrs. Wickstrom."

"Where did you sleep, Julie?"

"Upstairs. We each had our own room, and we each had a twin bed, and a bathroom, and we could go out into our parlor room and play games quietly, or read, or watch television. Sometimes there would be a program from America, like we had at home. I couldn't understand the Danish programs very well. One time I saw *Little House on the Prairie*."

"You did? Julie, did you ever go outside?"

"Sometimes we would go out in the backyard and play with a ball, or play a game of tag, like Neil and I used to play on the beach, and one time we had our lunch out on the grass. It was a beautiful, warm, sunny day. There was a big high wall around the yard so we couldn't see over it. Most of the time we just stayed inside."

"Julie, did Mr. Jenson have a wife?"

"I don't know. I don't think so. He spent a lot of time with Hans. I think he liked Hans the best."

"Do you remember seeing any other adults, honey?"

"Mr. and Mrs. Rosenberg were there, but we didn't see very much of them. Then, there was Mia, the maid. She was nice to all of us, too. We saw a man one day working outside, and he drove a big car once in a while, too. I think he lived over the garage, and one time I saw a lady out by the garage, and I think she was married to him."

"Did you see people come and go, Julie?"

"No, but we heard cars and car doors slamming sometimes, and then we could hear the doorbell chime. I think people came to buy the films we made."

"Julie, can you tell me some of the things they made you do?"

Julie stopped abruptly and withdrew her hand. Her eyes filled with tears, and her bottom lip quivered like an arrow shot from a hunter's bow. She just shook her head. Looking up at her father, she asked, "Can we go back to our room now, Daddy?" She pleaded, pulling on his sweater sleeve. "Please, let's go back now."

Rafe thought at that moment that his heart would burst. He bent to give her a hug and said, "Yes, Julie, let's go and see if Amanda has a nice cold drink for us. I know she bought some cookies the other day." Taking her hand, they turned and began to retrace their footsteps.

It had been only three weeks since they had arrived at the Lucerne airport. It had seemed more like three months. There were no tears shed at the parting. Instead, a long, deep look of complete trust and understanding passed between them. The tall, handsome, prematurely gray-haired man held the woman in his arms, and kissed her tenderly. Then turning, he hugged the beautiful, young, raven-haired girl. They clung together for a long time. Then, the man released her, and held her back so that he could look directly into her eyes. He gave her a reassuring smile, pinched her nose, kissed her on the forehead, turned, and walked to the gate to board the flight to London. Amanda, with her soft hazel eyes and shiny dark brown hair, took the child's hand; they stood together watching the attendant check the man's boarding pass. Rafe turned and waved. There was a smile on his face, and he blew them each a kiss. The woman and child smiled and waved, and blew him kisses, but before they turned to go, the man suddenly ran back to the attendant's desk and shouted, "Amanda, now I know who you remind me of! I'll tell you when you come home!" With a big grin, he turned and disappeared down the carpeted ramp.

After a lengthy dialogue with Charlie, they agreed that Amanda should write follow-up articles on the treatment and rehabilitation of the child abuse victims. The hospital administration gave her permission to interview doctors, nurses, counselors, and to talk to a few of the children who were patients in the hospital. The professionals were exceptionally helpful and cooperative; from the conversations Amanda had with the children, she gained a new perspective of the problem. Charlie had mentioned that reader interest was extremely high, and this gave her much encouragement.

Amanda concluded her summary article.

The importance of the sexual victimization of children cannot be over emphasized. Myths abound, and though we live in a sexually liberated society today, the subject of sexually abused children is real, not a half-truth. It is time for society to accept the truth, to lift its head out of the sand, to become aware of what is going on in the world, to cast aside its ignorance, to confront the problem—to punish the adult, not the child.

It is a sick society where so-called researchers and some psychologists insist that there is no harm in adults having sexual relationships with children, that the relationships may even be advantageous for the child. It is time to prosecute the organized associations in our country, as well as in foreign countries, who advocate and practice this atrocity. Research has shown that the sexual molestation of children is harmful and transmissible, and may carry over into adulthood. Where is it all going to end? It has become a vicious circle, a disease transmitted from one individual to another, and for society to treat it as though it does not exist is in itself a form of abuse.

Charlie commended Amanda on her coverage and editorial commentaries, and told her to go ahead on the Switzerland articles.

Rafe settled back in the window seat of the 747 and gazed out onto a world of billowing, snow-white clouds. Off in the distance he visualized an absolutely magnificent mountain range, but no, it was only a cloud formation. His thoughts went back to his childhood—a warm summer day, lying on the freshly mowed green grass, gazing up at the sky, dreaming that he was riding on one of the largest of the frosty looking clouds. He visualized all kinds of animals—lambs, poodles, ah, such perfect little white poodles. From his vantage point he observed the earth below, and pondered where he would like to live. His imagination had taken him all over the world.

"Sir, would you like something to drink?" the smart-looking, gracious young stewardess asked.

"Yes—yes, thank you very much. I'd like a soda, please."

Rafe sipped the cold drink, and popped some peanuts into his mouth. His thoughts turned to Julie. *How long would it be until she could come home and live a normal life again? Would her life ever be normal, really normal? Would the truth ever be revealed? What was Neil's connection with this man who wore a patch over one eye? Was Neil implicated in some way with the Copenhagen link in the porn ring? All of the adult participants at the estate were in custody, but who really controlled the racket? Was it organized crime? Thank God the children were not tortured in any way—or were they, and are they just too afraid to tell their stories? The perpetrators seemed to have had some degree of compassion, which was hard to comprehend. Someone in the estate had a concern for their welfare, but compassion?*

*What about the two older children, those who came from the streets in the first place? Hans—Monique—beautiful teenagers. What would be their fate? The streets again? A life that could be much worse, one that would only lead to disease, death, and final destruction? Was there any help, any hope at all, for them? The dark-haired boy, Alberto, handsome little fellow, would go back to his family in Florence. His parents could afford a psychiatrist, so there was at least a glimmer of hope for his rehabilitation. Alexander's parents were very wealthy, and they, too, could seek professional help. Would these young boys carry the marks of their abuse throughout their lives? As adults, would they abuse others? And, the lovely, beautiful Scandinavian girl, Kari, with the thick blond braids and sad eyes—how would she adjust to a normal life again? Would her ice skating help her to forget? Would these children have horrifying nightmares and memories for the rest of their lives? Would they be depressed, distant, unable to relate to their peers? Would they experience guilt beyond repair because of the sexual acts they were forced to perform in front of a camera? Would they harbor grief over the loss of what might have been a better life? Would they feel guilty because they actually enjoyed life at the estate at times? Would they feel that they, too, should be prosecuted for having participated in these lascivious acts?*

*Hmm—prosecuted. No, no, not the children, not the children, but the perpetrators—oh, they should pay dearly—pay and pay, pay and pay. They should each be locked up for life. The main characters in the fiasco—Jenson, the Rosenbergs—oh, yes, they should be punished all right—really punished. And, Neil—Neil.* Rafe's hands tightened in a steel grip. Every tendon was as taut as the strings on a mandolin. He realized his nails were digging into his palms. He felt such a surge of anger when he thought of Neil—and that man, Jenson—the guy with the patch over his eye.

"Sir? Sir—your dinner?"

"Oh—oh, yes—I'm sorry—here—now you can put it down. Thank you, Miss. Thank you." He drained the glass and shattered a chunk of ice with his teeth.

"Kim! Ken! You look wonderful! So good of you to meet me!" Rafe hugged and kissed Kim on the cheek, and gave Ken a bear hug. Ken guided the two of them away from the crowds, who were greeting friends and family, down the freshly polished concourse, to the escalator leading to the electric tram that would transport them to the luggage area.

Ken exclaimed, "It's just great to see you again, Rafe. I can't say that England was too hard on you, my friend, but hey, where'd you pick up those gray hairs?"

Rafe, with a twinkle in his eye, replied, "Oh, I just thought it would make me a bit more distinguished looking, so I put in an order for them. Kim, do you like my new look?"

"Do I? Yes, I'd like any kind of look on you, Rafe. Must say it makes you more handsome and better looking than ever."

There was a lot of small talk and chitchat about the Ripley family and mutual friends, until they got into the car, and headed north on I-5.

"Say," Rafe asked, "Do you ever see our friend, Neil Manning? Did he graduate?"

"Yes, he graduated," Ken replied, "But we don't see much of him around here anymore. I heard that he accepted a position teaching in a high school up in the valley somewhere, a small school I suppose."

Kim interrupted, "We heard that he sticks pretty much to himself. He was going with some girl up in Bellingham, but that broke off. As far as we know he's never married."

Ken added, "Someone told me that he taught all of the science classes in his high school. Guess you could say he was the head of the department—the only head!" They all chuckled. "You thought a lot of him, didn't you, Rafe? I remember the first time he came across on his boat to Whidbey—our last picnic of the season—he must have been a sophomore then, or a junior—I don't know. You got to be pretty good friends, didn't you? I know Julie thought he was something else—guess because he spent hours with her—reading, taking her out in the boat, swimming with her, playing ball, picking up agates and shells."

Rafe appeared deep in thought, then slowly replied, "Yes, we did become good friends as a matter of fact. Julie just loved him, and…" He didn't complete the sentence. "Well, I'll have to look him up. He was very helpful at Ann's funeral, and led one of the search parties for Julie, you know. Then, his father called and asked him to come back to the farm to help, so he took off, even before I left for England. He was a quiet, thoughtful kid—got good grades—couldn't always tell what he was thinking. Ann really liked having him around. He'd help with the dishes, even picked blackberries with us. Where'd you say he was teaching?"

Ken replied, "Oh, some wide spot in the road on highway two, up near the mountains—Gold Bar, Sultan, Startup—one of those small places. I don't know just where the high school is located, but I suppose the kids come in from all around that part of the country."

Rafe allowed the subject of Neil to drop. "How's Mike doing? Let's see—he'd be about fourteen now, wouldn't he? I suppose he's a freshman."

Ken proudly extolled Mike's accomplishments. "He's a terrific kid, Rafe—on the basketball team—really tall for his age, but with good coordination. He gets pretty good grades, especially in math, and declares math his favorite subject—next to girls. And, Rafe, speaking of girls, just wait 'til you see Erin. She's ten now, and in the fifth grade—has Kim's hair and eyes, my nose—poor kid—and height. We think she'll be a basketball player, too, though right now she's interested in figure skating. We have a new indoor rink, you know—best thing the town ever did for the kids. She imagines herself a Dorothy Hamill some day. You'll fall for her, Rafe."

Rafe smiled in agreement and thought of Julie—and Kari. Julie had said that the Norwegian girl had been a figure skater. He wondered if she were skating again—in Oslo.

"Say, do you suppose the Cascade Inn would be a good place for me to stay for a few days? I just can't make myself go back to the house—yet."

Kim spoke up, "The Cascade Inn? No way are you going to stay at an inn or a motel or a hotel. You're going to come right home with us, and stay just as long as you would like. Hear? You know we have an extra bedroom. We wouldn't think of anything else, Rafe."

"But, I don't want to impose. You're all busy. Well, it would be nice—just don't fuss over me. I'll come and go—I can eat out most of the time."

Kim replied, "We'll see about that."

Ken and Kim were like family to Rafe, but he had not written to tell them about Amanda and Julie. He couldn't explain why. Perhaps he had a guilt feeling since they had been so close to Ann. He wondered if he should tell them now. No, he'd wait for just the right time.

"Listen, friend, use the station wagon any time you need transportation." Ken added, "It just sits most of the time, and it would be good if it were driven."

"Thanks, Ken—I'll take you up on that."

When Rafe came in one morning, after having been gone over an hour, Kim noticed the drained expression on his face. She had the distinct feeling that he was concealing a hurt, but that it wasn't the time to share—yet. He told her that he had been out to the house, and could not believe how the blackberries had taken over everywhere. "They are about the best protection one could want, Kim. Would you believe, long feelers have grown across the front doors and some of the vines have gone as high as the roof, following the post-supports up? I'm going to have quite a job clearing them out and cutting them back. I think I'll just get rid of all of them." Somehow, he couldn't stand the thought of blackberries around the house anymore.

After dinner that evening, while enjoying a cup of coffee in the living room, Rafe said, "I've got something really important to tell both of you. I met a wonderful woman in Europe and we were married in Brighton over the Easter vacation…"

Kim interrupted, "You're *married*? Rafe, that's wonderful! How could you ever keep the secret so long?"

"I wanted to wait and tell you in person. You will both love her. Her name is Amanda Cates—well, Amanda Langley now. She is a reporter on the staff of *Today's World*. It's a magazine published in San Francisco.

"Wow! You stinker—keeping that terrific news from us! But, hey, I've read that magazine many times, Rafe, and yes, I'm familiar with that name," Ken replied.

"Well, where is she? Why didn't she come home with you?" Kim questioned.

"It's a long story, Kim. She stayed in Lucerne to be near Julie."

"*Julie*? Julie? Oh, Rafe, is Julie alive? How? What happened to her? Where has she been? You'd better start talking, friend. You have a lot of explaining to do!"

Talking late into the night, Rafe told them the whole story, how he and Amanda met, what she was writing about, their marriage, the videos, and how they found Julie. The Ripleys were flabbergasted and speechless. They could hardly believe that Rafe had actually found her while watching a video. It was a real miracle, and a definite answer to prayer.

Ken remarked. "You know, Rafe, I've worked with many child abuse victims, and I'd be happy to counsel and continue to work with Julie when she gets home.

"Do you mean to tell me that there is a problem with child abuse even here?" Rafe asked.

"You would be amazed to know just how much of a problem we do have, Rafe," Ken replied. "It's everywhere—a plague. It's—it's downright criminal….and a really big problem—right here."

"Amanda and Julie will be coming home in a couple of months, I hope. Julie is in a hospital on the outskirts of Lucerne that deals with these problems. The doctor there was very encouraging, and I have every confidence in the staff. I am certain she is just where she should be at this time, and I am confident they will be able to help her."

"I've read about that hospital, Rafe, and I understand it is one of the best to be found anywhere. They have a terrific reputation in dealing with this sordid business," Ken assured him.

"Say, Ken, do you suppose I could borrow the station wagon for awhile tomorrow? I'd like to take a drive up in the valley and look up Neil Manning. Also, I want to look around for a car for myself. Do you like your wagon?"

"You drive it for awhile before you make any decisions—see how you like it. It's great for a second car, and Rafe, you don't have to be in a hurry to buy, you know. Use it whenever you want. Just keep the keys—and don't lose them," he chuckled.

"Thanks so much. You guys are really something else. As I've said a hundred times before, I don't know what I'd do without you two. You're the best friends in the world. I'll never forget how you stood by me when Ann…" but, he didn't complete the sentence. They both understood.

Summertime in the Pacific Northwest could be miserable—wet, overcast, and extremely chilly, or it could be clear and sunny, with temperatures reaching into the 70s, 80s, and on rare occasions, in the 90s and even the 100s. Rafe enjoyed the forever-changing climate. He thought the Snohomish Valley one of the most peaceful pastoral scenes in the world, with the Snohomish River meandering lazily through the valley toward Puget Sound. He loved looking out over the green, fertile fields, the rolling hills and slopes, robed with the stately Douglas fir and the western hemlock. Cattle—black and white, red and white, or brown—dotted the pastures, barely moving as they munched the green grass. Rows of poplar trees acted as windbreaks out in the fields, standing as sentinels, guarding the livestock.

As Rafe drove east, he looked south across the valley to the Monroe Reformatory on the hill above the old highway. His thoughts went back to his childhood, to the stories his mother and father told about their teenage years.

Fry's Lettuce Farm, said to be the largest lettuce farm in the world at that time, covered a great portion of the valley. Though his parents knew each other in high school, it wasn't until that summer in the early thirties, while working at the farm, that they first experienced love. The small crew of eager workers in their group talked about the reformatory, conjuring fascinating, preposterous tales of hard-nosed criminals behind the high walls. "You kids quit talking and keep on weeding!" the foreman shouted.

Rafe grinned as he recalled his parents talking about those days on that farm. His mother had weeded lettuce for ten cents an hour the first summer, for fifteen cents an hour the second summer. *Poor Margaret, I'll never forget the day she tied a bandanna around her chest, fastened it in the back of her neck, and exposed her back to the sun. You should have seen her back at the end of the day. I have never seen such blisters in all my life. They were bigger than silver dollars. We all felt so sorry for her."* His mother's voice was so clear, so distinct in the recesses of his mind. *"And, Rafe, you should have seen the blisters on my knees. I had to tie rags round and round them. What a time we did have. You know, the first time I went out there I was only thirteen, and they weren't going to let me work because we were supposed to be fifteen. I just begged them to let me join the other kids, and when they did, I determined that I would stay out in front of the rest of the kids, work harder, cover more rows. I did, too, and they allowed me to stay on."* Rafe could still see her lovely smile.

It was a time when young people vied for work with the migrant workers. It was a time of depression, when every dime earned helped to feed and clothe a family. It was a time when kids picked wild berries to sell, when they went into the raspberry and strawberry fields to earn extra money. They received two cents a pound for the raspberries, but no one seemed to care how much they ate while working. They were happy to have been hired, and they hoarded the coins for something important, like a pair of jeans for $1.49, or dress material for ten and fifteen cents a yard. Cotton, wool, silk, and linen were sold in the yardage department of the J. C. Penney store. Rayon and nylon were unheard of at the time.

He heard his father's voice, *"Son, I hoed an entire acre of sugar beets for one dollar. Yep, they paid us a silver dollar for each acre, and I was determined to do one in a day. I was really proud of my self because I beat all the migrant workers."*

*"Gee, Dad, that was terrific. Did you have blisters on your hands?"*

*"Yes, I did, son, and I have to admit that I didn't go back the next day. That was a dollar well earned. I can't believe how far a dollar went in those days. Surely different now."* Rafe thought, *if only I could have them back for just one day. I would gladly give a day of my life for a few hours with them.*

Rafe's mother laughed when she told of the time she went into the woods where there had been a fire to pick the little wild blackberries. She filled her bucket and then went to a neighbor to see if she would like to buy them. How much did she ask for the full bucket? Twenty-five cents! When she got back home to tell her mother about it, her mom had a fit. Those little berries were a prize and to think that she sold them for a quarter! Rafe's mother exclaimed, "I never lived that mistake down!"

The rains came often to cleanse the earth, to give this part of the world a freshness, a newness one could not experience in an arid climate. As Rafe drove east on highway two, the valley narrowed and the mountains closed in. He noticed the leaves of the alders shimmering in the sun, and the blackberries in abundance everywhere—in the pastures, covering the fences, climbing an occasional tree, or completely engulfing an old building.

It was mid August 1985. School would convene in most small towns the day after Labor Day. Neil had returned from his parents' eastern Washington wheat farm to work on his own diminutive "stump ranch" near the Cascade Mountains, located about two miles north of the main highway over Steven's Pass. He had wanted to repair and shingle the roof of the shed before it caved in, and he intended to prune the blackberry vines around the four-room log house, as well as out by the barn. The vines were especially wild on the western side of the shed, growing densely on the slope leading to the gulch; many of the vines reached as high as the roof. It was definitely a challenge keeping the blackberry vines under control.

Rafe was deep in thought, enjoying the lush beauty of the countryside as he drove the stationwagon east. He whispered, "God help me control my emotions. Help me to know exactly what to do, what to say." Reminiscing, he recalled Ann's happiness at her celebration party. He saw Julie and the other children the first time Neil came across on his boat from Camano Island. He saw her face before going to the conference in the east. Julie, jumping up and down in her excitement, exclaiming, *"Oh, Daddy, please bring me a present! Will you, Daddy? Please!"* He could not erase the indelible impression inscribed in his mind when he recognized her in that lurid film, the physical and emotional pain he felt then, as well as later when he found her. He could hear her cry, *"Daddy! Daddy! Please don't leave me!"* How broken he was when her little arms reached around his waist, her lithe body shaking, convulsing in deep, agonizing sobs. Later, he had tried so desperately to understand her silence, her pensive moods, but rarely could he find the right words to say to her, his only child.

Rafe thought he had probably driven too far. He pulled over to the Gold Bar Gas Station and Grocery, got out, and walked into the small country store. A friendly young man was working behind the counter. "What can I do for you today?"

"I'd like a package of Double Mint, please. By the way, do you happen to know a young teacher around here by the name of Neil Manning? He teaches science in high school, I believe."

"Yeah, I had him last year in school. I worked on his car, too. But, school hasn't started yet—day after Labor Day."

"I know," Rafe responded. "By any chance, do you know where his place is located?"

"Sure, but you've come too far east. Here, I'll draw you a map." The young man drew a simple map showing Rafe the way to Neil's place. "This should do it for you. Now, don't get lost, Mister. Just go back west on the highway and go through Startup and Sultan, and on the other side of Sultan, on the right side of the road, you'll come to a metal build-ing—I think it's painted blue and white. Well, Rice Road is there, and you just hang a right on it, and follow the map from there on. You can't miss it."

"Thank you. You've been a great help, and I appreciate it." Rafe walked out of the store and jumped into his car.

The young man was correct. Rafe had little difficulty finding Rice Road. As he drove down the gravel top, he noticed the flourishing, pro-fuse, large blackberry clusters. They were everywhere, and the dark, pur-ple berries still hung in clumps, waiting to be picked. He glanced at his watch, noting that the minute hand moved listlessly forward. This gave him more time to think, to orchestrate a plan, a perfect plan. He must be discreet. He must take it easy. He must act, yes, act normal.


Neil was out cutting wood when Rafe drove up. As the car pulled into the yard, he looked up and squinted, shielding his deeply set blue-gray eyes from the afternoon sun. Rafe turned off the key in the ignition, and stepped out. "Hi, Neil!"

Neil stopped, put the ax down, and came over to the wagon. "Mr. Langley! Rafe! You're back from England! Gee, it's good to see you again."

"Nice seeing you again, too, Neil." Rafe gave him a bear hug, and shook his hand.

"Come in. Come in. Gee, this is really a surprise. How are you anyway?"

"Fine. I'm just fine, Neil. Well, I really don't have much time today—just wanted to get in touch with you and find out how you're doing. Why don't we just stay out here and soak up some sunshine? I could use a cold drink, if you have one."

"Sure! A soda okay?"

"Yes, that will be great—anything, thanks." Rafe's eyes followed him as he ran like a deer into the house. Neil had filled out. His shoulders were broader, his arms more muscular. He was no longer a boy. He had matured into an exceptionally handsome man. His sun-bleached hair was a striking contrast to the deep tan. Rafe thought, *probably got that great tan over in eastern Washington working on the farm, or out in his boat. Bet a lot of girls take science.*

A couple of minutes later, as they sat on the two lawn chairs near the back porch sipping their sodas, Rafe said, "Tell me about yourself, Neil. What have you been up to since I left?"

Neil appeared slightly nervous. "Yes, well, let's see—the next spring, after you left, I graduated from George, you know. I really missed your not being there, Rafe. After Ann's funeral, I went on home to help my dad on the farm with the harvesting. Surely felt bad about Ann—and Julie, Rafe. I just didn't know what to do, or say. It really shook me up—seems I just had to get away. Then, by the time I returned, you had already gone."

Without comment, Rafe permitted him to go on. "After I completed my senior year at George, and received my bachelor's degree, I started my fifth year in Bellingham, but I heard about this job up here—the teacher had to leave suddenly, so I applied for it. Even though I hadn't finished my fifth year, they hired me. I've been going to summer school to get my credits. Am also going to take one night class this fall. It really was a good deal, because I could be teaching at the same time. I guess I was lucky to get this position, even though it is in the sticks. The kids are great, and I like the staff, too."

"Well, you sound really happy, Neil. When did you get this place?"

"Oh, I bought it from a young couple about a year ago. I was living in a home—room and board—but decided that I wanted to go it alone. My folks helped me with the down payment. I think it has great possibilities. Do you like it?"

"From what I see—yes, it could be made into a very attractive little home." As an after thought Rafe added, "I see you have a battle with the blackberries up here, too."

"Yep, have to get at them before school starts. That's the Pacific Northwest for you, huh? They'll take over, if you're not at them all the time. As you well know, it's a constant battle. I sure do like to eat the berries, though. Boy, I'll never forget the jam and the pies Ann used to make."

"Yes—well—say, maybe I could come up next week-end and give you a hand. You surely did help us out plenty of times, Neil. I owe you."

"Naw, you don't owe me, Rafe. I was always happy to help you. I just loved being with all of you, and I really thought the world of Julie, you know. But, it would be nice if you wanted to come—if you're not too busy. I'll get some steaks and we can barbecue—if the weather'll cooperate."

"Well, that would be fine, Neil, but I don't want you to go to any extra work on my account." Pausing, he added with a grin, "Could you make mine medium rare?"

"Sure, that wouldn't be a problem. That's the way I like them, too. I'll whip up a salad and have some garlic bread, too."

"Well, that will be great. Say, have you found yourself a girlfriend? Any plans for marriage?"

"Well—ah—I did go with a nice girl up at Bellingham, but we broke it off. No one since. I don't know about marriage, Rafe."

Rafe got up, genuflected to get the blood circulating in his legs, and began walking slowly to the wagon. "Well, I have to get going. It was really good seeing you again, Neil. You're looking just great. Maybe next week? We'll have to take advantage of the time before you get too involved in school. Oh, why don't you give me your telephone number?"

"Here, let me write it down for you." Neil took a scrap of paper out of his pocket, and scribbled the number down. Handing Rafe the slip of paper, he shook his hand and smiled, "I want to thank you for coming, Rafe—really enjoyed our little visit. I'll be waiting to hear from you. Where are you staying? Your place?"

"No, I'm not ready to go back to the house yet. I'm at the Ripleys. I think you met them a couple of times."

"Yes, I remember them—nice couple—two kids older than Julie. I think I met them the first time I came over to your cabin on Whidbey."

"That's right. I remember your helping all the kids with their hot dogs—and smores."

Rafe got into the wagon, and rolled the window down. "Thanks for the soda, Neil!"

Neil bent over to look at Rafe. "Okay, Mr. Langley—Rafe. See you real soon."

Rafe started the engine and slowly pulled away, leaving Neil standing, one hand on his hip, the other clutching the soda can. Neil drained the can. His fingers tightened around it. He made it pop and snap as he crushed it. As he watched the wagon pull out on the main road, he wiped the beads of perspiration from his forehead with his shirtsleeve. He broke out in a cold sweat, and his t-shirt stuck to him as if it had been washed in Elmer's glue. As soon as the car was out of sight he turned and ran into the house, peeled off his t-shirt, and fell on the bed, totally exhausted.

During the next couple of weeks, Rafe and Neil met on several occasions. One time, they had lunch at the Candy Cane in Sultan, another time at the Dutch Cup. Rafe helped him cut and stack wood and pile it neatly by the side of the house near the back door. They picked blackberries together, the last of the season. He had never seen such thick, heavy vines, so dense on the sides of the barn, especially next to the gully where the berries were impossible to reach. No footing. Rafe thought it was pretty stupid to build a barn right on the cusp of a ravine—there must have been a reason.

An inexplicable darkness seemed to envelope Rafe as he secretly plotted and schemed. He had not wanted to involve the authorities—not yet. He wanted to get that confession himself—more than anything in the world. He had to know the entire story of what had happened—to Ann, to Julie, and just how Julie got to Copenhagen. He wanted to know about the connection between Neil and that Jenson fellow the authorities arrested, along with the other adults in the porn ring.

In his fantasy, he visualized a trial.

*"All rise!" the clerk cried. The judge swept into the room in his austere jet-black*

*robe, and sat in the brown high-back leather chair between the gracefully draped flags on their pointed brass stanchions. The great seal of Washington state hung behind him. An eerie glow bathed the judge as he peered down from the height of the judicial bench, elevated above all other furniture in the room. He slowly placed his magnified reading glasses on the tip of his hooked nose and picked up sheets of paper. When at last he removed the glasses and spoke, everyone looked up. He looked wise and kindly, yet firm and authoritative, a force, a power that all respected. "Counselor?"*

*Under the lights of banked fluorescent tubes, the district attorney made her opening statement to the jury. She said repeatedly, "The evidence will show..." With her eyes she made contact with each juror. They were transfixed by her dynamism, her every movement, her body language. She buttoned one button of her well-tailored dark navy blue suit, accentuating her narrow waist. The soft pink silk blouse, open at the neck, complimented her complexion, giving her cheeks a tinge of color. The jurors listened intently, hanging on to each word. "The evidence will show that the defendant..."*

*The witness stand was over on one side of the courtroom. She stood and asked the first witness to raise his right hand. The eyes of the young man at the far end of the jury box fell, transfixed by her shapely legs. "Do you solemnly swear to tell the truth, the whole truth, and nothing but the truth, so help you God?"*

*The witness, whose face was a blur in Rafe's subconscious replied in a firm, unwavering voice, "I do." At that same moment, the young man who was staring at the clerk, jerked to attention.*

*"Please state your name clearly, and spell it for the court."*

*Rafe saw faces in the juror's box—Alan Strickland, Abigail Lancaster, Dr. Berne, Ken and Kim, Ann (but why Ann?), Julie, and the children from the estate. He saw six men and eight women sitting in the jury box. Two of the women were alternates.*

*After the district attorney made her introductory statement, she sat at the table, her head bent over the thick manila folder of papers. She was just a slip of a woman, and so young—so very young. Could she do the job? A good job? Would she know the law sufficiently, the laws that related to the crimes Neil had committed?*

*Neil's attorney, a man in his forties with dark, curly hair and a short, full beard, sat at another table. His suit was a bit rumpled. Rafe noticed that he was wearing running shoes. The laces of one shoe were untied. Strange, for an attorney. A state trooper in uniform sat at a small table near the jury box, next to the bailiff. The room was crowded with spectators—friends, curious onlookers, the press, young attorneys wanting to learn new techniques, observing the experts in action. But, where was Neil? Rafe could not visualize Neil. He should have been there at the defense table, leaning over to consult with his attorney.*

*In his semiconscious state of mind, he heard the arguments of the attorneys. "Ladies and gentleman, you have heard all of the testimony in this trial. Now you must decide the facts. This man must be proven guilty beyond a reasonable doubt. What is reasonable doubt? Let me explain…" The judge's voice droned on, and on, and on.*

*"This is innuendo evidence! You cannot conjecture or convict on mere suspicion!" the defense shouted.*

*The voices of the attorneys began to fade in Rafe's mind, yet the remarks kept ringing in his ears, "At this juncture, the defense interpretation would have you believe…I will address this issue at considerable length, but first, you must decide the facts."*

*"Duplicitous! Concepts! Deliberative process! Nuances! Do you think you have heard the entire story? I must submit! Objection! Objection overruled! Objection sustained! Your Honor, may we approach the bench?" The weary looking judge spoke intently to the jury. "Ladies and gentlemen, you have now heard all the facts in this case. After a brief recess, you will return to the courtroom, and I will read the instructions to you. May I admonish you once again not to discuss the case among yourselves until I have dismissed you to deliberate. Please follow the bailiff." The jurors filed out, one by one. The judge rose and walked briskly from the courtroom. Those in the crowded courtroom rose, and looked silently at one another.*

*The jury would deliberate for hours, days, yes weeks. Finally, the six women, and six men, would return to the courtroom. The judge would look at them and say, "I understand you have reached the verdicts in this case?"*

*The first juror would stand and make the announcement. "Yes, your Honor, we have reached the verdicts."*

*The judge would continue, "Will you please hand the verdict forms to the bailiff, who will hand them to me." The juror would take the forms to the bailiff, and without looking at them, the bailiff would pass the papers to the judge. She would step back and wait while the judge perused the papers. Then, the judge would hand them back to the bailiff who took them to the jury foreperson.*

*The verdicts—the verdicts. Rafe heard a strange voice, a voice that seemed*

*to come from the very heavens, not the juror's voice. "Guilty of murder in*
*the second degree! Guilty of slavery! Guilty of kidnapping! Guilty of sexual*
*assault—count one, count two, count three!"*

The driver of a long, black Buick was laying on his horn, trying to make
Rafe aware that he wanted to pass. Rafe acknowledged the sign with
some embarrassment, pulled slightly to the right, and slowed down. The
driver glared at him as he accelerated the motor of his own car and
passed Rafe.

Justice would be served. Yes, justice would be rendered. If he could
only be patient and wait, if he didn't do anything foolish, like kill Neil
himself first. When he was with Neil he had to fight an impelling force,
a strong urge to wrap his hands around his throat, to squeeze unmerci-
fully until his eyes bugged out of his head, to strangle him to death. No,
he knew that he must allow the justice system to take care of Neil. If he
could wait, if only he could wait. He needed more time to perfect a plan.
Somehow, he would succeed. He had to get that confession from Neil.
He had to get it without the interference of the authorities, before the
FBI stepped in. He had to have some answers. *"May it please the court!*
*May it please the court! Guilty! Guilty!"* The words kept ringing in his
ears.

Rafe woke early, slipped out of bed, and quietly showered, shaved, and dressed. He hoped that he would not disturb any of the Ripleys. He carefully tiptoed out of the house and got into the stationwagen.

"Ken," Kim nudged her husband. "Where do you suppose Rafe is going at this hour, just a little after 6:00 a.m.—on a Saturday?"

"I don't know, sweetheart. Please lie down and cuddle up around my back. I'm chilly. Maybe we can go back to sleep." He turned over. Kim lay there, wide-awake, thinking, thinking. She felt uneasy. She didn't know why.

Rafe stopped at the Red Barn near Monroe for a sweet roll and coffee. It was the last Saturday in August, and school would commence the day after Labor Day, September 2nd. As Rafe continued driving the wagon east on highway two, the sweet roll in his stomach felt like molten lead. His heart beat quickened. He could actually hear the pounding and feel the blood pulsate through his veins. His face was tired and strained, lips tightened, jaw rigid. Every instinct within warned him to be careful. The small micro recorder was concealed in his jacket pocket, and he was determined to get the confession, one way or the other.

The sky darkened, and claps of thunder made the hairs on Rafe's arms stand at attention. Lightning flashed, and the sky continued to be enveloped in a dark gray, the kind of gray that makes every living thing a deeper shade. At first, it began to rain gently, then it came down in torrents, an unmitigated cloudburst. Pillars of rain hammered and beat mercilessly down upon the car. The windshield wipers raced back and forth in a fruitless effort to clear the windshield. Rafe's vision was so impaired that he could not see the yellow line on the highway. The mountains were invisible, but he could feel their mitigating presence. In the lens of his memory he knew the location of every peak.

Rafe had almost reached Neil's turnoff—just a few more miles. He remembered the little wayside chapel on the left side of the highway. *It must be along here somewhere.* Through the deluge, he finally saw it, turned his blinkers on, and pulled slowly over to the entrance. There was no one else around. He would go into the chapel, sit and meditate until the storm subsided. His brain was crowded with thoughts and ideas that whirled around like dry leaves on a warm, windy, autumn day. How could so many thoughts pass through the mind so quickly? How could they pick the blackberries now? They would be drenched. It would still take a few minutes to get to Neil's place. This was a drencher such as he had not seen since he was in England.

Excerpts from his conversation with Dr. Berne floated in and out of his mind, like debris rushing down a creek after a flood. *Child pornography is one of the worse kinds of child abuse—adults were betraying her— her intellect has been violated—it was sexual perversion that neither of us could dream possible—the perpetrators are reprobate, Mr. Langley—it is the exploitation of a child for the sexual gratification of an adult—a billion dollar business—your friend Neil was sexually and socially immature, and very naïve—the crime would be difficult to prove in a court of law. Thank God Julie was found.*

Rafe sat in the little chapel, replaying all the events of the past weeks. The howling wind whipped around the building, rattling the window shades. Ultimately, the storm tempered to a gentle, steady, earth-drenching rain. They needed the rain, and he gave thanks for it, even in the midst of his desperation. The rain finally subsided, and the storm veered southward. He walked quietly out of the chapel, started the engine in the wagon, and pulled out onto the highway again. He gripped the steering wheel until his knuckles shone white, and the skin stretching across them was as taut as the skin stretched over a pork sausage. Even his teeth were clenched so tightly together that his breath gave a slight whistle as he unconsciously breathed through his mouth.

Rafe drove into Neil's yard, turned off the lights and motor, looked around for Neil, and got out of the wagon. He thought it strange that Neil didn't come out of the house, or wave from the window, or yell from the barn door. He went around to the back door, knocked, and yelled, "Neil! Neil!" No answer. He slowly opened the unlocked door, and stepped into the kitchen. The coffee pot was on low. "Neil!" He walked into the cozy, small, rustic living room with the stone fireplace, and found everything it its proper place. He walked cat-like into the bedroom. The twin bed had been meticulously made, and a new pair of slacks and matching shirt were hanging on a hanger, hooked over the top drawer of the oak dresser. The kid was neat. Rafe shook his head. *Funny, he wouldn't—no, he wouldn't have gone without locking the doors.* He noticed a pornographic magazine on the stand by his bed. Few would ever have guessed.

Rafe walked out the front door, jumped off the side of the porch, and went around to the barn. "Neil! Hey, Neil! Are you in there?" No answer. He opened the squeaking barn door and peered in, taking note of the opened bundle of shingles on the floor. *Well, that's strange. Wonder where he could have gone. He must be near.*

He walked out of the shed toward the back of the building, which was built right up to the cusp of the gully. Here, on the slope beneath the barn roof's extension, the blackberries grew profusely, but no human being could possibly reach them. What a shame. They were hanging in thick clusters, waiting to be plucked.

Rafe stopped short, frozen to a standstill. The tiny hairs on the nape of his neck rose like a hairbrush, and a clammy chill of fear swept over him as he stared at the horrible scene. "Oh, my God! Neil! Neil!" he shouted. He was shocked, dumbfounded, repelled at the sight that met his eyes. A sour fluid worked its way from his stomach to his mouth, and he began to gag and retch. The sour, acrid liquid, along with small bits of the roll, gushed out of his mouth onto the sodden ground. He broke out in a cold sweat, reached in his back pocket for a handkerchief, and wiped his brow and mouth. In a stooped position, he forced himself to look again. He shook his head and blinked his eyes to clear the image.

Neil was suspended in the middle of the blackberry vines, and two vines, the largest Rafe had ever seen, were stretched straight across the upper throat, the barbs penetrating into the flesh, the blood oozing slowly down onto his shirt. His hands were clutching large thorny branches, blood oozing down the arms. He had literally been hanged to death by the blackberry vines. His shirt was covered with red stains, his eyes wide open, filled with terror, even in death.

He must have been up on the top of the roof shingling. The marks of the skidding were visible on the rotting shingles. The ladder on the side of the barn had fallen. The vines held him securely, strangling the very life out of his body, preventing him from falling into the ravine.

Rafe stood there gaping, fighting nausea, both hands holding his head. His thoughts flashed back to the first time he had seen Neil on registration. day. He had been a wonderful student–promising, bright. They had become close—real friends. . At that moment he thought of what Aristotle had said, *"What is a friend? A single soul dwelling in two bodies."* Yes, they had been friends in the beginning, and now he was dead. He stared at the body. "Neil, Neil, how could you? How could you have given her to those awful people? You loved her, and Julie loved you. We all loved you. Oh, Neil, what happened? What went wrong?" His voice startled him. It was not full of hatred, malice, or animosity; it was a voice full of compassion, caring, and love. *"Why,* Neil? What went wrong? What made you do this terrible thing? Were you mistreated as a child? Why did you do it? Why, Neil? Why?"

Slowly Rafe turned away, and walked back into the house. The phone was in the kitchen. He dialed 911 and explained the situation. Knowing that the troopers were always near, he picked up the phone again and dialed the operator. "Operator, will you please connect me with the state troopers?" After explaining briefly to the trooper, he hung up the receiver, and sat at the kitchen table. He waited about twenty minutes for the troopers to arrive. His mind was racing. It was over, all over. No need for a confession now. No trial. No conviction. No sentence. Rafe sat at that kitchen table, deep in thought, pondering and considering the life, and now the death, of this young man. He heard a still, small voice say, *"Vengeance is mine; I will repay, saith the Lord."* He thought about what his pastor had told him, *"Rafe, remember this: God never shuts one door without opening another. He has a way of working things out for the best."* But, was this for the best, was this for the best?

"Mr. Langley, will you sign these papers, please? Then, there will be no need for you to remain here any longer. We will take care of everything."

"What a terrible tragedy," Rafe whispered. "What a horrifying way to die."

"Yes, sir, this is the worse thing I've ever seen. I am sorry, Mr. Langley." The young trooper shook his hand, and Rafe walked hesitantly out the door.

Rafe drove with the window down, his left arm resting on the door. He needed air, fresh air, lots of it, to clear his mind. The sun was playing hide-and-go-seek behind heavy clouds, which were gathering, indicating the end of the storm. A beautiful rainbow arched over the mountains, reaching down to the valley below. The skies would once again be sunny and clear. His world had been bathed, cleansed by the deluge. He drove slowly, inhaling deep breaths of air.

When he came to the tiny chapel by the side of the highway, he pulled in and sat on one of the small benches. He sat there quietly with hands folded, staring straight ahead. Soon the signs of strain and anxiety on his face were replaced by an expression of serenity. He bent over and held his head in both his hands. The nightmare was over. He knew in his heart that he would never dream about the blackberries again. Thank God. *Thank you, God. It's over. I know the nightmare is over now.*

Back on the main highway heading home, he could not recall when he had seen the western sky so red and golden. A large cloud, shaped like a toy poodle glowed within, like precious amber, and all around feathered wisps surrounded it. He caught a glimpse of the Snohomish River in the fertile valley below, mirroring the colors of the sky. The dark evergreens along its edge were tinged in color.

When the sun peeked out from beneath the cloud, its light rested on all as far as Rafe could see. The air was clear and pure, and Rafe breathed deeply, filling his lungs. He switched on the radio. Willie Nelson was singing "On The Road Again" and Rafe, with a grin on his face, began to hum the tune, his thoughts full of Amanda and Julie.

On October 4, Rafe drove south on I-5 to the Sea/Tac Airport. He had transcended his moments of anguish, grief, and despair. At last he could envision a brighter future, a happier tomorrow. He possessed a greater depth of feeling, understanding, and compassion, and his faith had been renewed and restored.

He stood in the observation tower, watching the graceful 747 on its final descent. The plane made a faultless touchdown. It was right on time. He knew that it would take several minutes for them to come through customs. Waiting for the passengers seemed an eternity. His face broke into a big grin as he saw the two of them, and his heart skipped a beat as he watched the attractive young woman walk toward him. She had not as yet seen him. He couldn't miss that shiny brown hair styled so beautifully. There was an air of elegance in her carriage, in the manner in which she wore the brown tweed traveling suit, the jacket fashioned in long lines, the shoulders accentuated by large shoulder pads. Her skirt was narrow, and came just below the knee. She wore dark brown pumps, and carried a matching shoulder bag. Rafe thought, *great legs—so exquisite, and yes, she does remind me of…*

The young woman clasped the hand of a beautiful, raven-haired girl, neatly dressed in a navy blazer, with a blue and navy plaid pleated skirt, knee high stockings, and loafers, her long, black hair shining, her blue eyes sparkling with excitement. Excusing himself cordially, he pushed through the crowd and ran to embrace them both.

"Amanda! Julie! Oh, thank God you're here!"

"Rafe, my darling!"

"Daddy!" They embraced, and stood for a long time holding each other.

"First, let's get a cart so we don't have to lug all of these bags," Rafe said. Piling one piece upon the other, he added, "Did you have a good flight? How in the world did you two manage all of this stuff anyway?"

"We're strong, Daddy," Julie explained.

Rafe pushed the cart carefully, with his wife and daughter on each arm. Amanda turned to Rafe and smiling, asked, "Now, first things first, just who do I remind you of, Rafe? You said you'd tell me when I got home."

"Been worrying about that, huh?"

"Well, not worrying, just wondering…"

They all stopped. He turned to her and with a big grin said, "Well, my dear, you remind me of Jaclyn Smith."

"Jaclyn Smith? The actress from *Charlie's Angels*? She was one of the angels. Ironic, that's what I always thought I was. In fact, Charlie has often called me his angel. But, look like her? Really, Rafe, how in the world could you ever think that? I don't look like her. My teeth are crooked, my two front teeth are too long, and I have a mole over my right eye. She's beautiful! I'm not beautiful."

"Your teeth aren't that crooked, Amanda—only your eye teeth stick out a little. I wouldn't call that crooked. No, there's just something about the shape of your face, your smile. I can't help it. You do remind me of her."

"You're kidding. I can't see it, Rafe. Well, if that doesn't beat all. I surely never thought of that before. Do you think I should get braces?"

Rafe laughed as he started pushing the cart again. "Mandy, they aren't that bad, but you can if you want to. Just don't be in a rush and don't be silly—because I like your teeth! There is something there, though—something about you that reminds me of her. Perhaps it's your bone structure, your mouth, the shape of your eyes, your smile. You're prettier, though, honey. What do you think, Julie?"

"I think Amanda is very pretty, Daddy, but I don't know who Jaclyn is."

"Julie, she is a movie star, and Amanda, I mean it! There is something about you that is like Jaclyn Smith. Hey, I saw a few of those episodes on television, and I like them. Have you ever seen any of the shows?"

"Once, I think. I can't remember where I was. Perhaps at home with my mom. I know she liked that show, too. It was a bit unreal, but usually the storyline was good, at least that is what she said. The angels always seemed to come out on top of any situation. I might add, however, that there is one big difference between Jaclyn Smith and me which I might point out."

"What's that?"

"I don't have a contract in Hollywood. Though, if things begin to get tough, perhaps I could double for her." They both laughed. "Say, Rafe, do you mind if I bring Punky home to live with us?"

"Who's Punky anyway?"

"My cat."

"Your cat? Where is this cat?"

"She's been with my mother."

Rafe, turning to Julie, asked, "Julie, would you like a cat?"

"Oh, yes, Daddy, I'd love one. Amanda told me all about Punky, and she showed me a picture of her looking up at the Christmas tree. She's so cute, Daddy. She has a funny tail—part of the fur is missing."

"Punky? That's a great name for a cat. Well, can't see any reason why Punky can't come to live with us. Have you had her very many years, Mandy?"

"Yes, several, but she's still in her prime. I think you'll like her. She talks a blue streak, though. Just wanted to warn you."

"Oh, oh! Three women to contend with. Well, think I just might be able to handle that." They walked out the open doors to the street. "Okay, you stand here with the luggage and I'll go get the car. It won't take me very long."

"Daddy, I'll go with you. May I?"

"Sure, Julie. Come on—let's hurry."

"We'll see you in a few minutes, Amanda. Now, don't go running off anywhere." Rafe and Julie left Amanda at the curb and walked hand in hand over to the parking garage.

"With all of this luggage? Promise—I'll stand right here and wait. Maybe someone will come along and ask me for my autograph. By the way, Rafe, you remind me of someone, too," she called as they crossed the street.

"I do? Who?"

"I'll tell you later—on the way," she teased. She watched them together and her eyes filled with tears of happiness.

Julie seemed to be enjoying this game between her father and her new mother.

They were heading north on the freeway. "Now, tell me, who do I remind you of?"

"You worried, Rafe?"

"Of course not. Who? Come on, tell me."

"Robert Redford."

*"Robert Redford?* I wish! I wish!" Rafe laughed loud and long. "That's the best thing I've heard in years. Wow, what a compliment. Hmm, Robert Redford. Wait 'til I tell Ken and Kim that one." Grinning mischievously, he added, "Suppose the one big difference between us would be that I don't have a big ranch out there in Colorado or Montana, or wherever it is."

Julie was taking in all the banter. "Do I look like anyone else?" she asked seriously.

"Honey, you look just like yourself, and I wouldn't have it any other way," Rafe said.

"Nor would I," Amanda agreed.

Julie smiled, a pleased look on her face.

A little over an hour later, after a myriad of questions, and much chatter, they drove by the Ray place, and turned into the private driveway leading up to the old-fashioned stone house. There was a new sign on the left side of the road that read:

THE LANGLEYS
RAFE, AMANDA, AND JULIE

Graceful delicate blackberry vines with small clusters of berries had been painted around the words.

"Oh, Daddy, I love the new sign. Isn't that neat, Amanda?"

"Yes, yes, it is Julie," Amanda said. A tear formed in her eye.

Rafe drove slowly down the narrow driveway, and as they rounded the curve and came into full view of the house, he stopped the car and allowed the motor to idle. "Take a good look, girls."

"Rafe, it's beautiful. I love it!" Amanda exclaimed.

"I'm glad. I had hoped you would."

"Daddy, it's so good to be back home again!" Julie cried.

"And, you can't imagine how I feel having you both with me—my two gorgeous girls."

Rafe drove up to the front verandah, and they jumped out of the car. Hand in hand, they climbed the steps, and before Rafe unlocked the front door, he put his arms around both of them. They stood quietly, huddling together like a small football team. Their bowed heads touched, touched as one—a new beginning.

*Epilogue* – 2000

Art and Marilyn Manning continue to farm in eastern Washington State. Marilyn and her sister, Ellen Scott, often visit the cemetery beside the community church where Marilyn kneels beside her son's grave, arranging fresh flowers at the head stone. She looks up, searching Ellen's face for answers, commenting softly, "He was so young, so handsome. Why did he have to meet such a dreadful end, Ellen? He had so much to give." Ellen says nothing, but gently embraces her sister. She then walks over to place flowers on the grave of her former husband.

Rafe and Amanda Langley continue to live in the attractive old stone house in Snohomish County. All the blackberry vines near the dwelling have been cleared away, replaced by a natural park-like setting with a barbeque pit, shrubs, flowers, and cedar furniture. A new addition, boasting large view windows, is visible at the back of the house, and serves as a fully equipped, efficient, comfortable office with the latest technology. Rafe is chairman of the Science Department at George College, which has more than tripled in size, and Amanda Cates Langley works as a freelance writer, often sending articles to *Today's World*. Charlie Moore is in constant contact with her, assigning, encouraging, accepting. Several chapters of her first novel are securely saved, and backed up, on her laptop.

Ken and Kim Ripley remain close friends of the Langleys, and Kim and Amanda have a very special companionship. Ken's work at the clinic is more demanding than ever, but he still finds time for his best friend, Rafe, and occasionally they fly together in his Cessna around the Pacific Northwest.

Emily Ray died in 1990. Gordon Ray, who will be eighty-two on his next birthday, still maintains the family home, continues to be a good neighbor, keeps busy with volunteer work, and often shares a quiet evening with the Langleys.

Emol and Hilda Rosenberg both served time in prison. After Hilda's release, she obtained a small flat near the prison, visiting her husband daily until he was discharged. It is believed that they presently reside in Colombia, South America.

Abigail Lancaster and Charity Kendall agreed to leave the estate and move to a flat in Brighton. Together they traveled to the United States in 1992 to visit Rafe and Amanda Langley in Washington State. They never cease to exclaim how wonderfully the Langleys treated them and what a marvelous time they had. Through the years the Langleys have been in constant contact with them, and when Abigail celebrated her seventy-fifth birthday they surprised her with a visit. Now in their eighties, they still enjoy the morning paper over tea and crumpets. They were especially saddened over the death of Princess Diana, believing that it may have been a conspiracy, and they still wonder about the future of The House of Windsor. Together, over many cups of tea, they solve the many problems of the Royal Family, and they would like to voice their opinions, but no one will listen.

Cameron Jenson served several years in prison, working in the photo lab, the prison library, and taking his turn with the pots and pans. Upon his release, he moved to the Netherlands where he obtained a position in a museum in Amsterdam. He never married.

After a brief prison term, Astrid was released. Her whereabouts is unknown at the present time.

Mrs. Wickstrom went back to Stockholm to live with her daughter. Her grandchildren adore her and love to eat her cookies and abelskivers.

Hans Reiman was sent to live with his aunt, Renate Leiman, in Frankfurt. He was a better than average student in school and an outstanding soccer player. A high school counselor, John Hendrick, spent many sessions with Hans, listening and guiding this promising young man. After high school graduation, he attended one year of college, then joined the military. Now, almost thirty years old, he is happily married to Lisa, an attractive elementary school teacher, who is anticipating the birth of their first child. Hans has had a successful military career thus far.

Monique Marchant was sent back to Paris to live in a Catholic boarding school where she received counseling from the Reverend Mother. She graduated with honors. Monique decided to enter the Presentation Convent where she would be cared for, receive further education, and work in God's service. In 1992 she took her final vows. Now, Sister Mary Bernadette devotes her life in service to deprived, abused children. Very often one can catch a glimpse of a lovely, freckled-face nun in a long navy blue habit, red curls refusing to stay under the headdress, walking with two other sisters down the busy streets of Paris near the Moulin Rouge. They often stop to talk to the young women who stand in the doorways or stroll slowly down the busy thoroughfare.

Kari Johanssen's parents gave their daughter counseling and a fine education. At twenty-five, she completed her nurse's training at the University of Oslo and became a surgical nurse in the largest hospital in southern Norway. Her best friend, Carl Bostrom, is a senior in pre med. They are engaged and will be married after he finishes his internship. Kari, an attractive tall blond, became an exceptionally fine figure skater as well as an outstanding cross-country skier.

Alberto Giovani Lento was reunited with his family in Florence. He received counseling from Father Angelo, and now, almost twenty-three years old, continues to study piano and voice at the Florence School of Music. His goal is to become a concert pianist, marry, settle down, and have a large family.

Alexander Blenheim went back to London to live with his parents, receive counseling, and continue his education. At twenty-two, he is presently a fourth-year University student, handsome, quiet, studious, well-liked. His father wants him to pursue a career in the family shipping business. He is planning to attend Oxford for an advanced degree.

Julie Langley, lovely, yet withdrawn and reserved, has many casual friends, but no special male friend. She attends the University of Washington, is majoring in psychology, and hopes to earn a doctor's degree. Her goal is to work with neglected and abused children.

Today, millions of children are still suffering from parental neglect; physical, sexual, and emotional abuse; and other exploitations. Child abuse takes a costly toll on the troubled, tormented victims because of the long-term psychological damage it wreaks. Society is still failing to rescue, to save the victims. James Garbarino, the former president of the Erikson Institute, a child development center in Chicago, says:

> If you take almost any major social problem in America and treat it like those nested Russian dolls, what you will get to is that child abuse would be the last doll—because it is such a profound wound in developing children. That's why almost all the prisoners are child abuse victims. That's why over and over again what you find inside particularly troubled teen-agers are abused children.

The Oregonian, October 21, 1994.

## Bibliography

*Anchorage Times. Family Weekly. "The Shame of a Nation." By Ernest Volkman and Howard L. Rosenberg*

*De Young, Mary. The Sexual Victimization of Children. McFarland & Co., Inc. Jefferson, N.C. and Longdon. 1982.*

*Facts on File. Facts on File. New York. 1970 through 1982*

*Fodor's Travel Guides. Fodor's Great Britain. Fodor's Travel Guides. New York. 1985.*

*Fodor's Travel Guides. Fodor's Europe. David McKay. New York. 1984.*

*National Federation for Decency Journal. May/June, 1985. P.O. Drawer 2440. Tupelo, Miss. 38803.*

*McLean's. 97:62+. October 22, 1984.*

*Readers' Digest. December, 1985. Fox, John. Murder of a Polish Priest.*

*Time. 125:6. February 25, 1985.*

*The Oregonian. "Child Abuse: How Can We Stop It?" Chicago Tribune News Service. October 21, 1994.*